I0638508

Fearsome

By: S.A. Wolfe

All rights reserved.

Copyright ©2013 S.A. Wolfe

This is a work of fiction. Any resemblance of characters to persons, living or dead, is purely coincidental. The Author holds exclusive rights to this work. Unauthorized duplication is prohibited.

http://www.sa-wolfe.com

Cover Design by Damonza
Editing and Formatting by C&D Editing

One

There are young women in this city who are able to grab on to careers and romance with the zeal and ambition of an Olympic athlete. I, however, am not one of those women. I'll admit that I'm able to excel in parts of that equation, to a degree. I grew up in New York City, primed with a top notch education which has afforded me the ability to secure a great job in technology due to hard work and blessed prodigy talents, yet it hasn't made up for my less than stellar personal life.

The phone call from my Aunt Virginia's lawyer comes one afternoon when I am having an especially miserable day at work. Sitting in my cubby, surrounded by a dozen other techies also hunched over their computer monitors, I listen as Archibald Bixby informs me that my aunt died peacefully in her own bed a week ago and that she bequeathed all of her money and possessions to me. He's sorry he couldn't tell me sooner, but he had to follow Aunt Virginia's instructions.

I have a blurry image of my aunt. She was actually my great aunt; a generation older than my parents, and the last time I saw her I was six. I remember running through her big, old Victorian home, exploring the different rooms and all the remarkable things she collected. Artwork was everywhere. She was a painter and, over the years, she had collected other artists' work. It made me think of her house as something fanciful.

Before I can delve further into my foggy memories, Mr. Bixby's request that I come to his office brings me back to the present. He thinks it will be best if I meet him in person where he can fill me in on the details of my aunt's will. He says that my aunt left me her home and a significant amount of resources. He even suggests I pack enough to stay for a while so I can think things over.

"Think what over?" I ask.

"Miss Channing. May I call you Jessica?" he asks then, without waiting for my response, continues on, "Well, let's just say that Ginnie had some nice ideas for you and it's my job to convey her message to you as best I can. I think, when you arrive here, you'll understand more of what I'm trying to say. You'll want time to let this percolate on the brain, as they say, so pack a few suitcases and think of this as an extended vacation. I'll pick you up at the bus stop."

I take the subway back to my five-floor walk-up on Waverly while wondering why Mr. Bixby even assumes I have the luxury of taking a vacation, extended or otherwise. I don't. I've been working for 5 Alpha for almost two years, ever since I graduated college. I may have been smart enough to finish college and graduate school several years before my peers, but I'm still a cubicle-grunt at work. The hours are long and the opportunity to move up is highly competitive. It requires an

2

obscene devotion to the firm, including working weekends and nights; whatever it takes to debug the computer code we write all day and in our sleep.

I'm good at it and I get my share of mentoring from the management who like my ideas, but mostly, I stand out because I came to 5 Alpha at the age of nineteen, right out of M.I.T. My colleagues at 5 Alpha are all from the top of their graduate school classes, however, none of them are under the age of twenty-four and seventy percent of the employees are men. You'd think that would be appealing for a young woman, but to be honest, sometimes I still feel like I'm in high school and I haven't caught up with everyone else. Occasionally, I feel like the little duckling trailing behind, afraid to cross the road with the other, bigger ducks. Yes, I am a pathetic, nerdy girl who still compares herself to ducks.

When I enter my pre-war building, I smell a mixture of burnt microwave popcorn and curry, which I'm pretty sure comes from my apartment. There's also an undercurrent odor of pot, most likely from the stoner who lives below me.

I live in a great part of Greenwich Village, surrounded by brownstones that are being renovated by their wealthy owners, and I'm in close proximity to lively restaurants and shops. When you're in my aging building, though, you know you're in a place that caters to recent college grads.

The carpeting on the hollow staircase is a tattered, old, red brocade style that reminds me of lounge singers from the 1940's and the wooden banister wobbles as I grip it on my hike up to the apartment I share with two other girls, Kate and Marissa.

Our apartment is quiet when I let myself in; no TV blaring a primetime reality show that my roomies love to watch and no sounds of churning, burping water pipes, which always happens when someone is in the closet-sized bathroom. There are remnants of the destroyed popcorn left on the coffee table, clothes tossed onto the couch and there is a selection of strapless bras and slinky dresses displayed across a few kitchen chairs.

I can easily imagine what precipitated this. My roommates, after a dinner of burnt popcorn and disastrous, homemade chicken curry, decided to go out to a club, I'm sure. Naturally, they wouldn't wait for me because, as my roommates and I have been through many times, at a few months shy of my twenty-first birthday, I'm still not old enough to go out dancing and drinking with them. Of course, *sometimes* I'm able to slip in when a bouncer thinks I'm pretty and opens the velvet rope for me, but all too often, the female bartenders have gotten me tossed out not long after.

I can't blame my friends for going without me. They're twenty-three and want to get on with growing up and meeting men and, as much as they try to include me, sometimes it must feel like they have a little sister tagging along.

I pack the two very small suitcases I own with the few clothes I tend to wear constantly and stock my art box with paint tubes, brushes and my portfolio case with special watercolor paper. If inspiration strikes, maybe I'll get some painting done in the fresh country air. I complete a quick tidying of the apartment, picking up discarded clothing and washing the dishes, finishing with some light dusting.

I leave my roommates a note about my trip to Hera, New York with the assumption that I will return in a few days, and if I don't, to make inquiries and send out a search party for their "little sister". I also text my boss and let him know that I've had a death in the family and expect to be out of the office for a few days. He replies immediately, telling me to take all the time I need.

That's one very good thing about my job. Even though my boss, Nathan, flirts too much with me, he tries to be the boss everyone likes, so he's very accommodating. Sometimes I think he favors me more than the others and it's probably the universal perception that I am very young, therefore I must be very naïve and need all the guidance I can get.

Before bed, I double check on the computer for the bus schedule that will take me out of New York City and drop me off in Hera. I envision stepping off at a dusty bus stop surrounded by fields of wheat and not a single soul nearby, other than maybe a three-legged dog. Of course, that's ridiculous. The Catskills area is known for some of its very affluent country towns. A lot of New Yorkers set up second homes there while tourists vacation in the posh spa resorts in places like New Paltz.

I really can't remember Hera very well, though, so the idea of leaving a city of nine million people and going to a town of less than a thousand sounds more ominous than it should. Especially when, much to my dismay, there's no mass transportation. For a girl who has an unused driver's license because I take the train everywhere, I have a hard time wrapping my head around a town without a subway system.

Sleep comes late, I'm too anxious thinking about my aunt who is a distant image in my memory bank. I lie in bed on the first warm night of summer, listening to the street life through the open window; laughing couples, groups of friends talking too loudly and honking cars. These are the same sounds that have kept me company while I studied, lived and worked in the city most of my life; graduating high school at fourteen, graduating Columbia at seventeen and finishing my masters at M.I.T. at nineteen. I am the math geek that no one, especially me, ever dreams of being.

I also wonder why my parents haven't called me. Surely they must have been informed about Aunt Virginia's death. It's just as well, we rarely speak and, when we do, it's generic small talk about my work.

Two

Hera is truly a small town and, although it's not far from Woodstock, it's definitely not as famous. Well, not famous at all. In fact, most people drive through the main street in less than sixty seconds and don't realize they have passed through an actual town. I realize this when the bus stops without an announcement and the bus driver walks back to my seat to tell me we have arrived in Hera. I grab my two bags, as well as my portfolio case and exit the bus alone.

I scan the town, which is nothing more than a short stretch of low-scale buildings on either side of the main drag, just like in an old Western movie. However, there is no three-legged dog, only a thin man in a striped suit wearing a bow tie, who looks like what I would imagine of someone named Archibald Bixby. I smile because he looks more out of place than me; standing at a bus stop in his dapper outfit on a Saturday morning.

"Jessica," he says, reaching for my bags. "I'm Archie."

I let him take the two suitcases while I hold onto my portfolio and art supplies.

"Hello." I deliberate over adding Archie to my greeting, but it seems too soon to speak to him on such familiar terms. "Thank you for picking me up at the station... bus."

"Of course. I wouldn't let a young woman wander around trying to find her own way." I want to laugh, considering I've just arrived from one of the biggest cities and Hera is nothing more than a patch of grass, hardly a dangerous place for young women. However, Archie looks to be about seventy-five or older, so he probably doesn't realize how much freedom young women—especially me—have been given to roam and wander wherever they please.

"My office is only two minutes or so that way. Let's go sit and have a chat. We will have some tea and biscuits. I bet you could use some refreshment," he says in that old-timey way of his.

"Mr. Bixby—I mean—Archie, you know New York is only a couple of hours from here." I laugh. "You make it sound like I travelled across the country. Really, it was an easy trip, shorter than taking the Jitney to the Hamptons."

"I know. I forget that people travel everywhere at any time nowadays," he says while walking quickly with a tight grip on my bags. "You see, in the last fifty years, I have rarely left this town. Trips into the city are an ordeal for me."

"Why?" I ask, trying to keep up my pace with the spry old man.

"Fear. I suppose it's agoraphobia or something. I'm not afraid to leave my house mind you, but somehow I can't bring myself to leave the borders of Hera unless absolutely necessary. We have arrived," he announces as we approach a small, two story, wood-framed building.

It's painted a light blue and has black shutters. It's quaint, like a step back in time. A brass plaque by the door is engraved with *Offices of Archibald Bixby, Esq.* I find myself smiling again because there is simply something about the town; with its slowness and old-fashioned buildings stuck in a different time.

Before entering the office, I study the main street again. There are a handful of people and a few cars, but it's pretty quiet and sparse.

"Hey, Bixby," a deep voice says from behind us. Archie and I both turn to where a man has jumped out of a truck. He looks like he's in his mid-twenties or older; muscular build, very tall, dark brown, tussled, shoulder length hair and broad shoulders on a trim frame. He is definitely too handsome, too gorgeous and too intimidating for me. He's the kind of guy any woman would notice. He looks like he walked right out of a truck commercial. He even has the faded jeans, well-worn T-shirt and dusty work boots to complete the picture. I can't help staring.

"Carson," Archie greets, turning towards the man. "I'll bet you are anxious for that check."

"I am." As Carson approaches us, I see that his eyes are a steel blue. "I want to start building the new addition soon and I need the investor contracts." He is speaking to Archie, though his intense gaze is locked on me. His demeanor is neither openly friendly nor hostile, but he makes me avert my eyes nonetheless. Queasiness assaults me down to the pit of my stomach and I feel as if I've been revealed; that this guy can see past anyone's veneer.

"Jessica, this is Carson Blackard," Archie says with a smile and an extra-long look at both Carson and me.

Mr. Handsome tilts his chin up at me and then looks away. I don't even warrant a proper hello from him, so I only utter a quiet "hi" to the disinterested man. *Seventy-million! Seventy-million!* My brain's first protective reaction is to chant one of my favorite numbers. *Oh, to be cursed with obsessive, compulsive behaviors.* Left unguarded, I would probably sound like a rambling, lunatic parrot.

I follow Archie into his little two-room office with Carson looming behind me. I sense his urgency to get what he wants from Archie so he can leave and I happen to be slowing things down. Archie gets me seated with a plate of cookies and a can of seltzer. Thank God, he didn't give me a glass of milk in front of this Carson dude.

I nibble on a homemade oatmeal cookie and look around the front room, admiring the beautiful wood desk and built-in bookcases. I expected the room to be Victorian like the outside of the building; instead the furniture is craftsman style that looks too nice to have been mass-produced in a factory.

As I study the grain of the wood and the details in the table posts, I catch a snippet of Carson's voice in the other room. Then, he comes into view in the doorway and my attention is drawn to his butt, specifically how his butt fills out his jeans perfectly. He has a sexy, casual stance and I can't help ogling his exquisite form. Even though no one notices me, I feel a blush come to my face as I turn away.

Archie escorts Carson past me and out the front door before turning back to me.

"I'm sorry about that, Jessica. Carson can be a little rough around the edges. He should have extended his condolences, but I'm sure it merely slipped his mind," Archie says as he seats himself at the desk facing me.

"It's all right. He doesn't know me and it's not like I was close to Aunt Virginia."

"Well, in Hera it's not all right. We are a small, close-knit town and we know each other well enough. Children here are taught to use good manners all the time. Carson Blackard is a good young man and very talented, but sometimes he's so driven with work that he forgets the simple niceties."

I nod as if I understand the precarious nature of Carson Blackard when the only thing I know about this guy is that he sure knows how to put sexy into a pair of grubby work jeans.

"You really are a pretty young woman. You resemble your aunt. She had the same lovely red hair and brown eyes."

"Thank you. I'd like to see a photo of her."

"Oh, you will. Now, let's get down to the unfortunate task of business, shall we?" Archie pulls some papers out of a leather binder. "This is Ginnie's will. I want to review the details with you until you are satisfied." Archie pauses and looks at me with a solemn expression, exhaling a breath as if pushing out his sadness. "Before we start, I also want to tell you that Ginnie was my dear friend for many years, the last thirty years of my life, actually. They were the best years, knowing

Ginnie. She kept our circle of friends together and helped so many. There was no one else like this special woman, and I know you don't remember her, but she remembered you and kept track of you over the years."

"Why didn't she contact me? I mean, it wasn't until you called that I remembered her. I think the last time I was here was when I was around five or six and then my parents never brought me back, so it was definitely a shock when you found me. I know I have to call my parents to find out why they kept this from me, but why didn't Aunt Virginia call me? Email me? Anything?"

"I'm sorry you are finding out this way." He truly looks regretful with his furrowed brow. "All I can tell you is that Ginnie and your parents—well, your mother—had a falling out when you were a child. That's why Ginnie was cut-off from you. It's not my place to share the details. As per her instructions, she was cremated last week and her friends—the town—held a memorial service. She didn't think you should be there. Why start out on a sad note, right?"

Archie pulls a sealed envelope out of a packet and hands it to me. I reach for the ivory linen envelope that has my name elegantly scrawled across it in what must be my aunt's shaky hand.

"She explains everything in the letter. She wrote it this past winter while she was quite sick. After the paperwork here, I'll take you to her home—your home—and you can have some time to read the letter there."

I nod as a small wave of grief for a woman I barely remember washes over me. The loneliness of finding out about someone who cares about you, only to discover they have died before you can be with them, is another one of life's cruel ironies. It's the sense of losing that has been riding piggyback with me for the last twenty years. The anger I feel towards my parents prevents me from crying for my aunt; the family I could have had.

"My aunt's friends must think I'm a terrible person for not being here last week," I say, hearing my voice tremble a little.

"Not at all. They know Ginnie didn't want you to come to a funeral and remember her as a stranger. She wants you to be a part of her life now. It's all in her home and the friends she left behind. Everything about Ginnie is in Hera and she left it for you to enjoy. You'll see what I mean when we go to her house. I mean, your house." Archie gives me a reassuring smile. "Let's have you sign off on these papers and have a quick lunch before we head over to the house."

"Oh, Mr. Bixby—Archie, you don't have to take me to lunch—"

"Yes, I do. Ginnie wrote it in her instructions. 'Take Jessica to lunch at Bonnie's'."

I laugh, grateful that he is lightening the mood for my benefit.

Three

We leave my bags in his office and walk the fifty paces across the street to the diner with the sign, *Bonnie's*. I can't help thinking of this place as something out of an old cowboy movie, even though it's green instead of dusty with Toyotas and Hondas instead of horses and, of course, a diner instead of a saloon. Something about Hera is very calming and welcoming.

Inside the diner, there are quite a few patrons eating lunch at the tables and booths who all nod to Archie as we enter; even the curvaceous, sultry-looking waitress who is running around with a water pitcher gives Archie a smile and wave as we sit at the old-fashioned counter with its chrome, swivel bucket stools.

"Hi Archie!" says a pretty, blond waitress on the other side of the counter.

"Lauren. This is Jessica Channing. Ginnie's niece." Archie's slow enunciation of my name makes me feel special, as if people have been waiting for my arrival.

"Wow," Lauren says and puts her hand across the counter for a handshake.

I take her firm grip. "It's nice to meet you," I say.

"So this must be an awful shock for you," Lauren says as she hands us very large, laminated menus.

"Just two Bonnie Burgers, dear," Archie says to Lauren handing back the menus. "Oh, unless you're a vegetarian," he says to me.

"No, a burger would be great."

Archie winks at Lauren as if it's her signal to scamper off before I can respond to her comment about my sad news. I suppose Archie wants to protect me and I find that touching.

We eat our delicious burgers with gusto. For a slight man, even Archie seems enamored with the half pound of grilled meat that's slathered with mushrooms, Brie, roasted peppers and leeks. The waffle fries come with guacamole and a spicy mayonnaise. I am in a glutinous heaven, stuffing my mouth in a very un-lady-like manner as Archie slows down and begins telling me about Hera.

The population is nine hundred eighty-four and town picnics happen frequently at the end of the main street by the historic water fountain whenever the weather is nice and the mood strikes the town folk. He actually uses the term *town folk* and I giggle in between bites of food.

At that moment a stout, sixty-something-year-old woman comes out of the kitchen dressed in a blouse with a large flower print and an up-do I think originated in the 60's when aerosol hair spray was a necessity. She rounds the corner of the counter and waddles towards us to pat Archie's back with her chubby hand. Archie introduces her as *the* Bonnie of Bonnie's Diner and the other waitress, the curvy brunette, as her granddaughter, Imogene.

"Now you almost know everyone in town," Lauren jokes. "I hope you stay. I grew up here and I came back every summer during school break. Imogene and I work in the diner full-time and just hang out now. It's so relaxing here compared to city life and college."

I find out that Lauren and Imogene both graduated from Syracuse College last year and they are back in Hera trying to figure out what to do next. That puts them at least a couple years older than me and new to the workforce. I don't envy them trying to find entry-level jobs with degrees in English and History.

"Oh boy, here's trouble," Lauren says, looking over my shoulder. I turn around to see a very cute guy walk into the diner. He's what I'd call a summer boy, the Ralph Lauren ad; a tall, tan, athletic guy who sports sun-bleached light brown curls and a casually confident air. *Sure, I can surf. Sure, I play polo, who doesn't? Sure, I scuba dive, sky dive and ski off cliffs.*

Everyone is saying hello to the cute guy whose name I find out is Dylan. He makes a beeline right for us as he stares at me with a big grin and perfect white teeth. He's a stunning picture of good health and attractiveness. The Hera Chamber of Commerce should consider erecting a "*Welcome*" billboard at the entrance of town with Dylan's smiling face on it.

"I heard Archie has a visitor." He beams at me. I force the last bit of food down my throat, silently wishing I could rush off to the restroom to brush my teeth.

"Dylan, Jessica," Archie introduces, nodding towards me.

Dylan's smile is overwhelming. Up close, he radiates a sexual aura that enthralls me immediately. I smile and genuinely feel happiness soar through me as he takes my hand in his warm, calloused one.

"Hi there." I try to be as casual as possible even though he has made my nerves jump to new heights.

"Hi there, yourself," he says. "I'm glad I finally get to meet the famous Jessica. Ginnie talked about you a lot."

I can't believe these people know about me when I can barely remember my aunt. I wasn't even aware she was alive or that this community still existed less than two hours from my home in Manhattan.

My thoughts must have given me a slightly panicked expression because Lauren jumps in to remedy Dylan's bluntness. "It's okay," she says to me. "We know Ginnie wasn't in touch with you and that you didn't know that she was tracking you all these years."

"She only said good things about you," Dylan adds as I gently release his hand.

"This is all new to me," I say. "Twenty-four hours ago, I didn't even remember that Hera existed, and now I'm meeting all of you and hearing about my aunt. It's like finding out about a parallel existence in a way. I know that sounds dumb." I also now feel sort of dumb for saying that.

17

"You're right, dear. You were a specter in this town. Ginnie talked about you for years so we knew about you, but you had no real memories of Ginnie and our little town here," Archie says, pushing his plate away.

"My parents should have told me all of this." It would have been a sad, nostalgic moment for me to ponder about not having Aunt Ginnie in my life, but Dylan leans on the counter between Archie and me, filling up the space with his ruddy masculinity, and all I can do is swoon a little bit.

"I say, we go to the house and jog your memory a little bit," Dylan says to me.

"That's the plan," Archie says.

"I'll go with you and give you the tour. I know that place better than anyone. Carson and I are still working on Ginnie's To-Do list," Dylan says with contagious enthusiasm.

"List?"

"Dylan and Carson, that surly man in my office, have been doing a significant amount of carpentry for Ginnie," Archie says. "And now Dylan and his brother work for you."

"That's right; you're my client." Dylan smiles.

"That sounds like fun," Imogene says, approaching us with an armload of dirty dishes. "But, Lauren, it's time for you to get back to work."

Lauren gives Imogene an exaggerated eye roll and pushes herself away from the counter.

"Archie is going to convince you to stay, at least for a while, so Lauren and I will be up to visit you at the house real soon," Imogene says. "And, Jessica, I'm very sorry for your loss. I'm sorry you didn't get to know Ginnie the way we did."

As Imogene and Lauren leave to attend to customers, sadness and guilt sweep over me at the image of Aunt Virginia. To think I could have had someone besides my parents to lean on through my lonely years as my parents' only child, their prodigy. It would have helped me tremendously.

Archie pats my hand. "It's too hard to explain here," he says. "Dylan, bring that monstrous vehicle of yours around front and we'll take Jessica and her luggage up to the house."

"My pleasure," Dylan responds while looking at me. I have a stupid grin plastered on my face, like the inexperienced geek that I am.

Four

After Dylan fetches my bags from Archie's office, he comes back to the diner in a red Jeep Wrangler that is caked with so many layers of dried mud that it makes me wonder what this guy does for fun during his down time. The hard top has been removed from the vehicle, which I suppose is to be expected from an athletic guy who looks like he spends most of his time outdoors.

Archie is put off by the general filth of the vehicle and lays a hankie on the front seat before buckling himself in. I climb in the back seat and Dylan gives me another smile accompanied by a wink in the rearview mirror. That winking-smiling business is going to be the end of me. I can see how it can manipulate women like an addictive drug. I put on my sunglasses to block out his power, yet it doesn't seem to lessen his charm one bit. He keeps glancing at me in the mirror throughout the drive and I'm pretty sure he can tell I'm looking at him even with my sunglasses on.

It's about a ten minute drive to Aunt Virginia's home; off the main street and through roughly paved roads that have little to no traffic. I only see a few old homes along the way, most of them far back from the road with long, dirt driveways and acres of wild land. It's green, lush and absolutely nothing like my city life. As we bounce along a particularly bad road, Archie holds onto the roll bar above and an insect flies into my mouth. I'm horrified and struggle to spit it out while Dylan laughs loudly as he watches my comic antics through the rear view mirror.

Okay, bugs-in-mouth, that's one check against Hera. Hot gorgeous guy in Archie's office and cute guy who drives a rough and tumble Jeep with a sexy laugh to boot, that's worth at least ten checks *for* Hera.

"There it is," Archie yells over Dylan's grinding gears as he down shifts to climb up the dirt road to a large Victorian house.

"Wow."

The home is painted a hunter green with brown shutters. Since I have only lived in small New York and Cambridge apartments my whole life, any house seems large to me; however, Aunt Virginia's house—well, my new house—is outright huge. It has an incredible, wraparound porch and at least three stories with actual turrets and alcoves. It's beautiful, like a walk back in time to the 1800's, and I fully expect to see a woman with her hair piled on her head, dressed in a vintage white linen dress, gliding out onto the porch or veranda with an iced tea.

My imagination gets away from me as I analyze this enormous house that looks much too big for someone as small as me. Seriously, this is a house for a big family or a bunch of ghosts who are into some serious haunting.

"Wait until you see the inside, Jess," Dylan says. "It's a masterpiece." I'm still stuck on him calling me *Jess*, as though we already know each other so well.

As I push myself out of the Jeep, Dylan is instantly at my side, holding my arm to assist with the jump to the ground, but right as I'm about to step out, he grabs my waist with both of his hands and lifts me out.

"Oh," I say, startled and feeling incredibly brilliant with words because a handsome guy has surprised me.

"Thought I'd save you a step or two," he says, still keeping a firm grip on my waist.

I raise my sunglasses and prop them on my head, but can think of nothing to say to him.

"Come on, let's go!" Archie shouts with his back to us, already halfway up the stone path to the front door.

"Ah." Dylan puts his hands down and studies my face. "It's nice to finally have you here."

"Thank you," I say awkwardly. "Despite the circumstances, I think I'm happy to be here, too. At least, I'm intrigued."

I head up the walkway after Archie, and Dylan follows close enough behind me that I can hear his soft breaths. I've only just met him, however, this feels good and it seems right. I look up at the magnificent house and then at the blue sky as I wonder why my aunt orchestrated all of this for me.

"The first step creaks and sounds loose, but it's okay," Dylan says as we take the wide, wooden staircase up to the porch where Archie is waiting for us. "It's on our list."

"What list, again?"

"Carson and I have been working for Ginnie for the last three months. Redoing floors and cabinetry. Right now, we're working on the bookshelves."

"Ginnie decided that she wanted to fix up the whole house and add some new things," Archie adds.

"Why? I mean, she was ill; why did she want to work on the house? Oh, God. I'm sorry. That was a callous thing to say."

"No worries. She did this for you, dear," Archie answers.

"It's a great house," Dylan says. "Great bones. Ginnie wanted to preserve it even if she couldn't be here to enjoy it. She talked about making it a special place for you."

He pulls a set of keys out of his jean pocket and unlocks the heavy front door that looks as though it has been stripped and re-stained with a stunning vintage doorknocker added for those who don't know how to work a doorbell. I then realize there is no doorbell.

Dylan pushes the door open and lets Archie go through first. As I proceed to follow, Dylan jumps in front of me and I slam my nose into his hard chest.

"Ow!"

"Sorry, before you go in there, I want you to know that the whole place is a work in progress. Some rooms are pretty dirty and we have equipment everywhere."

I rub my nose and look up at him. *Hera sure produces tall dudes.* I judge Dylan to be about six-two, shorter than Carson, but almost a foot taller than me. "It's fine. If you saw my apartment, you wouldn't even be worried about such things."

"Well, you're going to be staying here and I want to make sure you're comfortable," he says softly, so Archie can't hear I presume. "Don't worry; your room hasn't been touched. Yet."

He grins and the heat rises in my face. What does *yet* mean? *Yet, he's going to actually repair things in my bedroom? Or, yet, meaning he's going to touch something in my designated bedroom? And why does my brain go on and on with these sexual thoughts?*While I have these thoughts he grabs my hand and leads me into the grand entryway.

"It's a mansion," I state, taking in the polished wood banister and staircase that winds up three more flights.

"No, but it's very large and requires quite a bit of upkeep." Archie appears from another room, glancing at our hands with his eyebrows arched. Dylan is still clenching my hand so I wriggle mine out and begin to walk around the front hall with a nonchalant air to shake off the Dylan effects.

"This young man is a little tuckered out, and yes, I'm referring to me, so I'm going to perch myself in one of those comfy wingbacks." Archie walks back into the living room towards the only chair not covered by a plastic tarp. The rest of the furniture has been pushed to one side and covered so a table saw and equipment can utilize most of the space.

Archie leans and falls into the chair as any stiff octogenarian might and the image of him makes me think of Aunt Virginia sitting there reading her paper as she drinks her morning cup of coffee while

Dylan and Carson work around her sawing away at something. In my vision, they make a racket, yet Aunt Virginia welcomes the noise and the company of two energetic, handsome men. Then, when it is time, she will make them a lunch that they'll enjoy on the porch's wicker dining set. Maybe it's the town, or the home from another era, but somehow I think my aunt had a wonderful life with her makeshift family and it was much more interesting than the one I lead.

"Dylan, give this lovely girl a tour of her home. You know these walls better than anyone," Archie instructs.

"Absolutely." Dylan turns to me. "Come this way, lovely girl."

I follow him up the winding staircase and, while I admire the rich buttery tones of the wood paneling and the modern touches of contemporary paintings to make the home brighter, I'm really focused on Dylan's cute backside. I try to suppress a giggle; I never find myself in these types of situations and it's highly amusing that I have this hunky guy to myself.

Dylan reaches the first floor and spins around. "What, lovely girl?" he asks. "What's so funny? You're bruising my ego with all that giggling behind my back."

"Nothing, I'm still in shock at being here, I think. And don't call me 'lovely girl'. It's sweet coming from Archie, but it's a little smarmy coming from you."

Dylan's smile fades and that alone makes me waver. I was only teasing him; I don't really think he's the smarmy type, so why did I say something that could possibly be hurtful?

"I'm sorry. It wasn't intended to be creepy."

"My fault. I'm very defensive. It's part of being an only child driven by obsessive, demanding parents." I give him a weak smile and a nervous laugh.

Dylan studies my face intently. For once I don't blush and look away like I normally would. I take in his baby-face good looks with his big blue eyes and full lips, and I know that he must have been very popular in school while I would have been the shy girl who watched him from a distance. I don't know how long the moment lasts, but it could go on forever for all I care. For the first time, I don't have to rush off to a class or work, I don't have to bury my head in front of a computer to get a job done and I don't have to dance with a guy who's attractiveness disappears the minute he opens his mouth or puts his hands on me in a way that gives me the willies. For once, I can breathe and simply stare at this person in front of me.

"Why would you be defensive about a compliment? I'm sure you've heard it a thousand times before," he says, sounding more serious.

"Heard what before?" I ask, distracted by our physical closeness as well as my wandering mind.

"That you're beautiful," he answers. I'm still studying his lips that said *beautiful* before I understand what he's saying.

"Oh, no. I mean, there's always someone who will say something flattering, but for the most part, my parents only complimented my grades and test scores," I say, listening to how stupid my explanation sounds.

"Your boyfriends must have told you how pretty you are. You know, attention from guys who aren't Archie? Guys under one hundred?"

I laugh, but I don't have an answer for him that doesn't make me look pathetic. *Yes, I'm twenty, but I've never had a real boyfriend because I'm a serial dater. One date per guy and then I dump them in disgust because I'm the smart, pretty girl who only attracts jerks. Please don't tell me you're a jerk because I'm having too much fun for this to end.*

"Okay, sure. Guys have complimented me before, so thank you for the compliment. Now let's move on." I forge ahead and end up in what must be the study.

I scan the room which is filled with leather couches, the old, cracked kind that you can sink into, stacks of books on the floor and in boxes, an immense desk piled with more books, a full wall of bay windows that overlook hills of green and two walls of built-in bookcases that are unfinished.

"This is the library. Carson and I have to finish the shelving and stain it, and when it's done, we're going to load about four thousand of Ginnie's books in here, and what do you mean, let's move on? Am I making you uncomfortable?"

"This room is fantastic." I ignore his question. "I can totally picture myself sitting at that desk with my computer and looking out at that incredible view." I have my back to Dylan now and I'm hoping that will stop him from asking about my personal life, or rather, my sorry-ass dating life. Nope, that doesn't stop him. He barrels around the desk, in his big, dirty work boots, stomping on my newly inherited floor and gets right in my face.

"Can I assume by your obvious jitteriness that you don't have a boyfriend?" he asks, putting his hand on my arm. His confident smile is back.

"No boyfriend." Cringe. Admit defeat.

"Shit. I mean, excuse me. Shit," he repeats. *Bingo, this is usually when I discover a guy is an ignorant, illiterate Neanderthal and I lose interest. Actually, Dylan, you've made it farther than most guys. You've held my interest for almost a full hour!*

I shake off his hand, walk to the window and pretend to take great interest in the large, ancient trees in the yard. "So when is all this renovation work going to be done?" I ask, facing the window. "When are you and your brother going to be out of here?"

"Oh, wait a minute." He laughs and turns me around. "You aren't getting rid of me that fast, and you aren't leaving this town without me getting at least one date with you."

"I just met you. How did we go from talking about finishing bookcases to going on a date?"

"No, you *think* you just met me. I've known you for years. Look around this room. Really look."

I don't know what he's getting at, but I look around the room. I see paintings on the floor, leaning against the wall. The paintings of people and abstract backgrounds are familiar; maybe something Aunt Virginia painted years ago. At least she and I have our art in common. Then the sun comes through the window and strikes a swath of golden light across the wide pine planks and the crackled leather couch and I remember those paintings hung on the wall where the bookcases are currently being built. How do I know this?

Another memory assaults me; I am jumping off the couch and being chased by a laughing boy. We hide under the massive desk, covering our mouths to suppress the laughter. Another voice calls our names. It's another boy, older than us. We hear him jump on the desk.

"He jumped on the desk to scare us," I say, staring at the distance between the couch and the desk caught in the sunlight.

"What?" Dylan asks. I turn back to him and I can tell he is excited that I'm remembering something he knew all along.

"It's you," I barely whisper.

Dylan puts his hands up to my face. He is gentle, but his firm touch and his scent give me a pleasant jolt. "Do you remember me?"

"I've been here before. In this room." Dylan nods, though he doesn't let go of my face. "You were the boy hiding with me under the desk, right?"

"Yes. You were five—almost six—and I was eight. We were hiding from Carson. Ginnie and your mom had him babysit us while they went to the farmers market."

"Carson jumped on the desk to scare us and we were laughing." I notice I'm shaking.

Dylan lets go of my face and rests his hands on my shoulders. "Yes, that was us. In this room. Laughing. I remember everything about that summer you lived here."

"I lived here the whole summer?"

Dylan nods his head. "Carson and I lived here that summer, too, and you and I played together every day. I didn't think I could stand being with a five-year-old, but you were so smart and we had a lot of fun together. It was right after my mom died and Carson became so serious. He was eleven and felt he had to watch over me. He stopped being fun. And then you came to town."

I take in everything he is saying and will myself to remember more. Dylan moves closer and puts his head down to mine. "I have been waiting for you to come back."

There is so much longing in that statement, but then I think I understand where it's coming from. We were children and maybe he feels I'm like a long lost friend, perhaps someone very special to him because I was regarded as unique. I was the smart, mouthy little girl who could play with boys and often act older than my age.

I feel a soft, forceful mouth on my lips. I open my eyes at the same time I accept Dylan's kiss. We both pull back simultaneously. I am confused and nervous while Dylan simply looks amused.

"I missed you, Jess. I've thought about you a lot over the last fifteen years."

"I can't believe you remember me. We were little kids and it was one summer of hide and seek and the baby pool. I remember that crappy little pool!"

Dylan laughs. "The baby pool that Carson would always turn over to make us miserable. Or he'd chase us with the water hose. Remember?"

"My God, I do. We were the troublemakers and he was the warden."

"Don't feel sorry for Carson; he got paid some mighty fine coin to watch over us."

"He didn't say anything when I saw him at Archie's office. He barely acknowledged me." I think of the cold greeting I received from Carson earlier that day.

Dylan shrugs. "It's been hard for Carson. He was devastated when our mom died and he felt it was his job to be the man of the house. Our dad was still alive then, but her death didn't stop him from disappearing for weeks at a time. Ginnie took us in. I mean, we had a home with our dad, but when he was gone, missing or whatever you want to call it, we stayed here with Ginnie."

"I didn't know any of this," I say with regret, but also with a touch of mounting anger. "My parents didn't stay in touch with my aunt and I didn't know what happened. I didn't know she was still alive. All these memories faded." I was getting worked up and about to cry.

"I know." Dylan's hands are back on my arms to comfort me. "I know, Jess. I know everything, but we promised we wouldn't find you and tell you. We promised Ginnie."

"But I'm here now. Are you going to tell me what's going on?"

"You better believe it. I've been waiting for this day. Come on, let's finish the tour to jog those memories and then we'll sit down with Arch to go over things."

Five

I'm surprised that our walk through three floors and a basement, all of which consisted of twelve rooms—five of which are bedrooms and five bathrooms—doesn't overwhelm me. I'm used to three people living in the space of a walk-in closet with one lousy, cramped bathroom.

Bits and pieces of memories come back as I enter each new room. Some haven't changed from what I can remember; the same worn furniture or an old-fashioned light fixture next to one of Aunt Ginnie's abstracts is enough to wake up some of my stored memories. Dylan shows me photos in my Aunt's room. Dozens of frames showing a beautiful, red-headed woman with various people. My aunt was stunning; the camera captured her vivacious joy. There are even a few photos of my mother, young and beautiful, with me and two young boys, Dylan and Carson.

Dylan takes his time walking me through each room and describing repairs that have been done or what needs to be done, however, underneath his calm exterior, he is anxious to talk about the years that have passed without me.

We finish downstairs in the pantry, a room of smooth, worn, wood counters and floor-to-ceiling cabinets. It's a space directly off the kitchen specifically designed for the cook who would prepare elaborate meals for the grand dinners that used to be hosted in the stately home over the last century.

"This pantry is about the size of my first off-campus apartment," I tell Dylan.

"There you two are! You forgot about me. I forgot about me. I fell asleep in that dusty chair and you were gone so long I think I missed my hundredth birthday." Archie stands in the low doorway to the pantry.

"Sorry, Arch. We had a lot of ground to cover," Dylan explains. "Jess remembers."

Archie takes in a long slow breath. "Oh my."

"I don't remember everything. Just parts of that summer I was here. Mostly images or events that were highly entertaining for a five-year-old. Most of those seem to include Dylan, but I'm missing huge chunks. Dylan said you'd both fill me in."

"Oh my," Archie says again. "I didn't expect all of this to happen so fast. I thought it would be discussed over days as you go through your aunt's possessions; however, I suppose the game has changed now that you have a new awareness."

"Isn't it great?" Dylan says as more of a statement rather than a question.

I'm still caught in a veil of confusion between the kiss and Dylan divulging that he has missed me all these years. Missed me in what way?

"Hmm," Archie says with a tentative smile. "Great it is, my dear."

"Don't do the Yoda thing on me, Arch," Dylan says. "I'm going to take Jess's bags up to the yellow room."

"That's my old room, the one with the white lilies on the yellow wallpaper, right?" I shout like I'm a game show contestant.

Archie is a little taken back by my enthusiasm. "If this is how it works, I can tell it's going to be an exhausting evening."

Dylan is laughing. "Isn't it a hoot? She's like an amnesia patient."

Archie looks horrified with that comparison. "Let's make this less morbid, shall we? First, we'll need food and beverages. Dylan, call Lauren and Imogene. We're going to need them."

"I seriously doubt they want to shop and cook for us after they've been working all day serving other people," Dylan comments.

"Of course, Dylan. I want you to order food from Bonnie's and have the girls *bring* it. We need enough for five of us, no seven. I'm going to call... you know what? No, wait." Archie taps his head with his finger.

"You're slipping into Yoda again. Make sense, old man."

"Oh, fine. Order enough food to feed seven and go down in the cellar and bring up three bottles of Bordeaux," Archie says, leading us out of the pantry and back to the front entryway. "Jessica, I don't want you to be overwhelmed with all these people trying to fill in missing pieces, but we'll make this a celebratory occasion, not a time for eulogies."

"Great, a party. Do I have to call Carson?" I sense that Dylan has no intention of calling his brother. There's some type of sibling conflict going on there which is lost on me.

"Well, Carson should be here, but our moody friend seems to have other things on his mind at the moment." Archie takes a cell phone out of his suit pocket. "I'm going to go outside and call Lois and Eleanor."

"You don't need to leave if you want privacy. I'll go upstairs and unpack," I say.

"No, dear. There's terrible cell phone service here. This house is like a vortex of technological mishaps. It drives me insane when I'm talking to someone on my phone and they simply disappear. It never seemed to bother Ginnie, though."

"You can help me," Dylan says, grabbing my hand and rushing me down the porch steps to his Jeep.

"Slow down, my legs are half as long as yours."

Dylan pulls me in fast, swinging me against his body and capturing me with his hands in my hair. I only get a glance of his determined expression before his mouth is warm and urgent on mine. I close my eyes and give in to the glorious rush of his aggressive kiss. I can't believe I'm letting him put his tongue down my throat, while at the same time I don't want him to stop. I pull away and gape at him, almost panting with my lips still wet and tender.

"God, you're beautiful," he says, edging closer to me.

"Why do you think you can kiss me like that? I wasn't your girlfriend at the age of five, so where do you get off pretending that I am now?" I'm not angry, yet I feel like I am losing control around him and that's definitely something that is new to me.

"It felt right," he says, moving even closer and letting his hands run up and down my bare arms. "There's something between us, right? You were kissing me back."

I groan in frustration and lean against his Jeep. "This has to stop. You move too fast, mister. I remember you as a little boy, I barely know you now."

"Yeah, I keep forgetting that, even though I've been thinking about you for over a decade, I'm new to you. I'll give you a little time to catch up," he says, giving me one of those damn winks.

"Why do you say it like that? That you've been waiting for me all these years? Why? A long time ago, I was your little friend for a summer, but we didn't keep in touch, so why do you have this exaggerated view of me?"

"You were special to me. You weren't like a sister, that's for sure. I kind of thought of you as a magical creature. You were so smart, even at five. The clever things that came out of your mouth would amaze me. Carson had to take a summer math program, and you'd glance at his homework then rattle off the answers to problems he needed a calculator for. Not to mention that your vocabulary was far beyond my level. You'd read the morning paper to Ginnie like a news anchor. Then there was your hair, it was just like it is now, red and long with blond streaks from the sun. It would get curly and wild after a rainstorm. You looked like some kind of powerful fairy," he explains with his hands miming my wild hair. "You look the same. Just taller and, well, more like a woman of course."

I am quiet as I dwell on his flattering comments. To be remembered and revered is an extraordinary feeling for me; I don't think my parents have ever thought of me as positively as Dylan does.

"Thank you," I say as I wrap my arms around myself.

"For what? For kissing you?"

"For telling me these things about myself." I pick up my art supply box while Dylan grabs the two suitcases and we start walking back to the house. "The jury is still out on the kiss."

Dylan laughs. "It wasn't good enough?"

Oh, it was good enough. Good and steamy. "My life is in New York. I don't want to make things complicated here while I'm visiting."

"We'll see about that," Dylan says as he holds the front door open for me.

Six

As the house fills up with people, I can hear the cheerfully raucous voices carrying up to the third floor where I am unpacking in my old bedroom with the faded yellow wallpaper. I hang a couple of blouses and a summer dress in the empty closet that smells like cedar. Then I put my jeans, T-shirts, and underwear in a creaky, stiff dresser that I don't recall being in this room.

"You know, you could stay in Ginnie's old room." Dylan enters my bedroom with my art portfolio case that I left downstairs. "It's bigger and has a nice view of the front yard. Plus, she renovated the master bathroom and put in one of those spa tubs."

"No, I want to stay in my old room."

"You forgot this." Dylan puts the portfolio on the bed.

"I think I'll take that down to Ginnie's studio. I brought my art supplies."

"Yeah, I heard you're a painter, too."

I nod and turn back to the dresser. "Dylan, was this here when I was a kid?" I ask, pointing to the dresser.

"No, I think that used to be in another bedroom. When you stayed here there was a giant basket full of toys against this wall and a little rocking chair. Those are in the basement."

"Could you push the dresser to the right for me?" I ask, studying the wall to the left of the dresser.

Dylan doesn't question my request; he simply lifts the left side of the dresser as if it weighs nothing and gently pushes it aside. I drop to my knees and look at the red crayon scrawled on the wall. *Jess.*

"Hey, would you look at that," Dylan says, crouching down next to me. He grins. "I told ya you were smart. You were marking your territory, even at five."

Our faces are inches apart. I smile, happy that these memories are bringing back a flood of good emotions.

"You know, I'm harnessing the strength of one hundred soldiers right now, doing everything in my weakening will power not to kiss you." His warm breath caresses my face.

"It's very admirable." I stand up before my body tries to betray me by kissing him first.

"Okay, I guess that's enough temptation. How about we set up your studio?" Dylan suggests.

Eventually, Dylan and I make it back downstairs to join the others who have come to visit. After dinner, the dining room is covered in dirty dishes, empty wine goblets and remnants of the fried chicken, mashed potatoes and various salads Bonnie made for our impromptu dinner meeting. I sit between Lauren and Dylan and across from Archie and Imogene. Lois and Eleanor, Aunt Virginia's dearest friends, sit at either end of the table. They are both in their sixties, and very striking and pretty, showing off every well-earned wrinkle along with fashionably styled hair that doesn't hide their silver and gray. They look very fit in their bright linen tunics and the yoga pants they say they prefer to wear.

"Keeping up your physical health at our age is full-time work, so we do yoga and Pilates five days a week. Might as well keep the pants on," Lois says to me in an exasperated tone. "Sometimes I get so sick and tired of bending over and having to look at someone else's rear end in front of me. Honestly. Not to mention all these new-age people and their phony 'namaste' greetings. Between the expensive classes, retreats and the clothing lines, this yoga business is really a racket. It would be nice to take it beyond the pants, if you know what I mean."

"We're opening our own studio in Hera soon so we don't have to keep driving to Woodstock for classes," Eleanor adds. "Oh! I just thought of a name for our studio, Lois. Beyond The Pants!"

Lois and I both laugh. Imogene and Lauren give each other shrugs. They are used to this type of banter among people who are more like family than friends. I'm not. My parents are both uptight prudes who found their soul mate by seeking out the only other person in the tri-state area that was born without a sense of humor. My family doesn't hang out and laugh. We argue and debate. Rather, my mother and father argue and debate with me, their only child; the kid who is supposed to live up to all of their expectations.

After several hot and heavy stolen kisses from Dylan earlier and the laid back sassiness of these women, young and old, I am very comfortable in their company.

I'm not a big drinker since I'm not of the legal drinking age, so the half glass of wine I drank is making me tired as well as unbearably aware of my proximity to Dylan and his muscular leg, which he has conveniently positioned against mine. It does not go unnoticed by the others when he rests his arm across the back of my chair as if we are a couple at a dinner soiree.

Archie briefly glances at Dylan with a raised eyebrow. "I think we've had time to get to know Jessica. It's probably time we talk about how she got here," he announces.

The letter from Aunt Ginny is still sealed in the ivory envelope. It is now damp from my sweaty hands having clutched it in my lap all through dinner. I rest the letter on the empty place setting before me as Imogene voluntarily walks around the table collecting dirty dishes.

"Ah, would you like to read that alone?" Archie asks me.

"I'm not sure." I look around the room at everyone.

"If it helps any, Ginnie was not the kind of person that liked to surprise people. She was always very direct. I don't think there will be anything unusual in the letter. It's more like a goodbye message," Dylan says.

Archie clears his throat and Dylan glances at him.

"I mean, it's probably a 'Hello, Jessica' letter, 'Welcome to Hera'," Dylan redirects. His thoughtful attempt to ease whatever sad blows I'm expecting is touching. I'm becoming alarmed at how easy I'm falling for this cute guy because falling for such males is not in my genetic make-up. I come from hard-driven people with an unforgiving view towards the sentimental.

"I'll read it now. You were all her family, so it seems appropriate that you hear it, too."

A loud crash, a banging door and something heavy falling to the floor comes from the front entryway and disrupts our silence.

"Sweet Jesus!" Lois exclaims.

"Shit." Dylan stands abruptly and his chair falls back and clatters to the floor.

We all scurry to the front door to see Carson standing there with a drill box at his feet.

"No wonder you didn't answer your phone. You're already here," he speaks angrily to Dylan.

"Carson, what are you doing?" Archie asks. It sounds like he's trying to be as soothing as possible to calm Carson down.

"Dylan and I have been working on the library at night. You know I have a day job," Carson hisses to everyone, but then he looks at me. "So you're staying here?"

"We didn't say we were working tonight. Besides, Jess is staying here, so we have to change our hours back to days. She's not going to be able to sleep through the drilling and pounding," Dylan says before I can answer Carson's question.

"Carson, do you ever stop working? Honestly, you need some Zen," Lois tells him while Eleanor and Lauren nod in agreement.

"Huh?" Carson grunts.

Other than the same tall muscular physique from hard labor and an inherent handsomeness, Carson doesn't really resemble Dylan. His serious blue eyes against his dark hair, sculpted cheekbones and strong chin are nothing like Dylan's cute baby face charm.

"So," Carson directs to me. "Are you here to marry me?"

There's an audible gasp from Lauren.

"Say what?" Imogene asks in a laughing tone.

"What?" I whisper.

"Ignore him, Jess," Dylan says. "He always has something cynical up his sleeve."

"Maybe you forgot, little brother, but this woman said I'd be her husband. Let me see, I think her exact words were *'Carson Blackard, you can be quite a nasty boy when you want, but someday if you're nice, I'll marry you.'*"

Everyone, but me, Dylan and Carson, is howling with laughter.

"I remember when you said that, Jessica," Lois says. "It was when you discovered Carson had eaten all of your homemade cookies and he blamed it on Dylan. We were having dinner outside and you made this announcement to him and stormed back into the house. You were so cute. We had such a good laugh watching you scold Carson and then declare he'd be your husband."

"I don't remember that," Dylan says, shaking his head.

"You were a bossy little piece of work," Carson says to me, although he doesn't smile as you'd expect when people are sharing humorous stories.

His eyes quickly take me in from head to toe. He looks like he's glaring, but I catch his roaming observation even if the others don't. He's checking me out and I get the impression that he's not

thrilled to see me. Maybe he sees me as problem—
an obstacle in their daily life—and a distraction for
Dylan who is supposed to be working with him. Or
maybe he liked Aunt Virginia's home without me in
it because I'm a reminder of a time that was
painful. Perhaps Dylan saw me as a godsend, the
friend he needed, and Carson saw me as a new
responsibility, the bratty kid he had to babysit.

"Sorry, but I don't remember that at all. Which
is a good thing, I suppose," I say. "And by the way,
the wedding is off."

Dylan and the others laugh and I'm pretty sure
I see a tiny smirk break Carson's clenched jaw.

"Sorry to hear that, Jess." He picks up his drill
box.

Hearing my name on his lips gives me a
moment of surprise. The emotion coursing through
me is pure elation. He used my proper name and
not *Babycakes*, the nickname that has come back to
haunt my images of this house. He sees me as a
woman now and not the annoying five-year-old who
apparently bossed everyone around.

"I'm going to drop this off in the library before I
go." Carson takes the drill box up a few steps and
then pauses to look back at me. "Babycakes, let me
know when I can get back in here to work, okay?"
My spirits sink again. *Babycakes.* I hold no special
regard for that name, especially when it's said in a
snide voice.

"Right, Babycakes, the little spitfire of that
exciting summer," Archie nods. "I had forgotten
that nickname."

"Babyyyyycaaaaakes," Lauren and Imogene
croon in unison. "How sweet."

"There will be no Babycakes while I'm here," I retort. "Understood?" I hear Carson laughing from upstairs.

"I prefer Jess anyway," Dylan consoles.

After the incident with Carson, we take our coffee and pies onto the porch, which is filled with citronella candles in clear glasses lining the railing and positioned on tables. They give off a dreamy, yellow glow as they keep the bugs away. The porch is very wide with two wicker couches, a coffee table, several wicker chairs with end tables on one end and then a big rope hammock that takes up the other end.

I sit next to Lauren on one of the loveseats and lean forward towards the coffee table so I can read Aunt Virginia's letter by the light of one of the candles. Everyone stops chattering and focuses on me. I start tearing open the letter as gently as possible when I hear the front door creak open and close. I look up to see Carson fold his thick arms and lean against the doorframe. Our eyes meet and then I look down again at my letter. I begin to read out loud:

Dear Jessica,

It is with a very heavy heart that I write this letter. Had I been a braver woman, I would have ignored foolish family protocol and contacted you years ago. I hope being in my home, which is now yours, reminds you of me as well as the people that loved you and missed you terribly for all these wasted years. I was a fool for not staying in your life. I let your parents' anger and judgment dictate and, for that, I am sorry. Sometimes we broads screw up. Let that be a lesson."

I pause as Lois and Eleanor laugh.

"Onto more interesting things. You were a lively, precocious girl who brightened my home, my life and those around you. I saw the spark of your talents and intelligence and watched them ignite into powerful flames. I wasn't with you in person, but I watched you from afar. Your extraordinary gifts in academics made me so proud when you graduated college at an age when most are beginning. Your expressions in painting are dazzling. Whatever you do in life, never, never stop painting.

It must be a shock to hear from me. I would understand if you are hurt and angry over the conflict between your parents and me. Let me say again how sorry I am for that. Years ago, your mother and I were very close until I made the mistake of trying to come between her and your father. Your mother was similar to you in academics and art, however, with no slight intended to Michelle, she was a watered down version of you. Nonetheless, she was my only family at the time and I felt marrying your father would be the death of her independence. I will no longer belabor that issue. It's in the past. Now I want to make sure I leave you with a sense of family and belonging for I know you have led quite a solitary path through your young years.

Hera became my home over thirty years ago when I was at a down point in my life. No husband and children of my own, I was thrilled when you and your mother came to spend that one summer with me. *Unfortunately, the period that brought you and I closer together, drove your mother and me farther apart. Your parents demanded I not see you while they also created the ridiculous scenario of my death or non-existence, yet in a sense, I never left your side.*

Right now, everything I love and hold dear is in Hera, including you. I hope the house inspires you and gives you space to create your beautiful pieces. And I hope you find comfort and joy among my friends. They remember the little Jessie who took charge of this house one bright, happy summer. If you need any help with my estate or personal items, please know that Archie, Eleanor and Lois are there for you, as are all of my friends. Please don't be afraid to ask Carson for help, he can fix anything."

I glance up at Carson and he looks just as surprised as me to hear himself mentioned in the letter.

"This is another beginning for you. Embrace it and be happy. And please, please, love and take care of Bert.

Love,
Aunt Ginnie"

"Bert?" I ask.

"Sweet Potato Pie!" Lois shouts. "I forgot to bring Bert!"

Everyone is laughing, but I'm still feeling misty-eyed from the letter and can't imagine who Bert could be.

Carson notices my confusion. "Bert is Gin's two-year-old bulldog. He's been staying at Lois's house for the last week." I appreciate that he speaks to me in a normal tone without the sarcasm.

"I've inherited a dog, too?" Now I know this won't work out. My New York apartment can't handle a dog and neither can my roommates.

"I'll bring Bert by tomorrow when Carson and I come back," Dylan tells me. "Once you get past all the farting and snorting, you'll love Bert."

"You're going to be working here tomorrow?" I ask.

"Is that a problem?" Dylan and Carson are both looking at me, gauging my reaction I suppose.

Time for your big girl pants. I remember that was one of my aunt's favorite lines she used on my annoyed mother. Carson's unforgiving glare brings that memory back. I shake my head, still feeling befuddled by the last twenty-four hours. It's all too much too soon.

"Damn. I knew this wasn't going to be easy," Eleanor says to me. "Ginnie left us with a lot of explaining to do. It's a nice letter, but it doesn't help in the real world; right, sweetie?"

"Oh my," Archie says and I fear that this is his standard response to most things. "I just don't have the intestinal fortitude for this. I'm very happy Jessica is with us now, but it's all so tragic."

I don't know what to say to these people. They seem to have very high expectations of me and my head is swimming with information while my emotions are running on high-speed. Plus, now I find out that I'm a dog owner. They might as well have told me I'm getting a baby in the morning. I've been managing my own dull life crafted out by working hard, saving money for future non-existent plans, and living on a lot of ramen noodles. Now I have a huge, beautiful though aging home to maintain and a farting dog.

Why did Ginnie have to die before I could get to know her? I could use some type of adult guidance right about now. I know I'm supposed to be a grown-up, but most of the time I feel like a kid in an adult's body. The only time the big girl pants make their appearance is when I'm talking about computer simulations and code.

I've been bamboozled. I get a super deal at an unbelievable cost, a furnished house and potty-trained dog, but I never get to see Aunt Virginia again while the people of Hera are supposed to be a replacement for my family. I don't have to read between the lines to understand what my aunt was trying to convey in her letter. It's a peace offering attached to a lot of people she wants back in my life.

Lauren gets up to serve more coffee. Everyone is jabbering while I put myself through this mind maze, it's like a data surge on my brain.

"Hey," Carson says quietly, coming over to replace Lauren's empty seat next to me. "Are you okay?"

Oh, God. His eyes turn me into a quivering blob. To think I had the audacity as a child to say he'd be my husband. It makes me wish I still had that confidence to speak my mind. I look into Carson's eyes and search his face, completely forgetting to respond to his question.

Dylan takes notice of Carson's attention towards me. "Jess?" he asks, bringing my focus away from Carson.

"She's overwhelmed," Archie says.

"You're going to stay for a while, right?" Imogene asks. "At least live here for the summer?"

Lauren nods along with Imogene's comment as if they've come up with a splendid plan.

"I have a job in New York. I have an apartment in New York. My life is there, my career," I say half-heartedly.

"Jessie, Lois and I will be helping you go through the house and Ginnie's things and we'll tell you whatever you want to know. We'll do it nice and easy," Eleanor says. "Can't you take a leave of absence from your job?"

"It doesn't work that way. There's always someone to replace you. I'm not in a position to take a summer off."

"She'd get bored here," Carson comments. His voice is deep and strong; there's no sign of that caring tone from a moment ago and there is a hint of something else, maybe distrust or cynicism. "She'd want to run back to the city after one week in this place."

"Carson, stop being so negative," Imogene snaps with her hands on her hips. "She may get bored being around your sorry, crabby ass, but Lauren and I are boatloads of fun."

Carson scoffs.

"Fun! Fun! Fun!" Imogene kicks Carson's leg three times as she says it. He doesn't even flinch in pain.

"Whatever. I have to get going." He gets up and leaves my side. I feel an instant loneliness with his departure. I wish I could run down the steps after him and ask him to take me on a nighttime drive.

Anywhere. Anyplace where I don't have to make decisions. "See you in the morning, Dylan. Bright and early!" Carson shouts from his truck before driving off.

"Great, just what I love, working at dawn on a Sunday," Dylan says to me. Somehow I don't think he really minds, though. There's something brewing between his golden locks besides a pretty face. He likes his brother's attention and he wants me to notice that he's needed.

"What could you possibly be doing at dawn?" I ask. "Chop down trees and hunt bears?"

Dylan laughs, but my imagination shows them doing exactly that, swinging axes.

After the dinner is cleared up, the dishes are done and I'm given several more overloads of the history I can't remember, everyone bids me goodbye. Dylan lingers and is the last to leave.

"If you get scared staying in this big house all alone, just call me. I'll run right over." What a flirt. I've had plenty of guys hit on me, mostly drunk frat types that want sex, but none as sweet as Dylan. He's the kind of guy who has always been out of my league. They notice me, but turn away once I mention my major or my work.

Dylan would fit in at the Hamptons with a pretty, pedigreed girl on his arm who excels at society benefits and interior design.

"Bye." I push him out the door.

"You can't get rid of me. I'll be back tomorrow," he calls out into the night.

Sleep does not come easily. The country makes its own kind of racket that's different from the city, yet even louder. Crickets chirping, owls—or something—hooting and buzzing insects outside my screened window. The moon casts dark shadows across the bedroom and I am amazed that I slept here as a child unafraid. Of course, then the house was full of people; Aunt Virginia, my mother, Carson and Dylan in the rooms next door. There are no humans within a mile of me now and it terrifies me.

I keep my mind busy with things I must do. I'll need to call 5 Alpha and ask about an extended leave from my job and health coverage. I need to call Kate and Marissa to let them know I'll be gone awhile and that I'll mail my rent check to them. Call my parents and scream at them, or alternatively, never speak to them again. I need to go to the bank in Woodstock and sign papers for the account Aunt Virginia left in my trust. Fix this house up and decide if I need to sell it. I rethink that idea and consider Dylan, his attractiveness as well as his evident interest towards me and what I might be able to have if I stayed here longer.

I continue to mull the same thoughts and ideas over and over until the room brightens a bit and I know it will soon be sunrise. The last things I think of in my big, lonely house are wishing a subway line ran under the foundation so its rumbling vibrations could lull me to sleep and Carson Blackard's blue eyes waiting for me to answer him.

Are you okay? No, Carson, I'm not, but my aunt says you can fix anything.

Seven

A wet, grunting sound persists in my dream. I am at a party back in New York. The guests are not people I recognize and more than one guy has asked me to dance even though there isn't any music playing. I am walking away from the party and down a hallway, but someone is following me and there's that wet grunting sound again. I know I'm dreaming when I become very analytical in my dreams. Sometimes I can force myself to wake up while at other times it's like I'm heavily sedated and I don't have the will to pull myself out of the drugged-like state.

Something warm and wet touches my leg. No, licks my leg. I pry my eyes open and, in that moment, I see a lump of blubber with giant jowls resting next to my leg. He is panting with a thread of saliva hanging from his mouth. He grunts, shakes his head so his spittle hits my face and then plops his head back down on the bed as if he is satisfied with his new owner.

"Ah, you must be Bert," I say to the bulldog.

His eyes perk and he glances at me upon hearing his name.

"I bet you are the worst roommate," I say groggily and decide to go back to sleep.

Violent pounding underneath my bed jolts me awake. Hera doesn't have earthquakes, at least not ones accompanied by hammering and sawing. The commotion makes my bed jump and Bert and me with it.

"For the love of sarsaparilla!" I shout, now fully awake.

"Hey, good," Carson says, appearing at my door. "You got your country on. Glad to see it. Now get up or you're going to suffer much worse."

"What the HEY are you doing down there?" I yell.

"Dylan and I are finishing the library shelves, Babycakes. Nice to see you and Bert getting along so well." He smiles and leaves.

"Why do we need bookcases?" I yell after him. "It's the digital age, in case you haven't noticed."

Bert looks at me with his tired, red-veined, droopy eyes.

"It was a pretty good comeback." Bert merely closes his eyes and feigns sleep.

I realize I have been sleeping on top of the covers in a skimpy, sheer white T-shirt and bikini panties which means Carson got a good gander at my almost naked body. Either he wasn't impressed or he was being polite about it. Somehow, I doubt he's the polite type.

I put my long hair in one of those messy top knots with curls and frizz spiking out; the kind of grab-and-go do that is always a no-no in public, however, women do it anyway. I do it because, really, whom do I have to impress? After a quick hot shower, I throw on a pair of very short cut-off jeans, a green tank top and some flip-flops. The house doesn't have air conditioning of any kind and I already feel the oppressive heat of an early summer day coming on.

As if he knows I'm in charge now, Bert automatically jumps off the bed and follows me downstairs to the second floor where the construction nightmare is taking place. Dylan is the first person I see when I walk into the library and I quickly regret not fixing my hair and putting on some make-up. He's up on a ladder with wood planks and a drill in his hand.

"Good morning, gorgeous." He gives me a big smile.

"Hi," I reply back, wondering if I should go back upstairs and make myself more presentable, however, that would be too obvious.

Bert grunts, snorts and waddles over to Carson who is across the room sanding boards. He kneels down and pets Bert. "Hey, little buddy."

"I assume you brought Bert here this morning and put him in my bed?" I say to Carson.

"We brought him with us, but he ran upstairs and let himself into your room." Carson begins roughhousing with an eager Bert.

"He was probably hoping to find Ginnie," Dylan adds. "And when he didn't, he must have searched the other bedrooms. Then he saw Sleeping Beauty and decided to join her."

Carson lets out a snicker at Dylan's flirting, but I don't mind. I like the flattery. I smile and bat my eyelashes at Dylan until he laughs. Carson frowns at me and throws his work gloves on the floor. "Dylan let's break for lunch," he says curtly.

"Lunch?" I ask. "I was just going to put on a pot of coffee and make some breakfast."

"Listen, Babycakes, you're going to have to rise earlier if you want to keep up with what goes on around here. We started at six to prep these boards at the shop and now it's almost noon, so we need to eat lunch," Carson says.

"It's Sunday," I retort. "Who does construction on Sunday? In New York this is when we go out for brunch. You know; eggs, pancakes and mimosas."

Carson isn't amused and brushes by me on his way downstairs. The contact of his bare arm against mine is electric. Carson turns back enough to catch me suck in a quiet breath. He doesn't look too composed either before walking out of the room. What was that? My body and brain don't react to men like that.

"He's grouchy. Don't take it personally. I'm sorry we woke you, too. I wanted to let you sleep in, but Carson wants to stick to his rigid schedule." Dylan climbs down the ladder and removes his gloves as he approaches me.

"It's okay. I should have gotten up earlier. I need to learn my way around this house and inventory my aunt's possessions. That sounds very insensitive of me, but there are so many books and canvases and wine." I am amused at the idea of me being a wine collector.

"It can wait." Dylan lifts a strand of hair off my face. It is an intimate gesture that sends those sweet shivers down my body. I wouldn't mind a summer fling for once in my life. He is simply too cute. A part of me wants him to kiss me now, fast and furiously. He stares at me intently and for a moment I think he's considering it, too, but then he pulls his hand back. "Get your breakfast and meet us on the porch." I suppose my admonishments from the previous night have forced him to use some restraint and avoid a kiss.

The kitchen is in the back on the east side of the house. The remaining morning light still fills the room, making it bright and cheery. It's a dated kitchen, not one of those high-end jobs where you can entertain and feed your guests at the same time. Some of it must date back to the late 1800's, like the wooden slat walls. There's also a large, stained and slightly chipped porcelain farmhouse sink, a round, oak table with four mismatched, ladder-back chairs and one of those small, round-edged refrigerators from the 1940's that hums loudly and is inefficient at keeping perishables cold.

While most things are out of style, Aunt Virginia did at least invest in an expensive eight-burner Viking range and an elaborate coffee and cappuccino machine. I can't cook, however, I sure do love infusing my body with high doses of caffeine.

There are a few bags of gourmet coffee beans on the counter along with a grinder and, having worked at a coffeehouse while I was in college, I manage to figure out how to work the complex coffee machine fairly quickly.

The fridge is stocked with local farm eggs, cream, butter, pre-cut carrot and celery sticks and apples, which tells me Archie must have made sure I had some staples. The cupboards are the same honey colored stain as the walls. I search through them and find granola, bread, peanut butter, jelly and a few cans of chicken noodle soup. Underneath the counter I find bags of dog food. Bert sees my discovery and then trots over to the far wall where, below the rotary phone with the long dangling cord, there are two metal dog bowls. Bert nuzzles one and returns to me with a mouth full of dry, crunchy nibbles.

"Good. It looks like someone knew enough to leave you food and water. Just so you know, I've never owned a pet, so you'll have to speak up if I forget to feed you." Bert keeps chewing while he looks at me as if we have a perfect understanding of one another.

As my cappuccino finishes gurgling and frothing into my waiting cup, I grab an apple and then take my breakfast out the kitchen door that leads to the porch on the east side of the house. As I walk outside, I find Dylan and Carson seated not far from the door at a bistro-style table with three chairs. *How quaint. I get to dine with the two giant lumberjacks,* I think to myself as I carefully juggle the oversized mug and apple over to the table. Dylan jumps up and pulls out the empty chair for me as Carson continues eating his sandwich without even so much as looking at me.

"Is that all you're going to eat?" Dylan asks.

"I'm fine. I'm still stuffed from all the food yesterday. Really, an apple is all I need."

"Let me go make you an omelet," Dylan offers.

"Shit. She does quadratic equations for a living, she can manage on her own," Carson snaps.

I am touched by Dylan's attentiveness and keenly surprised by Carson's awareness about me.

I know my aunt kept them informed about my life, but to think Carson has been making a conscious effort to understand my work is a little mind-boggling. He's a little too aloof or cocky to be interested in me, so it must be Dylan's attention towards me that irritates him, as if I'm undermining their work schedule.

"I'm trying to be polite." It's the first time I see Dylan register anger. "You could try it."

"You can find your way around the kitchen, right?" Carson asks me in a measured tone meant for his brother.

"I'm fine; thanks for your concern," I say and drink my coffee.

"We need to get back to work." Carson directs to Dylan, although he's looking at me. He grabs his paper lunch bag and can of soda. "Come on," he barks to Dylan.

I gather I'm a thorn in Carson's side. I don't know why and I don't care. I kind of like that I annoy him.

Dylan looks flustered. We both expected to have this opportunity to talk, yet Carson is the taskmaster. I pretend to not care that they are leaving my company unexpectedly, so I take my cell phone out of my pocket and try to look very busy.

"Sorry for rushing off. If you want company, come hang out in the library." Dylan winks.

"Knock it off." Carson smacks the back of Dylan's head.

"Shit. What's that for?" Dylan rubs his head.

It's pretty evident that Carson isn't keen on me hanging out with Dylan.

"Oh, don't worry," I say, trying to smooth things over. "I have plenty to do. I have people I have to call; you know, work, my friends." I hold the dead phone to my ear as if I'm waiting for someone to answer. The battery is completely drained, but I keep holding the phone to my ear like a fool.

"She doesn't want to be in the same room as the sawing and hammering," Carson says, holding the kitchen door open for Dylan who reluctantly leaves. I give him a little parade-wave good bye without taking the stupid cell phone from my ear.

Before Carson closes the door, he leans back out. "If you need to make a call, you'll probably have to take ten paces off the porch to get service." I nod while remaining extremely committed to following through on my fake phone call. "And by the way," he continues. "I found your phone charger on the second floor, so I put it on your dresser this morning while you were sleeping." Then his mouth curves slightly at the corners and I know the jig is up. I put my dead phone down on the table.

"Thanks. You're a peach."

He chuckles as he leaves me alone with Bert.

"I don't know if I'm cut out for this country life, Bert."

He is sprawled on the floor at my feet as if he's overcome by fatigue. Looking at him makes me tired and I get the feeling that this is pretty much what Bert does all day.

"My aunt should have named you Hangover."

Eight

I head back up to my room and plug my phone into the charger, which Carson not only left on my dresser, but also plugged into the wall socket buried behind the dresser. How he moved the heavy furniture this morning without making a sound is beyond me. Thinking of him standing inches from my sleeping body leaves me slightly breathless. I have a brief thought of him looking at my naked body that was completely visible through my see-through T-shirt. *Oh my,* as Archie would say.

Next, I head to Aunt Virginia's painting studio, which is on the second floor at the back of the house. It is separated from the library by the playroom that is sandwiched between them. The playroom was created the summer I stayed here and it is where my dollhouse and other artifacts of my shared childhood with Carson and Dylan still reside.

I only take a quick glance around the room, wondering what I should do with all the board games and baskets of toys lining the walls. Why did my aunt hold on to these childhood items all these years? The toys and our beanbag chairs on shaggy throw rugs are evidence of the times when we were sequestered inside by rainy days. I don't want to spend time going through each and every item that

61

will only bring back the happier memories I've been expected to forget.

No sooner do I think this when another vision returns, Carson picking up after Dylan and me while telling us to start behaving. I also recall following him around a lot, demanding answers to impossible questions. I remember Carson being incredibly patient sometimes, letting me help with his Lego models or having me stand on a chair next to him while he made us sandwiches.

I know I'm intelligent. Everyone has always overused the "you're so smart" phrase with me. The I.Q. tests my parents have made me take tell me I'm a genius, so how have I let my brain block out my memory of these people and this place?

The pounding from the library becomes deafening again, so I head in the opposite direction to *my* studio. Aunt Virginia was a tidy artist. Her oils and acrylics are stored neatly on a worktable along with clean brushes organized by size and material, horse hair and synthetic. About a dozen of her large, finished canvases lean against two walls.

I open my large portfolio case and take out eight of my finished paintings. I tack them on the bare walls with poster putty so they won't get damaged. I know other artists wouldn't do this, but I don't really consider myself an artist and I can be very careless with my pieces. For me it's all part of the process. I enjoy making something I like to look at. It's about expressing myself through paint in ways that I cannot communicate through language. Perhaps that's why I have trouble with the rules of dating. I have neither the patience for nor the comprehension on how to speak to men.

I scan the walls filled with my paintings and am pleased to be surrounded by familiar images I've created. There are two empty wooden easels and a large drafting table in the room. I set my watercolor paper on the drafting table, and study a handful of my charcoal and ink drawings that I will enhance with watercolors.

My current project is a young woman in a ballerina costume and combat boots. She stands in the middle of a busy section of midtown New York City with cars and pedestrians passing by and skyscrapers looming above. An old man who could be homeless or just tired and haggard is standing next her with an expression of defeat. The young woman appears to be enraptured by her surroundings. Her arms float at her sides as if she is dancing while her long, puffy ballerina skirt twirls.

I begin to drizzle watercolors down parts of the drawing, painting in the girl with vibrant colors to offset against the black and white grimness of the man. I've been doing these types of paintings for a few years and I enjoy them so much that I obsess about future ideas while I'm doing my day job or hanging out with friends. My mind is always thinking of new images I want to explore.

My roommates and colleagues at 5 Alpha call my paintings grunge art because I combine so many images of pop culture and world news, blending the humor of society with the grimness of reality. Some people seem to really like it, but others have told me it's kind of scary.

When I gave a couple of pieces as gifts to my boss, he got me hooked up with a friend of his who owns a gallery in Chelsea. I didn't think much of it, yet the art dealer, Tom, was persistent. He came to my ramshackle apartment and insisted on taking ten of my paintings to hang in his gallery. When I didn't initially jump at the chance, Tom reminded me that having a dealer asking to represent you was like winning the lottery and no artist can afford to be self-deprecating. That shut me up. I handed over all of my paintings with gratitude.

There are starving artists everywhere wanting to get noticed. I realized that, however, he didn't seem to understand that I never started out with the intention of selling my paintings. I did it because the images hounded me until I put them down on paper. I did it to escape from the daily grind of work as well as to escape the numbers that plague my brain. It's true.

Sometimes, my brain feels like it's an automated system running code on its own and I'm forced to visualize the numbers as they scroll through my mind. I can be eating lunch and some random number will pop in my mind and I'll whisper out loud, *"Seventy million."* Seventy million what? The numbers change and they generally come to me during stressful times when my brain is deliberating over a predicament. I'm really not sure what it is; if it's an affliction, a form of anxiety, a part of obsessive-compulsive disorder, but I manage with it while, at the same time, I find that it compels me to draw and paint more.

Once I finish a piece, I feel an incredible release and sense of freedom. Katie says it's an *art*gasm because I haven't gotten laid. She's blunt like that. It's what makes her a good roommate. Besides, maybe she's right. I've dated enough and done plenty of things over and under the clothes, but even with the guys I think I could fall in love with, I reach a point where I realize I don't want to have sex with them.

I never wanted to be a twenty-year-old virgin, yet for some reason, I'm holding back. The last guy I dated was a pretty good catch, enough so that one night I was naked in his bed and doing just about everything. We were both eagerly horny and sweaty; however, when he climbed on top of me, I immediately pushed him aside and struggled away. The desire had deflated in a flash.

"Nope, this isn't going to work," I said to him. I wasn't angry, scared or weepy; I just realized I didn't want that with him. He was pissed. Watching him trying to put his pants on with an erection and then wrapping his hoodie around his waist so he could escape my apartment, left me wondering if I was a lesbian and just didn't know it. Sharing a tiny bathroom with two other women tells me, no, I definitely love the male body. I also love having crushes and the idea of falling in love with a man.

Yep, when I saw Dylan, that rush of lust and desire hit me like a bug on a windshield. Splat! Could I fall in love with Dylan? I don't know about that, especially since I keep thinking about his rude older brother. If I want a summer fling, Dylan seems like a sure thing. He's sending all the right signals, but I'm very good at making things not work out. I'm very good at taking the hard road, which is probably why I'm attracted to Carson.

I laugh to myself and then, without thinking, I whisper, "Fifty million."

"You still do that?" A deep voice startles me, a voice that I like very much.

I turn around and find Carson standing at the open door to the studio. He is incredibly handsome with his chiseled, serious face and his broad shoulders that veer down into a muscular torso. A leather tool belt is slung low on his narrow hips and it simply makes him sexier.

"What?" I ask.

"That whispering thing. You used to whisper numbers to yourself all the time."

"I did? You actually remember that?"

He nods and then enters the room as if he was waiting for a safe time to pass between us. He walks around the studio and studies each painting I stuck on the wall. He is quiet as he takes his time with each piece. It's almost more difficult than if he saw me naked. After a few minutes, he turns back to me and his expression has all the earlier tension and crankiness washed from it.

"These are good. Provocative," he comments.

I pause and then stammer, completely surprised by his compliment.

"Thank you. I didn't think you'd like them."

"Why?" He stares at me as if it's a standoff.

"Because you always thought I was a pest. At least, that's what it sounds like even though I don't recall it being that way when I was a kid."

Carson laughs lightly and comes closer to me. "You're talented. I knew that then and I see that now. You've grown into something that is your own. Not many people get to be so fortunate."

I savor the praise coming from his deep, alluring voice and I feel lucky to see him smile. Is that a rarity for him? I suspect so.

"You weren't a pest," he says, now close enough that I can see the pulse in his neck and his bicep, strangled by the snug, short sleeve of his T-shirt. He didn't shave this morning, and there are a few spots of sawdust caught in his stubble and across the hairs on his arm. He is filthy from work and normally I wouldn't let someone like that walk into my clean space, but on Carson, it's so appealing.

"Wow," Dylan says as he walks right to the wall of paintings. "Cute girl with a grenade and a bear holding a peace sign. Weird stuff."

Carson gives me a sympathetic shrug. It's the first time I feel that he is on my side. Maybe I've done something to win him over.

"Ginnie did some pretty neat abstracts, but these are really out there," Dylan continues.

"Do you like them, though?" I ask.

"Yeah," Dylan says. "They make a bold statement without being pretentious."

"All right, that's enough of that." Carson rakes his hand through his dark, unruly hair. "Back to work." He looks at me a moment and I am captivated by his blue eyes and long eyelashes. I think I just got caught staring with a little too much interest on my part so I turn away quickly.

Carson leaves, but Dylan stays. He fills the spot that Carson has just been occupying and I catch myself breathing in all the maleness that surrounds me. I have never welcomed so much testosterone at one time. The men at 5 Alpha are colleagues that I've never been attracted to; however, Dylan and Carson have my insides fluttering like a butterfly on high-octane. I don't know what to do with my hands or my gaze without appearing to be swooning. I grab a fistful of paintbrushes and a bottle of gel ink to keep my hands busy. Dylan follows and is right behind me, closing in on all the empty air I was planning on using to breathe.

"Hey," he says softly. "Would you go out with me for dinner?"

"Um." I fidget and think of all the possible reasons why this would be a bad idea, but then the obvious one hits me in the face. My first dates never turn into second dates and if things are going to go sour with Dylan, how does that affect me being in the same town with him? Even if I sell this house, he's doing all the repair and renovation work. "I don't know if I can."

"Tomorrow night. I'll take you to this nice little restaurant in Woodstock. I'd like to get to know you without everyone else hovering around us."

"I'm calling my office today and I may have to head back to the city tomorrow and then finish up here next weekend."

"You don't have to leave tomorrow, Jess. Call your boss. He'll tell you to take your time."

"How do you know? My company believes in working around the clock. You know what people do during their time off? Work! That's what they do."

Dylan smiles at me and then swoops in for a kiss. It is a long, lingering kiss that excites me and leaves me wanting more before I finally push away.

"Dinner tomorrow night," he says, looking just as heated as I feel. "I have to work in the shop tomorrow. We have a lot of orders so I won't be here during the day."

"What shop?" My voice is weak. I really want to kiss him again.

"Carson's workshop. We make furniture."

"I didn't know that," I say, thinking they were handymen. Archie had mentioned something about furniture, but I must have forgotten that they have actual jobs other than working on Aunt Virginia's house.

"I'll take you there sometime and introduce you to the crew. They're more fun than Carson."

"I need to make some calls now, but I'll let you know about tomorrow night," I tell him, thinking that I'll have to turn him down.

"Oh, we're going. That's not an issue." Dylan heads back down the hall to the library where Carson has been hammering away.

First I call my boss, Nathan. I sit on the front stoop of the house with my phone, catching the afternoon rays.

It's a Sunday, but it's not unusual for people in our office to call each other on weekends or vacations if there's a computer glitch that has to be fixed immediately. I've probably spent more time talking to Nathan on my cell phone than I have in person.

Surprisingly, Nathan is very accommodating. He is amazed that I have inherited a country home and suggests that I stay longer to figure out what I'm going to do with the property. He also says he'll send out a computer and other equipment with some of the guys from IT and then I can work from the house.

"I'm not letting you resign, Jessica," he says to me. "We have too many good projects cooking with you. I may even come out and visit my little country mouse."

Nathan's plan is surprisingly good. It never occurred to me to work from here, at least for a while. Plus, the IT guys will do all the set-up; they'll bring in a few nice, big 27-inch monitors and a printer along with whatever else I need here. Nathan is even going to wire the house for Internet service since Aunt Virginia didn't even use a computer. Apparently, she counted on her cell phone for access to the Internet and she only got that when she left her home.

Next I call my roommates. Marissa picks up and then Kate gets on the other cordless phone. "Oh. My. God!" they say in unison.

"Who gets a whole house when someone dies?" Kate asks.

"Um, a lot of people inherit property," I answer.

"Yes, but who do *we* know that gets a house you can vacation in? This is unbelievable!" Kate says excitedly, as if she won a prize.

"Sorry, for your loss," Marissa says, trying to get Kate to tone down her jubilation over my ill-gotten gains.

The conversation is short and ends with me reminding them to deposit my check and pay our landlord on time, since I'm the one that usually handles all the bill paying. I beg them to tape a large note about the bill due dates on the fridge. Before saying goodbye, Kate inquires about a pool or local amenities in case she and Marissa want to visit for a weekend. I explain that it's an old house without modern day conveniences, but the luxury it offers is scenic solitude. That doesn't seem to deter Kate, not after hearing that my workmen are attractive, hunky young men.

"Shit," I say after ending the call. Bert is leaning against my back and does a partial roll into me so his stubby legs are in the air and I'm pushed farther off the step. "Honey, if this is how you're going to spend your day, we've got a problem," I tell him.

A small car comes up the driveway, leaving a trail of dust in its path. I abruptly stand up to see who it is and Bert rolls off the top step, crashing into my feet. He gets up with a grunt and shakes himself off before moving back into the shade of the porch. "Come on, Hangover, it's time to get up already."

"What did you call him?" Lauren asks as she and Imogene get out of the little car with beach towels and tote bags.

"Hangover, that's funny," Imogene comments.

"We're here to sunbathe. Figure you could use some company and we have the afternoon off to work on our tans," Lauren says.

"I'm not much of a sunbather. I'm as pale as they come," I say. "But I sure could use some company. This pooch doesn't talk much."

"Bert is sweet, but he's lazy. You'll never see him playing catch or anything like that. We always lie out over there." Imogene points to the west side of the house to the open sunny grass under the library window.

"Okay, that sounds good." I help them carry a grocery bag of chips and water out to the designated spot.

They've brought a beach towel for me, too. I spread out the towels as they peel off their tank tops and shorts to reveal very skimpy bikinis underneath. Lauren is a very tan, willowy, blond with the perfect figure you see in catalogues and magazines. She piles her lengthy, blond hair on top of her head like me, showing off her long, graceful neck.

Imogene, on the other hand, is a full-figured gal with a large bosom. She isn't shy about wearing a bikini which offers no support for her heavy breasts and ample waist, though. She has fairer skin than Lauren, so I'll probably have to nag her about sun exposure and skin cancer. Being a fair-skinned redhead, I'm big on SPF and hats, even though I have allowed myself to get a hint of a tan and sprinkle of tiny freckles across my nose so I can show some skin in the summer.

"I didn't bring a suit," I say. "I had no idea I'd be relaxing in the sun when I planned this trip."

"We know that, dummy. I brought you one of my suits." Lauren pulls a red one-piece out of her tote bag and hands it to me. "Don't worry; it's clean, practically brand new."

"All right," I say hesitantly. "Let me go change upstairs. Did you bring sunscreen?"

Imogene holds up two bottles. "Of course."

I stand in front of the dresser mirror, turning to get a good view of my rear. The swimsuit is a very bright red, but I have to admit, it's flattering in a 1940's pin-up girl sort of way. I don't have a big chest, yet the halter makes me look fuller on top and the ruching on the sides with the high-cut leg openings makes my legs look very long and slender.

Since I don't have the instant power to give myself bigger boobs or longer legs, I decide that I'm pleased with how I look. I grab one of Aunt Virginia's large, sombrero-style sun hats and head back downstairs.

As I pass the second floor, I hear "What the—" from Carson as he sees the flash of red dashing down the stairs.

Lauren and Imogene have brought out a serving tray from the kitchen and have it loaded with beverages, bowls of chips, and pretzels.

"You can't wear that hat! You won't get any sun," Lauren exclaims. "It looks like you have an umbrella on your head."

"That's the point," Imogene remarks. "She doesn't want to burn. Wow, Jess, you look fabulous in that suit. Very sexy for a one-piece."

"Very," Lauren adds.

"I like it, too," I agree. "Thanks for bringing it."

I plop down on one of the towels and lean back on my hands. The view is majestic. Rolling green hills, blue sky, and it's *my* view.

"This is heaven," I say.

"Hmm." Lauren is on her back, arms raised above her head for even tanning. It makes me giggle.

"Don't laugh," Imogene says. "She's a pro at perfecting the killer tan. Too bad that someday it may kill her."

"Leave me alone," Lauren says without opening her eyes.

"I wouldn't mind a little more color for my date, so I don't look like death," I say before kicking myself. I may have resigned myself to the idea of Dylan's dinner invitation, but I didn't want anyone else to know that I was going out with him. At least not yet, not on the heels of my aunt's death; the part about me being new to town and looking like a cheap hussy bothers me.

"Date?" Imogene shouts. "With who?" She and Lauren both prop themselves up on their elbows, waiting for me to respond.

"Dylan is taking me out for dinner tomorrow night."

"Dylan. Of course. He's been all over you," Imogene notes.

"That's fast even for Dylan," Lauren says. "He's a great guy and so cute, he gets the women, but we only see him hanging out with them at bars or parties. He never dates one person, Jess."

"Yeah, he gets his pick of women, that's for sure," Imogene adds. "I've seen him rolling down the street at dawn, coming back from a one nightstand, but I don't think I've ever seen him on a real date. He's one of those guys that goes out with a group of people and ends up sleeping with different women every time."

"Ugh. Well, then maybe I shouldn't go. I mean, I'm not looking to date someone. I assumed this was just a friendly dinner invitation, but now it sounds like a bad idea."

"No, you should go," Imogene insists. "He's sexy hot and he obviously likes you a lot. I would go in a heartbeat if a guy like him asked me out, but not Dylan. He's a like a brother to us."

"Yeah." Lauren makes a little face to Imogene who shakes her off. They're hiding something from me. "We can't date Dylan. Not that he'd ask us. He *is* too much like a brother. I am a little jealous, though. I've lived here my whole life and I've had some crappy boyfriends and, no matter what I do, I can't get that idiot Leo to even notice me. You're here two days and you have a stud hot on your tail."

"Who's Leo?"

"One of the guys that works at the Blackard workshop. He's very quiet around women," Imogene answers.

"I bet Dylan is taking you to Cucina," Lauren says. "He loves that place. If he's taking you to a place he loves, then that's a big deal. It means he's sharing something important with you."

"I think you're reading too much into this. I don't really live here. Remember? I have a job and a place in the city. I don't think Dylan thinks it's more than dinner." I say this more to convince myself, however, after those kisses, I don't even know if I can buy my own story. He's a guy; he wants sex and so do I. Finally.

"When are you leaving? I thought Archie convinced you to stay a while?" Lauren sounds genuinely sad.

"I guess I'm not leaving any time soon. I spoke to my boss and he's setting up my office here so I can work long distance and I received some money from my aunt. I also have some in savings, so I'm still paying my share on my rental. So, no, I'm not leaving anytime soon, but I have to come up with a real life plan. I can't go on with all these balls in the air."

Imogene laughs. "Life plan? You're twenty. God, I keep thinking you're older because you are so mature, but you do look like a teenager."

"Okay, good, that's settled. You're not leaving and you have a real date with a cute guy," Lauren says. "You suck."

She lies down again and closes her eyes.

"Good for you, Jess." Imogene takes a cigarette out of her bag and lights it, taking a long drag on it before blowing the smoke out slowly.

Lauren, who is lying between us, waves her hand to get the smoke away from her face.

"You'd both like my roommates, Kate and Marissa. You two are similar to them."

"College educated and unemployed?" Imogene asks.

"If you mean employed in fields other than what they studied for, then yes. But the whole dating scene, too. Kate and Marissa either have bad dates or go through dry spells. Why is it so difficult? I don't know anyone in a good relationship. It's odd. In high school, I was too young and it didn't help being a skinny geek, yet finally, by the end of college, it was working out for me. I thought. I looked infinitely better and I was getting plenty of one-time dates, but no winners."

"You started college at what? Fourteen?" Lauren asks. "How many serious boyfriends did you have?"

"Serious ones? None."

"Have you had your heart broken?" Imogene turns her head away from us and blows another plume of smoke towards the butterflies hovering around us. I imagine them all dropping to the ground with black lung disease.

"No, I've never been in love."

"I think I'm in love with Leo," Lauren says.

"You have to have a conversation with him for that to happen." Imogene laughs.

"What are you going to wear on your date with Dylan?" Lauren asks.

"More importantly, should the opportunity arise, if you know what I mean, are you going to sleep with him?" Imogene asks.

I decide to put all my cards on the table. I like these two and, if they can offer any advice on improving my romantic life, or lack thereof, I want in. "If that happens, it will be a first."

Lauren shields her eyes from the sun with her hand and studies me. "You're serious, aren't you? You're a virgin. You've honestly never fucked a guy?"

"It makes sense," Imogene says more delicately. "She's so much younger than everyone, she's just catching up. But you're very pretty; you have to expect guys to hit on you."

"Back up a minute here," Lauren says. "What about other stuff? Blow jobs and hand jobs. Did you ever go down on a guy? Did a guy ever go down on you?"

"Leave her alone," Imogene slaps Lauren's arm.

I'm not bothered by her questions. When I was sixteen and studying with a bunch of nineteen-year-old sorority girls, I was intimidated, but now my confidence is stronger and I'm not terrified to be imperfect. I'm only a little nervous.

"I've done plenty, but not the actual deed." Truth be told, I tried to give a guy a blow job once, but holding his penis in my hand made me realize I really disliked the guy. There was also one time, when a guy pulled my panties down, I suddenly didn't want his face between my legs. It wasn't the sexual acts, it was the guys. They always turned me off somehow; they were simply wrong for me.

"You mean the actual fucking, penis in and humping and bumping?" Lauren continues her questioning.

"It sounds lovely when you put it like that."

Imogene and Lauren laugh and then I join in.

"Maybe Dylan will be your lucky stud," Imogene says.

"Maybe he'll hammer it home for you," Lauren says, still laughing. "I bet he's good in bed. He probably delivers a great orgasm."

"I'll settle for a good grilled steak, heavy on the butter." I get up while they howl with laughter over my comment. "I'm going to the kitchen to make some real drinks. I found vodka in the freezer."

They're still laughing, so I toss my sombrero on the ground and walk back to the house.

I'm mixing vodka with cranberry juice as I pour it into tall tumblers when I hear someone's intake of breath behind me. I turn around and Carson is staring at my legs and working his way up to my face. I'm generally not the kind of person who feels comfortable walking around in a bathing suit unless I'm at a beach or pool with others similarly dressed, I wish I had thrown on some kind of cover-up, but I forgot to bring one outside.

"Hi," I say. He has that serious face again, not the soft, contemplative expression from earlier in the studio. "I'm making vodka cranberries for the gals. May I make a couple for you and Dylan?"

"No, we're working." He's authoritative, almost scolding me with his eyes.

"It's getting late; don't you want to quit and have some of your weekend—"

"Dylan said he's taking you out tomorrow night," Carson cuts me off, definitely not interested in my suggestion about ending his workday.

"Yes, that's right. He asked me out for dinner."

"Why are you doing this?"

I'm a little insulted that he's talking to me with accusation ringing in his tone, clearly blaming me for something.

"Dylan asked me out for dinner. It's pretty straightforward. Is there a problem with me going out with him?"

"Yes."

Now I am more than frustrated, I want to scream at his stony expression. "Would it be possible for you to use a few more nouns and verbs, so I know exactly *why* you have a problem with me going out to dinner with your brother?"

Carson takes a couple long strides and is in my face before I can count to one. He has to lean over to be at my eye level. He places his hands on the counter on either side of me so I'm trapped. "He thinks you're going to stay here for good. He thinks he has a chance with you. I want you to be honest with him and explain that you'll be going back to your real life in New York."

He moves so close to my face, I find myself staring back into his beautiful eyes that never leave mine. He is nothing like Dylan; I can see that in this moment. Carson is only three years older than his brother; however, he might as well be twenty years older. He carries a weight—a burden in him—that is marked by a serious, unwavering demeanor. I think a part of me remembers this about him and another part of me remembers trying to coax the fun side out of him. I know I have seen him laugh, the memory is there, buried with all the other fuzzy images, yet right now, I only see a man who is trying to look strong because there's something that worries him.

If he's trying to be intimidating and rouse my anxiety, it's working. After a short stare-off between us, he moves back. My small victory is that he seems to be at a loss for words, too.

"I haven't decided what I'm doing. My boss gave me a great opportunity to work from here, from this house."

Carson looks surprised and crosses his arms. "So you're staying here? You're going to live in the house full-time?" He doesn't sound convinced at all.

"That's my plan, at least for now."

"Ah, at least for now and how long do you think 'for now' will last?"

"Well, Carson, I don't know that," I snap. "I want to try something new and fun; something where I get to work from home and I can have a real studio for painting. Besides, what the hell business is it of yours anyway?"

"It's my business when it involves my brother."

"He's not a child. He's twenty-three-years-old." I'm getting angrier. "He's older than me and can take care of himself."

"You don't know anything about Dylan. This may be a new, fun thing for you. Isn't that what you called it? Something new and fun? This is Dylan's life."

"It's my life, too." I'm good at sounding like a petulant child. "What the fuck are you talking about?"

My sudden rage startles him; I see him physically back off and gather his thoughts, bringing it down a notch.

"I didn't mean for it to come out like that." His tone is nicer, though forced. This is a painful subject for him to talk about and it will probably put me on his permanent shit list. "The thing is, I don't want Dylan to get his hopes up and then get hurt."

"Hurt by me?" I sound incredulous. "Dylan, the big flirt? He's somewhat of a womanizer from what

I've heard. You think I'm going to hurt him? That's rich."

Carson shakes his head and rubs his hand back and forth on his jaw. It's a good move on him, very cool and sexy. I wonder what he's hiding.

"This is too difficult to explain."

"Hey, I'm the woman who does quadratic equations. You said so yourself. I think I'm capable of understanding whatever dilemma you think we have here."

"I wish it was that simple. But I know you'll get bored living in this little town. You'll want to go back. New York has more to offer you."

"Really? You're a psychic, too? That's amazing. 5 Alpha could probably use your abilities." My sarcasm is almost palpable. I have been fighting for years to be taken seriously as an adult and here I am behaving like a child.

"I'm not trying to be an ass. I'm sorry. You've made a lot of people happy coming here." I believe him, although I also don't think he's one of those happy people.

"Thank you."

"I don't want you to break Dylan's heart," he mumbles.

As much as I want to scoff at that hilarious concept, I don't. I shrug, feeling completely naked in this vivid red bathing suit that is meant for someone more glamorous, so I cross my arms.

Carson senses my discomfort. "You look really good, Jess. You were a little hellion when you were a kid, but you've become a very beautiful woman." He instantly looks like he regrets saying that and heads quickly for the door.

I love that he says that to me while, at the same time, I know I want more of that from Carson. *From Carson*, my big fat brain tells me.

"I've never broken anyone's heart," I blurt out before he's out of earshot.

At the kitchen door, he turns back around and produces the slightest smile as though it distresses him.

"Yes, you have," he says and leaves.

Whose heart? Aunt Virginia's? My parents'? The last guy I dated who slept with the neighbor girl after I kicked him out of bed? Carson is using a code I can't decipher. I want to chase after him and demand that he explain what he's afraid of between Dylan and me, or more accurately myself in general.

I want to be near Carson, end of story. However, experience has taught me that guys are turned off by brainiacs. Even if I wear a push-up bra and sex up a dress, I invariably let something slip; an innocuous comment about science or math, it doesn't matter, it's enough to send the gorgeous, good-looking guys for the hills.

One man I met at a glitzy party on the Upper Eastside seemed terrific, intelligent and handsome. I thought it was a sign that my bad man-luck had changed. After a nice dinner at Cesca, he swooped me into his arms for a kiss. I was overjoyed and started to say something I thought was clever when he covered my mouth with two fingers and actually said, "Please don't talk. I really want to take you home and fuck you." His balls got to meet my knee up close and personal before I stole his cab.

Nine

"What took so long, partner? I'm mighty parched," Imogene says as I set the tray of drinks on the grass.

"A little hold-up with Carson. Apparently, he is not happy about me going out with his brother."

"Carson is very protective of Dylan," Lauren tells me.

"Why? Dylan seems pretty capable of fending for himself."

"He is," Imogene adds. "But they went through a lot together as kids. First their mom died when they were very young, then their dad was pretty useless and Carson had to take over at a young age."

"That's the summer they moved in with Ginnie. You and your mom were here," Lauren says.

"Shit, I have to call my mom," I say and then immediately brush the thought away. "Okay, so they moved in here that summer and then they moved back with their dad?"

"That's just it; their dad never really came back. Not to parent them at least. Carson took Dylan back to their home and he did everything. Carson has always been the parent to Dylan," Imogene says. "They had a trailer home and not a nice one. Their dad would float back into town when he felt like it or when the money from his sales job ran out."

"He was a drunk," Lauren adds. "I remember him stumbling into Dylan's class to pick him up and he was so intoxicated that the school had the police pick him up."

"Then that part of their life ended when their dad killed himself," Imogene interjects.

"Oh," I say. "I didn't know."

"It was pretty rough for them. They were close to their mom. When she got sick, that whole family fell apart, especially their dad. When she died, that was the first time their dad disappeared," Lauren explains. "That's why Ginnie had them come spend that summer here, so she could help them figure out what to do next. They could have stayed in Ginnie's house forever, but Carson wanted to show he was brave and strong. I think it was more likely that he was really afraid to be dependent on people again. Besides that, though, he wanted to move Dylan back to the trailer park and get him back in school. Carson believed he could make things normal for his brother and himself."

"And he did," Imogene says. "Although, I think the only reason they got under the radar of the state was because Ginnie would help out with groceries and utility bills. I was in awe when I'd see them walking to school, doing everything on their own. Carson was very serious about being in charge and keeping his brother in line. Then their messed up dad came back and blew his brains out behind the trailer one day."

"Oh, God," I exclaim. "I can't believe what they've gone through. Why didn't they go into foster care when their dad died?"

"Because Carson was eighteen, he got approval to be Dylan's legal guardian or something so they could stay there. Between their parents' deaths, they spent seven years raising themselves; well, with the help of Ginnie and my mom who did a lot of cooking for them. Really, the whole town was watching over them," Imogene says. "It seems so long ago, but it really wasn't. Then, when Lauren and I went off to college, Dylan was already gone. He got into Colgate. We came back every summer to work at Grandma's diner and by then, Carson's business was growing really well."

"Wait a sec, Dylan went to college and Carson stayed here?"

"Carson couldn't go to college," Lauren answers. "He had to stay here. Dylan was only fifteen, so Carson forfeited his scholarship to Columbia, but he made sure Dylan went to college. They're both smart, but Carson has something wicked going on in that brain of his. Dylan went to Colgate on scholarship, too, while Carson helped pay his bills. By then, he had started his furniture business. He learned the trade from a local guy who was retiring. Carson was like an apprentice before his furniture and woodworking skills became very popular with some of the wealthier residents and tourists so he got good contacts at high-end stores in the city and around the country. He did go into the city for part-time classes at Columbia as well, but he never got his degree."

"Carson is doing all right for himself. As well as for Dylan," Imogene says. "Lauren and I should go work for Carson 'cause so far our college degrees are not landing us jobs. And Carson pays more than my grandmother."

"So it's all working out for them," I muse. "Dylan is a grown man with a college degree and his brother is worried that I'm a distraction?"

Imogene laughs and reaches for another cigarette. "No, he doesn't think that. He's trying to keep Dylan focused on his career, I suppose. He wants to make sure Dylan's life is more stable now. The last fifteen years were a struggle to get where they are now."

"What is Dylan's degree in?"

"Geology and business. Isn't that interesting?" Lauren says. "All he wants is to work for Carson, though. They're very talented. Have you seen the furniture they make?"

"I think I saw some of it in Archie's office."

Imogene nods her head with her cigarette clenched in her mouth as she reapplies sunscreen.

"Dylan is adorable. I think it's sweet that he's interested in you," Lauren says. "He got excellent grades when he was off at college, but apparently he had a little too much fun with the ladies. He could use a sensible influence like you in his life."

"I thought Carson was a sensible influence."

"I mean the female kind; you know, to settle him down," Lauren says.

"Gee, I don't like the sound of that. What was he doing with all these women?"

"Screwing around," Lauren answers with a shrug. "What does any handsome guy with a dick do? Fuck 'em and leave 'em."

"Then why the hell would I want to go out with him?"

"Lauren," Imogene scolds before turning to me. "Jess, Dylan has matured. A little. He's not the same playboy he was in college."

"A little. Huh? But he's still a playboy, right? Just a different kind of playboy."

"Oh, he likes you. Imogene is right. Dylan has grown up a lot in the last couple of years. I can totally see you together," Lauren says.

"Carson believes otherwise. Honestly, why do you think he doesn't want me going out with Dylan?"

Imogene shrugs. "Carson is kind of a mystery. We know he was seeing some woman who worked in one of the New York showrooms, one of his distributors, I think. Anyway, I think he stopped seeing her a while ago. Whoever he was dating, he never brought her around here. Maybe if Dylan gets paired off with someone, Carson is afraid of being alone," Imogene suggests. "Hey, maybe I'm onto something here. Carson keeps whatever personal life he has a complete secret from us. If he isn't at the shop, he's roaming around in his big house."

"Does Dylan live with him?"

"God, no, they'd be at each other's throats all the time," Imogene says. "It's enough they work together. Carson built a very nice house up the road from here. He has the same views as you, but his house is one of those eco-friendly, green designs.

It has a lot of glass and concrete, but it's very comfortable. I've only been there a few times for company parties. Dylan lives with Leo."

"They're in an old farmhouse that Leo is renovating by himself," Lauren says. "Dylan would rather pay rent to Leo than live for free with his brother. I think he wants to get out from under Carson's control."

"Lordy, we have to get out of our parents' houses," Imogene says.

"Amen," Lauren agrees.

Before I can ask more questions, we're interrupted by a loud, appreciative whistle. Dylan and Carson are walking over with their tool belts resembling holsters. If they were wearing cowboy hats, they'd look like gunslingers by the way they swagger towards us.

"Bathing beauties." Dylan winks at me.

"I fed Bert and gave him clean water," Carson directs towards me. "You have to remember to take care of him. He's your responsibility and, if you don't think you can handle him, tell me now and I'll take him."

I'm taken aback by his rudeness.

Dylan shoots him an icy glare. "Hey."

"Geez, Carson. Lighten up. Bert's fine," Lauren says.

"I saw Bert had food this morning," I say timidly, hoping he doesn't see I'm a little tipsy from one cocktail.

"Our porky friend, Bert, is okay," Imogene says. "Stop being such a control freak." After three drinks she's pretty mouthy.

Carson winces when Imogene says that, but then he turns to me and his expression softens. "Bert goes through a lot of water. Gin would keep a dish in the kitchen and one on the porch for him," he says. "Thought you'd want to know."

"Thanks. I'll pay better attention."

Carson nods and heads back to his truck.

Dylan kneels down next to me. "We're done with the bookcases. We have to strip some of the dead branches out here. Gin asked us to do it two months ago. The tree over there is dead." He points to a brown lilting tree. "We're going to cut some things down today and haul it later if that's okay with you." He is waiting for my answer, but I know nothing about home care and trees.

"Ah, yeah. I guess that's okay. If my aunt wanted it done, I guess you should do it."

"Good call," Imogene says, slurping down her diluted vodka and cranberry.

"Good." Dylan smiles at me and then heads back to the truck. Carson hands him a chain saw.

"You okay there?" Imogene asks. "You look a little worried."

"This whole house business is new to me. I don't know if I'm qualified to make decisions about houses and trees."

"You can always ask Carson or Archie for help," Lauren offers. "Damn, it's hot." She begins spritzing herself with the water sprayer.

"Carson doesn't like talking to me. I'll ask Archie for help." I slather on more sunblock.

"What's that? I don't like talking to you?" Carson stops next to us with a chain saw propped up in his gloved hands. Dylan is already checking out the dead tree about one hundred yards away from us.

"Nothing. Go do your choppy thing." I make the international chopping motion with my hand.

"My choppy thing?" I can see a twinkle behind his sunglasses. His T-shirt is drenched with sweat and I see some trickle down his neck. I look away. Guys shouldn't be allowed to look that good when they are filthy and sweating.

Lauren giggles like a drunk.

"Just go chop your trees and things," I repeat, waving him on and putting my sombrero back on to hide my face. He walks off, chuckling. "Hope you don't lose your pecker," I mutter so he can't hear.

Imogene and Lauren laugh so loudly Carson sneaks a glance back at me.

For a while after, the obnoxious noise from the chainsaws drowns out any conversation. We watch them scale trees, take down dead limbs and make piles. They are far enough away from us so we're not in danger, but we're close enough that we can admire their muscles in action.

"Pretty hot," Imogene shouts over the saws. "And I'm not talking about the sun."

Lauren props herself on her elbows to watch Carson and Dylan. "Oh, here we go, ladies. The shirts are coming off. It's show time."

She's not kidding. As Carson walks farther away to the dead tree, he puts his saw on the ground and takes off his shirt. As he wipes his neck and forehead with the wet T-shirt, his abs ripple on his flat stomach while the muscles in his shoulders and biceps look impressively taut. I ogle him, knowing I'm safely hidden under my sombrero.

Dylan is muscular and tan, though skinnier and an inch or two shorter than Carson.

"I had no idea the country had this kind of entertainment." I'm mesmerized with Carson's waist and the muscles flexing just above his jeans. "Wow."

"Yes, our country boys got it going on," Imogene says in a country twang.

Carson stands with his back to us and starts up his saw again. The sound is so sudden and loud all three of us girls flinch and laugh loudly. He certainly jolted us out of our butt-gazing frenzy.

The tree is not as tall as the ancient one next to the house, so after a few swipes with their saws, Carson and Dylan are able to push it over. It snaps free with a clean cut. Dylan looks over at us and gives a thumbs up.

"If they are going to do this every day, I am staying here the whole summer." I peer out from under the brim of the hat and continue watching them.

Imogene laughs. "Quick, Jess, this would be a good time for you to run over there and give them your SPF speech. You can apply the lotion for them."

"Dylan would love that," Lauren says. "Carson would have a cow. He's kind of conservative when it comes to public displays of anything."

"Yeah, I'm not doing any of that. My eyeballs are already in sensory overload just watching those two."

"Here comes the beefcake. They are so fucking obvious, strutting in front of us. Everyone, lie down and close your eyes. Don't give them the satisfaction of an audience." Imogene puts a towel over her face.

"How drunk are you?" I ask. "They saw us watching them hop around the trees."

"Ladies," Carson says as he walks by us to his truck. I'm too busy to respond, studying the eye-catching tan line below his stomach where his jeans keep dipping, exposing skin that is paler.

"Carson," Lauren acknowledges him even though her eyes are closed while she works on her glorious tan.

Dylan stands in front of me and blocks the sun. "I forgot to tell you that Carson is going to come back tomorrow to put the library back together and then you can set up your computer in there." He's so bright and chipper compared to his brother.

"My computer?" I attempt to think back to my conversation with Carson.

"Yeah, Carson said your office is sending it over so you can work from here. How cool is that?" Dylan says.

"Very cool!" Imogene and Lauren say in unison and a little too loudly, as only drunks would do.

Carson blasts the truck horn impatiently. He's already got the equipment loaded in back and is in the driver's seat. His hand hangs out the window to bang the side of the door loudly to get Dylan's attention.

Dylan sighs. "The boss calls. I have to get back to the shop. Tomorrow night, we're on."

"I'll see you then." I try to sound casual, but I feel Lauren and Imogene's eyes on me.

"Bye, ladies." With that, he dashes off to Carson's truck.

I watch them drive away, knowing that the girls are still staring at me with grins.

"Well?" Imogene asks. "He likes you, so the big question is, what are you going to wear?"

"I don't know. I was thinking of clothes, maybe some jewelry, maybe both," I answer. "I'm definitely wearing panties."

Imogene chuckles while Lauren says, "Skin. You want to show skin. You want Dylan to be heaving with desire to the point that he wants to jump you."

"Oh, brother," Imogene groans. "Guys don't need to see skin to be horny. They find any woman desirable if she's walking around with a vagina."

"Unless he's gay," I remind her.

"Yeah, don't worry. Dylan's not gay. You could wear a garbage bag and he'd still be crazy about you. I can tell," Imogene says. "So, are you going to sleep with him?"

"Absolutely not. No first date fucks." I want to sound as tough as them.

Ten

After too many vodka cranberries in the hot afternoon sun, Imogene and Lauren take over two of the empty bedrooms and nap away until the evening. I keep myself busy in the studio, painting until my buzz has worn off and I know I can't keep avoiding my parents.

"I can't believe you didn't call us when you found out," my mother says over the phone.

"I can't believe you didn't tell me Aunt Virginia was still alive," I practically shout into the phone.

My mother is silent on the other end. I am holding the vintage phone in the kitchen tightly to my ear, listening for any signs of life on the other end. My mother finally sighs.

"I'm sorry, Jess. At the time, I thought it was the right thing to do. I was very close to Gin when I was a child and as a young woman, but then she came between your father and me. I took you to stay with Gin when your father and I had a rough patch in those early years. We had great fun, I remember it well, but your father came to take us back."

"Why couldn't we have all stayed with Ginnie that summer? Dad, too?"

"Your aunt disliked him. She made that known to him as well. She believed that your father wasn't good enough for me because she thought he was very controlling."

"He is!" I shout into the phone. "I love Dad, but he is very stodgy and very controlling and you know it. He chose my college and he chose my field of study. He's always had the final word on everything I do or you do."

"I'm sorry to hear you say it like that. It's his way of loving people—to take care of them."

"Controlling isn't the same as loving. Why did you run to Aunt Ginnie's that summer?"

My mother is silent for a moment. "Robert cheated on me. I found out that he had been having an affair with a woman in our circle of friends for two years. I took you to Hera so I could figure out what to do next. Your aunt adored you and loved having us there. We were her only living family."

"How could you take that away from her? From me? I loved being here. I know that. You tried to scrub my memories, but they're coming back, Mom. Why did you forgive Dad for cheating, but you couldn't forgive Aunt Ginnie for butting in?"

I hear my mother crying softly on the other end, sniffles she tries to hide. I wait patiently and listen to her as I wonder where my father is and why he hasn't bothered to pick up the extension like he usually does.

"It wasn't that simple, Jess. I still loved your father and I didn't want to lose him. He gave me an ultimatum. We couldn't see your aunt anymore."

"How could you be so weak to agree to those terms? It goes against everything you two have taught me about being independent and strong.

What did Dad have to gain by giving you the ultimatum?"

"I'm pretty sure at the time that he would have divorced me if I hadn't cut off ties with Ginnie. Don't think badly of your father. A lot has changed in the last fifteen years; our marriage is stronger and he is much more respectful and loving."

"If that were true, you and he would have reconnected with Ginnie and given me my aunt back." I fight the tears.

"I know your father is concerned about you."

"Ah, you mean he's worried that I'm making bad choices and he wants to tell me what to do."

My mother sighs, almost as if she's agreeing with me. "He loves you."

There's a silence on the line, neither of us know what to say, yet we don't want to end the call.

"What are you going to do while you're there? What about your job?"

"My job is fine. Nathan is letting me work from here for a while. I'm figuring some things out on my own this time. Archie Bixby and Ginnie's friends are helping me with the house. I'll let you know what my future plans are, but for now, I'm staying here to think it out. I've never really had a vacation, so I'm using part of the summer here to take a break from the city. That's all."

"All right," my mother says. Her voice trembles so I know she's still crying. I don't have memories of her crying, so I'm not sure if she's crying about losing her aunt or if she thinks she's losing me.

I hear my father in the background. "Michelle, stop crying, you're making it worse.

"Mom," I say. "You should cry. This is a terrible and sad thing."

"Take good care of yourself, Jess. And I am sorry. You need to know that. I wish we had handled it differently and you'd had some years to spend with your aunt before she died."

"I'm sorry we weren't with her during her illness and at the end of her life. I think that makes us horrible people, a horrible family," I retort.

"Robert and I are responsible for that, not you. Sometimes, family loyalty is misplaced and we can't undo the hurt we've caused. I never thought I'd be that kind of mother. I'm sorry."

"Bye, Mom."

"That didn't sound good," Imogene says. She and Lauren are peeking in the kitchen, waiting for a safe time to enter.

"It's kind of typical with my mother and me."

"That sucks," Imogene says. "I can't imagine not being close to my parents and my grandmother."

Lauren nods. "My parents drive me crazy, but we're close."

"You were probably raised on Harry Potter books and funny sitcoms. My parents entertained me with quantum physics and '60 Minutes'. We were never the fun family."

"This is depressing. We need food," Lauren says as they scrounge through the fridge.

I hang up the plastic receiver of the rotary wall phone and it accidentally falls and conks me on the foot. I make another attempt and, this time, when I latch the phone on the chrome cradle I notice a phone number scrawled in pencil on the side of the phone. It's my apartment number in New York. Underneath it is another phone number with a line through it, which is my old phone listing for my college dorm. Aunt Ginnie must have thought of calling me several times over the last few years, but couldn't bring herself to break the archaic, destructive promise she made with my parents.

Imogene makes us delicious bacon and cheese omelets and we polish off the cranberry juice and orange juice, without the vodka this time. Our heads all ache a little, but we want to enjoy the nice evening out on the porch. I like their company and feel more connected to the town and the house because of them. We laugh hardily like longtime friends and then I suggest they both spend the night. I can't tell if we're still tipsy or entering the hung-over stage.

While they head off to their self-appointed bedrooms, I put fresh water in Bert's bowl and then head upstairs to the studio to paint some more. I end up painting until after midnight. My back is sore from sitting on the tall stool and leaning forward to drizzle vibrant colors down the watercolor paper. It's hypnotizing watching where the paint will puddle and if it swirls into other colors. I love this part of my process, the beginning. There's no messy middle to deal with yet. Like the beginning of a relationship or a work project before the computer code becomes riddled with bugs and the clients become demanding. Beginnings are exciting and offer so much hope.

I finally turn in for the night as Bert snuggles next to me in the bed. This time I make sure to set the alarm on my cell phone for eight in the morning, hoping this will be before any dangerously handsome workmen can find me half-dressed in bed.

I roll on my side and hug Bert who eagerly licks my face and grunts.

"God, is this what it's come to, Bert? Me hugging a slobbering dog? A farting dog, no less? And, geez, can I just say the obvious?"

Bert looks at me and waits for my answer.

"You stink. You have the worst breath. I've never had a dog; is this what they mean by dog breath? 'Cause I gotta say, this is what I'd call a WMD, buddy."

He perks his head at me.

"Weapon of mass destruction. That's what you got going on and you'll never get the ladies with that breath." I scratch roughly behind his ears the way he likes and then can't resist hugging him again.

"I'm so lucky I have you," I whisper to him.

Eleven

The pounding begins when I'm still in a wonderful, dreamy position with the cool sheets wrapped around me and the down pillows are scrunched below me in all the right places. I jolt up and realize someone is repeatedly slamming the doorknocker as if they're trying to raise the dead.

"Jesus Effing Barnacles!" I scream. Bert bolts off the bed and runs down the stairs to happily greet whoever has come to ruin my morning.

"Traitor!" I shout after him.

I push my knotted hair back and put on a mint-green silk robe that belonged to Aunt Ginnie. I don't bother looking in the mirror and fixing myself up, I figure whoever thinks calling on me at seven in the morning is okay deserves a good scare.

When I reach the first landing, the front door is open and I see Carson letting in two of the 5 Alpha tech guys, Matthew and Ken. Carson is saying something to them I can't hear before he notices me coming down the stairs.

"You are definitely not a morning person," he declares. "And you've got an impressive temper."

I sigh and thump down the stairs, ignoring his remark.

"Hey, Jess," Ken greets.

"Hi guys," I reply. "I'm surprised Nathan made you leave so early. I didn't even know you were coming today."

"We wanted to beat the traffic. We brought everything," Matthew voices. "We'll have it all set up and be out of your way in an hour or so. Tell us where you want it."

"Oh, but I want it in the library, and Carson still has to put it together and clean it up today."

"It's done," Carson addresses me with a slight smile.

"What? I thought you just got here. How could it be done already?"

I turn around and begin jogging back up to the second floor with all three men following me. I am shocked when I walk into the library. The bookcases are complete; stained, polished and shining. The pine floor is glistening clean. The furniture is unwrapped and Aunt Ginnie's entire hardcover book collection has been arranged on the shelves. Two new chairs have been added that blend well with the rustic leather couch. These pieces have high backs and smooth, contoured seats. A new, huge, square coffee table has been placed in front of the couch. The wood is a bit more weathered and unfinished, which adds to the rustic look and makes it more eclectic than a traditional library. They must have come from Carson's shop. The room looks pristine and incredible, like a page out of an interior design magazine.

"You can set up her monitor here. I turned the desk around so she can face the view outside," Carson explains and then Matthew and Ken leave my side. They follow Carson and listen to everything he says since he seems to be the authority on this room. They talk amongst themselves and then leave to retrieve boxes from the SUV they have out front.

"What is going on?" Imogene asks. She is still wearing her bikini with a T-shirt over it and, with her smudged raccoon eyes and disheveled hair, she could pass as a crack addict. Lauren, who also woke up from all the shouting, doesn't fare much better in her Hello Kitty T-shirt. They both look like they're in agony from their heavy drinking in the hot sun.

I ignore them both and turn back to the one guy who seems to think he's still my babysitter.

"When did you do all this?" I ask Carson, who is adjusting the desk position and what looks to be a new table lamp.

"This morning while you were sleeping."

"What time did you get here?" I know I sound very rude.

"Four-thirty."

"Who does that? Seriously, Carson, you can't let yourself into my house while I'm sleeping and work at these ungodly hours."

"Carson, that's insane," Lauren agrees.

"You don't like the room?" Carson asks me.

"Of course I like it. You know I do and you also know that I call the shots in this house, not you."

Carson smiles a little bit at that. He's not a grinner like Dylan, but Carson seems to have moments when he wants to smile yet tries very hard not to.

"I knew these guys were coming early, so I thought I'd have the room ready."

I must look as deranged as I feel. "Whoa. How did you know they were coming this morning? *I* didn't even know."

"When we were here yesterday I heard the call come in on the answering machine. I assumed you listened to your messages last night."

I want to scream at him. I want the information that he's only willing to deliver in cryptic sound bites. "What answering machine?" I raise my voice. "There was nothing on my cell phone."

"Settle down, Babycakes." He puts his hands up to block my bad vibes. "Gin's machine is on the kitchen counter. That ancient black box? You can't miss it. Your boss, Nathan, must have had trouble reaching you on your cell phone and got the number to the house from information. I don't know. Oh, and by the way, he also sent flowers. I put them on the dining room table."

I'm huffing and puffing like a child, angry that I am so clueless about the house, what's going on and that I'm sleeping through everything. I hate that Carson must consider me a spoiled princess compared to what he's gone through. I probably come across as an ungrateful brat.

"Sorry for the Babycakes remark. Next time, I'll come later," he says. The tension between us is palpable.

"Next time?" Although my voice is calmer, I'm still angry. "You're going to do this again?"

"I still have more work that I promised to finish for Gin, but if you want me to send someone else, or we could hire out a different crew, you let me know."

"The room looks nice." It's more of a hiss than a compliment. "I need to go take a shower." I walk out of the room, stomping up the stairs. *Why did I mention the shower? Now he's picturing me naked in the shower. You wish. Oh, shut up, you have a date with his brother.*

"Maybe if you and your friends weren't hungover, you could get up at a reasonable hour like the rest of the world," he shouts up the stairs.

"Argh!" I shout back and slam my bedroom door.

I stay in my room for at least two hours. I take a long, hot shower, shave my legs and deep condition my hair. Then I spend forever drying my hair with product to remove the frizz. Plus, the process of making long, loose curls takes a half hour and ten finger burns on the curling iron. The make-up is easier; I only apply a little eye shadow, some mascara and gloss my lips with a red tint. My appearance is vastly improved since that horrible wake-up call and my monstrous behavior. I have very few clothes with me, but I did bring a flattering pair of Capri jeans that go well with my white sleeveless blouse. As I head back downstairs the smell of coffee and bacon is divine. I make it to my fabulous new library on the second floor and discover Imogene and Lauren, having showered and dressed, lounging on the couch with Bert, along with coffee and a few newspapers.

"I made coffee and bacon," Imogene tells me as I come into the room. "It's in the kitchen. Oh, and did you know that Carson brought fresh croissants? I guess he picked them up at the bakery, hot out of the oven, before he came over here and set-up this fantastic room for you."

"Hmm," Lauren adds. "Pretty nice of him. I can't believe how you raked him over the coals. Ouch."

I pinch my mouth shut. I don't like where this is going.

"And you have Internet access!" Lauren announces, waving her tablet in the air.

"And those flowers from your boss are gorgeous. Time to come out of your cave, Miss Channing, you're missing the day," Imogene says.

"Ech," I say. I notice all my equipment, including five large computer monitors, are set up on the desk. "Where's Carson?" Then I hear hammering. "Never mind."

Bert follows me downstairs and we find Carson holstering his hammer in the living room.

"Thank God, you're putting that away," I say as he adjusts his tool belt. He's stingy with his smiles; however, I get a small one.

"How's your head?" he asks, gazing at me thoroughly.

"I'm fine—oh, my gosh," I say, realizing the living room is immaculate. The tarps and the table saw are gone. The furniture has been put back in place. The floor is polished and the paintings on the wall have been uncovered. "You're like an elf. You come and work in the night and I wake up to these little miracles."

"It's a nice room." He nods. "And, F.Y.I., no guy wants to be referred to as an elf."

I laugh. "Yeah, well, okay."

"Still hung-over? There's breakfast in the kitchen."

"I'm not hung-over and, don't worry, I plan on eating the breakfast."

"By the way, I had no idea you had so many computers. They block your view outside. I assumed they'd be setting up one monitor, so if you want me to move the desk to the side of the room, I can."

"No, I like where it is. This way, the glare from the sun won't affect my screens. It will be fine, thanks."

There's an awkward pause, since I don't know what to say to Carson. His tall, hunky, workman handsomeness makes my hormones stupid and I can't help gawking. Bert leaves us and waddles towards the kitchen so I take that moment to excuse myself from Carson's lascivious aura. "I'm going to go eat."

I pass through the dining room and notice Nathan's ginormous bouquet of yellow roses and wonder what they represent. Roses don't seem appropriate for condolences. The note is written in Nathan's messy scrawl. "*You're the best!*" He's such a nerd. I don't even know what he means.

My escape to the kitchen is short-lived. I am leaning against the counter, munching on a croissant and bacon together, when Imogene and Lauren thank me for the hospitality and head off to the diner for their day shift. Then Carson appears again and my chest constricts as perspiration beads across my forehead.

"So all of our equipment is out of here, but I still have to come back and tick minor things off

Gin's list. I have to measure for some new appliances in here and Gin wanted me to strip the face of the cupboards and paint them."

I nod and wipe croissant crumbs from my mouth. I would like to avoid looking at him because being near him makes me fumble, verbally and physically, however, he's not getting the hint.

"Can I ask you what you do at 5 Alpha exactly? Gin, told me you work in software, but she didn't have specifics."

I'm flattered he wants to know more about me, although he is the type of person who pays attention to details. They seem to matter to him greatly, whereas Dylan is more about enjoying the moment.

"I have a few different project teams. One of them does the engineering designs to make integrated circuits. The other team designs software for analyzing resistivity." I decide not to provide a more detailed explanation because this is usually the point where people nod along and then nod off—I sound that boring—but Carson looks genuinely interested.

"I know what you're talking about. Those two guys said you are a hotshot at the firm. I believe it."

"Ken and Matthew are being generous. 5 Alpha hires hotshots. I'm nothing special there."

"Liar. They set up a special office for you here because they don't want to lose you. I'm going to Google you." Oh boy, he flashes me a wide grin.

I know I'm blushing. Fair-skinned redheads turn a rosy pink rather easily.

"Too bad you don't have your big hat to cover up that lie," Carson says and I smile. *For him*, I think to myself.

"So, you still think I'm a lousy influence on your brother?"

"I never said that."

"But you think I'm wrong for him."

"I never said that, either. I doubt you're wrong for anyone." That floors me. "But I'm not sure Dylan can handle anyone. There's a difference."

"Care to explain?"

"I'm not sure it's my place." His demeanor instantly becomes more subdued again. What is it with these up and down moods of his?

"Why not? You seem very good at butting into other people's lives."

"Yeah, I probably deserve that, but with Dylan it's different."

"So, you're being overly protective of him, but you won't really tell me why and I'm having dinner with him, which you may or may not find objectionable. Thanks for making things clearer for me," I snap.

"I'll say this. Dylan is a good person and he means well. I have my reasons to be concerned about him, but I'm not going to get into that right now."

"That was nice and cryptic. I could be going out to dinner with a serial killer and you're not telling me."

Carson doesn't look amused at all. I'm pushing all the wrong buttons now.

"He really likes you," Carson says as though it pains him to admit it. "So are you going to start working today?"

"Are you trying to change the subject? No, I can't work, oh wait. Did Lauren mention that I have Internet now?"

"Yes. The cable guy was here this morning, too. Gin already had the wiring, the cable guy only needed to install the box. I had him put it in the pantry behind the door so it's easy to get to."

"Then I guess I am working today," I say, relieved I can keep collecting a paycheck.

Carson walks to the front door while Bert and I trail right behind him. He's like a wall of muscle in front of me. Thoughts of him coming back to work in the house override the plans of my upcoming date with Dylan. I'm still daydreaming when he stops abruptly to pick up his toolbox and I bash right into his back. Perfect. Didn't I already do this with Dylan?

Carson drops the box and turns around to catch me. "I'm sorry, did I do that?"

"No, it was me." I rub my nose.

He's holding me by the waist, pulling me into him, but it's not a déjà vu of Dylan. Carson is something else—something I like very much—and I suspect that being torn between two men in my own imaginary, lovelorn world is a sign of my immaturity. At least, that would be the first thing my mother would say before she asks what they do for a living. My hands are wedged between us, resting against his hard abdomen.

Carson doesn't let go, as if he's thinking of something to say or thinking of pulling one of those fast Blackard kisses. "This could be awkward," he says and releases his grip on me while his hands remain hovering by me.

I'm not sure if he's having the same thought as me, that a kiss would be awkward since I'm going out with Dylan, or if it's awkward because he sees me as some virginal geek and he's never touched one in person before. *It's awkward because I'm over-thinking the whole scenario!*

Quickly, I step up on my tippy toes and kiss his cheek. "Thanks for the library. I know I'm a crab in the morning, but thanks for coming in early to fix it up for me."

Carson doesn't move. As the aroma of his freshly laundered T-shirt mixed with sweat pummels my brain, it hits me. Dylan is the light version of Carson. Dylan is a dream guy for any woman, even me, but if you want to amp it up and make it more interesting with a guy who's complex and intellectually challenging, my bet is on Carson. Unfortunately, he's difficult to read and I'm too inexperienced to pursue someone like him.

Dylan is more my speed, laid back and sweet, and I have agreed to go out with him. That little reminder makes me push back completely from Carson's arms. Once out of his grasp we both look at one another. Is he considering the lost moment? What may have happened between us? Therein lies my problem; I'm between them. I tell myself that I'm playing a dangerous game even if I think I've chosen the safer path with Dylan. I'm hardly an expert on this topic and the tight flutters in my chest tell me that I'm not fooling myself.

"I'm going to get to work now," I say.

"Yeah, I have to get going, too. We'll be back to work on the kitchen when the new appliances come in." He lingers in the doorway, as though he wants to say something else, but I cut him off before he can consider it.

"Bye."

"Goodbye, Jess."

I close the door so I don't get caught watching him walk to his truck. Then I jump up on the staircase and peek through the small, decorative window to admire his swagger, lugging his heavy toolbox. Damn that swagger.

Twelve

Dylan rings the doorbell at exactly six o'clock right as I finish tying the vintage halter top around my neck. I found it in Aunt Virginia's closet along with an assortment of well-maintained retro pieces. The halter is black crepe with ruffles around the edges; very elegant and rather sexy, especially paired with my short black skirt. My legs are bare and have a nice, sun-kissed hue to them.

I traipse down the stairs, carrying a pair of black, sling-back sandals with a kitten heel. It's the best I could do considering I expected to be here wearing mourning clothing and not dating attire. My red hair is down, voluminous and curled. I will regret it later when it's wet and sticking to the back of my neck, yet right now, I'm going for maximum effect.

I fling open the door and get the reaction I expected from Dylan, who falls over himself to be generous with compliments.

"Wow, I thought you were stunning in that red bathing suit yesterday, but now, you look even more gorgeous, if that's possible," he says with a wide grin.

I'm glad I dressed up because Dylan is a vision of male beauty. He's having another Ralph Lauren moment in his black dress pants paired with a fitted, white dress shirt. His shoes are polished and there's no mud in sight. There's not even a Jeep. Behind him, parked in the driveway, sits a shiny, black sports car.

"Thank you. You look nice yourself." I slip on my shoes and grab my clutch off the stairs.

"You're sure I don't look like a waiter in this get-up?"

"Ha! Absolutely not."

I lock the door and hold Dylan's arm as we walk down the stairs to the path. He immediately shakes my hand off his arm and catches it in his hand. He holds it firmly and it's thrilling, of course, to have his eager attention.

"Fifty-two million," I whisper before I can silence myself.

"What?" Dylan asks as he opens the passenger door for me.

"Nothing." I just want to forget about my whispering number habit.

"I love when you do that. It's cute."

"I didn't know you noticed."

"You've always done that." He winks.

I sink back into the comfortable black leather seat as he buckles himself in.

"Is this your car?"

"No, it's Carson's. I wasn't going to drive you in my dirty Jeep with the wind blowing you around."

"This BMW doesn't seem like Carson."

"He uses it when he goes to the city for meetings or to see clients, but I call it his date car." The thought of Carson on a date leaves me a little sad and jealous.

Dylan is a confident driver, relaxed and smooth. He maneuvers us quickly out of the bumpy driveway and hits the main road at a high speed.

"This isn't the Indy 500. You don't have to drive like a New York cabbie on my account," I say as he turns on some music.

"Am I making you nervous?" He smiles.

"This isn't *The Fast and The Furious Part 25.* I wouldn't mind a nice, leisurely drive through the country at a safe speed," I say loudly over the heavy metal music blasting through the speaker system.

Dylan laughs. "Okay, whatever you want." He turns down the music, taking quick glances at me.

I look away and study the scenic farms outside my window. "Being here makes you want to slow down and enjoy life instead of running at top speed, chasing after things that only seem important," I say.

"Good. Another reason for you to stay."

We pull up to the restaurant and I chuckle.

"What's so funny?"

"Lauren predicted you'd take me to Cucina."

"It's my favorite place and it's not like we have a lot of restaurants to choose from, but this one is good." He leans over and kisses me with one large palm holding my face. I kiss him back as the image of Carson pops in my head and doesn't leave until the kiss ends. Damn.

"I'm not a bad cook, but I'll take you to any restaurant anywhere, anytime as long as you kiss me like that," he says with his forehead against mine.

"I'm hungry," I divert him from our eager libidos and my anxious nerves that don't know what to do with a guy like Dylan.

Dinner is excellent and Dylan is charming. He frequently picks up my unoccupied hand and holds it like he's about to propose. Then he kisses it and says, "It was just sitting there doing nothing."

I catch the wait staff watching us, I suspect because Dylan is strikingly handsome and takes over a room when he's in it. The pull of a beautiful creature like Dylan is powerful; his magnetism has an orbit all its own and it sucks you in. Unfortunately, that lovely thought about Dylan reminds me of his womanizing past, and makes me wonder about other women he may have brought here.

"People can't stop looking at the beautiful redhead with the most exotic eyes I have ever seen," he says and, with the way his eyes never leave me, I don't think he's really noticed the other people in the room. Either that, or he's a very good actor.

We end up back at my house and kick our shoes off in the living room. I offer to make coffee or open a bottle of wine, but Dylan has other things on his mind. He pulls me onto the couch and pushes his weight on top of me. His groin is hard against my thigh and despite previously considering his brother, Dylan turns me on.

My interests are fully focused on his body. His mouth is all over me—my lips and my neck—while his hands grope my thighs and move up under my halter. He fondles my breast. The halter loosens and moves to the side. I moan as his warm mouth reaches my nipple and then squirm under him, excited and nervous. He responds by kissing me more fervently and palming both of my breasts, his hand rough against my hard nipples. I reach down and stroke his hard bulge and he hisses loudly.

"God, I want to take you to bed," he says into my ear. "I can't stop thinking of you in bed with me."

I know this is the perfect time to finally have the sex I've been waiting for because Dylan is the perfect guy to do the deed, however, there's a nagging voice in my head that tells me I'm going too fast. I've known Dylan three days and this goes against all the practical advice I've given myself and the rational choices I have made in life. For Dylan, there's no reason to analyze lust, you act on it and feel good. I'm not wired that way. I always believe there are consequences to every action.

As his fingers slide under my panties and begin a rhythmic rubbing, my defenses weaken. It's either stop this now or go all the way. Every part of my body, my senses, is reacting to him. They want him. I'm having a heated internal debate with myself.

"Stop. Dylan, we have to stop." I move his hand away.

"Really?" he asks, panting.

"We barely know each other, and I'm not a one-night-stand girl."

"I don't want you for one night," he says, fighting for control of his body back. "I want you for every night."

"I like you, I'm enjoying this, but I can't jump into bed with you." I sit up and smooth out my skirt and tie my halter back behind my neck.

Dylan sighs and lies back on the couch with an arm behind his head as the other reaches out, takes a hunk of my curls and wraps them around his finger. "We can slow down," he says. His hand drops my hair and then cups my breast before resting on my leg. "I'm not going anywhere. Are you?"

That's a loaded question. He knows I've made the decision to stay in town at least for a while, but beyond the summer, I haven't committed to anything. He's supposed to be older and wiser than me, how can he be asking me to make final plans after only three days into this new life? It could be a temporary life, yet the hopefulness in his face makes me want to tell him whatever he wants to hear, even if it's a lie.

"What happened to Dylan the playboy? I heard you really got around in college."

"That was then, this is now. It's not like I was a criminal or a junkie. I went out with a lot of women. Don't judge me by what I did in the past, Jess."

"Fair enough, but don't expect me to change my mind because you've got a party in your pants."

He laughs. "Come here."

I curl back down against him on the couch with my head on his chest and his arms wrapped around me.

My hand rests where his shirt is unbuttoned and I feel his fast heartbeat. I have never been this comfortable and felt this safe with any guy. After being so close to getting naked with Dylan, I am glad to be here now, in our own little web of comfort.

"I could hold you like this all night, Jess," I feel him kiss the top of my head and I marvel at the sensation of being adored and perhaps being loved in this way by one man forever.

"This is nice, Dylan."

"Let me know if you do change your mind. I can adapt at a moment's notice," he says, sounding sleepy.

Pressed against his very warm body, only separated from his skin by the cotton shirt, I smile at his resolve.

"I know you're smiling," he says, his voice dropping an octave with fatigue setting in.

We lie entwined for a while before I hear the soft, labored breaths of him sleeping. The rise and fall of his chest relaxes me and I soon drift off to sleep as well.

Thirteen

As Dylan wakes up early and unfolds himself from me, I reluctantly wake myself up, but stay sprawled on the couch with my tangled hair fanned out around my head.

"You can go back to sleep," he says. "I have to get to the shop. Carson likes us to start work between six and seven so he can let the other guys off at three to be with their families."

He puts on his dress shoes and stands up to tuck in his shirt.

"At this hour, you look like a gigolo leaving his one night stand," I say, admiring how men can pull themselves together in the morning with very little effort. He's every bit as good-natured a soul at dawn as he is at any other hour.

"You look like a goddess," he says, smiling.

"You're sweet, but I know I must look like the whore of Babylon with the breath of Bert." I cover my mouth with three fingers.

Dylan sits back down and swoops in for a full on kiss. His tongue and hands are on me before I can hold him off. I run my hands through his thick curly hair and the desire in me rises, urging me to finish what we started last night. Dylan's hand is under my panties and cupping one buttock. When he squeezes, my groin reacts and the little nag inside shouts at me to stop. *If I do this with Dylan, what door do I open? If you have to keep asking yourself that, then you're not ready.*

He's hard and on top of me again. "Say the word and I can be naked in less than a second," Dylan says into my neck.

I savor him pressing on top of me, the sexual heat, the fantasy of being naked with him, the longing to feel what it's like to have him completely, but then I hear Carson. *I don't want you to break Dylan's heart.* Damn, damn, damn.

"You stopped," Dylan says, unlocking his lips from mine and lifting his head to look at me. "What's wrong? This feels so right. Why aren't we running up to your bed?"

"As much as I love this, and I do, I..."

"You're not ready," he finishes for me. "Is it me or is it a general feeling that you need to wait?"

"It's a general feeling. It's too soon." I know it's a lie as soon as I say it.

Dylan nods. "Okay, I can live with that." He gives me a quick peck on the mouth and then stands up to resume his grooming.

I berate myself for not being honest. *I want to sleep with you, Dylan. I want your sexy body, but I want to leave our hearts out of this equation.* I want the sex, but Carson's words linger with me, his once womanizing brother needs to be treated with care? Why? Why can't we just have sex with no strings attached?

We let Bert out and he does a wobbly trot to the yard to do his morning poop. I have no idea where he goes and I don't know if I'm supposed to be cleaning up his piles or if it's eco-friendly here in the country to leave them.

Barefoot, I walk Dylan to the sports car.

"So are you going to be working all day?" he asks, putting his arms around my waist.

"That's the plan. I may walk in to town later to pick up groceries."

"Why not drive?"

"I don't have a car. Remember, you drove me here."

"I meant Gin's car." He points to the detached garage on the side of the house.

"I assumed those were old horse stables full of junk or something."

"They were horse stables, but now they hold Gin's Prius and all the garden equipment. She left you a car. The keys are hanging on a hook inside the pantry. There are extra house keys there, too."

A smile spreads across my face. "I've never had my own car. I've had a driver's license for four years and I've probably driven less than a dozen times. It's too hard to maintain one in the city, but this is great. I have a car! Maybe Bert and I will go for a drive."

Dylan is beaming. "Then you have to come visit us at the shop. Come see what we do and then I'll take you to get groceries."

"All right, I suppose I could come around my noon time break." Bert returns from his nature call and walks between us, looking at me and licking his jowls.

"Someone is ready to be fed," Dylan comments.

"Oh, is that what that means? He's always slobbering around me."

Dylan kisses me again, a peck only. "I'll see you soon, around lunchtime. Do you know how to get back to town? Our shop is going to be on the left just as you enter. It says Blackard Designs."

"Got it. Drive straight down the one road, look to my left."

"You're a genius."

I watch him drive away before Bert and I go inside to make breakfast.

I sit in my bra and underwear and spend the whole morning trying to find one persistent bug in my program. The library is a beautiful, comfortable room. I admire the view from its window and think I could get used to this working environment. A little before noon, I shower and change into a T-shirt and shorts. I put my hair in a high ponytail and grab my purse.

"Come on. Let's go!" I call to Bert. He scrambles down the stairs with me and follows me out to the garage. I pull open the barn-style door and find the shiny, clean, silver Prius waiting for me. It's such a rare treat for me, a kick of independence. I back the car out, excited to be driving. Then I jump out and run around the passenger side and open the door for Bert.

"Come on. Get inside. I'm letting you sit up front."

Bert plants his rump on the ground and all the excitement is drained from his body. I grip his collar and try to lead him, but he won't budge. It's like trying to drag a fifty-pound sack of flour. I manage to get him on his feet and move forward about three steps before he grunts and pulls me back six steps.

"This is ridiculous. I thought you'd want to go out on the town with me." Bert lies down with his head between his paws and looks up at me with dread.

"Fine. You stay here. Back inside!" I point to the house. He charges back to the house, gleeful he won the battle. I let him back in the front door and then jog back to my car.

It's not too difficult to find my way back to the town. The dirt road from my house leads to the main road that goes right through Hera. I pull over when I see the black metal sign for Blackard Designs. It looks like a renovated barn with a glass front so people can see not only the furniture, but also the craftsmen at work. I park along the side of the building next to Dylan's Jeep.

When I enter the modern, industrial-looking shop there's a receptionist desk up front made of metal and wood. To the left of it is a large showroom with finished furniture displayed in various settings. On the right side is the work area. Four guys around the same age as Carson and Dylan are sawing, carving, sanding and putting together actual furniture that doesn't come from an IKEA box. An attractive young woman sits behind the counter talking on the phone and signals to me with her index finger, but I see Dylan come out of a back room and he reaches me as the woman puts down the phone.

"You made it," he says. "Daisy, this is Jessica. Daisy runs this whole place. We'd be lost without her."

Daisy reaches across the counter and shakes my hand. "I've heard so much about you." She gives me a friendly smile. "I'm so sorry about Ginnie, but we're so lucky to have you here."

Maybe I'm a jaded city person because I don't think I could ever believe that a town is lucky to have me, yet from her it sounds sincere.

"Thank you. I'm having a very interesting time so far."

"I'll bet," she says. "I hear ya got plenty of action goin' on up at the house."

Mortified, the image of Dylan and I grappling half-naked on the couch comes to mind. I look at Dylan and he bursts out laughing. "I told her that Lauren and Imogene have been hanging out with you. And she already knows Carson and I have been working there."

"Yeah, it's been busy at the house," I admit.

"I want to introduce you to the guys." Dylan puts his arm around my shoulder. Daisy smiles at me as if she's got Dylan and me all figured out.

As we walk through the workshop area, the men put down their tools and silence their equipment so they can hear Dylan.

"Jess, this is Thomas and Daniel." He points to two men at the table saw, both bearded with brown hair. I'd never be able to tell them apart.

"Hello!" they both bark loudly and I wonder if they're all going deaf from the noise of their equipment. Then I see them pull earplugs out.

I nod and say hi.

"This is Jeremy who just started a couple of weeks ago." Dylan points at a young man about Dylan's age. He takes off a work glove and leans over a table to shake my hand.

"And this is Leo," Dylan says after I shake Jeremy's sweaty hand and give him a little hi. "We go way back. We've known each other since we were in kindergarten and he has his own style here." This is Lauren's Leo. He gives me a shy wave and an inaudible "hi". He's painting the trim on a rustic table that looks like it's made from barn wood. His style is whimsical and colorful, and I can see why his pieces would be popular.

The door to the back office swings open and Carson steps out. Our eyes meet and then he goes back inside, closing the door behind him. Well, shit me. Someone doesn't want to see me.

"That's the office, nothing to see there," Dylan says. "Okay, time for groceries." He bids goodbye to the staff and we head about fifty yards down the main street to the small grocery store. It has a sign that says, *The General Store*. I laugh.

"A lot of people shop at the super stores out on the interstate. They only go here for emergencies or gourmet items," Dylan explains. "I like to support Harvey's business."

He holds the door open and I walk inside to the nineteenth century. The floors are unfinished wood planks, there are wooden barrels of gourmet items and a long, wooden front counter supports the cash register and freshly made treats. Behind the counter are floor-to-ceiling shelves with cans of caviar and other delicacies I've never eaten. A ladder on rails makes everything accessible to the large man in the white apron.

"Dylan!" the husky man exclaims, stepping off the ladder. "Sushi man is here today. And you must be Ginnie's niece. I'm Harvey."

"Jessica." I put my hand into his giant palm.

"Sushi. You like sushi?" Dylan asks me.

I nod as he takes my hand and grabs a wicker shopping basket at the counter. We weave through aisles of fresh produce and baked goods that are displayed in baskets.

The ambiance reminds me of Eataly, one of my favorite places to shop and eat in New York, although this store is infinitely smaller and not crowded with tourists. The back end of the store actually has a sushi station with two chefs making hand rolls. We select a few varieties and perch ourselves at a dining bar where a few other locals Dylan knows are eating sushi as well.

"See, now you can move here. We have sushi," he says, wolfing down his pieces in whole bites.

"This is a surprise. Fresh sushi in the country. Weird." I have an inner debate over how much wasabi I can use if I'm going to be kissing Dylan in the very near future. I decide to omit it all together.

After we eat, Dylan stays to peruse the aisles with me, carrying the basket that is growing extremely heavy with all the items he thinks I must have.

"You have me mistaken for someone who cooks." I look at the homemade sausages and eggplants he has put in the basket. "I'm good with apples and instant ramen noodles."

"Don't let Harvey hear you say that. He doesn't stock ramen or instant anything."

"Well, I don't know how to cook eggplant."

"I do. These are from local farms. It's the best produce. We also have a local couple that makes artisanal sausages and cheeses. You're from the city; I thought you'd have refined tastes."

"I was raised on Ding Dongs and baloney sandwiches. Don't get me wrong, my parents eat out constantly at all the best places, but at home, they wouldn't know how to work an Easy Bake Oven. I know that because I actually received an Easy Bake Oven for one of my birthdays and my mother had no clue how to operate it."

"You're cute." Dylan laughs and shoves more items into the basket. "I'm going to cook for you."

"What makes you such a good cook?"

"No parents, but I had nice women who offered to feed us. I watched them cook and picked up a few skills." His face doesn't register any grief or the wish to expand on his comment. I regret asking something that would bring up his sad childhood; however, it doesn't seem to bother Dylan.

He takes my hand and leads me back to the front register. When I reach for my credit card, he stops my hand. "I've got this."

"Why? It's my food."

"I've overloaded your basket. I'm cooking for you."

Dylan collects the three burlap shopping bags that Harvey packs my groceries in. Yes, The General Store is eco-friendly and makes you purchase and carry re-useable bags, unless you bring your own. I'm racking up my commitments to Hera after less than a week.

He puts everything on the floor on my passenger side and then comes back to my side of the car and leans in the driver's side window.

Dylan is so tall that he has to bend really far over to face me in the window of the small car.

"Tonight," he says. "What's a good time for you? Five? Six?"

"Six is fine," I say a little excited. I may have some doubts about the Blackard brothers, but this insistent one knows how to turn the dial up to *thrill.*

He kisses me slowly and I reciprocate. It's too easy to respond the way he wants. After a minute, we end it, though Dylan brushes his lips against the side of my face.

"Does everyone know about us?" I ask.

"I hope so." He looks as delighted as ever with our public kiss. "I've been making it a point to tell everyone about you."

I have no doubt that he has been referring to me in a possessive way with every resident in Hera he knows. Plus, knowing Dylan, he's probably on a first name basis with all nine hundred eighty-four residents.

Fourteen

When I return to the house, the big, black monster truck is in my driveway. Carson. I had no idea he'd be back today to work on one of his projects for Aunt Virginia, or, now me. He didn't bother to say hello to me at the shop, so I figured he'd had enough of me. I drive on the other side of his vehicle and park in front of the garage so I can unload my groceries. As I walk around to the passenger side and open the door, Carson is already taking long strides to my car with Bert jogging alongside him.

"Let me help." He grabs all three burlap bags in one hand and closes the door with his free hand.

"I didn't know you'd be here today," I say, following him back to the house.

"I'm fixing the kitchen pipe. I noticed it leaking the other day. I brought a replacement. It will only take a few minutes to fix and then I'll be out of your way."

"I don't mind. I'm going to be in the library working for the rest of the day."

In the kitchen I put away the groceries while Carson gets back to work. He wedges his big frame under the kitchen sink and takes a wrench to the leaky pipe.

"Shit!" Carson slides out from under the sink with the decayed pipe in one hand and wet, black gunk splattered across his chest. He puts the broken pipe on a paper towel spread on the floor then he takes off his T-shirt to remove the offending grime.

I am completely captivated by his splendidly buff physique. His muscles and rippling abs up close cause me to lose my voice and any rational thought. I fold and re-fold the burlap bags, trying to play it cool as if I'm used to handymen stripping down in front of me. This always happens to single chicks in New York.

Carson balls up the dirty T-shirt and puts it on the floor. "Will you hand me the new piece there?" He points to the shiny, curved pipe on the counter near me.

Speechless, I grab the pipe and hand it to him. Our eyes lock as we both grip the pipe at the same time. The seconds pass quicker than I want, but long enough for me to realize there's an attraction between us. Either that or I'm an idiot. I decide I am indeed a delusional idiot.

Carson ducks back under the sink and installs the new hardware while I watch the rise and fall of his chest and follow the path of his bare skin down to the top edge of his jeans which have inched below the rim of his underwear. I sigh a little too loudly as Carson climbs back out of the cupboard and he looks at me with amusement.

"Kitchen plumbing exciting to watch?"

"Huh, not at all. I've got a lot of work to do," I mumble and head back upstairs to the library.

After a couple hours of programming that includes finally finding and fixing the bug that was driving me and my team crazy, I take a breather and peruse the Internet. I do a search on Blackard Designs and find more than a dozen articles on Carson, the furniture, their retailers along with interviews in Dwell, Elle Décor and Architectural Digest. There are a few photos of Carson posing with some of the furniture and at work in the shop. He's wearing jeans and T-shirts in all of them and in some he's covered in sawdust or hasn't removed his dirty work gloves.

I like that he doesn't primp and get cleaned up for the photo shoots. I can imagine him telling the photographer to get on with it and take his photo as is. Perhaps it's his indifference to others' opinions that I admire. I spent too many years worrying about fitting in, while Carson spent those years worrying about his brother and their general survival. I hear clomping on the stairs and quickly close the screen window on the image of Carson Blackard.

I swivel around in my chair as Carson enters the room and drops onto the couch in a casual slouch. *Damn, he has a new T-shirt on.* He must keep extra clothing in his truck for these types of mishaps.

Carson rests his arms across the back of the couch and stretches out his long legs, crossing his clunky work boots at the ankle. Bert comes in and jumps up on the couch, snuggling into Carson who picks up a magazine from the coffee table and flips through with disinterest.

"May I help you?" I ask, observing his confidence at making himself comfortable in my new work place. "I thought you left a while ago."

"Nope. I figured that since you were up here, I could finish the kitchen measurements and then I ordered the new appliances. Nice, huh? I'm just waiting for dinner."

"Oh. Um. I'm not cooking. I mean, Dylan is coming over to make dinner for me."

"Yeah, I figured as much. I saw the eggplant and sausage." Carson laughs. "That guy can cook and eat. You don't mind if I join you, do you?" This is a side of Carson I haven't seen; cocky and taking great liberties. I assume this is to piss off Dylan. Whatever is going on between them, I'm being left in the dark, or rather, bounced around between them.

"I don't mind." I really don't mind, either. Carson's sporadic coldness is somewhat attractive. Isn't that the mistake women always make with men; they seek out the sexy, inattentive ones that are bound to be troubling disappointments? I could tell him that I plan to dine alone with Dylan, but I don't and Carson seems to be completely aware of this.

Dylan's reaction is evident. I'm at the end of the hall in the kitchen doorway when Carson answers the door and Dylan's face drops. "What the fuck are you doing here?"

"Hi, brother," Carson greets him with a smugness in his voice. "I was working on the kitchen and thought I'd stay for dinner. I see you're making your eggplant parm. Wouldn't want to miss that." He holds the door open for Dylan who storms through with two bottles of wine in each hand.

"Oh, fuck you," Dylan snaps and head towards me. He kisses me on the cheek. "Hi. So we've got company." He shakes his head at me.

"Here, let me open the wine." Carson squeezes between Dylan and me, grabbing the bottles. "You cook. Jess and I will drink this fine vino you've brought us."

"I didn't bring it for you," Dylan counters.

Carson studies the wine label and raises his eyebrows. "You've dropped an impressive little bundle on these two gems. Can't wait to drink it."

Dylan ignores him and makes his way into the kitchen where he begins to pull items out of the fridge along with pots and pans from the cupboards. I'm caught in the middle of some brotherly dynamic that is foreign to me, so I stay out of it and keep quiet.

Carson uncorks a bottle of wine with a switchblade he pulls out of his pocket. I don't know whether to be unnerved or impressed that he carries a knife and knows how to open a bottle of wine with it. He makes one slice around the seal, thuds the base of the bottle against one of the vertical beams along the wall and then pulls the cork out with his teeth. I've never seen anything like it. He looks even sexier merely by doing that little move. His hands are full with the bottle in one hand and the knife and cork in the other, so he pulls a kitchen chair out with his foot.

"Have a seat, milady, and join me in a glass of the grape," he mimics a thick Scottish brogue.

"Oh, please," Dylan says over his shoulder as he slams pans on the range.

I laugh and sit down. Carson smiles at me and pours a tiny amount of the wine into a juice glass for me. I take a little sip and nod approvingly. I know nothing about wine.

"Mm," Carson hums after a sip. "This is too good not to decant."

As he leaves the kitchen, Dylan turns to me. "You can ask him to leave."

"That would be rude, Dylan. Carson has been working all afternoon on my house."

Dylan shakes his head as he resumes his chopping and cooking. Carson returns with a wine decanter and crystal wine glasses. "Just so you know, Gin keeps these in the buffet in the dining room."

"I don't even know how to use a decanter," I answer.

"It allows the wine to breathe." He pours the wine into the decanter and then takes the chair right next to mine, which means Dylan will have to sit across the table from us. "This is fun," Carson deadpans.

"It's interesting," I comment.

He fills a small amount into our wine glasses. "Cheers."

I gently tap my glass to his and we drink.

"You need to pour a glass for Dylan," I tell him.

"Right, keep the cook happy." Carson fills another wine glass and puts it on the counter for Dylan.

The food is delicious, however, the company is tense. Carson is the most talkative I've ever seen him, telling me stories about his company and enjoying an audience. Dylan responds with terse comments when Carson engages him.

"Dylan, your cooking is superb," I compliment, noticing that Carson doesn't thank him. "Thank you for taking me shopping and making this wonderful meal."

"You're welcome," Dylan says, "Milady." He smiles at me from across the table.

"Good grub, brother," Carson interjects.

Dylan grunts an acknowledgement from him.

I am full from the rich food and cannot finish half the plate. Carson keeps refilling my wine glass so I'm woozy. I put my napkin on my plate and push it away. "I'm done," I announce. "So are we going to talk about the elephant that's sitting at this table with us?"

Carson and Dylan both look at me. I turn to Carson who stares at me and settles back in his chair with his arm across the back of mine; a blatantly territorial move I would expect from Dylan, not Carson.

"Oh, come on," I say to Carson. "You're going to play dumb now? What's going on here? It's obvious you've been taunting Dylan and you're using me as the bait."

Carson doesn't say anything, so I look at Dylan for a response. He says nothing also, simply keeps shoveling food—his third helping—into his mouth.

"Okay, how about this? It's my house, my rules. Tell me what the hell is going on between you two because it's like watching a tennis match without a ball. You guys are lobbing jabs at each other and I want to know why."

"It's nothing for you to concern yourself with, Jess," Dylan says. "Brothers fight. It's no big deal."

"No, she's right," Carson says. "I've decided that it's time for me to stop hovering over Dylan. I'm not his parent."

"Then why are you here," Dylan hisses.

"I like hanging out with Jess."

"Hah!" I scoff. "Two can play at this game of sarcasm. You're as believable as a..." I go blank. I'm usually good at rattling off comebacks, must be the wine.

"I'm not being sarcastic and this isn't a game." Carson finishes his glass of wine. We've polished off two bottles between the three of us. I'm drunk and they're sober as well as angry. "I forgot to mention, Lois is having a party in a couple of weeks and wanted me to invite you," Carson continues, changing the subject. "She said she left a message on that antique answering machine over there, but you must have forgotten to check it."

"I did forget," I admit.

"I saw her before I came out here," Carson says.

Dylan watches Carson with hard, cold eyes.

"That's sounds like fun," I say.

"Good. You want to go with me?" Carson asks.

Fifteen

In a fury of flying limbs and dishes, Dylan overturns the table and slams against Carson. However, Carson is faster, stronger and more adept at combat maneuvers. He blocks Dylan's swings and manages to flip him over, throwing him to the ground. Carson has Dylan pinned with his arms secured behind his back underneath Carson's weight.

I have never witnessed an actual fight, so I just stand there with the table and food upturned at my feet.

"Do you want to rethink this one, Dylan?" Carson growls into his ear.

"Get the fuck off me!" Dylan yells. Dylan's pupils dilate. He looks angry and fearful at the same time.

A panic rises in me and all I can think of doing is getting as far away from them as possible. How could these two nice people, brothers, be so violent with each other? I turn and run. I run down the hall and out the front door. I fly down the porch steps and turn towards the garage.

Imogene told me the other day about Barron's Creek—a nature walk people take—and the trail runs by my house. She said that if I went beyond the garage I would see the opening for the dirt trail. The sun hasn't set completely, so there's still enough light for me to see. Bert is at my heels, panting and trying to keep up. He stops abruptly when I find the opening to the trail where the grass ends and the forest begins.

I turn to him. "If you're coming with me, let's go!" He sits and stays in place. "Fine. Stay with the lunatics."

I take the trail and keep running. The rubber flip-flops don't provide any traction on the rocky path, so I slow to a jog and keep going, watching the trees break the light of the setting sun. After about ten minutes, I slow to a walk and breathe heavily. The panic hasn't left me; I'm shaking as the mosquitoes now begin descending on my uncovered legs and arms. I swat them away and realize I'm fully alert, there's no trace of the haziness left by the wine.

The sound of a babbling brook becomes more distinct and then I see the wooden footbridge Imogene told me to look for. It's long. First it runs alongside the creek and then angles across the water to the other side. I step on the bridge when I hear my name being called.

"Jessica!" It's either Dylan or Carson, but from this distance I cannot decipher which man it belongs to.

I walk to the center of the bridge and debate with continuing on the trail, yet I don't know where it leads and I don't want to get lost in these unknown woods at night. I lean over the railing and take long, slow, deep breaths. "*Sixty Million, Forty Million, Seventy Million.*" I repeat numbers over and over to myself. The water is about five feet below the bridge and runs shallow over rocks and tree limbs.

"Jessica!" the voice shouts. He is at the entrance to the footbridge. I look up, trying to discern if it's Carson or Dylan. I cannot tell, but the voice is deep, so I'm guessing it's Carson. If I keep running in the other direction, I won't know where to go and he'd only follow me, so I stay where I am as the figure jogs towards me. In the fog of twilight I see that it is, indeed, Carson. I feel the vibration from his boots pounding on the bridge and in a few long strides he is by my side.

"Are you okay?" His concern and thoughtful expression seem sincere and far removed from the beast I saw in the kitchen.

"Please leave me alone." I keep my voice even.

"I'd never hurt you."

"I don't want to be a part of this. Whatever is going on between you and Dylan, it's not for me."

He comes close enough to put one hand on the railing in front of me and his other hand on the back of my neck. I flinch away and he looks startled.

"I didn't hurt Dylan. Is that what you think?"

"I don't understand what that was all about," I say angrily. "You knew Dylan and I were having dinner together and you showed up to goad him. You were cruel."

"You need to see Dylan for what he really is."

"What? A nice guy who is helpful and asks me out?" I try to laugh, but tears pool at the corners of my eyes. I'm thankful it's getting dark because, I assume, Carson can't see them. He is relentless, however, and steps closer to me again, closing in on

140

my safe distance. Carson rakes his hand through his hair, trying to think of a good explanation to give me.

"Dylan is a nice guy. You know I love my brother," he stammers.

"That wasn't love. He was angry at you about something and you kept pushing him. It was almost sadistic." He takes my hand and I jerk it away. "Don't touch me."

"Dylan has some serious problems and you needed to see that," he says.

"See what? Where is he? Did you—"

"I didn't hurt him, Jess. We always yell a bit, but I let him go and he left."

"Left where? He went home?"

"I don't know, Jess. This is what he does. He gets angry, falls apart and leaves. Sometimes he's gone for a while."

"What do you mean 'we always yell a bit'? Do you two fight like this a lot? Is this a regular thing; you being so violent?"

"I'm not a violent person," he says.

"You threw your two hundred pound brother to the floor like it was nothing. Then you pinned him like a wild hog."

"Dylan has always had these episodes and I'm the only one who can subdue him. I can only hope that it doesn't get him into an impossible situation someday. I worry about a fight with a stranger, police, jail time or worse, someone uses a gun against him."

Carson is talking about someone else. It can't be the same guy I have a mild crush on; the guy who is playful and sweet, the one I fooled around with and snuggled with all night on my couch. Carson started the fight. He's the bad guy in this.

"You can't tell me that Dylan is the violent one," I say, but then I think of Dylan's red, tense face with a protruding vein at his temple as he charged Carson. Dylan threw his body into Carson with the intent of hurting him. The revelation must have been written on my face. I look up into Carson's worried expression, my mouth gaping.

"Dylan suffers from severe depression," Carson says slowly.

"Millions of people do. That doesn't make them violent."

"Dylan is different. This started after our mom died. It started happening about a year after you were here. He sunk into a very deep despair over our mother's death. His depressive mood swings increased with our dad's drinking and absences."

"Okay, so Dylan suffers from depression. Half the world does and they can get help."

"He's gotten help. That's what I'm trying to tell you. He had some bad episodes in college and I'd go help him. He's been seeing doctors since he was in high school. He was doing pretty well on medication, but the spark kind of went out of him. I had to make sure he took his medicine. Whenever he felt good, he'd take himself off his meds and then he'd have an episode like what you saw tonight; where he can't control his anger and he goes into a rage. He's been in a few fights with guys, but mostly he storms out and disappears."

"Where does he go? Where is he now?"

Carson shakes his head. "Now that he's an adult, it's not like I can barricade him in the house. He takes off in his car, sometimes for days."

I turn away because the thought of crying in front of Carson is intolerable. My back is to him as he puts his hands gently on my shoulders.

"I was afraid he wouldn't tell you and that worried me because I could see you two becoming more involved. He's a very fragile person, Jess."

"That's why you said you didn't want him to get hurt. You meant with me. He could fall into a depression again."

"I'm sorry if I was a jerk about it, but Dylan was never serious about any woman until you came along. I can't let people keep leaving him, he can't handle it." Carson's voice is kind.

"And you think I'd leave him because you think the odds are against me staying here."

Carson turns me around. "I know he thinks he's in love with you, but so am–I can't let him get hurt," he says more forcefully.

"Okay, I get it. I think." I push him aside and walk back the way I came.

"Jess, wait," Carson shouts to my back, but I keep going.

Sixteen

Dylan returns three days later. I have no idea where he went and I don't ask. I refuse his calls. I even leave Carson a message on his cell phone to hold up on the kitchen repairs and appliances so I can work in peace.

It's now been two weeks and I've done nothing other than work in the library every morning, taking calls from my team at 5 Alpha and focusing on current as well as new software programs. Every afternoon I take a walk to Barron's Creek and beyond. Bert won't go with me, so I hike for a couple of hours every day by myself, going further into the woods and climbing the nearby hills. Then, every evening, I eat an apple and some ramen soup I picked up in bulk at Target, and I paint in the studio until it's time to sleep.

Imogene and Lauren come over every other day when their diner shifts permit and we watch movies on my computer and gab about everything except Carson and Dylan. Lois and Eleanor come by several times to help me clean out Aunt Ginnie's closets. I keep the good jewelry and some vintage clothing, but I donate a lot of other items.

After we finish up, they like to have cold beverages and sit on the porch while our pores steam open in the humidity, but I don't mind. They are good company, telling me everything about

Hera; the local gossip, Aunt Ginnie's life and their funny stories from their yoga classes. Apparently, I'm a big part of the local gossip, however, Lois and Eleanor gloss over that part, especially since I have a sign posted on the front door, "*No Blackards Allowed*." Yes, it's juvenile, but effective. If the sign wasn't there, Carson and Dylan would let themselves in my home whenever they please, using a repair job or something else as an excuse to work in the house.

Carson has only called once and left an apology on my cell phone. I saved the message so I can listen to his nice voice whenever I want. Dylan calls and periodically leaves notes or flowers by the front door. He's sweet and I want to see him. I want to see them both, but I don't know what I should be doing.

One day, Carson shows up with the two bearded fellows from the shop and they clean the dead tree and branches from the yard. I watch them from the library window, sawing the tree into smaller pieces and then loading the debris onto two separate trucks. Carson glances up at both of the windows where he knows I spend most of my time, the library and the studio. I keep my head buried between the monitors so he can't see me, but it soothes me, nonetheless, to have him near me.

"Sweet mustard seeds," Lois says one afternoon as we lounge on the porch. "How long can this go on? You can't avoid those two boys forever."

"I bet I could make it last forever," I say. "I have incredible endurance. You should see me reading through hours and hours of code. I'm like a stone statue. I could do it forever."

"Why would you want to?" Eleanor asks. "Honey, life is too short to carry the hatchet around all day." I look at her funny. "I meant to say 'life is too short not to bury the hatchet,'" she explains.

"They really are fine young men. You need to work this out," Lois says.

"It's easier to avoid them. I don't want to be tangled up in their messes."

"Jessica, life is messy. People are messy. They make messy mistakes and guess what, you cannot live happily without people," Eleanor says.

"I have people. I have you two, I have Lauren and Imogene, and Archie has been a big help with the accounting and taxes, and I have my friends at 5 Alpha. I have people in my life."

"Oh, sweet butter biscuits; I know you have friends, but you need love," Lois says.

"Please, I dated Dylan for five minutes. It wasn't love. It was just a little crush and now it's gone." Both women look at me in an odd way, bunching up their wrinkled faces. "It's true. Dylan has issues and he kept a big secret from me. I'm doing him a favor and it really was at the request of Carson. I'm doing what Carson wanted all along. He didn't think Dylan could handle dating me. Me, of all people. Apparently, I'm dangerous."

Lois and Eleanor share a moment, a knowing look with one another. I pretend not to care and sip my iced tea.

"So, everyone knows I'm going to have my party," Lois says. "Tomorrow night. And all my friends are invited. That includes you, Jess. I never got your RSVP.

"Sorry about that. Are Carson and Dylan going to be there?"

"Of course. You can't have a party without the handsome Blackard crew," Lois says.

"You'll have to figure out how to get along with them, live in peace and all that jazz," Eleanor says.

"And if you don't come to my party, I will be offended," Lois adds.

"Nice," I reply.

"Ginnie wants you to come to my party." Lois gives me a scolding look.

"Oh really, now you talk to the dead?" I raise my eyebrows at Lois.

"She also thinks it would be very nice if you brought a homemade key lime pie," Lois tells me.

"I don't bake."

"Gin's secret recipe is in the recipe box on the counter. It's not so secret," Lois says.

Eleanor chuckles.

"I can't follow recipes, really, I'm awful at it."

"Then I suppose you'll have to call Dylan. He's an excellent cook and baker," Lois says. "Or Carson. He'd be willing to help you."

"Yeah, that's not going to happen."

Lois looks deadly serious at me. "It was Gin's last wish!"

Eleanor bursts out laughing.

Seventeen

After ignoring him for two weeks, I miss Dylan, or maybe I miss the opportunity I could have with Dylan. Now that I know his big not-so-secret secret, I'm less scared. I've spent enough time daydreaming over my computer monitors, thinking about Dylan, his brother bullying him and his sweet disposition. I can envision myself being with Dylan despite his issues. We all have issues and maybe I could be the one to help him. Perhaps my presence will be a good thing for Dylan and I could fall in love with him.

He has left flowers at my door step almost every other day and countless messages on my phone, however, now I can't locate him. I give in and call Carson to explain about Lois's invite and the pie request as well as the fact that I need to patch things up with Dylan, at least to the extent that we're on speaking terms.

Carson arrives at my front door within the hour. He has bags of baking supplies, fresh limes and whatever else I rattled off from the recipe card.

"You ready to do this?" Carson holds up the "*No Blackards Allowed*" paper he yanked down from my front door and then crumples it in his fist. I can tell he showered before coming over. His hair is damp and pushed back as if he keeps running his hands through the wet locks. He's wearing a clean white

T-shirt that hugs his muscles and broad shoulders as it shows off his tan forearms and face. He smells like soap. I want to step into his embrace and fold myself into his strong body, but it isn't offered.

"Let's give it a go," I answer.

We work side by side in the kitchen for a few hours, speaking only about the recipe along with the fixtures and items in the house that still need to be repaired. We don't mention Dylan, yet he's there, hanging between us. By the end of the evening, we've made two pies that look like they are the first attempts of a fourth grade home economics class.

"Not bad," Carson says.

"Not great, either. Think they're edible?"

"Who cares? I'm here because you called. It's nice to see you."

"It's nice to see you, too. I handled that evening... I handled Dylan poorly. I shouldn't have run off."

"No. I handled it poorly. It was out of line for me to put that kind of responsibility on you."

"Is that what you were trying to do? Hand off Dylan to me so you wouldn't have to watch over him anymore?" I ask. "I think I wanted you to believe that I'm someone who is capable of being... worthy of being with Dylan."

Carson tosses the oven mitts on the counter and comes closer to me with concern in his sharp blue eyes. "Jesus, no. I never thought you weren't worthy of being with Dylan. You're too good for him. I was worried that he was too needy and it would be too much of a burden for you. And I—"

"What?" I ask, studying his expression.

He thinks for a minute before responding with a well-crafted, safe answer.

"You're very young, Jess. Dylan does not have his depression under control. It's not something you should feel obligated to endure or try to fix. Dylan isn't trying hard enough to help himself, so it's not fair that he subjects other people—you—to this."

"That's not very nice. Dylan deserves help with his illness, and it was horrible for me to not take his calls over the last two weeks."

"You misunderstand me. Dylan has received a great deal of medical help and help from our friends. He's the one who keeps rejecting it or taking himself off medication. When things are good, Dylan sabotages the treatment. I don't want to see you get sucked into Dylan's emotional rollercoaster."

"You can't make those decisions for me. What if I want to be involved? What if I like him so much, I want to help?"

"You like him that much?" Carson mumbles and runs his hand slowly through his hair. It falls in lanky spikes around his face. I can tell he is worried as he casts his eyes down before taking both of my hands in his. "Dylan's feelings for you are real, even if he might blow them out of proportion. It's part of his nature to be overly dramatic, high on life, before he crashes. It's a horrible thing to watch, it's even worse to be a... don't take this the wrong way... a pawn in his game of life."

That hurts. I try to pull my hands from his, but he grips them tighter. "I'm sorry," he says. "That came out wrong. Dylan doesn't intentionally use people, but he becomes attached in an unhealthy way and they become like accessories for him. I know that I sound mean, but I'm trying to explain that Dylan doesn't realize what he's doing. He doesn't see what we see. He's an emotional tornado that grabs everything that isn't tied down and pulls them into the eye of the Dylan storm and tosses them around like a rag doll. I'd hate myself if he did that to you."

"I thought you were worried about *me* hurting Dylan. You thought I was a lousy influence," I say, letting him hold my hands longer.

"I was hoping to discourage a relationship between you two, to avoid this very scenario."

"Sixty-five million," I whisper to myself.

"Are you scared?" Carson asks. "You whisper larger figures when you're anxious about something."

"How do you know that? I don't think I've even made the connection between my emotional state and my whispering," I say, perplexed.

"Like I told you before, you did that when you were a kid, usually when you were worried about something. Then I noticed it again when you first arrived here a month ago, you did it all the time. It's not hard to connect the dots."

"Sometimes you amaze me, Carson Blackard." I begin to smile.

He seems pleased when I say that.

"This is not the Carson I met in Archie's office on my first day. You barged by me like I was nobody."

"Oh, I knew who you were. Believe me, the minute I saw you outside Archie's office, everything

I knew about Jessica Channing was bombarding my brain. I didn't know how it would affect me to see you in person again after so many years. I was—"

"Were we like a family that one summer?" I query excitedly. My mind is racing with explanations. I don't let Carson respond. "Is that why Dylan latched on to me? When you saw me, did it feel like a long lost sister was returning home?" I sound very hopeful, like someone who always wanted siblings.

Carson grips my hands tighter and pulls me into his chest then looks down at me with exasperation. "Not once have I thought of you as my sister. Do not confuse me with someone you think is like a brother." Ouch. He's tough.

We're so close our eyes are inches apart. I can see a thin white scar by his ear which is hidden by a lock of hair. My gaze drops from his magnificent eyes to his seductive lips. Carson doesn't have the adorable cuteness of Dylan; he's a bundle of steely masculinity with little interest or talent in being a playful flirt like Dylan. Yet I am naïve and presumptuous, entertaining such ideas that Carson could ever take an interest in me. He is merely putting me in my place, prompting me to stay on track with his goal of helping and protecting his brother. He must have taken my reaction as discomfort because he loosens his grip and then lets go of me altogether.

"Your aunt talked about you plenty. I knew what you looked like in junior high, high school, and I saw enough photos of you from college to know exactly who you were when I walked into

Archie's office. Whatever your aunt had in private photos, she had more in public documents. Things that Archie would find on the Internet; school achievements, awards, anything and everything."

"How did she get all these photos of me? Did my mother send them?"

"Hell, no. Gin's relationship with your parents was so fucked up. Sorry. Gin hired a private detective to keep tabs on you."

"Seriously?"

"You lived in New York City, isn't that the perfect place to have someone followed without them ever knowing?"

"True, tourists with cameras are everywhere. A man or woman carrying a full-size SLR camera wouldn't turn a head. They could be a tourist, a journalist, a TV crew, a crime scene photographer. Hmm. Weird."

"We should get going soon." Carson begins clearing the counters and putting dirty dishes in the sink.

His fluctuating moods keep my mind preoccupied while we clean the kitchen. One minute he's very attentive, sometimes thoughtful like his brother and then the next minute he's scolding me like I'm a misbehaving child. It occurs to me that he is torn between accepting me as an adult now and maintaining some kind of guardianship over Dylan and his illness without driving his brother away. That seems to be the crux of it all.

I have to accept Carson's words as truth. I know so little about him, but if he's telling me that Dylan suffers from serious bouts of depression and erratic behavior, then I have to honor Carson's wishes. His brother has an illness and I can either be a hindrance or a help with his wellbeing. If Carson is attempting to scare me away with the reality of Dylan's prognosis, then Carson knows less about me than he thinks.

I may be a late bloomer when it comes to relationships and people in general, however, in my short time here, I have developed some feelings for Dylan. At first, I thought it was a crush, falling for a handsome guy that I thought was out of my league, although to be fair to myself, I am a cautious person when it comes to men.

Being much younger than my classmates and work colleagues has taught me to be careful when it comes to deciphering the overtures of men. Youth has worked against me in the arena of love and I have had to deal with a greater learning curve than most women.

When I replay the scenes with Dylan over in my mind, as well as Carson's revelation about Dylan, they have made me see this serendipitous moment for what it is. Dylan does care about me and Carson is making it clear that he sees me as an adult, not a child; a woman mature enough to be with Dylan and to help him. I'm sure I can love Dylan or rather, I can let myself fall in love.

I watch Carson's back as he does the dishes while, at the same time, I formulate a new resolve to be a different woman, a stronger person.

"You okay there?" Carson asks, watching me daydream in the middle of drying a mixing bowl.

I step towards him to hand off the bowl, catching one rubber flip-flop on top of the other and stumbling right into him. Carson catches me in a tight grip as the metal bowl clangs across the floor.

"Barnacles!" I exclaim.

He laughs. "Yeah, you're real fine." He holds me tightly and pulls me back up. "You need to wear real shoes or you're going to get injured in your own home."

Home.

"Yeah, yeah." I laugh and push away from his grasp.

I could berate myself over and over for getting gushy over a man saving me, but I have to look at Carson in a new light. I need him as a friend because he's right. I have a new home, new friends and a potential new man that is good despite coming with some baggage. After all, who doesn't have some type of baggage? I have two critical, demanding parents that repel my friends, I have a job that bores the bejeezus out of anyone who asks me about it, and socially I'm not known for my exciting affairs. I was the nerdy wallflower who happened to inherit a couple of good genes; pretty and smart. It's time to make good on them.

Before we leave for Lois's party, I take a quick shower and change into a summer dress. Carson waits impatiently downstairs so there's no time for make-up or taming my hair.

My dress twirls up over my thighs as I run barefoot down the stairs. Carson lets out a low whistle, so I quickly brush the linen fabric down with my hands to cover myself up, although it's not anything he hasn't seen before.

"Nice legs," he says in a sexy voice that I don't think was intentional.

I will just have to accept that I view Carson as a lusty man. Every time he speaks to me or flips his hammer in his hands, I think everything about his body and gruff personality exudes a dynamic masculinity. I look away from him and search for my dressy sandals in the hall closet.

"I can drive myself to Lois's house. That way you can go home and change," I offer.

"Change? Why do I want to change?" Carson's holding both pies and his keys.

"Because it's a party. Don't you want to look nice?"

"We're not going to a ball. This is how I always look. I think everyone is used to me as I am," he says. "Why? Do you think I look bad?"

Of course not. He is splendid. However, I can't arrive at the party with Carson if I want to see Dylan.

It's as if Carson can read my thoughts as I bite my lip and ponder the situation. "It's fine," he says rather forcefully. "This isn't a date and no one will think it is, so don't worry; we can go together."

"I'm not worried what other people think," I say in a huff. I lock the front door and take one of the pies from him. I walk rapidly to his truck with him right on my heels. Seriously, I feel like one of his big boots is going to crush me.

The pies are still warm as they rest in my lap, making me perspire even more. We ride in silence as I resist the urge to glance over at Carson. I suspect he's aware of my plan to renew my interest in Dylan. If Carson thought he'd sway me otherwise, his strategy has done the opposite. I'm eager to see Dylan and I'm pretty sure that Carson is on to me. His deep sighs periodically break the quiet tension.

I laugh to myself. I have the world's laziest dog, *Hangover*, I have a quasi-boyfriend who is too cute and unstable for his own good—*Hotty*—and my new protector or guardian, who I can only think of as *Lusty*. What a cast of characters.

Eighteen

"Why are you so jumpy?" Carson asks when we pull in on the grassy area where everyone else has parked in front of Lois's quaint farmhouse.

There are guests milling around the front porch and admiring the gardens around the side of the house. I search the unrecognizable faces.

"He'll be here," Carson says harshly.

"I didn't say anything."

"I know, but you're jittery as all hell. Dylan will be here." Carson slams his door before walking around the truck to meet me by my door. I'm not moving towards the house; I'm frozen there, holding two pies.

"How do you know? I wasn't very nice to him the last few weeks. I wouldn't even speak to him."

"He's not angry at you," Carson reassures me. "He blames me for coming between you two, but even then, Dylan is a very forgiving guy. Even on his worst day, he doesn't hold grudges."

"Good. I'm going to give Lois the pies and look for Dylan." I head for the party without waiting for him, though I do hear him utter a terse *"fine"* behind me.

I make my way through the crowded porch and living room, nodding to people who say hello. I am searching for Lois so I can hand off these damn pies, but I'm really looking for any sign of a head with golden curls, any sign of Dylan. Lois comes out of the kitchen and puts out her two hands, reaching for my pies.

"Look at you! How pretty you are! I'll take these to the buffet table," she greets. "Where's Carson?"

"He's not far behind. Probably on the porch or out in that living room crowd," I answer, my head bobbing around, looking for Dylan.

"Oh," Lois starts. "Well…"

"Well, what?"

"Didn't you come with Carson?"

"Yes. We made the pies together and he drove me over here."

She looks pleased at that and then I realize she assumes I'm *with* Carson.

"We're not on a date, Lois. Carson was my ride."

"Okay, dear." Lois sighs.

"Have you seen Dylan?"

"I think he may be out milling around the garden," she answers, sounding disappointed.

Lois's garden on the side of the house isn't your average sprinkling of flower plots. The area of the garden is vast, covering much more land than her home. The entrance of the garden is adorned with abstract stone sculptures and white fairy lights wired through the trees and hedges.

I enter the sanctuary and am immediately dazzled by what I see. A magnificent, old fountain lights up in muted shades of pink arches of water over its three tiers. The fountain is the focal point and large enough that twenty people could climb in it if they got drunk enough and daringly stupid. I imagine my old roommates Kate and Marissa doing this. I realize then that in my mind I have referred to them as my *old* roommates. Have I decided to stay in Hera?

Various garden paths lead away from the fountain where different beds of roses and lilies are in abundance. There are also a number of herbal plots that send an aromatic blend of lavender and thyme across the pleasant evening air. I can't see the entire garden from the entrance, it's too large. The paths go off into hidden areas where other party guests have settled themselves on stone benches or delightful antique swings. I can't see everyone, but I can hear laughter and conversation rise up from the tall hedges that create a wonderful mystery maze.

I begin to roam the gravel path, looking for the familiar face I am so desperate to see. Dylan. The thought of his beautiful smile looking down on me and his strong arms wrapped around me sounds like the best antidote to my sexless life. Maybe he's not just another playboy and he actually has feelings for me. Maybe it doesn't even matter. I want to be with him, I need to be with someone. It's safe to assume it's lust, but my gut tells me that I can get closer to Dylan if I try and perhaps a relationship with him is worth pursuing after all.

I eagerly turn a corner into a secluded alcove of arched tree branches over a marble sculpture that looks like some Greek god. As I consider how much planning and work went into this spectacular garden, I hear a twig snap and the sound of crunching gravel nearby, so I look behind me.

"Hey," Dylan says. His voice is low and tentative.

I stare at him for a moment; first because I'm surprised to see him after realizing that I did miss him over the last two weeks, and second, because he is shockingly handsome. His curly hair looks blonder and he's definitely tanner, so he must have spent a lot of time in the outdoors while we were apart.

He steps into the alcove with me where we are alone; far removed from the other guests and the musicians that have begun performing some joyful Mozart sonatas.

"Lois has really outdone herself with this garden," I say, my hands fumbling at my sides.

Dylan smiles and looks relieved. "It took her a few years and a lot of arguments with architects and landscapers to get to this."

I wonder how I can continue to be overwhelmed by his sweet beauty when I seem to have the same thoughts about Carson's lustiness. I have never been like this with any other guys. I could have a mild crush or interest in someone in the morning and by lunch, I'd write them off as a dope. Am I simply so inexperienced in love and relationships that I crumble when I'm around these two brothers? I'm all nerves and adrenaline with Dylan standing before me and it's only Dylan and Carson that do this to me. There's no future with Carson, he's made it clear that he's around to make sure Dylan and I don't screw up our lives. Dylan is around because he and I have an unmistakable attraction to one another.

"I owe you an apology." I find it difficult to look into his soft eyes without feeling a stab of guilt.

"No, you don't." He smiles.

"It was horrible of me not to take your phone calls. I could have answered the door, too. I was rude. Thank you for all the flowers you sent. They were beautiful."

"Lois cut them from her garden. I kept running to Target to buy more vases so I could leave them at your door." He laughs and the sparkle is back in his eyes.

I step forward, wrap my hands around his neck to pull him down into a kiss and he responds without pause. His soft lips on mine and his tongue circling in my mouth make my desire more intense, so I press firmly into him, aggressively searching for what I was missing. Dylan reacts with the same vigorous force as though we can't get close enough to one another. One of his hands travels up my back and positions securely on my shoulder blade as he works his kisses down to my neck and bare collarbone.

I wish I were the kind of person who could drop all inhibitions for once and tumble to the ground with Dylan, pulling each other's clothes off. I have a dreadful, nagging inner voice that warns me of being reckless, though. I push the nag aside. For once I want to be recklessly in love, I want to be naked against him. The hardness from his groin strains against his pants and presses against me while my nipples spring into rigid nubs as his hand fondles my breasts.

"I didn't see your Jeep. Did you drive here?' I ask between heavy breaths.

"Yes," Dylan says wickedly into my ear before sucking on the lobe.

"Let's go to my house. Now."

"Yes," he says again, pulling away. "Now."

He takes me by the hand and leads me out of the garden maze. We don't stop to chat or even say hello to people who smile as we stalk by as fast as we can. When we pass the front porch, I see someone turn from a group of men who are laughing loudly. It's Carson who watches Dylan settle me into the passenger side of the Jeep. I look down and pretend I haven't noticed him, but as we drive away, I look back up directly into Carson's unreadable gaze.

Nineteen

My bedroom is stifling. Dylan races around and opens the windows. He shuts off the overhead light and turns on a small antique lamp on the dresser that gives off a yellow glow. He also shoos Bert out of the bedroom and closes the door. I hear a click as he locks it. I stand by the side of the bed, excited and feeling silly at the same time. Dylan strides toward me, pulling off his T-shirt in one fast move. He's walking and removing his jeans at the same time. I'm impressed with his cheetah-like reflexes and watch him as if it's a private show for me.

In seconds he stands before me in his briefs and begins removing my dress, which happens in the blink of an eye. Then we are there, together in the darkened room, with romantic lighting, sheer curtains billowing in the light warm breeze and the two of us stripped down to our underwear.

Dylan towers over me, solid, thick muscles, making him look like he has been created to resemble the perfect Romanesque sculpture. He puts his hands on either side of my arms and waits for me. I unfasten the front clasp of my lace bra and wriggle out of it. Dylan's hands slide down my arms and cup my breasts. The excitement of his touch sends a tremor down to my center where a tingling sensation torments me.

I really have no interest in long, slow foreplay. I've waited too long for this and Dylan is the perfect candidate to take my virginity.

"I can't keep waiting." I yank Dylan by the hands so he falls with me onto the bed. He is on top of me and laughs as he leans on one arm and pulls off his briefs. I wriggle beneath him and pull off my lace panties.

Even in the dim light, we can see each other's bodies perfectly. My fair skin against his enormous erection instinctively makes me open my legs and pull my hips up so my thighs can wrap around him.

"Oh God," he says, looking down at me. He reaches for the nightstand where he has tossed a couple of condoms when he came in. He moves quickly to open one and put it on. I don't know whether to be impressed by his speed or concerned with his skill and dexterity at doing it with one hand. How many times has this guy been in a condom emergency? How many women has he slept with or should I call it what it is, fucking?

We kiss and I run my tongue over and under his teeth. I want to bite him, but I manage to contain myself. I feel his arms hitching underneath my knees pushing them up higher. I'm a little worried. I have no experience to really base this on, however, Dylan is a tall man, his penis seems unusually large and I don't see how he can fit inside of me. I glance down as he rubs against me, making me wetter. He looks into my eyes as if sensing my nervousness.

"Don't worry. I'll be gentle, the first time," he says and then smiles. He's joking, making light that we'll have several rounds of sex. I wonder if that's a line men always use with women, pretending they have to tone down their superhero sex powers so they don't hurt the little lady. He has no idea that his first time with me is my first time ever, and I'm a little too nervous to appreciate his Thor humor.

We kiss again. This time it becomes more frantic as Dylan rubs himself against my soft, wet folds. I groan, never having been this close. Then I reach down and replace his hand with mine. His hand comes up to my breasts, which he palms before placing his mouth on my nipples, sucking them roughly. This alone could be my undoing.

"Now," I say, trying to push him inside of me.

"Wait," he whispers. He removes my hand from his body and pins both of my hands above my head with his one strong hand. His other hand probes inside my wet, tender center. I wriggle beneath him, raise my legs higher and wrap them around his back. He keeps my hands and arms locked firmly in place as he continues to suck and nibble on my breasts while pushing his fingers further inside of me.

"I'm so ready, Dylan," I say, feeling liquid seep out of me. "I can't get any wetter or any hornier than this." The desire is completely overwhelming I can't spare any time to be embarrassed over what I'm saying.

"I know," he says and pulls his fingers out of me. He looks down between us and positions himself about a half-inch into me before he begins thrusting gently forward.

"Oh," I moan with surprise rather than pleasure.

"Does that hurt?" he asks, slowing down.

"No, keep going." I lie. Yes, it hurts a little, but I'm not going to tell him that.

"I'm not about to stop," he rasps. He thrusts harder and faster and it feels good and painful at the same time. He keeps it slow with short thrusts and the tingling starts in my clit and then sends little signals out to my limbs before it reaches a small crescendo of pleasure. As I begin to want him to go deeper and faster, Dylan does. He lets go of my imprisoned hands and props himself up higher on his hands, driving his pelvis deeper into mine, grinding into me. He grunts as his thrusts become longer and he plunges further into me. My brain goes mindless with a brief spasm of ecstasy until the thrusting actually begins to ache too much. The minor enjoyment I was experiencing is gone and there's only sharp discomfort followed by Dylan groaning.

I close my eyes and hold him tighter, letting him settle on top of me with all his weight, still inside of me. This togetherness is an extraordinary sensation and so new to me. No pushing a guy off me or rolling away to excuse myself from their reach forever. This is what it feels like to have someone enthralled by your body, mindless and lost in a titillating oblivion. It certainly doesn't last long and it didn't have the gratifying end result for me, but I have a sense of satisfaction as Dylan buries his face into my neck and his exhausted body goes limp.

Fluids leak out of me, those once precious liquids and membranes we are supposed to protect like jewels. I stifle a giggle as I think of my parents dropping sex education books on my bed at the age of six. Cute books with a bashful, naked, chubby couple who make a comedy team out of procreation. The book ends with the chubby couple happily holding a chubby baby.

I don't want to procreate with Dylan. He'd certainly make gorgeous babies, but it suddenly strikes me that all this time I've been with Dylan, I've only wanted sex. Sex, not love, not the hope of a future relationship.

He rolls off me as I stay immobile on the damp sheet.

"I'll be right back," Dylan says. The bed creaks and springs up as he leaves for the bathroom to take care of the condom. I am content not to move, to enjoy the moment of keeping my body as motionless as possible, still reeling with delight.

The bed sinks again as Dylan lies next to me. "Hey," he says softly. "Jess, are you okay?"

I open my eyes and turn to look at him. "I'm great."

"I should have made it last longer, but it's our first time with each other. Kind of difficult to hold out. I almost exploded before we got to the bed."

I laugh which makes him smile. If he only knew that I feel like a fraud. I'm not the sweet girl he thinks he's falling in love with. I'm not the innocent girl any of them assume I am. I'm enraptured with Dylan's body and what it can do for me. Perhaps it's due to years of only allowing boys, and then men, grope, fondle and kiss me; endless sexless encounters that drove me to this point of wanting actual sex with a man who exudes a tremendous amount of sensuality in every move. The thought makes it sound dirty and selfish, however, I know there's a part of me that cares about Dylan.

He stretches out next to me and holds my cheek for a quick kiss. "I'm crazy about you." He looks at me lovingly, his eyes wide and sincere. No words come to me, so I smile in return.

"I'll be right back," I say, prying myself from his embrace and getting up from the bed.

"Okay." Dylan lounges on his side, propped on his elbow. He grins as he watches me walk to the bathroom. I turn my back on him and shake my naked ass to get a laugh out of him.

In the bathroom, I use a washcloth and shower gel to clean off the sticky blood that is drying against my inner thighs and my nether regions. "Well, that's done," I say out loud to myself. "No more wondering." Of course Dylan must know. There must have been blood on the condom.

I freshen up as much as possible and brush my teeth and hair before returning to the bed and the seductive man waiting for me.

Dylan looks relaxed and content, stretched out on the bed.

I lie on my side next to him and he pulls a sheet over us. I snuggle into his warm, hard chest with his strong arms wrapped securely around me. Ironically, a sense of liberation and safety sweep over me, despite being completely engulfed by him. He kisses the top of my head and I bury my face in his neck, taking in his natural scent that sends erotic thoughts through my sex-addled brain.

"Are you happy?" I ask, whispering into his neck.

"With you and this? Of course. I just got laid, what do you think?"

I laugh. "That's not what I meant." I look up at him.

"I know what you meant. I'm very happy. I knew you were going to Lois's tonight and my gut told me that we'd be back together. I didn't know we'd do this..."

"Ha!" I pinch his arm.

"Hey, you pushed for this. Literally. You pushed me onto the bed."

"Yes, I did."

"Are you happy?" he asks and I can see in his eyes the seriousness that lies behind the cheerful demeanor. The anxious boy that sometimes takes over the confident man.

"I am extremely content," I answer.

"That's not good enough. You need to be deliriously happy."

He kisses me lightly on the lips and then doesn't stop. It goes deeper and I feel my tingling hormones surge again with desire. His mouth leaves mine and works its way down my neck to my breasts. I arch into him as he sucks hard on my nipples, but then he continues on to my stomach, his tongue circling my belly button. I'm sore and not sure I'm ready to do it again, but this time he really is gentle and only uses his tongue. Yeah, he definitely knows I *was* a virgin.

He positions his hands underneath each of my butt cheeks and then his head is between my legs. His tongue is inside of me and I groan, letting every muscle in my body go limp as my legs open wide to receive him. As he works my desire over with his relentlessly probing mouth, my thoughts spin with the image of Dylan. Quickly Dylan's face changes into Carson and it's Carson's splendid, naked form that brings me to a climax. That fantasy coupled with the building *delirious happiness* throws me over the edge into the most intense orgasm I've ever had. I cry out, relieved that I didn't shout Carson's name.

This is too good to be true, I tell myself. Finally, I'm compatible with someone I don't want to kick out of bed.

"I'm in love with you, Jess," Dylan whispers into my ear.

For a moment I am paralyzed with fear, not knowing how to respond. I like Dylan, I'm infatuated with him, but I can't say that I'm in love with him. I hope I will fall in love with him, but I can't utter false words now, not in this moment when he's being honest and I have a bad habit of thinking of his brother. Instead, I look at him and smile as I bury my face and body back into his inviting embrace. I'm good at deflecting and I am too tired and sated to say or do anything.

The last thing I remember is drifting off, still cuddled next to his naked body.

Twenty

Over the month of July, I find myself in a rather nice routine. I rise early and walk Bert as far as he'll go, which is usually to the end of the driveway and back. After breakfast, I spend four to six hours in the library handling 5 Alpha work. I don't take on any new accounts, so I can keep my workload manageable and part-time.

Nathan is obliging because I am reliable and produce good work. I'm thankful because even with Aunt Virginia's money from the trust, I still need an additional income so I can pay the rent on my New York apartment and put a substantial amount in savings every month.

I have a fear of poverty. I shouldn't. I grew up in a home with everything that I pretty much desired and, as an only child, I'll inherit everything from my parents' savings and assets. Of course, I now own a home free and clear as well, but I still worry about being alone and being penniless. I suppose a shrink would tell me it's because I never allowed myself to become attached to anyone in a real commitment.

Yet, now there's Dylan.

Every afternoon I work in the studio and paint and, when I finish, Dylan arrives with groceries in hand to make dinner for both of us. We hang out on the porch or watch movies on one of the computers in the library before heading off to bed. I can't say that I'm falling in love with him, however, I'm fond of him and completely in lust, looking forward to our nightly bouts of adventurous sex that leave me so exhausted that I sleep like the dead and wake up every morning feeling refreshed.

Sometimes Lauren and Imogene stop by for lunch or dinner depending on their schedules at the diner and I look forward to their company; our growing friendship is one of the reasons why I don't think I could leave Hera.

I have also started taking yoga three times a week at Beyond The Pants, which Lois and Eleanor opened during a scorching hot day in July. It was one of the few places with working air conditioning, so they got a lot of customers during their grand opening.

When I pass through town to go to yoga class, or stop in to see Archie about my trust and house accounts, I'll sometimes see Carson. It's usually from a distance and we never say anything to one another. I never see him at Bonnie's diner or any of the dinner parties among our mutual friends, either. I wonder if he is avoiding most people or just me. Dylan doesn't mention him even though they work together every day at the shop. He talks about clients or projects, but manages to leave Carson's name out of it as if he senses that I think about Carson.

I do. I think about the night I was on the footbridge with Carson at Barron's Creek and the afternoon we baked those ridiculous pies together. Of course, that look he gave me as I drove off with Dylan to begin a relationship that has become increasingly more serious on Dylan's part is ever present in my thoughts as well.

I enjoy the physical aspects and the sweet company of Dylan, yet I'm aware now more than ever that he floats around on a cloud of love while I'm more pragmatic about it. Sadly, a month of spending every free moment with Dylan hasn't changed my initial feelings for him. I work, I paint, I have friends, I have a stubborn dog and I have a cute boyfriend who can dish it up in the kitchen and the bedroom.

Dylan appears to be happy and I don't want to change that, but I'm concerned that his growing love and affection for me is way beyond what I may ever feel for him. I should be content with this, right? This is a pretty good life I have carved out for myself. A lot of people would be overjoyed to have this type of contentment. Maybe safety and faithfulness are more important than falling head over heels in love.

I finish a phone call with the 5 Alpha IT guys and sit back in my chair, daydreaming about a painting I'd like to do when Dylan surprises me by coming home early. I hear the front door slam and him bounding up the stairs to find me.

"Hey!" he says, slightly out of breath. "We knocked off early for the day so I thought you and I could do something special."

Dylan's face is flushed against his tan skin. He is radiant. He comes over to give me his usual greeting kiss and then spins me in my office chair, which makes me laugh.

"Well, I was planning on painting this afternoon. What did you have in mind?" I let my fingers brush against his groin, which immediately goes hard.

He removes my hand. "Not so fast. We'll get to that, too. I thought we could go up to the Ridge and have a picnic. Take a bottle of wine, a blanket and then that other stuff you love so much." He smirks.

"A picnic." My voice is flat and Dylan's smile fades. I'm afraid I may have dampened his expectations. "Oh!" I try to recover the mood, but I sound artificial. Before I can say anything else, the sound of a car driving up to the house interrupts the awkward moment.

"Who could that be?" Dylan asks with concern and I wonder if he's hoping it's not Carson. Secretly, I'm hoping it *is* Carson and he's deciding to come back to work on the house projects. I miss having him nearby, but of course, I don't say this.

We both look out the second floor window of the library and watch a black Range Rover park before a well-dressed man in a suit gets out. He slings his suit coat over his shoulder and holds it with one finger while he walks with a confident gait up to the house.

"That's Tom!"

"Who?"

"My art dealer. Well, the guy who took a few of my paintings last year. He sold a couple pieces."

"You didn't tell me he was coming out here today." The hurt in his voice is almost annoying and I feel mean for thinking that.

"Because I didn't know," I tell him, running out of the room to answer the door.

Tom is in his late-thirties and looks very youthful and fit. His clothes are expensive and his grooming is impeccable without appearing finicky. His blond hair is buzzed against his scalp and his face is plain, though it has strong Scandinavian lines giving him a very masculine edge as though he is someone who could have been a sailor or oil rigger before becoming accustomed to finely tailored suits. I don't know Tom's history, but I like to make these things up in my head as I go along.

I introduce Tom to Dylan and then we all decide it would be nice to sit on the porch with our cold glasses of water.

"I haven't seen one of my favorite artists in a while, so I thought I'd come out here and see what all the fuss is about." Tom reclines back on the wicker loveseat and puts one ankle across a knee. He looks very comfortable and Dylan seems completely uneasy about that. "Nathan told me how to find you."

"This is a nice surprise. I didn't know you made house calls." I'm sitting on the loveseat next to Tom and Dylan sits across the coffee table from us. I can tell the distance from me makes Dylan even more uncomfortable.

"I make house calls when artists make me money." Tom reaches into his suit coat and pulls a white envelope out of the interior pocket. "This is for you."

I take the envelope and open it. I pull out a check and my eyes must have popped because Dylan comes to my side to see the figure.

"Twenty-four thousand dollars?" Dylan asks. He's not smiling, but I am.

I am giddy. I can't believe my paintings are selling.

"This is incredible," I say.

Tom smiles and shrugs. "Your work is unique and it moved well. I actually raised the prices on the last three pieces. Do you have more for me? I'm ready to give you a show."

"Seriously?" I am so excited I jump out of my chair and give Tom a kiss on the cheek. "Let me go upstairs and get the other paintings." I leave without looking back at Dylan's confused face. I run up the stairs to the studio and begin taking down the completed paintings from the wall. I collect twelve of them and put them in a large portfolio case.

When I return to the porch, Tom is talking to Dylan about his gallery, but Dylan appears to be waiting nervously for me with a troubled expression.

"I have twelve more here." I hand over the hefty portfolio to Tom.

"It's a good thing for me that you work on paper and not canvas," Tom says, trying to lighten the tense mood that Dylan has created. "So I was thinking of perhaps doing a show in mid-December before everyone shuts down for the holiday season. You wouldn't be the headline, but you'd be shown with two of my strongest artists. I'd like to have at least twenty-five pieces total from you. Is that doable?"

"Absolutely. That gives me four months to paint. I can do another thirteen or so; I have so many ideas in my head. I can even cut back on my hours at 5 Alpha—"

"Wait, slow down, babe," Dylan interrupts. "Don't knock yourself out over this. You already have a stressful job; you don't have to put more pressure on yourself by trying to paint day and night."

My first inclination is to yell at him to stay out of my business; my art is the only thing that I have that is all mine. *Slow down*, I think. *He's right. Dylan is only trying to be a good boyfriend, to be supportive*, I tell myself. So why does it seem like petty jealousy? Is it because my paintings are selling or that Tom is here delivering the news in person? Is Dylan jealous of Tom? The guy has no interest in me, other than the money I can bring in to his gallery. Tom is a single, wealthy man in Manhattan, who has plenty of women. Is Dylan so insecure or paranoid in thinking that Tom has nefarious intentions towards me?

I can't read the expression on Tom's face, but he is definitely questioning Dylan's role in my life. Tom looks quizzically at Dylan before turning back to me.

"If this is too much—" Tom begins to say.

"No, of course not," I cut him off. "I have plenty of time to do this. I paint all the time. It's my favorite thing in the world and I'm very pleased that you're selling my work."

Dylan stiffens and reclines back in his chair. He knows he went too far. His emotional outburst will have to be discussed later. This is business and, like his furniture business, you don't let your personal relationships slip into discussions. He humiliated me in front of someone I respect. I know Dylan's aware that he really screwed this up and made me look unprofessional. He remains fairly quiet for the rest of Tom's visit, which is short.

After Tom goes through my new paintings and takes some notes, jotting down titles he'd like to use, and then doing a short tour of the house with me alone, he leaves. As I watch his very clean Range Rover drive away, Dylan comes up behind me and places his hands on my waist.

"You can never do that again, Dylan," I say, looking out at the amazing landscape from the porch to avoid facing him.

Dylan kisses my neck. "I know. This guy likes you and it made me feel envious that he can talk about your art with you. It was immature of me, but I wanted—"

I wrench away from his caresses and face him. "You wanted to show him that you live here and sleep with me. It was stupid, Dylan. Also, for the record, Tom isn't attracted to me. He likes my paintings. Actually, I don't even know if he likes my paintings so much as he likes the money my paintings make for him. I am lucky to have his representation and you had no right to interfere like that."

Dylan rubs his jaw with his hand—a move that reminds me of Carson—and he looks genuinely remorseful. "I'm sorry. I started imagining this guy taking you out to celebrate your success and I felt scared. It was like I was losing you already."

"That's ridiculous. You're letting your imagination get away from you and it isn't fair to take it out on me. Are you afraid of my potential success? Do you want me to fail?"

"Of course not. I know I didn't react the way I should have, but in the moment I wasn't thinking clearly. I see this successful guy pull up in his expensive SUV, he hands you a huge check and says he's giving you a show. In my mind, he's taking you back to New York and you're going to be successful there. In my mind, I saw you leaving Hera, leaving this," he says, holding his arms wide. "Leaving me."

Leaving me, his words echo through me. How often have I felt that I was alone, having to do everything on my own, to figure the world out, to figure myself out because my parents didn't talk about personal needs or desires, or how a young girl is supposed to navigate an adult world before she's on equal footing with everyone else? Am I still so naïve and foolish that I cannot truly see the wonderful man in front of me who cares about me?

I place my hands on Dylan's chest and feel his strong heartbeat underneath the thin T-shirt. He is so attractive that I begin to consider lewd thoughts to dismiss my earlier anger. Without deliberating further, I start taking off his T-shirt. He looks a little bewildered, but assists in removing his shirt. I rub my hands up and down his muscular torso and push him back towards the porch wall. Then Dylan watches as I unbutton my blouse. A wanton expression overcomes his face as I stand before him in my see-thru lace demi bra. I step out of my skirt and underwear and begin kissing him as I put my hand down his jeans, aggressively groping his hardness.

"Okay," Dylan rasps and then he turns me around so my back is against the wall.

He unbuttons his jeans and pulls a condom from his wallet then hoists me up using his weight and the wall to brace me in place before he's in me. I wrap my legs around his waist and move frantically with his thrusts.

I want more; I want it faster and harder. I want my body and mind to explode so I can feel good and not think about us arguing over the time I spend on painting and work versus the time I give to Dylan. At least that's what goes through my mind as the term *"fucking my brains out"* races through my head.

It also occurs to me that anyone could drive up to the house and see Dylan's naked ass nailing me against the house in broad daylight. Then I imagine Carson driving up and seeing us just before that image of him turns into the image of Carson screwing me here against the wall. I keep my eyes closed as Dylan pulls my bra down to fondle my breasts, imagining that it's Carson's tongue on my nipple and Carson ramming himself into me, bringing me to the edge.

"Oh God, I love this. I love you," Dylan groans and rubs two fingers on my clit. "I want us to come at the same time."

I can tell he's ready to climax, but he strains to hold off until I'm a moaning mess. I shudder and fall into Dylan; spent, both physically and emotionally.

"So, you still want to go on that picnic?" I ask as we retrieve our clothing from the porch and quickly dress.

"It's not that big a deal. I was planning on just screwing around with you since we'd have a blanket and a nice view." He smiles. "You beat me to it."

"Oh, so the picnic part was really an excuse to have sex in another location."

"Yep."

"I'm hungry," I whine, ruffling his blond curls.

"Then I'll cook for you." He kisses me softly on the lips, quickly enough to be tender, yet innocent as though he wants to prove that not all of our physical encounters are about sex.

Dylan outdoes himself on our dinner. He grills rib eye steaks on the old charcoal Weber out back and sears scallops and leeks in the kitchen. He also makes some kind of buttery asparagus and mushroom dish that is divine. He tops off all the butter and fatty foods with homemade pie and ice cream from Bonnie's.

I watch Dylan finish his second serving of pie. "I'm going to get fat if I keep eating like this," I tell him. "I think I've already gained a few pounds."

"You haven't gained an ounce. I know. My hands have covered every inch of your body."

"Funny. But I'm serious. This food is delicious, but you're going to turn me into a cow with these meals."

Dylan pulls me into his lap and begins kissing my neck. "I worship your body. Even if you gained a hundred pounds, I would still love you."

"I call bullshit," I say and stand up. "Guys always say crap like that. It's such a lie, though."

"I don't say crap like that," Dylan says. "I'm serious. Do you think fat women are unloved?"

"Oh, don't turn it around. I didn't say that. Of course there are fat couples who love each other. This is a stupid conversation!"

"You started it."

"No, what I started was a conversation about how men say things they don't really mean."

"Fine. Here's what I know. I love you now. I love you thin and I'll love you fat, should it come to that." He laughs.

"Sure, plenty of guys still love their girlfriends when they get fat, but then they stop having sex," I say, putting dirty dishes in the sink. "Then the relationship goes to crap and that's when the guy resents the woman for gaining weight."

"And this is based on?"

"Oh please, it's part of our culture. Don't play dumb."

I have constructed a towering mound of dirty pans and dishes in the sink and I contemplate how they will get clean when Dylan wraps his arms around me.

"I love you, Jess. You worry about so many things that you don't have to worry about." He is so tender and kind, I want to believe him. I want to feel as sure about him as he feels about me, however, I don't. I'm as anxious and cynical as I ever was.

I sigh and continue to study the mess in the sink as though it's a great conundrum.

"You know those dishes can't be washed when they're jammed in there like that," he says.

"I know. I'm waiting for that damn dishwasher Carson said he'd install."

Dylan takes me by the shoulders and leads me back to a kitchen chair where he sits me down. Then he pours a glass of red wine from an open bottle and places it on the table in front of me. "You, relax. I'm going to do the dishes."

I sip the wine and watch Dylan's back as he works over the sink. I wish I was in a more forgiving mood, but I'm still angry about his behavior in front of Tom.

"Dylan, what you did while Tom was here; you can't ever do that again," I bring up the conversation again.

He turns around and dries his wet hands on his thighs and leans back against the sink. Dylan's expression is kind and confident, nothing like what I saw earlier on the porch.

"I thought I was helping you. I was trying to be supportive, hoping you wouldn't take on too much work."

"You made me look like I don't have control of my own life. You looked like a jealous boyfriend in front of someone I respect, someone who is the only person who supports my artistic endeavors."

"I support your art."

"When was the last time you walked through my studio? The day I set it up? You never ask about my paintings or ask to see them," I say, trying not to sound angry.

"When was the last time you came to the workshop to see what I was working on?" he asks, although his tone isn't accusatory like mine.

"Exactly. You've made my point, Dylan," I reply. "We've been spending a lot of time together, but let's not pretend that we are so close that we can make career choices for one another." I hear what I'm saying and yet I don't stop. I feel sick by my own words, but I continue. "We do not share in life changing decisions."

"I'm not pretending, Jess." Dylan's hands clench the sink edge as his arms flex. "You *are* my life changing decision and, whatever you are passionate about, I want to support you."

"What do you mean?" I ask. My voice goes from angry to timid. "How am I a life changing decision for you?"

"I'm here every day, Jess. We both work and then we're together every night; every dinner, every movie, every walk out by the creek, every night in the same bed." He walks over to where I'm sitting and leans on the table, hovering over me. "Do you think I take this lightly?"

"We're dating, that doesn't make you a decision-maker in my life. It makes you my boyfriend."

"Are you sure? Because I don't think you've ever had a boyfriend like me, right? Did you ever date anyone that you let stick around?"

"No, I wasn't serious with anyone and you know that because I already told you."

"I guess the question is, are you serious about me?" Dylan's voice becomes angry and it causes Bert to perk up from his slumber and leave the room.

"Now you've scared Bert. I hope you know what you sound like." I'm saying any stupid old thing I can think of and it sounds lame even to me.

"Answer the question," Dylan demands. "Are you serious about me? Because your reaction to

Tom and this idea that working around the clock doesn't have anything to do with me, makes me wonder if I'm even a priority in your life."

"Of course, you are," I say quietly, looking up at him. "But my reaction to Tom was about the work he was offering, not Tom himself. You seemed jealous—"

"I am jealous. I'm jealous of any guy who can make you smile the way you did today. You were jumping out of your chair like a kid. I'm jealous that he can give you something I can't. I know you love painting more than designing computer software. I get that. I get that you need to spend hours every day in your studio and it makes you very happy. I'm jealous that there's a guy in New York City, hell, there are a lot of guys in the city who can sell your paintings so that you'll feel like a real artist."

"I'm not interested in Tom," I add.

"I know that!" Dylan yells. "I already think of you as an artist, but you don't unless you're being paid for your work. You need validation from others, experts like Tom. He makes you feel like a real artist and I don't. That's what pisses me off. I want to be the one..."

Dylan backs away from me and then goes back to the sink. "Go paint. It will make you feel better," he says in a soft tone. He's not being glib. "I'll finish up the kitchen; you go work in the studio. Okay?"

"Yeah. Dylan?"

"Jess, I don't want to argue," he says with his back to me as he resumes washing dishes. "And you need to paint. Go. I'll meet you in a bit."

I walk over and wrap my arms around his waist and hug his back. He stills to let me have my moment. Then I plant a kiss on his back between his shoulder blades.

"The kiss doesn't count unless it's on bare skin," he says. "Go paint."

I paint until midnight, hours of uninterrupted painting, and I only decide to go to bed when Bert's noxious gas makes my studio unbearable. I change into a slip of a nightie and look for Dylan. I find him in the library, sitting on the couch with his long legs stretched out resting on the coffee table. He's working on his laptop and has a pen and pad of paper next to him.

"What are you doing?" I ask.

"Surfing porn sites."

"Really?"

"No, I'm kidding. I'm reading the Fed announcement that came out today. It moved the market one percent."

"Really, you're reading that at this hour?"

"No, I'm kidding. I'm just catching up on some work."

"Oh, you're a funny man when there's a full moon." I sit down next to him.

He's perusing the website of a high-end store in Manhattan I recognize. It lists locations in Brooklyn and D.C.

"They're a client," Dylan informs me. "I want to see what they currently have on hand and if I need to push our New York sales rep into adding more pieces. I have about fifty sites I like to go through every month. Sometimes I find new stores I think would be a perfect match for our product, so I send notes out to the sales reps."

"I didn't know you handled the business end, too. I thought you made furniture all day."

"That's my primary job, working in the shop, however, Carson has me going out into the field more, meeting store buyers and talking to sales reps. I help train them with our furniture. I like talking about the wood, the work, the process. Then I think the reps are better at selling it."

A slew of spreadsheets pop up on the screen and I watch as Dylan flips through them. Revenue, Inventory, Sales Expectations, Current Orders, Sales History. His eyes flit around the screen quickly as he reads the numbers before going to the next screen.

"So you're a businessman, too. You help Carson with the financial part?"

Dylan looks at me amused. "Well, golly gee, I think I can add and subtract a few numbers, Ms. Channing," he says in a Gomer Pyle imitation.

I laugh and am relieved we're back to our regular banter, that the tension from earlier is gone.

"I don't know, Dylan. These fancy numbers and charts and that sexy accent are kind of turning me on."

Dylan puts the laptop on the table and then lifts me like a bride as he stands. "We're going to have to do something about that right now," he says as he carries me off to bed.

I wake when it's still dark, my mind murky with a dream that is now fading. The nightstand clock says it's three o'clock in the morning while Dylan's quick breaths tell me he's awake, too.

"Dylan?" I turn towards his back. "You awake?"

"Yeah," he says, rolling over to face me. "Did you have a bad dream?"

"I don't know. I can't remember. Something woke me up. I'm usually a heavy sleeper, but sometimes those owls and crickets make a peep and then I'm wide awake. Country noises are creepy compared to the city."

I can see Dylan's smile in the moonlight as he reaches over with one arm and pulls me closer.

"Why are you awake?" I ask him. His smile is not convincing, I sense something closer to anguish from him. "What's wrong, Dylan?"

"Sometimes I have insomnia."

"How often?"

"A lot, but then sometimes, on the weekends, I crash and sleep like a log."

"How long has this been going on?" I ask, wondering if it started with my arrival.

"About six months. I stopped taking the anti-depressant I was on because it made me sleepy. Ironic, isn't it?"

"Dylan," I say urgently. "When was the last time you saw a doctor?"

"I saw the shrink about a year ago. I took the pills for about six months and then stopped. Except for the sleepiness, I was feeling pretty good. You don't have to worry about me, Jess. I'm fine."

"Don't you think you were feeling good because of the medication? It's supposed to balance you out."

Dylan gives a tired laugh. "Jesus, I know what the meds are supposed to do and I know Carson told you I've been at this a while. I'm fine. I'm taking on some new responsibilities at the shop and I don't want to let Carson down. Maybe I've been worrying a little too much about it and it keeps me up at night, but it will go away."

"Why can't you see your doctor, or a new doctor, and try a new medication that doesn't make you tired?"

"I don't need another anti-depressant or anti-anxiety drug. I've taken so many pills since I was a teenager, enough to disable an elephant. I'm done with the pill regimen."

"That's not how it works and you know it. You took those meds over many years. The doctors didn't keep you loaded and drugged up."

"How do you know?" Now Dylan is propped on his arm, in my face. "Do you and Carson discuss my medical history a lot? Do you think I'm sick?"

"I didn't mean to be intrusive," I say, my voice trying to find a soothing tone. "I think you're trying too hard to be perfect. Believe me, Dylan; I know what it's like to worry about pleasing other people and always trying to be the best. I lived like that my whole life, living the life my parents wanted for me, but you don't have to do that."

"Jess," he snaps. "Don't talk to me like a child. My brother has done that enough over the last twenty years. I may not have a fucking Ph.D. like you, but I know how to take care of myself."

I fall back on the bed and roll away from him.

"Sorry I yelled at you. I think if I exercise more, I'll sleep better," he says, putting his hand on my shoulder.

I'm not giving into to his gentle apology again. I can't decide if I'm completely enraged with him for dropping his treatment or if I feel sorry for him. I can't look at him. "Dylan, you already put in thirty miles a week running. Uphill. You should be sleeping like a baby every night."

I'm watching the shadows of the tree limbs cast by the moonlight as they dance across the wall like nighttime fairies. It's so strange to be in a home that is now mine with a man that shares my bed every night. I no longer hear my roommates arriving home loud and drunk or the neighbors jamming horribly on their guitars and drums. I'm supposed to be an adult and Dylan, who I found to be sweet and comforting in the beginning of my Hera life, is making me question my own sensibilities. I have misgivings about him, which doesn't bode well for either of us.

"Besides, I don't have a Ph.D.; I have a master's degree. See how little you know about me?"

"I know, you have two masters," he says. "Okay, exercise is probably not the answer to my problem, but I don't want to go through a gauntlet of drugs again, the insanity of trying to find the right match. It's too hard. Besides, I've been happy since you came here. You're my drug, Jess."

He pulls me on my back so he can see my face.

"Dylan, I'm not enough. I haven't managed my own life without assistance from caring friends, especially people in this town. Do I look like someone who can take care of a home, manage a career, start a new career based on a dream and take care of a dog? I haven't been doing this by myself. Besides you, there are a lot of people helping me. If you think I'm enough to help you through this, you're wrong. Your brother loves you, he wants to help you."

"I know. It's not that you can't help me. It's that you don't feel the same way I feel about you."

"I didn't say that."

"You didn't have to. Every time I tell you that I love you, you change the subject."

"Because this is happening so fast and it's new. It's exciting, but it's overwhelming," I stammer.

"You don't have to explain or justify your feelings to me. I'm not mad. Do you think I'm angry at you?"

"How could you not be? You're doing everything right and I'm coming off as some unappreciative bitch."

"I never think that and you shouldn't, either." His fingers trace lightly up and down my arm.

"I can't help feeling that way. I have something so good here and most people would envy my situation. I'm squandering my good fortune, but I can't make myself fall in love before I'm ready."

"Or ever," Dylan says.

True. Sometimes I feel smothered by Dylan and I know I wouldn't if my feelings for him weren't waning or based on something more solid than our sex life.

As much as I want to help Dylan and keep thinking I'll eventually fall in love with him, I'm not as happy as someone should be in my situation. I spend an awful lot of time daydreaming in my country home. Most of the images that loop endlessly in my brain are homey scenes of me painting and relaxing on the porch with friends. The only man in every single scene of my domestic tranquility is there because I put him there. Carson.

Twenty-One

When I wake up, Dylan's side of the bed is empty. He usually leaves for work before I rise, but today there is no cute little note on the kitchen counter with his plans for our dinner or night out. He didn't even leave me a fresh a pot of coffee.

I feed Bert and shoo him outside so he can do his business. Then I check in with 5 Alpha to tell my team that I'll be out for the morning, but that they can reach me later in the afternoon. I put on a tank top and some running tights, which I bought last year when I thought I'd become a runner, only to discover that I can't run unless I'm trying to catch a cab or get the last muffin at Magnolia Bakery. I grab one of the yoga mats Aunt Virginia had stowed in her closet and head out. Bert refuses to walk with me so I let him back inside to wile his hours away in blissful slumber.

I make it to Beyond The Pants in time for the nine o'clock yoga class with Imogene and Lauren. The instructor is a striking woman in her forties with silver hair and deeply tanned skin. Lois is up front, following the moves at her own graceful pace while I like to hide in the back of the class.

The yogi's voice is deep and smooth; she manages to make her way over to me frequently to adjust my hips or put a palm on my back to guide me into a better position. She has me contorted into some kind of pretzel move that requires quiet breathing and that's when it occurs to me that it's conceivable that I really don't fit in Hera. As much as I have come to love my new little town and how my life seems to be better, maybe I'm a poison for the town, or rather Dylan. I contemplate this and replay last night's conversation in my head when I realize I can't move.

"Sweet mother of nuts," Lois says, bending down to look me in the face. "What the heavens are you doing there?"

One of my legs is tucked under me and the other is bent across the front. I can't move because the leg under my ass has fallen asleep and that crazy, painful, tingling sensation of paralysis makes me stay put. "I think I did it wrong," I say.

"Well, if you could see your purple face you'd sure as heck know it isn't right." Lois laughs. Imogene and Lauren burst out laughing, too. The class is finished and everyone is milling out with their rolled mats under their arms; except for me, pretzel girl. The instructor comes over and gently removes my bent leg and massages both so I can stand with minimal pain.

"I didn't get much sleep last night. I think I'm having trouble following directions this morning." I rub my leg.

"Dylan must be voracious," Lauren says in low voice as we exit, but loud enough that Lois looks back at me and grimaces. I smile and hurry the girls outside.

"Did you have to say that in front of Lois?" I ask Lauren. "You made it sound like I'm the town hooker."

"No, I didn't. I only said—"

"I know what you said. Everyone heard what you said. Did you see Lois's face? She looked pissed."

"She's not mad at you, Jess," Imogene says as she lights a cigarette.

"How can you smoke after yoga class?" I ask.

"Easy, I keep the cigs and lighter in my yoga bag. Just light, puff and blow."

I cringe. "What is going on with Lois?"

"She's not a fan of you and Dylan dating," Lauren answers. "Actually, she told us a couple of weeks ago that she didn't think it was a good idea for you and Dylan to date, but I suppose now she's aware you're sleeping together. Thanks to me, I guess."

"I thought Lois liked me. Are you going to tell me the rest of the story? Why is she opposed to me dating Dylan?"

"Oh, sweetie, it's not you. She's opposed to anyone—"

"Lauren!" Imogene scolds. "Jess, Lois is concerned that you and Dylan may be rushing things. That's her problem, not yours."

A look passes between the two women with Imogene winning the stare down battle and ultimately whatever it is they are keeping from me.

"I don't believe you two. I don't have time for these guessing games. I have work to do," I say and then head down the main street for my long walk home.

I make it as far as The General Store when I see Carson coming out with a bottle of water.

"How's the yoga going?" he asks with a forced smile.

"Oh, geez. Not you, too," I say, trying to pass him on the sidewalk.

"What?" he laughs and intentionally blocks my path.

"I came down from my crumbling house on the hill to get my Zen on and relax for a change and I've had nothing except the weirdest encounters with everyone this morning. Go ahead, make your crack so I can be on my way." I stand my ground with my yoga satchel in one hand and my New York Yankees cap in the other.

"Hera has Zen? How do you get that on?" Although this is a rare moment for Carson and someone should record it, I'm too annoyed for anymore evasive or humorous conversations at my expense.

"Step aside, cowboy. I need to get going."

"Where's your car?"

"I walked."

"Ah girly, you and your citified ways," he says in a Hillbilly accent and I have to laugh. "We don't walk here. Come on, cowpoke; let me give you a ride home."

I'm actually relieved that he offers to drive me. I'm not cut out for long, hot, country walks. I climb into the truck's cab and Carson turns on the air conditioning full blast.

"That's heaven," I mumble and close my eyes, letting the cool air chill the sweat on my face.

"Can I ask you something?"

"If I say no, you'll ask anyway." I look over at him as he drives with one hand while the other one does that Blackard tic of stroking his chin, which means he's ready to be all serious again. "What?"

"Has Dylan been acting a little different?" he asks. This is not an impromptu question. Carson has been thinking about this for a while and is trying to say it as delicately as possible without causing me to be alarmed. He's a planner and I can see that it is difficult for him to ask someone else about his own brother; the boy and the man he has been raising for a lifetime.

"In what way?" I ask in a meek voice I haven't used in a long time.

Carson glances at me and then back at the road in front of us. "He's been too low key. Very quiet and distant."

"Doesn't his anti-depressant medication do that? Calm him?" I ask, hopeful that maybe Dylan is secretly getting treatment, but wasn't ready to tell me.

"It calms him, but it doesn't make him indifferent," Carson answers. "Jess, I told you he went off his medication and hasn't been very stable since then."

"I know. I was just hoping you were going to tell me his behavior was a good sign."

"Do you think he's doing well?" Carson asks me. "He's quiet at work. He does his job, although he's less talkative. He uses his lunch hour to go running, and before he used to hang out with the guys and eat and shoot the shit. Now he runs like a maniac. Excuse me, poor choice of words. You see him more than I do. That's why I'm asking."

"No, I don't think he's doing well. He told me last night that he doesn't want to go back on any treatment program. It's a sore point between us."

"I'm sorry," Carson says under his breath. He parks his truck in front of my house.

"Well, thanks for the ride."

"Yeah, about that. Sorry to tell you, but I'm coming in. I've got my equipment in back and I have to rip out some of the kitchen cabinets we can't save, so we can slide in your new appliances which will be arriving on a delivery truck in approximately two hours, or less."

"It's a good thing I don't cook or I'd be really pissed off at your lack of notice. I have to get to work anyway."

"How is that going? Working from here?" Carson asks as he begins unloading equipment from the truck bed.

"Pretty good. I like the quiet of the library. It's kind of lonely not having my colleagues around and people to eat lunch with, but it's a pretty good trade-off with the views and the peacefulness. Other than Bert, I have very few distractions."

"Except for Dylan," Carson says. "Have you given him his own set of drawers and a closet yet? He spends more time here than anywhere else."

One minute Carson is concerned about his brother, the next he's taking jabs at me as if he's resentful of me or Dylan, or both. I'm too stunned to reply. Carson carries a toolbox and a small ladder, and I follow him into the house.

"Wait a minute," I say. Carson sets his equipment down on the kitchen floor and turns back to me. "Do you think I've caused Dylan to behave this way? Do you think this is my fault?"

"No." Carson shakes his head in exasperation. "Forget I said anything." He leans down to pet Bert.

"It's hard to forget when you keep bringing it up."

Carson gives me the once over and shakes his head. Then he retrieves Bert's food dishes to give him fresh water and the dry smelly pellets he eats.

"I was going to do that." I point to the dishes.

"Don't be so defensive. I'm trying to help out; I'm not blaming you for Dylan or for Bert's dirty water dish."

"Jesus. Something is going on. Between you and Lois and the others, I swear something is going on and no one is telling me. I feel like I'm the star in some crazy Fellini movie, except I'm the only one who doesn't have a script." I swing my arms in frustration and whack my hand unintentionally against the doorframe. "Fuck!"

"Are you okay?" Carson comes towards me.

"Leave me alone." I hold my hand up so he doesn't touch it. "I have work to do." I leave and jog up the staircase to my bedroom, pounding my feet as hard as I can.

After a shower and an hour of sitting in front of my computer screens, I realize I never ate breakfast or lunch and my stomach is gurgling. Carson is making a racket, demolishing part of my kitchen, though, and the last thing I want to do is slink down to the kitchen to grab some food while he's there.

I continue to work, plodding through code that I should know well, yet my thoughts are distracted so I might as well be translating a foreign language. I should be celebrating after what Tom has offered to do with my paintings, but other than Dylan, I haven't told anyone my good news. The fact that Dylan did not mention it again last night and did not congratulate me or seem happy in the least strikes an unsettling chord.

By late afternoon the house is quiet. The demolition has stopped and I see a large delivery truck pull up in the front yard. I let Carson handle the order since it's been organized by him and I'd only get in the way. I sit in the bay window and watch the delivery men roll the stainless steel appliances off the truck ramp, Carson directing the way.

I go back to work, joining in a late afternoon conference call with Nathan and my team to go over changes they want to make in one of our software programs before a final product is presented to the client. I listen, but say little. I'm too busy doodling on my notepad, thinking I'd rather be in the studio right now, playing with my paints and inks. I hear the delivery truck drive away and Bert perks up from his place on the couch as I get off the conference call.

"I think it's safe for you to go down and eat now," I tell him. He cocks his head and then does a wobbly stand before stumbling off the couch and running out of the room.

I stare past my computer monitors to the large tree outside the bay windows, mesmerized by a swaying branch. I don't even notice the plate being put in front of me until Carson speaks. "Thought you must be hungry."

He made me a peanut butter and jelly sandwich with apple slices and a glass of lemonade. This is the same meal he used to serve Dylan and me when we were kids.

"Thanks. I'm famished," I say, finally looking at him.

"The kitchen is almost done. You can use it now, though. I still have to put the new cabinet fronts on, but the appliances are all hooked up." He perches on the edge of my desk while I eat. His great ass is awfully close to my keyboard. Talk about a distraction.

"Did my Aunt's trust cover the expense and did Archie already pay you for everything?" I keep my eyes on my plate.

"Everything is in order. You don't have to do a thing."

I nod and hold up an apple slice before biting into it. "Really? You think you have to cut up my apples like I'm a five-year-old?" I smile.

Carson shrugs and chuckles. "Habit. I still slice my apples, too."

I nibble the apple while he watches me, and it seems an odd turn of events that Carson is here instead of Dylan, and that we can be close to one another in this pleasant state without any friction bordering the edges of the air between us as it does when I'm with Dylan.

Being with Carson, I don't sense that I'm on the verge of something disagreeable taking over. He's black and white, easy to read. He's either pissed or pleasant. I may not know why, but I can always read his emotions. By comparison, Dylan is made of many hues in between that I can't interpret. Dylan is a palette of paint that I don't know how to brush on paper, no matter how long I stare at the various color combinations. Nothing clicks with Dylan, unless it's sex.

"Did Dylan tell you my good news? About the art show I'm going to be in this winter." I say it joylessly.

Carson senses my disappointment. "No. He didn't say anything about it. Congratulations, Jess. Gin would be very proud of you."

I want to stay in this lovely room with its warm wood, smells of worn leather and old books and keep talking to Carson. This is where I want to be, but I have to remind myself that he is not mine. I have chosen to be with someone else and it's a mistake that is entirely my fault.

Dylan arrives with Leo and Daniel from the shop, and they help Carson finish the new cabinets in a matter of hours. I spend the time painting in the studio. In the evening, Dylan brings me down for the unveiling of the new kitchen.

"A dishwasher!" I exclaim and the men laugh.

They even transferred the old food to the new fridge and cupboards and mopped the dust off the floor. Carson is right; I don't have to do anything.

They crack open a few bottles of beer and talk for a while about business and then Leo and Daniel load the tools into the back of Carson's truck.

Before he leaves, Carson stops at the front door, turns to me and puts his hand on my shoulder. "Congratulations, Jess. Your show will be great."

"Thanks, Carson." I want to do more. I want to hug him for this, but I can't. Not in front of Dylan.

Dylan closes the door. "You told him about the show?"

"Yes. I wanted to share it with someone. I was surprised you didn't tell him this morning at work."

"I forgot, that's all," Dylan says, but his dejected expression says otherwise.

"Dylan, this show is a big deal to me and I thought you'd be happy for me. You're acting like I've been called for duty and I'm going off to war."

He doesn't say anything. I follow him around the first floor as he shuts off lights. "Dylan, what's going on? Is this because of our conversation last night? Is this because you're depressed again and you won't get help?" I ask, pleading.

"I don't want to talk about it," he raises his voice. "You and Carson both, lay off."

"I'm sick of you acting like this doesn't affect the rest of us. It has everything to do with me and Carson and your friends," I say. He avoids eye contact with me, closing windows, shutting off lights and locking doors. I'm right behind him because I need to resolve this.

"Let's go to bed."

"You can't fuck your way out of everything, Dylan!" I shout. "I'm sick of you being so glum, and your answer to avoiding your problem when you're with me is to screw. You can't decide that you'll be happy only during sex and then miserable the rest of the time. You may think that works for you, but it doesn't work for me."

Dylan stands on the first landing and stares at me, shocked by my rant. I try to run past him up the stairs to get to my bedroom, but he grabs my arm and pulls me back to him. "I don't want to make you miserable," he says. "I thought we were becoming closer. I want to live with you. I thought you'd want me to move in."

"What? Live together? Dylan, we can't even work out the problems we have now. You think moving in together and combining our belongings will solve our problems?"

"I practically live here as it is."

"Yes, I know. And we don't seem to be doing very well outside of the bedroom." It's too late to take back my harsh words. "I shouldn't have said that."

Dylan lets go of my arm. "I haven't done everything the way you think I should, but I do love you. I know if we live together, I'll get back on track so my—my mood swings are under control."

"No, Dylan, you have to do that anyway, whether you live with me or not. You have to get professional help. I can't live with you. Not like this. This is how wrong the situation is; you were thinking of moving in together and I was thinking we need to take a break from us."

"You're breaking up with me?" He looks down. His whole body seems to deplete whatever energy it has left. He's not the Dylan I met two months ago, the gregarious personality that took over a room. The strength and effervescence is seeping from this Dylan. He's becoming hollow and muted and he won't let anyone help him.

"We both need to be apart from one another for a while, but—"

"Don't say '*we*.' It's you that needs to be apart from me," he says without any hostility. He walks slowly back down the stairs and I want to go after him, but I have nothing left to give him. Dylan picks up the keys to his Jeep from the hall table and walks out the front door without looking back at me.

I sit down on the step and cry, sparsely at first and then it pours out of me. I have never cried over a broken relationship, I've never been in this situation where my stomach hurts and my heart aches for something I've done, somebody I've hurt.

With Dylan's absence, my bed seems enormous. Bert takes it upon himself to hobble up on the covers and join me. I am awake most of the night, wondering what I could have done better to make things right, however, even a genius can get it wrong most of the time. I get up and find my cell phone. I think about calling Marissa and Kate to make plans to meet them back in the city, instead I text Lauren and Imogene, asking if we can spend Saturday together. I'll be turning twenty-one and I'd rather have people around me so I can pretend to be happy.

Twenty-Two

On Saturday it rains, bringing with it a cool wind and some relief. It allows me to sleep in and make up for all those late-night wake-ups.

Imogene and Lauren plan to come for the day and spend the night. They show up with overnight bags, junk food, a bag of limes and tequila. "Happy Birthday!" they scream when I open the front door.

"How did you know?" I ask, hustling them off the wet porch.

"Archie told us," Lauren answers. "He knows everything. He's like a wizard or something."

"It's official; you're old enough for margarita night." Imogene holds up the tequila.

"I am so glad you guys are here," I say with a timid smile before the crying starts.

Imogene and Lauren usher me over to the living room couch and I gladly sit down and bawl uncontrollably.

"I really screwed up," I say between sobs.

"We heard all about the break up; you don't have to say anything. These things happen every day. You'll be fine." Imogene puts her arm around my shoulders.

"Don't listen to her," Lauren says. "You can tell us anything. All we heard is that Dylan has been crashing at Leo's again. He told us the other day at the diner."

I wipe my eyes with the tissues Imogene gives me. "Great, now everyone knows."

"No, only the people at the diner." Lauren sighs.

"Yep, that's pretty much the whole town," Imogene adds.

"Carson was right again. He's the wizard. I should have listened to him," I say. "All this time, he knew this would happen."

"No, he didn't," Imogene says. "What did he say to you?"

"I haven't seen him since Dylan left, but when Dylan first asked me out, Carson didn't want us to start anything. He said I'd hurt Dylan and I did."

"Even Carson could not predict this. Besides, you didn't intentionally hurt Dylan. You look pretty broken up, too, so it's fair to say that it took two people to make this happen." Imogene rubs my back.

"Leo says that Dylan hasn't said a word about what happened. He said Dylan is barely speaking at all." Lauren's eyes bug out to emphasize Dylan's awful state.

"So you finally started talking to Leo?" I ask.

"Oh, God, no. He's still afraid to talk to me, I guess, but he talks to Bonnie and I stand right there to listen in."

Imogene shakes her head. "They are so pathetic. They're both too terrified to ask the other out so they have conversations through my grandmother. Honestly, my grandmother is afraid she'll have to go on a date with them."

Imogene and I both laugh at that.

"See, Jess? I'm not doing much better than you. That's why I have brought the best movies to get over heartbreak." Lauren digs through her tote bag.

"Like what?" I ask, expecting a slew of sappy romantic comedies.

"I have *Goodfellas*." She hands me the DVD case. "I have *Dog Day Afternoon*, one of the greatest love stories ever told, by the way."

"Aren't these bloody, violent films?" I ask.

"Lauren has a thing for mob movies and crime flicks," Imogene says.

"No, I watch what my dad watches. It's our thing. I also brought *Raging Bull*, *Fargo*, and I have two seasons of *Boardwalk Empire*. There is a lot of romance in B.E.; all we need are the margaritas and we can get this party started!" Lauren cheers with a jump.

"I don't think these movies are going to be much help." I fan through the gloomy DVD covers.

"It's going to be fun. Besides, it's not like we can go out. The rain is coming down sideways. We can't go out driving in this weather," Lauren says. "The news said the hurricane has turned into a tropical storm and it's coming inland. It's going to get worse before it gets better."

"Fine," I say as Imogene pulls me into the kitchen after Lauren.

We mix drinks and fill big bowls with chips and Cheetos, a forbidden food in my parents' home because my father thought the orange powder was unhealthy, this from a man who stocked our home with Oreos and pudding.

Imogene is rummaging through cupboards, which have been re-arranged by Carson and Dylan when they finished the kitchen. "Where are the friggin' margarita glasses that Gin used to have in here?"

"I don't know where anything is," I say.

"The boys did an amazing job on the kitchen, but I want those fucking giant margarita glasses!" Imogene shouts. Then she lets out a loud gasp that causes Lauren and me to whip our heads in unison.

"What?" Lauren asks.

"Oh. My. God." Imogene turns around and we see the small, velvet ring box open in her hand with a solitaire diamond ring nestled in it.

I'm staring at it, hoping that we find a scrap of information to go along with it, something along the lines of a love letter from one of Aunt Virginia's former lovers, but I know this cupboard has been wiped out within the last week and anything in there now—groceries or diamond rings—are from recent purchases.

"Shit almighty. That looks real," Lauren says.

"It is. The bag and receipt were next to it on the shelf." Imogene hands me the receipt so I can see the proof for myself. She timidly holds the ring box in her open palm.

I study the receipt. The ring was purchased in the city at a jewelry story in midtown Manhattan, the diamond district. It's dated last week, the night of my blow up with Dylan. He came home and helped finish the kitchen then hid the ring on a shelf where he knew I'd never look because I can't cook and never scrounge for dishware.

"Dylan bought this," I say. Imogene holds the ring out to me, but I can't touch it. I shake my head and step back as if it's radioactive. "This is worse than I thought."

Imogene and Lauren huddle and snatch the ring from its velvet cradle. Lauren holds it up to the kitchen light. "Is this three carats? This is unbelievable. What was Dylan thinking? Men don't propose marriage after a few weeks of dating."

"Tell that to my parents. You remember them, Pammy and Mark? Our cooks? They got hitched after three dates and guess who was born eleven months later?" Imogene points a finger at herself.

"No one says '*hitched*,'" Lauren adds. "But on the bright side, that's a great story with a happy ending."

"No. No," I say. "This is unbelievable. I had no idea Dylan was thinking about marriage. This is crazy." I run down to the hall to get away from the ring. I'm getting good at fleeing rooms. Apparently the country life and having so much space to run in my home has taught me how to flee any scene like a crazed chicken. The girls follow me with a tray of margaritas.

"We put the ring back in the cupboard. Tonight we celebrate your birthday. We shall not speak of you-know-who," Lauren says.

"I can't ignore this. I'm going to have to talk to Dylan about this and I'll have to return the ring."

"That's not going to happen tonight, so for now, put it out of your mind, if that's possible, and bottoms up," Imogene says.

We slam back the cocktails like shots. After my drama, there seems no point in pretending this is a regular girls' night out.

I burp. "That was good. I'll need a bucket of these."

"Oh no, we forgot the toast," Lauren says. "Here's to twenty·one." As the three of us clink our empty glasses, we hear a popping sound in the house and then we are submerged in complete darkness.

"Shit! A power outage!" This comes from Imogene.

"Where do you keep the flashlights?" Lauren asks.

"I have no idea," I say to the two dark figures.

The rain outside has turned into a full·on apocalyptic thunderstorm and the only light we get is from lightning strikes close to the house that wash the room with a white haze before going dark again.

We hear a crack outside and something hits the house. We let out blood·curdling screams and laugh at the same time. It's a like a cheesy horror movie.

"I think one of your trees just lost a limb," Imogene points out.

"Wait! I do have a flashlight on me. I forgot my dad gave me this for my car." Lauren stumbles in the dark somewhere by the couch. "Ah ha! Found it." A little light comes on in Lauren's hands. It's a tiny key light, enough to cast a dim glow across her face.

"A key light?" Imogene asks. "Lauren, that isn't going to help; I still can't see my hands or feet, all we can see is your mug and you look crazy, lady."

"It's not great, but look, we can point it at the floor and use it to guide us to the basement. I bet Gin has a stash of tools down there and there must be at least a few flashlights. She's lived here forever and has been through a few bad storms, she must have kept emergency supplies somewhere."

"My phone has a flashlight app," I say. "Except I have no idea where I left the phone."

"Perfect," Imogene huffs.

"Let's go with Lauren's idea," I suggest. "I know there's more than wine downstairs. There's a ladder and an old saw, so maybe there are some flashlights and batteries."

"Fine," Imogene says. "You lead, Lauren. We'll follow your itty bitty light."

Imogene holds my arm and guides me as we shuffle down the long hallway towards the kitchen and cellar door. We jump every time we hear a crack of thunder. Before we're halfway down the hall, there's another blinding flash of light coming from the living room windows and a crack follows too closely as if the lightning hit the house. At the same exact moment the front door swings open, banging against the hall console, and we see a tall, hulking, dark figure in the doorway.

Imogene produces another movie-worthy scream and then Lauren joins her. I am too terrified to scream or move. A flash of lightning illuminates the face of the stranger, and I see it's Carson looking drenched and wild-eyed, but oh so sexy with his shirt plastered to his chest.

"It's Carson," I yell. Imogene and Lauren are still screaming as if he's an ax murderer. I decide that I must remember this moment because, should we ever find ourselves in a similar crisis, at least I now know that these two women are the type to panic first and react later.

"Jesus, stop screaming," Carson says, walking towards us.

"Carson, how did you get here?" Imogene asks. In the darkness I see her grabbing on to him.

Lauren shines her little light in his face.

"Get that thing off my face," he says, so she points it at his neck. "Are you all okay?"

"We're fine," Imogene says. "We were celebrating Jess's birthday when the power went out."

Carson searches for my face and we lock eyes for a second when another flash of lightning strikes. "Let's get you some flashlights," he says.

"You're in a suit; did you come from your house?" Lauren asks.

"No, I was at Mohonk when the power went out. I left the flashlights I had in my truck with some people at the hotel," he says. "I got a text from Archie, Pam and Bonnie. They all said the power was out down here, too, and they couldn't call you, but they could text me. I told them I'd check on you. I made Gin an emergency kit and put it in the pantry so it would be close by."

"God, we're so lucky you came to our rescue," Imogene says. "We were going to go hunt around the scary cellar for flashlights. I'm so glad you got here first."

Carson leads us in the dark back down the hallway to the pantry. "It's the lower cabinet behind the door," he says. I hear him banging things around and then a light comes on. It lights up the whole pantry. "These are LED lanterns."

"Awesome," Lauren says. "Are there more?"

"There are ten lanterns and at least six flashlights. They're all LED so they should last a while. There's also a box of new batteries in every size so let's start filling these." He hands out the camping lanterns and handheld flashlights.

We assemble all the lanterns and place one in all the downstairs rooms so we have light in every room. The lanterns give off a ghastly whiteness like moonbeams. We all look like the walking dead.

"Carson Blackard, you have saved the day—I mean night," Lauren says. "Now we must continue with our party because I sure as hell can't sleep in this."

"So my parents called you because they thought you were home and could roll down the hill and check on us?" Imogene asks Carson. ""Hmm, interesting."

"What?" Lauren asks. She's refilling our margarita glasses from the pitcher as I eagerly hold my glass out for her. Carson is checking the window frames or something manly that guys think they should be doing in a storm to look busy and productive.

"Carson is in a suit," Imogene says and at that we all turn to look at Carson who tosses his wet suit coat on the couch to reveal a wet, white dress shirt that clings to his superbly defined muscular chest. His wet locks are disheveled and only help to make him look more attractive. Fuckity-fuck. I can't be around him without getting all worked up.

"A very nice suit," Imogene continues. "And he just told us that he was at swanky Mohonk which means he must be on a date. I bet he left a lovely lady up at the hotel where she probably has a nice room and a candle light dinner waiting for him."

"Who are you two? Cagney and Lacey? The power went out at Mohonk, too," Carson says which doesn't sound like much of a defense to me. Little pangs of jealousy are rattling me, thinking of Carson at a nice resort with another woman.

"Ha! But you are on a date and she *IS* up at Mohonk waiting for you!" Lauren shouts.

"So what?" Carson says and glances over at me. I put on a show of loving my strong drink too much to even consider participating in the conversation. I'm actually seething, thinking of some pretty woman waiting in a hotel room for Carson. What's his type? Bombshells with boobs or leggy, skinny models?

"Just saying," Imogene says, a little drunk. "You never bring women to your home. You are a true mystery, Mr. Blackard. You take a date to Mohonk for a fabulous dinner and stunning ambiance. You book a room so you don't have to share your home with her. Then, to make it less personal, you get a text or call from my parents and you tell your date to make herself comfortable while you go to check on three women, but you'll be back in time for sex."

"Yes! That's it." Lauren points her finger at him.

"You're all drunk," he says, loosening his tie. "Don't sleep upstairs. Ride out the storm down here, okay?"

"Did you at least get dinner before the power went out?" Imogene grins at Carson. "Who's the woman, Carson?"

"No one special," he mutters.

"Is that why you didn't invite her to your home?" Lauren asks. "You only date out-of-town women? Locals aren't good enough for you?"

"Do you have everything you need here?" he asks me, ignoring Imogene's and Lauren's taunts.

I nod and he looks at me a moment longer than necessary. My eyes linger on him, too, as I wonder what Dylan has told him. I consider that Carson is probably angry with me and wants to shout, *"I told you so!"*

"You can't drive in this weather," Imogene says to him.

"What are you talking about? I drove down in this weather, I can drive back. I have my truck. I knew the weather would be bad. I didn't know it would be this rough, though."

"You can't leave us now. Besides, I have some things I need to discuss with you," Imogene says, sounding drunker by the minute.

"Where's Bert?" Carson directs at me.

"Oh my God, I don't know." I put down my drink. "He's in the house somewhere, but I completely forgot about him when the lights went out. I'll go search upstairs."

"No. Don't," Carson says. "Come here."

I follow him into the dining room, which looks more austere and eerie than the living room.

"Look," Carson says, pointing under the dining room table where Bert is hiding flat out on his stomach with his face buried in his front paws. "It's his go-to place when he freaks out. Thunderstorms always freak him out."

"Oh, honey," I say, bending down to see Bert. "I'm sorry."

"Put his dishes under there and he'll be fine," Carson instructs. I nod and realize I'm afraid to speak to Carson. I'm anxious and worried that he's pissed off with me and frankly, I'm tired of disappointing people, especially him.

"Come and join the party, Carson," Imogene says from the living room. Lauren is dancing to a Michael Jackson cassette tape on an old battery-operated boom box that was in the pantry.

"I don't think so," Carson says so quietly that only I can hear him.

We're standing together, alone in the dining room. I don't know why he doesn't race back up to New Paltz and his hot date instead of taking the drunken abuse from Imogene and Lauren. Somehow, he doesn't seem in a rush, though. Besides, I'm not in a rush to see him leave. In the chaos of the stormy weather outside and the drunk women laughing in the other room, this moment alone with him in the dining room seems private and rather intimate.

"Are you okay?" he asks me, breaking our silence.

"We're fine. Thanks for finding the lanterns."

"I meant you. Dylan doesn't talk to me about you, but I know you two had a—"

"Break-up," I finish for him.

"Yeah."

"Please don't get the wrong idea by what you see here. Imogene and Lauren came over to cheer me up. I'm not happy about what happened between Dylan and me."

"I would never think badly of you." His voice is soft and understanding. "Dylan is closed off. That's nothing new. I wanted to make sure that you're all right. That's the real reason I came down here tonight. I know those two can handle themselves in this storm, but it gave me a good excuse to come check on you."

My breath hitches in my throat; I'm surprised by his admission.

"Did you really leave your date back at Mohonk?"

"She's in good company. We met some nice couples at the dinner we were invited to, so she'll be fine without me."

"Hmm, she'll probably be ticked off that you left her to go check on three young, drunk women. Did you tell her that part or did you tell her you were checking on seniors?"

Carson laughs softly. "I told her a friend was worried about her granddaughter's safety."

"So she thinks you're checking on a baby. Good one."

We both laugh and then a thunderbolt cracks, causing me to duck and shudder with it. Carson holds my shoulders and moves closer. "It's fine. That's at least two miles away."

I try to look brave. "Sure. I'm fine."

"Hey, happy birthday."

"Not really. I expected twenty·one to be a great celebration, but the timing is horrible."

"Don't let a little thunderstorm ruin your night. You have two very good friends in there who want to have fun with you."

"They are good friends. It's not the storm," I say and then I begin to hem and haw because I'm afraid to tell Carson about the ring.

"What is it?" His smile fades and he looks concerned.

"Tonight, before the power went out, Imogene found a ring in the kitchen cupboard. We were mixing drinks and you know I don't cook or really know my way around a kitchen, so if you wanted to hide something from me, where would you put it?" I'm rambling while Carson stares at me, waiting for me to get to the point.

"In the cupboard? And?" Carson's tone is heavy with worry. His brow furrows.

"Dylan bought a ring and hid it in the cupboard, Carson. It's a big, fat diamond ring that was purchased last week. I saw the receipt. He put it in there the same night we argued and he left."

"Did you and Dylan talk about marriage?" His voice is less friendly.

"No, of course not. We never even talked about living together until that night. Dylan brought it up. I thought we were moving too fast and I wanted to slow down, take a break."

"A break up, you mean. Taking a break is a break up," Carson clarifies.

"Yes."

"Did Dylan have any idea that you wanted to end it?" There's that accusatory tone again.

"I never said I wanted to end it, Carson. I said it was moving too fast and I wanted to slow down."

"You wanted to break up. No guy is stupid enough to believe that slowing down isn't the same thing as saying you aren't that in to him and want to break up." His voice is stern.

"I didn't realize that after less than two months, Dylan would want to live together and that he was actually thinking of proposing. Maybe we're wrong about all of this. We're just speculating about this ring."

"We're not speculating. He bought a ring." Carson spits out the words at me.

"But he never gave it to me. Maybe he changed his mind."

"Or maybe he didn't have a chance to propose because you kicked him out."

The blood rises in my face. Now I'm pissed at Carson and any sweet thoughts I had about him are quickly being erased. "I didn't kick him out. He left on his own without saying a word to me!"

My shouting attracts the attention of Imogene and Lauren. They stop dancing and drinking to join us in the dining room.

"Carson, you know that Jess is not responsible for what Dylan has done. She didn't know he was so serious about her," Imogene says, sounding pretty sober.

"I know that!" Carson shouts.

"Stop yelling at my friends, Blackard," Lauren snaps.

Carson undoes his tie completely and opens the top two buttons of his dress shirt.

"What? Are you getting ready for a fist fight?" Imogene asks.

Carson ignores her and turns back to me. "I warned you about Dylan."

"You said he's very sensitive. You didn't say he was intensely serious. I like Dylan, I didn't want to break it off completely, but I was not ready to live with him. I had no idea he was considering marriage."

"She just turned twenty-one for fuck's sake." Lauren is much drunker than Imogene. "Dylan was her first real boyfriend. She was expecting sex, not a husband."

Carson glares at me as if I'm responsible for Lauren's crass words.

"Dylan may be in worse shape than we think," I say.

"You think?" Carson says loudly. He has every right to be mean and sarcastic. It's his brother I screwed around with, but I can't stand being scolded by him.

"I want to help," I say. "I told him to see his doctor. Dylan wasn't listening to me. Tell me what to do."

"I'll tell you what to do. Stop trying to help my brother," Carson says, so enraged that Imogene and Lauren gasp. "Don't date him, don't talk to him and definitely don't fuck him." He walks to the couch and picks up his jacket before going to the front door to head out into the rain.

I run after him through the blinding sheets of rain, ignoring the pleas from Imogene and Lauren to let him go. I chase him down to the truck and grab his arm.

"Carson, wait!"

"Get back in the house!"

Instead I open the driver's side door and climb in the truck cab. Carson follows and slams the door as I scramble to the passenger side. The rain beats down on the truck roof and it's like being inside a drum. We're drenched and I'm freezing. Carson swings his wet jacket around my shoulders. My hair is plastered to my head like a wet blanket.

"That was stupid," he says to me in a calmer voice.

"You can't blame me for Dylan," I say, shivering.

"I don't. And I'm sorry for yelling at you back there." He nods towards the house. "I hate you seeing me like that."

I pull his coat in closer around me.

"I blame myself and I blame Dylan. You're not the cause of Dylan's behavior, you're a symptom. We're all part of the fallout whenever he does something like this. He's very emotional and he sometimes lives in another world all his own."

"So you don't think my rejection of him is the cause?"

"Well, it didn't help. He had problems before you got here. I saw the signs, but you were a distraction, at least temporarily. Then, when his depression started creeping back in, he thought he could cover it with more drama, moving in with you, I suppose. I don't know what he was thinking. He didn't talk to me about this, but I'm assuming he thought ramping up the stakes to living together and a proposal were the way to go. He's probable feeling very desperate to find an antidote to his melancholy and he believed falling in love with you and escalating the relationship would make him better."

"Are you saying he doesn't really love me? That he's crazy?"

"No. Of course he has very strong feelings for you and he's not crazy. He simply overdramatizes things in his head. In his mind everything is on fast forward because it's like a drug; he keeps reaching for his next hit to make himself feel better, feel happy, or at least make the pain go away."

I am shocked and a little hurt to think that Carson thinks I am a participant, even if unknowingly, in Dylan's delusions, as he implies. That Dylan isn't really in love with me. At least, I feel like a dope for not comprehending what Carson was telling me weeks ago when the relationship started. I did not heed Carson's words seriously and I know nothing about the mindset of someone who suffers from extreme depression. I was the ninny who assumed she would be an enormous help, a saving grace for Dylan.

"Dylan said I was his drug, the only one he needed. I thought he meant that he was so in love with me that he didn't need medication because I made him happy, but you're telling me that he latches on to people. That I could have been replaced with any other woman and he would have reacted the same way?"

Carson cups my cheek with his hand. "God, no. That's not what I meant. He is in love with you, or at least, it's his idea of love. It's real to him. Are you in love with him?"

I shake my head slowly. "No," I whisper. Carson's face gives away his relief.

"What I meant is that a drug for Dylan is any idea that he gets in his head. It doesn't have to be a person; it could be an activity like when he was racing motorcycles in college, or it could be his work. He's asked for a bigger role in managing our business accounts and he's obsessive about it. In this case, you did become his drug. He's obsessed about you, thinking you will keep him distracted enough from his illness. His feelings for you are genuine; however, he's not really in a healthy enough emotional state to tell the difference between caring for a girlfriend and asking her to marry him. He's not thinking clearly."

"That's what I thought," I say. "You have to believe me when I say this started out fairly innocently. He flirted, I liked him and I thought we'd date and have fun. I should have listened to you in the beginning. Dylan was becoming so intense that I should have stopped him then or told you. When we found that ring tonight, I felt sick to my stomach. I think of how I must have led him on; that if he's feeling rejected and it's exasperated by his depression, then I know I have a hand in that."

"No. Stop," Carson says, shushing me. "We'll... I'll get him help. If I have to do it by force, I will."

"I'm so sorry, Carson. You have to believe that if I could take all this back I would. Even if it meant I never came to Hera and never made these new friends. I'd give it all back to take all this pain away from Dylan."

"That's a nice thing to say, but Dylan is like the weather tonight. He's been a storm that was brewing. As long as he refused treatment, refused going to therapy and taking his medication, this was going to happen. Maybe in a different way, maybe worse, but it was going to happen in some way."

"Lauren says he's living at Leo's house again."

"Yeah. He's there and he's lying low. He comes into work early every morning. He's quiet, but he's working hard. He wants me to send him out to visit some accounts in other states. If he was on medication I'd say yes, right now, though, I have reservations about letting him leave town. He's okay. At least I know he's with Leo, who is a very good friend to Dylan. My brother is safe, that's what I know."

My eyes pool with tears. I wipe them with the sleeve of Carson's suit coat. Then I take it off and hand it back. "Maybe you don't want to wear this now that I slobbered all over it, but you probably need to get back to your date before she feels completely deserted by you."

"I'm not going back there. She has a room at the hotel so she's not stranded. I'm going to head back to my house." He sounds as though he wants to make sure I understand explicitly that he is not sleeping with his date tonight.

"Really, you're going to disappoint the lady?" I laugh, although I'm very relieved. I don't want him with another woman. I don't care if Dylan is with another woman, but the thought of Carson touching his date makes me feel very territorial. "Who is she?" I want to sound nonchalant, but I'm really dying to know what kind of woman attracts Carson.

"She's someone I know through my business."

"But you brought her all the way out here and then you stood her up?" I tease.

"She asked me out. She asked if I'd meet her at Mohonk because she was meeting other business colleagues there. I didn't stand her up. We were done with our dinner when Imogene's parents contacted me. So I cut the date short. She'll live," he replies. "There wasn't any chemistry going on there anyway."

"Ah," I say, trying to not sound so happy about that.

"Hey." He leans in quickly to give me a peck on the cheek. "Happy birthday, Jessica Olivia Channing."

My breath catches. He knows my full name and says it so beautifully.

"How do you know my middle name?"

There's that lopsided smile. Small, but it's there. "Archie and Gin showed me the will."

"Oh, right. Well, thanks." We look at each other for a moment. It's awkward after yelling at each other, yet the high-octane atmosphere in the truck cab is fueled by the intensity of the storm raging outside of our small, enclosed space. "I should get back to my drunk friends," I say, but I don't really want to leave and Carson doesn't acknowledge my statement. He merely runs his hand through his wet hair and continues to look at me. It's as if we're both waiting for the right words to come to us.

If being with Carson is right, then I suspect we'd have plenty to say. That sentiment along with the thought of all the grief I may have inflicted on Dylan is upsetting. I'm stupid enough to get romantically involved with Dylan and harbor a crush for his brother at the same time. I am pathetic, the type of person I wouldn't trust.

"Before you go, I have something for you." Carson reaches across me and opens the glove compartment to take out a small gift box with a bow. My mouth drops open and Carson must have mistaken my surprise for alarm. "Don't worry. It's not a ring."

"You got me a birthday present?"

"Yeah." He says this as though the drama of Dylan's diamond ring has already overshadowed any gift Carson could give me. "Open it."

I unwrap the paper and open the box. It's an old fashioned skeleton key. I turn it in my fingers. It's gold with *HERA* engraved on the side and it's attached to a delicate gold chain.

"Not so impressive after seeing Dylan's gift," Carson says.

"It's beautiful. A goddess key," I say. "Hera, wife of Zeus, goddess of marriage."

Carson looks down and I'm not sure if it's because he's uncomfortable that I make the gift sound more personal than he has intended. I try to change his discomfort as quickly as possible. "It's very cool. Where did you get this?"

"One of the estate auctions nearby. The key belonged to some local banker from a hundred years ago or so. He had these keys made for his personal use."

"Hera doesn't have a bank."

"No, it doesn't," Carson laughs. "It's a yoga studio now."

"That's funny. And this is very thoughtful."

"It's nothing special, I guess, but I thought of you when I saw it. Maybe it will bring you better luck here."

I slip the necklace over my head. "It's my favorite present." He could have given me one of his grungy hammers and it would have been my favorite present. I like Carson more than I've ever liked any man and being with him sets my insides on fire. I've known this all along. I should have been honest with Dylan from the beginning.

Carson's tense face relaxes as he gives me a one-sided shrug.

"I should let you go," I say. I'm getting really good at lying to men.

"Take my coat and use it to cover your head on the run back to the house." He hands the coat back to me.

"Thanks."

"Was Dylan really your first boyfriend?" he blurts out. "Lauren said that in there."

"I dated some dweebs and jerks in college, but, yes, Dylan was the first really nice guy I would call a boyfriend," I say. I know he's fishing. What Lauren implied correctly was that Dylan was the first guy I've slept with and Carson is really asking me about that; however, considering we're connected by his brother in a very awkward way, he doesn't pry further.

"Do you still have feelings for Dylan?"

I'm about to open the door, but I pause.

"Carson, I never felt for Dylan what he felt for me. After what you told me tonight, I don't even know if Dylan's feelings were authentic. I'm really confused about all of this."

"I get that, but Dylan's feelings aside. Were you ever in love with him at any point?" He's already asked me that, but this time he adds *"ever",* as if to clarify for himself.

I shake my head slowly. "No."

Carson doesn't say anything. I lift his coat to cover my head. "Fifty million," I whisper to myself and Carson chuckles.

"This is Armani," I say, looking above my head at the label.

"So? It's a suit, who cares?"

"We'll have to take this to the dry cleaners. And what about the ring? I forgot to give it to you."

"I can't deal with the ring right now. I'll get it later."

"I saw the receipt. Carson, he spent thirty thousand on that ring. I can't let it sit around with the Domino Sugar and the Jif."

"Damn, Dylan," he says. "Put it in one of the upstairs closets and I'll come by to pick it up in a few days. Will that work?"

"Sure," I say, but I'm already on to another thought that strikes me.

"What's wrong?"

"He spent thirty thousand on that ring and that's right after I got a check from my art dealer for close to the same amount. Do you think that means something?"

"You think it has something to do with Dylan's idea of self-worth and the need to give you something comparable to what you just earned? Could be, but even that's a little convoluted for Dylan. Numbers are your thing, remember?" He laughs lightly.

"That's true." I drape the coat over my head.

"Be careful on the path. I don't want you to fall. Can I walk you back to the house?"

"No. I'll be fine." I hesitate. "What's your middle name?"

"Phineas," he says with a slight eye roll.

"You must have been loved dearly to receive such a beautiful, impressive set of names. Goodbye, Carson Phineas Blackard." I open the door fast and jump out. Right before the door closes, though, I think I hear Carson say, *"I'll see you soon, Jessica."*

Twenty-Three

The power comes back on late in the morning and, with the exception of a few small tree limbs and branches sprinkled around the yard, we've survived. Even my new fridge spared the food from spoilage and Imogene is able to fry up eggs and bacon for breakfast. We all have headaches so we guzzle glasses of water and wear sunglasses as it turns into another hot and humid day.

Carson calls to tell me that he'll clean up the storm debris when he comes by for the ring. When I hang up all I can think about is the next time I will be able to see Carson. Regardless of Carson's demand that I not see his brother, I do have a responsibility to see Dylan, even though I dread it.

I think back on my behavior with Dylan—the school-girl giggles, the lust and sex—never once did I think that it would come to this. I don't want to believe that I was very cavalier with Dylan. Yet it's true. It all went to my head. I was finally old enough and pretty enough to catch the hot guy. I wanted a boyfriend like Dylan, but I got more than a casual fling you can drop when it gets boring.

I hate that I became one of those selfish women I hate seeing with nice guys. They take them for granted. Even if Dylan's depression played the biggest role, I, too, had a starring role in this disaster.

"I wish you guys weren't going to work today," I say as Imogene washes dishes and Lauren reads on her tablet.

"Are you lonely here by yourself?" Lauren asks.

"Yes. Bert doesn't talk much and he certainly doesn't know how to have a proper cocktail hour." I pout.

Imogene pulls the rubber gloves off her hands and joins us at the table. "Do you miss Dylan or is it just having a boyfriend around that you miss?"

"I miss being with someone, but I don't want to be back in that situation."

"Of course not," Imogene agrees. "Even if you weren't in love with the guy, Dylan is pretty terrific. You had a live-in stud. But Dylan needs to do what's best for him right now. We've all known he's bipolar, but Carson is the person who manages him when he won't or can't manage himself. So now it's time for Dylan to help Dylan."

"Bipolar," I repeat. "So you all have known this?"

"For years," Lauren says. "At least since Dylan was a teenager. It's not anything new. A lot of people are bipolar."

"Why didn't you tell me?"

"It wasn't our place," Imogene answers. "Dylan should have told you. He did, right?"

"Carson told me Dylan had issues. I didn't know the full extent of his problems and Dylan didn't say anything until after Carson told me. By then, Dylan was in a full-blown obsession with me or really our relationship. I was in the dating stage and Dylan was way ahead of me planning our wedding."

"Unfortunately, that's part of Dylan's problem and you got dragged into it before you knew what was going on," Lauren says, but there's an edge of annoyance to her voice and I suspect she's irritated with me for some reason.

"I wanted to end my virgin status. I didn't want it to blow up in my face."

"Listen to you," Lauren snaps at me. "Is this really about you? Our dear friend, Dylan, is falling apart and you're still blubbering on about yourself. I'm going to say this once. You are so fucking lucky. I know you're smart and you've worked hard, but you also got the lucky gene. We all pray for the lucky gene while most of us never get it. You got it. You're smart, you're pretty and you got Dylan. Even if it was short lived, you got a great guy. I'm sorry he's out of the picture now. It's for the best, but still."

My humiliation is obvious; I sense my face reddening.

"Lauren," Imogene scolds.

"Jess, I like you a lot, but I've only known you for a few months. Dylan has been my friend my whole life. He's had a history of wild behavior and a trail of women, but he's a good person. At least you lost your virginity to a nice guy who cares about you and not some lame geek you dug out of the library stacks."

Imogene and I look at one another and burst out laughing.

"Fair enough," I say.

"It's amazing that you didn't fall in love with Dylan," Imogene says. "Usually it's the inexperienced girls that fall really hard for the first hunk, but you're so..."

"Pragmatic," I tack on. "It's our family motto. Why fall hopelessly in love when you can be practical?"

"Ew. Really?" Imogene asks. "My parents have been working side-by-side in that diner forever and they argue over dinner orders or ketchup, but they are real romantics at heart. My dad still can't keep his hands off my mom. Sometimes it's like living with lovey-dovey teenagers."

"That's nice." I picture my parents, content with their rigid routine of work, eating at the same restaurants and going to the same benefits where they can be seen by people they call friends, but who they secretly detest. "My parents are not affectionate people and they pushed me into the early college program, assuming I'd skip over all the pesky puberty and dating business. They got their wish. Almost. I think they would have preferred if I was a eunuch so they'd never have to deal with the possibility of me having a boyfriend or worse, a husband."

"Nonsense." Imogene laughs. "Be grateful they made sure you got the education you received. Your accomplishments are remarkable."

"But it's lonely always being the youngest person in the dorms, in my classes, in my office. Even here, everyone treats me like a naïve school girl."

"No, we don't. We don't think of you like that," Lauren says.

"Well, maybe a little," Imogene adds.

"Carson always lectures me."

"That's how Carson is," Lauren says. "Do you know how many times he's lectured Imogene to quit smoking?"

"Hey, I haven't seen you smoking lately," I note.

"I quit. And I'm fucking irritable. Can't you tell?"

"No, you're doing great. Did you do it cold turkey?" I ask.

"Yes."

"Tell her why," Lauren says.

I look back at Imogene who rolls her eyes up to the ceiling and lets out a dramatic sigh. "I happen to like someone who has asthma. Wouldn't ya know?"

Lauren giggles. "It's perfect. She has to quit smoking because Jeremy is asthmatic. He told Imogene when she offered him a smoke. He actually said his future family will live in a non-smoking environment." Lauren is beside herself with laughter.

"It wasn't that funny," Imogene says. "I was trying to break the ice, get the conversation going, and we were outside a pool hall. Everyone smokes there, but not the one guy I'm interested in."

"Who's Jeremy?" I ask, excited to hear about someone else's dating woes.

"The new guy at Blackard Designs," Lauren answers.

"I met him. Dylan introduced me to him," I say. "Really, you're into this guy? Like seriously enough that you'll quit smoking?"

Imogene glares at me. "He better be worth it. I gave up two packs a day for this guy, but the upside is that now I can afford to buy new shoes."

"The upside is now you can breathe," I say. "Have you gone out?"

"Oh, no, she hasn't even gotten that far. Miss big mouth over here, who tells the rest of us how to date, can't get up the nerve to ask him out, so she's hoping she'll bump into him again and then the magic will really happen."

Imogene shrugs. "What can I say? I'm a little shy around guys I'm attracted to."

"It sounds very promising," I add.

"What about you, Jess. Are you going to talk to Dylan? Mend things? I don't mean get back together, but find a way to speak to each other like friends?"

"Carson would rather I stay away from Dylan right now."

"We all heard what Carson said to you, but Carson's no expert. I think it's pretty nasty for him to say you need to be cut off from Dylan. Dylan isn't a leper and maybe a come-to-Jesus conversation with you will help him after all. You could be the push he needs to get back into treatment." Imogene sounds so sure of herself. "Dylan really likes you and he's had time to calm down since he's been back at Leo's place. He's rational again. Isn't that the time to talk him?"

"I don't know. I trust Carson on this," I answer. "I don't want to make things worse again." I'm afraid to see Dylan. That's what I can't admit. Afraid because I don't love him and it makes me feel like an awful person; the one who should be persecuted. I have no doubt that I would have been the first woman burned at the Salem witch trials if I had been born during that era.

237

"Enough about these men," Lauren says. "I'll never get Leo to speak to me, Imogene will never ask Jeremy out, Dylan won't face reality and Carson and Jess will dance around each other, avoiding the obvious forever, so let's move on to another topic like our jewelry business."

"What about Carson and me?" I ask, bolting upright in my chair.

"Lauren thinks she has a sixth sense for these things. She thinks you and Carson are really better suited for one another and that's why he antagonizes you," Imogene says. "I don't know. I can't think straight since I quit smoking, but you know the old saying about boys who tease girls they secretly like."

"For the boss of his own company, who doesn't need to do the actual labor any more, Carson sure spends a lot of time over here," Lauren says.

"He was hired by Aunt Virginia," I say.

"Carson has a crew for his contracting business, Jess. They go out and do the house renovations. I'm not talking about his employees at Blackard Designs. Those guys make the furniture. I'm talking about Carson's high-end carpentry and renovation work he does in private homes. He has a huge crew for that. He has two very successful businesses and he doesn't pick up a saw or a hammer, but he's over here every other day repairing or building things. He's here because of you." Lauren nods her head after her solid closing argument. "I saw that sweet little necklace he gave you. Is that the key to his heart?"

"Key to his heart?" Imogene barks with laughter. "Okay, it sounds lame, but Lauren, you may be on to something."

I look down at the necklace that I slept in. I fiddle with the key, hoping it is a way to Carson. It seems inappropriate for me to comment about Carson and the attraction I have felt for him since I was sleeping with his brother. The whole idea of telling them sounds crude, so I avoid Lauren's remark entirely.

"Tell me about your jewelry business," I say.

Imogene and Lauren look at one another, debating whether to let me change the topic or not.

We spend the next hour, before they have to leave for their shifts at the diner, discussing re-purposed vintage necklaces. Imogene and Lauren have been making necklaces, bracelets and earrings from pieces of vintage jewelry they buy at estate sales or as lots on auction sites. They take the old jewelry apart if it is damaged or has missing pieces and then they use the undamaged components in their own creations. Their pieces are quite elaborate and require a lot of labor, yet they enjoy the work and doing it together. Their online presence in a community store for artists brings in good sales, but they want to expand with their own website and figure out how to make it a full-time career, so they can stop waitressing.

It's exciting to hear them talk about it and they promise to bring their jewelry cases over next time for show and tell. They want to get professional photos of their work and would like me to help them create their website. When people hear that

I'm good with computer coding and design they seem to think I have some kind of supernatural abilities. If that were true, I wouldn't feel so alone.

Losing track of time is easy when you don't have to be anywhere. My office, my home and my studio all blur together. I spend more time painting, staying in my pajamas, working on 5 Alpha projects before going to the studio. I eat at odd hours. Apples are easy to eat any time and in any room.

It's easy to wallow in self-pity and loneliness, it's also unattractive. Hair goes unwashed, showers get skipped, clothes get over-worn and even man's best friend starts to get turned off.

Bert stops sleeping on my bed and moves to the floor when my moping becomes the overbearing third person in the room. His dog sense tells him that his master needs to get her act together.

Lauren and Imogene are often at the diner or working on their jewelry business out of Bonnie's home's basement. I look forward to when they make time to see me, like a kid waiting for their parents to take them to the circus.

It's the end of August and I'm wearing a flannel, granny nightgown because it's the last clean sleeping garment available. I'm sitting in the bay window of the library, eating a bowl of dry Cheerios because I ran out of milk three days ago. My thick hair has grown longer and it's flat with grease build-up. I tuck it behind my ears and munch on my cereal when Carson's big, black truck pulls up in front of the house and he and Leo get out. They inspect the large tree closest to the house and the branches on the ground that were brought down by the storm. Carson looks up at the library window and sees me. I wave my spoon and continue eating.

A few minutes later, the slamming door and his boots pounding on the stairs makes me think I'm reliving some kind of bad school play. I expect to see the star football player-slash-theater major barrel onto the set with his overeager entrance.

Carson swaggers into the library and I think, *Here's Carson!*

He takes in my flannel nightgown and fuzzy footies. It's only ninety degrees outside. "What has happened to you?"

"I've been busy with work," I mumble through a mouth full of cereal.

He continues to look at my unkempt hair, the paint under my long fingernails and my miserable meal.

"No time to get my hair and nails done. Big project at work and I have all those paintings that I need to finish," I go on.

"Uh-huh," he says. "When was the last time you left the house?"

"I take Bert out every day."

"You mean you open the door everyday so Bert can go out."

I shrug and continue to eat my dry, tasteless food. I'm not even swayed by the fact that Carson is freshly showered and I can smell his scented deodorant along with a whiff of the shampoo from his wet hair. He takes my cereal bowl from me and puts it on the windowsill. Then he walks me upstairs to my bathroom.

"Shower," he demands. "Put on clean clothes and meet me downstairs when you're done." He leaves and I hear him jog back down the stairs.

I decide to use Aunt Ginnie's master bath instead because I've never used the enormous claw tub in there. I fill it with her herbal-scented bubble bath and then discover a long rubber tube with a showerhead that screws onto the faucet so you can wash your hair while taking a bath. Either that or it's to give yourself an enema.

When I sink into the hot water, I slip down far enough to realize that the tub could easily hold two people comfortably. Why did I always rush through showers when I could have taken a long, hot bath and soaked as long as I want? I have no place to be.

I take my time, shaving my legs, deep conditioning my hair and trying out one of my aunt's mud masks. It's a very slow process to wake up all of my senses, but after a half hour in the tub, I feel like I'm coming back to earth.

My hair takes a while to dry with the low wattage hair dryer, so I swing my head upside down to help hurry it along. Then I slather on body oil that smells like roses and makes my skin baby smooth. Then I dab on one of her perfumes and find a simple cream-colored cotton sheath dress in her closet to wear.

My aunt left behind a lot of little luxuries I never noticed in her room when Lois and Eleanor helped me clean out her closets. Her friends obviously saved some of the special toiletries and clothing for me, and it's a treat to discover everything I missed up until this point. I imagine my aunt getting ready for a date, going through the same rituals with the same products I've used. She was very beautiful and I suspect she had admirers and lovers even in old age.

Before I leave Aunt Ginnie's bedroom, I take the jeweler's bag from the closet shelf. I haven't looked at the ring since the night Imogene found it. I kept it in the bag with the receipt and shoved it in the back of the closet. *As if that would stop me from thinking about it*, I laugh.

I pad barefoot back out to the porch to watch Carson and Leo haul the rest of the yard debris onto the truck bed. I lean against the porch railing and watch them lift the heavy broken limbs. Carson glances at me only briefly, before giving his full attention to the yard work.

The sun beats down on them as they haul the heavy branches over their heads with loud grunts and a final ARGH as they dump it on a flatbed hooked up to Carson's truck. They use cables to secure the large limbs from rolling and then take a break from their hard work. Carson wipes his sweaty brow with the bottom of his t-shirt and slugs back a full bottle of water.

I wonder if some of this Paul Bunyan activity is for my benefit.

When the yard is cleared and the truck is loaded, Leo takes out his cell phone to make a call. He sits half in and half out of the cab of the truck talking to someone. *What Lauren wouldn't give to see this*, I think.

Carson makes his way over to the porch and eyes me with suspicion. I am groomed and dressed, nothing like the zombie he encountered earlier.

"Feel better?" he asks, stepping up on the porch.

"I wasn't sick. Seventy million," I whisper.

"You do that around me a lot." His shirt is soaked with perspiration and his face has droplets that I'm tempted to touch.

"I'm sure I've done it around many people, but they were polite enough not to mention it. I know Dylan caught me at it."

"Do you only do it around guys you're interested in then?"

"Hah! I don't think that's how it works," I tell him.

"I do. I think it's a nervous tic that happens when you're with—"

"Why are you here?" I cut him off.

"What do you mean? I told you I'd come clean the storm debris."

"No, I mean in general. You have a contracting crew that does all this work. I know that because Lauren told me you never handle the work at a client's home."

"Gin was more than a client. She was a friend, like a second mother."

"She's not here. I am. And you've been coming to my house for months doing an awful lot of work when you could have had your men handle it."

"They're working up at the Peterson house and the Tuturro place. I need them on those big projects. Is there a problem with me being here?"

"No," I answer. We look at each other quietly for a moment and then he looks at the pretty little gift bag in my hand. "The ring." I hold it up for him. "Take it with you."

"It doesn't feel right, but I will. I'll give it to Dylan."

"Thank you."

He takes the bag and his calloused fingers brush against mine. The sensation of his rough skin against mine sends a firestorm of lascivious signals screaming through my body. Carson lets his fingers linger and at one point we're both holding the ring bag.

"I like being around you," he finally says. "That's why I'm here."

I consider his words for a moment, trembling with joy that he would say that, however, I'm realistic enough to know that I had already made my choice when I slept with Dylan. I sabotaged this from the beginning. To think I could then move on to the next brother and start over sounds incestuous and ugly. I don't want to be a woman who does that.

He looks frustrated by my unresponsiveness to his confession while he stands there a bit longer, waiting for me to acknowledge him.

"I have an errand to run, so I have to get back inside, but thanks for doing this and tell Dylan... well..."

Carson regards me with disappointment.

"Never mind." I head back into the house so I don't have to see Carson's confused, handsome face.

Twenty-Four

As the yoga class ends, I'm doing one last stretch when I see Dylan look through the front window, directly at me. His face is expressionless. It's similar to viewing someone who has the same disease as me, the loss of will to move on quickly and the ability to flounder in one's own world. Like me, he's lost some weight and his general spark has been diffused. I hear Lois call my name and I turn away for a moment. When I turn back to the window, Dylan is gone. Perhaps he wasn't really there to begin with and now my guilt is haunting me.

I leave Beyond The Pants and head across the street to Archie's office. We spend some time on the investment accounts and he hands me another check from the trust. There are investments that Archie was instructed to liquidate upon Aunt Virginia's death. The taxes take a huge chunk, but the remaining balance is supposed to go into a special interest-bearing account to cover house maintenance, Bert's expenses, and general needs for living in a home that's much too big for me with property that extends beyond what any single person could possibly need.

"What do you think the house is worth?" I ask Archie.

This catches him off guard and he studies me with a slight frown before responding.

"I'm not sure exactly. Comparable properties in the area have sold between six and seven figures. It would have to be appraised. Is there something you want to tell me?"

"I'm not sure I should stay in Hera." I try to think of a way to explain it without all the dramatic parts included, yet it seems impossible.

"That would be a tragedy," Archie says softly. He places his hands on the stack of papers in front of him and lets out a deep, wounded sigh. "I thought life was going well for you here. Am I mistaken?"

"It's a wonderful town. I've made some very nice friends."

"But that whole business with Dylan didn't help," Archie includes.

"You know about that?"

"This town has no secrets. That's what you get with a small place like Hera, but it's also one of the reasons to live here. Ginnie thought this would be the perfect remedy for you."

"Remedy for what?"

"Oh, let me see how Gin put it," he says, thumping his fingers. "Ah, yes. She said 'your life in New York was utterly conventional with you being one of the many Generation XYZs or whatever they're called today. They're all working long hours in jobs that make them miserable while being saddled with student loan debts in a terrible economy which only makes the recipe worse'. She wanted Hera to be a refuge, a home where you pursue art and all things grand. Nice, isn't it?"

"That's a lovely idea, but I actually have a good job. I'm kind of the exception for my age group. Plus, I went to school on an academic scholarship and my parents helped cover whatever else I needed, so I'm not buried in debt. I had a few lousy jobs during school, but I'm not one those college grads who can really say I'm struggling."

"Point well taken. How about this then? Gin wanted to give you something wonderful. It's certainly your right to sell the property and you could put a tidy sum of money in your savings, but would you really be happier?"

"It's not about happiness. It's about getting out before I cause more damage."

"I see you have a talent for the dramatic flair like your aunt. Let me stop you before you go any further with your creative storytelling. I have an idea I think might appeal to you."

"You're a crafty one, aren't you?" I tease him. "I'm listening, Bixby. Tell me what you've got."

The idea of grilling pizzas like they do in restaurants sounded like a good idea, but we burn three crusts until they are nothing other than charred, black discs. Imogene and Lauren launch them like Frisbees across the yard. Upon the failure of our brilliant plan, we decide to take our unused pizza toppings and make an antipasto plate along with a pot of linguine swimming in olive oil, garlic and herbs. We feast in the dining room and open a nice bottle of red wine that Lauren brings up from the cellar for our special celebratory occasion.

After Archie told me his idea, I couldn't wait to share it with Imogene and Lauren. I don't know why I didn't think of it earlier. Having them in the house instantly lifts my spirits as we gorge ourselves on our rich cuisine. We're reaching for a toast when the front door slams open and Imogene plunks herself back down in her chair.

"Not again," she says.

Carson and his angry testosterone army of one comes whirling through the living room and pushes a dining chair aside to lunge across the table at me. His fists are on the table and his face is inches from mine. "So you're going to run like a coward?" he shouts at me.

I'm frozen, holding my glass of wine as my mouth remains hanging open.

"What the hell are you doing, Carson?" Imogene yells back. She stands and yanks him away from the table. "Where do you get off storming in here in your goddamn muddy boots, yelling at Jess in her own home?"

"Archie said you're thinking of moving back to the city." Carson points a finger at me. He's really good at dramatic entrances and he never hides his anger. This makes the night he wrestled Dylan to the ground look pretty tame.

"Get your finger out of her face and calm down," Lauren interjects.

He puts his hands on his hips and leans forward like he's getting ready to smash the table, the only barrier protecting me from him. I put my wine glass down and walk around the table to meet him. "We can discuss this outside so my friends can enjoy their meal," I tell him. "Let's go."

"But I want to hear what's going on," Lauren whines as Carson follows me out to the porch.

"First of all, don't ever talk that way to me in front of my friends." I am terse, though not shouting. "Second, stop walking into my house whenever you feel like it. You don't see me storming into your home, ever. Third, you don't know the full story, and even if you did, you have no right to judge what I do with my life."

"So you're moving back? You're selling everything Gin worked so hard to give you, just like that? You're going to take the money and run?" He looms over me, but speaks in a much more measured tone.

"Archie didn't tell you that." My fingers nervously fiddle with the key necklace Carson gave me. He glances at the necklace and then back at my face.

"Not in so many words. He said you inquired about selling the property and that you have reservations about living here. Why? Because of Dylan? Or is this place too boring for you?"

"No and no. I am a little worried about how I'm going to talk to Dylan and for a while there I did tinker with the idea of moving back to the city. There were a few weeks where I thought this place was a bad idea and that I had really screwed up. I hurt Dylan and I've never felt responsible for someone else. No matter what you told me, I did think that I had some serious part in his breakdown or whatever it was. Being here, alone in this house, became pretty oppressive. I didn't know what to do. That's why I went to talk to Archie about selling the house."

"But you're not?" he asks and I think I see something that resembles hope in his eyes.

"Why do you care so much about what I do, Carson?" My voice cracks as I ask it. "You're really good at showing up and giving me a piece of your mind."

"You think I'm an asshole, don't you?"

"No. I have never thought that about you, but I'm not Dylan. You can't force your way in and tell me what to do. I can't stand your lectures."

"That's understandable," he says.

"So why do you care so much about what I do? Is it the house? Are you afraid of losing a pleasant part of your childhood? At least, I assume the time here with Aunt Virginia was a nice time."

Carson smiles a little. "I love how you analyze and try to get in other peoples' heads like a shrink, but sometimes you miss the bigger picture, Jess."

"Then what's the big picture? What's lit a fire under your ass?"

He's quiet for a moment and we stare at each other. Yelling or not, his beauty upends my reserve. He cranks my anxiety dial up to the maximum and the excitement of being near him draws me in.

"It's you. I don't want you to leave." Carson says it more as a demand and my stupid insides swoon a little bit. "I told you I like coming around here to see you. I meant it."

Every thought and image I have of Carson, from the first day I saw him in Archie's office scowling to this moment, plays like a montage in my head. The nerves in my body swirl with elation and I want him to hold me close like he did that night on Barron's Creek, yet the woman in me says

I'm rushing into something blindly again. Dylan is no longer in the picture; however, it would be vulgar for me to throw myself at his brother while Dylan is in the midst of working out his issues. I'm not supposed to be going near Dylan or talking to him, but I'm pretty sure I shouldn't be doing anything with Carson, either. Anything that gives off a romantic vibe has got to be off limits.

I maintain my composure and give away nothing. "I'm not leaving. In fact, Imogene and Lauren are moving in. They need to get out of their parents' homes so they're going to pay rent while also setting up their jewelry business upstairs in the old playroom, since I never use it. It was Archie's idea and I think it's a pretty great one. We were celebrating our new living arrangements when you came in and blew a gasket."

"I'm not like Dylan. I don't fly off in unexplained rages," he defends. "Okay, I admit I can yell, but that in there was me being mad. Nothing more. I don't hold it in when I'm pissed off. I say something." Carson's fear of being compared to his brother is unnecessary. After knowing him for several months, I would never consider them to be alike in any way.

I smile. "You do *mad* really, really well."

"It gets old," he confesses. "I spend too much time trying to control things, trying to contain Dylan."

I lean against the porch railing and Carson walks closer, perching himself next to me.

A confidence soars in me. I am more like my true self when I'm with Carson than I ever was with Dylan, who took attentiveness to a painstaking level. Dylan couldn't wrap his head around my art and my need to paint at any given hour of the day or night.

It's exciting being near Carson and I know he has made a point of figuring out my likes and dislikes with a genuine interest in what makes me tick. I am deeply moved by his declaration of *I don't want you to leave.* He may not be interested in me beyond a simple affection, but I matter to him and that's something significant to my weak ego. Yet I also want to be more realistic about men in general, right down to reading the signals correctly and owning up to my poor decisions.

"You know, at some point I will need to talk to Dylan. I owe it to him and to myself. We can't live in the same town and pretend we're strangers." I study Carson's face for any sign of jealousy, but of course, there is none. I suppose he's not that kind of guy and I'm not the kind of girl he'd feel that way about.

"Do you think you still have feelings for him?" he asks in a very clinical, non-emotional way.

"No. I told you no. I'm concerned about him, though."

"You should see him, but not now. There will be a better opportunity when the time is right, to clear the air. Dylan is going to get better. He'll be fine."

Carson picks up my hand and looks at it while holding it gently in his own. "You're wearing the necklace."

I nod.

"Would you come see my house?" His steely eyes are serious as he waits for my reply.

"Ninety million," I whisper.

Carson chuckles. "Am I making you nervous?"

Yes, and if you keeping holding my hand and caressing my palm, my body is going to shatter.

"Maybe. This doesn't seem like a good idea. I haven't seen Dylan in over a month and I should probably talk to him before I see your house," I say and then realize how idiotic that sounds.

"You want to ask Dylan for permission to see my house?" Carson laughs.

"No, of course not. That's not what I meant."

"I'm joking. I know what you meant. You don't want him to see you with me. You're afraid he still has feelings for you, no matter how irrational they may be. Like I said, Dylan will be fine."

"How do you know? Before today, you were pretty sure I needed to stay away from Dylan. Now, you think he'll be fine. You seem awfully sure about all of this."

"We've already looked into a residential treatment program and it looks like a good fit for Dylan."

"Dylan is agreeing to this?" I ask. I'm both amazed and ticked off that Carson didn't tell me this sooner. "Carson, this is the news you were supposed to lead with when you came crashing through my door."

"So, now will you come over to my house?"

Twenty-Five

I drive up the solitary road that narrows with trees arching over the dirt road like a secret entrance. It's September and the autumn colors are beginning to take over the closer I get to Carson's home. I navigate my car through the heavily wooded patch of red and yellow trees before I burst upon a scene of unbelievable beauty.

With the trees behind me I am overlooking the valley, the same view I have from my home, but I'm more elevated up here, therefore, everything appears more majestic and vast. In the middle of it all, before the drop down to the valley, is a lone house.

Carson's home.

It's a contemporary design with straight lines and glass, but instead of looking grotesquely modern like an "office building" type structure, it has organic qualities of wood and shades of neutral tones that give it an earthy appearance. It's huge, bigger than my Victorian house.

I park near his detached garage, which is a low structure covered by a green screen of living plants. As I get out of the car to view my surroundings, Carson steps out of the house and walks towards me with a casual gait. No tool belt hanging on his hips and no muddy boots. He's barefoot, in jeans and a white T-shirt.

"Hi," he greets, smiling. His intentions are clear. He wants to be with me and I have every inch of desire in my body and brain pushing me towards him. The way he looks at me is all I need to feel wonderful and special.

We're surrounded by clean, crisp, cool air and it makes the mood incredibly promising. It's just us with no pretext of doing anything else. I'm here to see him and he looks happy. I don't know what to make of this homebody. I've only known the work-driven, hard-edged Carson who's usually covered in saw dust or dressed for an unwanted occasion. This is the most relaxed I have ever seen him and it causes me to smile in return.

"I'm really glad you're here." He puts a hand on my back and guides me towards the house.

"I had to see the house that is forbidden to all of Carson's dates."

"That sounds like something Imogene and Lauren cooked up." He leads me through the front door. The first thing that strikes me is the thirty-foot high ceilings, the polished concrete floors and the floor-to-ceiling windows.

"This is amazing," I say with my head swiveling around.

"Thank you. I know most people think it looks too stark, kind of bleak, but it's really very comfortable. I wanted a casual place. I don't have a lot of possessions, but everything is made for comfort, not show."

It's so Carson. There's no clutter, no nick-knacks. Everything has a purpose. Two leather couches and Blackard chairs grace the living room that opens into a dining area with a massive

Blackard dining table and chair set. The dining room wall is one of those retractable windows like you see at a gas station. There are a few area rugs, some exceptional works of art on the walls and a wood-burning fireplace that comes down in the middle of the living room. It's simple, tasteful and very masculine.

"It looks very comfortable," I agree. "So have you brought a lot of your dates here?"

"Why do keep bringing up my dating life?" Carson looks flustered by where I'm going with this.

"You implied that Imogene and Lauren were making up stories. They said you've never brought women here, meaning the women you were or are dating. Is it true?"

Carson smiles. "You're here."

"You're not dating me. Then there are Lauren and Imogene, they've seen this house and you're not dating them, either."

"I've never brought a date here," he admits. "It's true. You're the first." He's smiling when he says this.

"Mmm, I suppose this is a date," I say as I walk around the fireplace to the dining area. I stop and pause, staring at one particular framed painting. It's positioned on a narrow wall between two large windows, a special exhibition space, a place where guests have to pass by it on their way to the dining area so they will notice this piece.

It's my painting, one of the originals I gave to Tom's gallery last year. It's a dark image of a man in a grubby suit and hat grasping a bottle of whiskey, shuffling through Bryant Park with his head hung low, surrounded by neon explosions of splattered paint and dancing girls.

"That's one of my favorites," Carson says from behind me.

"Did you buy my painting at Tom's gallery or did Ginnie buy it and give it to you?"

"I bought it. I was visiting one of our stores and stopped in at the gallery."

I'm still staring at my painting. "This was one of the first pieces that sold. I remember Tom calling me."

"'*Searching for Hope*," Carson says.

It dawns on me that he's telling me the title of my own painting.

"That's right. It's '*Searching for Hope*, but I thought it sold with two other pieces."

"It did. I purchased those, too."

I turn around and stare at him in disbelief. He's full of surprises and I want to kiss him. Not a thank you kiss, but a full on, passionate I'm-crazy-about-you kiss.

"You don't believe me?" he asks. "Let's finish the tour and you'll see the other paintings."

"I believe you. I'm surprised, that's all. Dylan thinks my paintings are strange."

"Consider the source." Carson reaches out and brushes a lock of my long hair back, his hand resting lightly on my shoulder as though he's contemplating what to do next. "I like strange. I like different. I like intelligent, beautiful, smart-alecky and funny. I like it all."

I presume he's describing me, yet I'm so muddled with opposing thoughts that suddenly the autumn chill forces me to pull my baby-doll cardigan across my chest. The thin material does nothing to warm me or hide the fact that I am nervous, though.

Carson doesn't miss a beat on reading my anxiety. He moves his hand back to my shoulder blade and propels me through the kitchen, highlighting every component that is made of recycled or sustainable materials. Sleek, modern appliances, bare counters and more poured concrete flooring.

"The house is so modern, but it's rustic at the same time. It's really you," I say.

"I hired a good design team. A friend of mine does this. He knows me well, so I didn't have to tell him to avoid anything with flowers and patterns."

"The kitchen is immaculate. Do you even eat meals here?"

Carson laughs. "I can't cook like Dylan, but I make a mean peanut butter and jelly sandwich and sloppy Joes. Mostly, though, I depend on my housekeeper to take care of everything."

"You have a housekeeper? I don't know any guys your age who have a maid. Unless they're rich, I suppose, like my boss, Nathan." I chuckle at the image of a housekeeper bossing Carson around in his own home.

"Is she a stout, little, old, gray-haired woman who makes her own bread and cleans everything with white vinegar?"

"No, she's fairly young and strong. She's Polish and blond. Her name is Talia. She's here three times a week, cleans, does the laundry and leaves me dinners in the fridge. She's great. And, yes, I can afford her."

I hate her.

"You should hire her."

First he's telling me how awesome this young woman is and then he's suggesting I hire her? "You think I'm a slob?"

"No, not at all, but you inherited a very big house and you have to admit you have some dust going on there. Gin's housecleaner moved away a few months ago and she was going to hire Talia, but things happened. Gin died and I got caught up in finishing the work around the house; I forgot to mention the housecleaner to you."

"I can't afford her anyway." I sound a little miffed, not about hiring a maid, but about this fabulous woman in Carson's home.

"Yes, you can. Gin included it in the house maintenance money going into the checking account every month. You haven't really used that account have you?"

"Archie has been going over the accounts with me."

"Yeah, but you haven't used the checking account Gin provided."

"I've been using my own. I have enough money and I am using some of the money that came from the checks Archie gave me when some assets were liquidated. Besides, my paintings are selling, in case you didn't hear."

"Don't do that. Save your money and use the money Gin left you. You're making it harder on yourself."

"How do you know so much about Ginnie's accounts?"

"She trusted me. She had me sit in on the meetings with her and Archie when she was deciding how to set everything up for you. Let me talk to Talia about coming to your house at least once a week. Cleaning only. You can trust her and you can concentrate on your job and your painting. That's why I'm suggesting her. You can focus on work instead of managing that big house. I need her to do so much here because I work long hours at the shop and, honestly, I hate doing laundry and house cleaning."

"Well, Carson, who doesn't?" I lean against the cool concrete counter and admire the spectacular view of fall foliage behind him.

"The view is something, isn't it?" He grins. "You have to see the rest."

He nudges me and I follow him back to the hallway where we head up a suspension staircase with wires and clear glass panels so no views are obstructed. The second floor is really an extension of the first level with an open hallway that overlooks the living room, four bedrooms and a sun filled room that Carson calls the office, although it's practically bare.

I walk right up to my painting, "*Laundry*", a scene of neighborhood residents at the local Laundromat and all the activities that go on while they wait for their clothes to wash and tumble dry. The clothes are emblazoned in more neon splatters, including some underwear with a super hero logo. All the people in the painting are drawn in black ink down to the tiniest detail. I smile nervously revisiting that one.

"You don't really work here." I look at the Blackard desk and chair set with a lamp made out of some vintage mechanical equipment. Except for a few papers on the desk and a stack of books, the room is bare. One wall is another retractable window that opens the whole wall onto a large terrace. The terrace has bamboo flooring and glass panels as well as a set of chairs outside. The scenic view of the valley with its palette of red, orange and yellow colors is lovely and uplifting. "If I lived here I would drink my coffee out here every morning and my easel and paints would be all over this room," I ramble it off so quickly before I realize that I have embarrassed myself.

Carson's smile is kind. He regards me with a thoughtful expression and my instincts tell me that he'd like to say something, but for now he'll keep it to himself.

"Yeah. I should use this room more often."

I shrug and walk past him to look at the bedrooms. There are no feminine touches anywhere. It's minimalism to the extreme; however, the rustic wood tones of the Blackard furniture and a few area rugs make the rooms warm and inviting. Carson also has some very fine paintings and sculptures displayed so they stand out. He walks quietly behind me, listening to my compliments. I start to wonder if everyone says the same things when they tour his house and if he is bored with the same reactions.

I'm not paying attention when I walk into the last room and take notice that it's Carson's personal space, the master bedroom. The first thing I notice, other than one of his T-shirts tossed on the rumpled bed—*Talia must not have cleaned today*—is my other painting, my self-portrait titled, *"Girl"*. I painted it when I turned nineteen.

The *girl's* hair is a fire engine-red, the eyes, a little sad, are an unnatural brown with gold bolts, like lightening. The mouth is questionable; it's hard to tell if the girl is about to smile or closer to crying. It was one of those pieces I almost didn't let Tom have, but he insisted. And now it's in Carson's possession. In his bedroom, three feet from his bed.

"In case you weren't aware, that's supposed to be me," I say.

"I figured. That's why I bought it." He shoves his hands in his back pockets and looks perfectly at ease.

"You don't think it's kind of strange that I was seeing your brother and during that whole time you had this painting of me in your bedroom?"

Carson shakes his head slowly. "Nope."

"Well, I feel weird. Actually, I don't know how I feel. This situation is strange."

"I like strange, remember?" he says, smiling.

"Okay, now I don't know what you're talking about, I—"

"Relax. Jesus. I didn't put this up when you were dating Dylan. I bought this painting long before you moved here. Besides, I'm the one who tried to stop you from going out with Dylan, remember that part? I knew that would be a disaster."

"Dylan and I would be a disaster, or you trying to stop me, would be a disaster?"

"Both. Shit." He laughs. "You're so fucking analytical. I really do love that about you."

263

Goosebumps pop up across my lower arms, sending shivers through my whole body. I desperately want to whisper a very large number, but Carson is observing me, thoroughly.

"I guess we're done with the tour. I should go and get back to work." I'm not very convincing since my feet haven't moved an inch. I suck at first dates.

"Don't go. Not yet." He steps forward, closing the small space between us so our bodies are touching. His arms circle around my back and, although Carson looks nothing like Dylan, the familiarity of the move and what follows, send a surge of remorse through me.

"Carson, I only stopped seeing your brother a couple of months ago. This seems like a bad déjà vu."

"I'm. Not. Dylan." It's the uncompromising Carson again, the one that is intimidating and sexy at the same time. It's the one I've had a crush on since my first day in Hera when I decided to settle for a more eager and attainable Dylan.

"Why did you want me to see your house?"

"Because Imogene and Lauren were telling you the truth. I've never brought any women here that I dated. The only women who have been here are my housekeeper and friends."

"So you're trying to tell me that we're friends?" *Please don't say yes. Tell me this is really a first date.*

"Ha! No. Obviously, I'm not good at this. I'm trying to tell you that I couldn't bear it if you moved back to the city. Because... I'm in love with you."

I stare at his mouth, hanging on those words. "Uh-huh," I mumble.

"That's why I tried to talk you out of going out with Dylan and why I had it out with you a few times at your house. Those weren't my best moments. Not well-played in the least."

The heat from his body and the firm grip of his hands on my lower back makes me want to melt into his arms, to have the kiss I have imagined over and over, but it's all a little too good to be true.

"You didn't try to stop me from dating Dylan because you were in love with me. You'd only known me for like a day or two. I thought you tried to stop me and Dylan because he was in a very precarious emotional state and you knew I could be the tipping point that threw him off edge again." I pull my hands off his warm, hard chest and try to push back, but Carson doesn't loosen his grip.

"Jess, I was already in love with you then. When Gin talked about you, when I bought your paintings, I knew I was concocting a plan to be with you. That's why I didn't want my brother going out with you. Yes, he's a fuck up when it comes to relationships and I didn't want him doing that to you or himself, but I really wanted you for myself."

"That's a very good answer." My heart is racing as I relax my palms on his chest again, letting Carson come in for a crushing kiss. He pulls me in fiercely with his powerful hands and his mouth devours mine. His lips are everything I've imagined; soft and relentless. His tongue caresses my lips and sweeps around my mouth before plunging, dueling with me. My heart is beating so fast that I fear it must be audible to Carson.

"I have wanted to kiss you for three hundred and sixty days," he says between kisses. "How's that number for you?"

"I'm not sure it's accurate," I say through breathless pants.

"It's probably closer to three hundred and ninety-two days, which is when I bought your paintings."

He kisses me between my neck and collarbone. I let out a sharp breath from the electrifying sensation taking over my body.

"Stay with me. Here," Carson says, coming up for breath. "In my bed. Now."

"Uh-huh," I mumble, being reduced to the same cave man dialect as him.

Carson slips off my cardigan, then I fumble with removing my tank top and jeans as quickly as possible. He removes his shirt and I can't take my eyes away from his spectacularly muscular arms and chest. I study his scars up close, which only add to his sexiness. His legs are not sinewy like a runner's; they are thicker, more powerful, like someone who does a lot of bench squats or tosses tree trunks for fun.

I scramble backwards onto the bed with my panties and lace bra still on. Carson climbs over me, corralling me onto the middle of the bed. He is naked except for his briefs, which are bulging against me.

"Let me be perfectly clear here," he says with bated breath.

My hands are all over his body, feeling his hard muscles as I listen to him.

"We will not mention his name in this room again," he demands. "This room is about you and me. Understood?"

I nod eagerly and then a look of alarm must have passed over my face as he reaches into his nightstand and removes an entire box of condoms.

"You must be very good at this if you think we need a whole box of condoms."

Carson laughs. "It's never been opened. I hope they're not expired."

I laugh as he struggles to be suave while he tries to open the condom with one hand and then his teeth since he's still perched over me on his other hand. I grab the condom from him and open it. "Let me."

Carson's expression darkens. Without taking his eyes off me, he pulls his underwear off. I look down and, once again, my inexperience shows. I blanch at the size of his erection, but not wanting to ruin the moment, I reach for him and begin to slide the condom on. He moans as I slide my hands down between his legs and stroke him then trail my fingers slowly up his sides and back down around his firm ass. He's looking at me with unabashed lust.

He follows my hands as I slide my panties off and wriggle out of them. Then his eyes move slowly up my body as my fingers unfasten the front clasp of my bra. My breasts are already perky, waiting for him. Carson takes in one ragged breath before running his tongue across my nipples.

I open my legs and hold his cock, rubbing it against me, getting more wet with each stroke. Carson moans, yet doesn't rush me. As he sucks on my breasts and circles my nipples with his tongue, I move his hardness in small circles against me, prodding a little inside and then pulling him back. We're both losing control.

He's on my mouth again, kissing, using his other hand to pinch my hard nipples, which are straining along with my lower body that is dripping and trembling. I pull my legs up and wrap them around Carson's waist to urge him into me.

"Wait," he says, gently pushing my hand away from the appendage I'm desperate to have inside of me. "I want you to be ready for me."

"Carson, I can't get any more ready," I moan.

He begins rubbing my clit with the pad of his thumb and my eyes roll back into my head. It feels too good with him touching me. His tongue is sweeping through my mouth again and I feel his fingers go inside of me, swirling gently and then rubbing my clit over and over. I reach underneath him and stroke the soft skin under his balls.

"Ah, fuck, yes," he hisses into my ear. "I need you."

I grab his ass and arch towards him, pushing him inside of me. There's no more desire to keep it slow when he enters me in one powerful thrust. I yelp with pleasure, but then he gets control of himself and thrusts in and out at a slower pace to make it last.

"Carson," I whimper.

"I knew you'd feel like this. So good. So perfect." He struggles to talk and I like that I'm causing this.

I run my hands across all his hard lines. I can't get enough of him and it feels as if he can't push into me all the way. Either I'm too small or he's too big. He doesn't seem to notice. His eyes are half closed and it seems he can't decide whether to keep his mouth on my breasts or keep kissing me. I love that his smooth composure has collapsed and he's as frazzled as I am.

He does a grind, circle, thrust move that begins the aching momentum in me. I look up at Carson's intense face and blue eyes as I run my hands through his hair. At that point, he thrusts harder and faster, never taking his eyes off mine. I only close my eyes the moment he rubs against me in that perfect way that sets off a completely shuddering climax.

I'm still coming when I hear him utter a curse. His long thrusts slow down and then he pounds into me with deep grunts of enjoyment. When the last wave of gratification subsides, I open my eyes. Carson regards me with what I can only describe as complete satisfaction. He closes his large frame around my body and kisses me tenderly.

"I do love you," he says into my hair so I can't see his face. "But you don't have to say anything. Just think about it."

"Of course, I'm thinking about it."

His lips hover above mine, brushing against me. He pulls off the condom and wraps it in a tissue before returning to lie by my side. I turn to face him and want to tell him that I'm falling in love with him, too. That I've been crushing on him for months, however, the mood is perfect as it is.

It's late afternoon, our bodies entwined as we hold each other and offer tender kisses when it occurs to me that I missed a conference call for work.

"Oh, shoot. The team meeting. I missed it. I have to go," I say, looking around the bed for my underwear.

"No, not so fast," he says. "You already missed the meeting and we're not done here."

He pulls me back down on my right side, pinning me in place with my back set against his chest. I hear him opening a condom and rolling it on. He doesn't get any protest from me. *Yeah, I'm really dedicated to my job.*

His hand comes over my hip and he forces his fingers between my legs, rubbing and probing as he brings my senses back to the brink. His bottom hand pulls my lower hip back just as he enters me from behind. I can't move, but he manages to pull my leg over his and thrust deeply back and forth with enough strength to move both of us together. I put my arms in front of our bodies to brace myself as Carson plunges in and out of me, rocking the mattress across the platform bed.

Between his thrusts and his fingers rubbing me, I'm going wild with excitement. I push my rear end back harder to meet his driving cock, waiting for it to be my undoing. Carson's breathing becomes heavier and louder and I know he wants to come, although he is doing everything he can to make me climax first. His fingers are wet from stroking my slick center and he slides himself easily back and forth when I come. I tighten all my muscles around him as it takes me over.

"Oh damn, that feels good," Carson groans through heavy breaths as his body erupts.

I'm facing the wall and the portrait of me. I close my eyes and enjoy this moment of being in Carson's bed.

"Don't move," he commands from behind me. I hear him peel the condom off and then he gets up from the bed. He's in the bathroom and then back, hugging me.

"I really have to get home and call my boss," I say, yet my voice is as tired as I feel.

"If you're going to blow your work day—which you already did, by the way—you might as well go big," he suggests. I haven't turned around to face him, but I can hear the smile in his tone. "Take a shower with me."

I feign a small protest, but I walk into the spa shower with its three shower heads and the naked man whose presence makes me never want to leave. The man I'm pretty sure I'm in love with.

Twenty-Six

It's still light out when I leave Carson's home. He threatens to drag me back inside, but I manage to give a convincing case that work really does beckon me. Nathan has left three messages on my cell phone.

I drive down the narrow road through the woods, but I'm not worried about finding my way back home. It's still fairly light out and there's only one way in and out. The wooded drive opens onto the narrow road that eventually merges onto the larger county road. I keep my eyes on the lookout for the old, wooden bridge that crosses over a stream with at least a fifteen-foot drop. It must be a scary road to navigate if you drive too fast or it's covered in snow.

Just as I cross the bumpy little bridge I see a vehicle up ahead coming from the direction of town. As I'm about to pass it, I recognize the Blackard delivery truck with Dylan at the wheel. Our eyes lock for a moment before he turns his gaze back to the road ahead of him. Something in my gut is crawling out of me, a sickening feeling that Dylan is headed to Carson's home and he knows that I've just come from there.

Before I can put the thought of him out of my head, I hear a deafening crash. I pull to the side of the road and slam on the brakes. My car is at an angle, so I can see back far enough to the bridge where one side of the wooden rail is gone.

"Dylan," I whisper to myself.

I get out of my car and start running back to the bridge. As I get closer, I know it's Dylan's truck that went through that railing. He saw me, his eyes were glazed over with indifference. The tracks from the truck are prominent where they left the dirt road and drove onto the wooden bridge. He must have stepped on the gas and then drove right through the railing instead of straightening out his wheels.

I run to the edge of the bridge where broken beams are hanging. The Blackard truck is lying on the driver's side almost flipped over. The bile rises in my throat, but I can't scream, there's no sound in me and no one around to hear me if I could scream for help. I take my cell phone out of my cardigan pocket and call Carson.

"Get in your truck and drive to the bridge now! It's Dylan!" I shout when Carson answers.

Next I call Archie and tell him to call for emergency help because I don't know how to explain my location or the names of the crossroads. I tell Archie I'm at the bridge that enters onto Carson's property and he immediately hangs up to call others for help. I'm no help. I'm the problem, not the solution.

Maybe it's five minutes or longer, I don't know. I'm crying too hard to even see. Someone leads me out of the way when a state patrol vehicle and an ambulance arrive. I see Carson down by the crashed truck with a team of men and then, through my blurry vision, I see people in uniforms carrying a stretcher up the gully to the waiting ambulance. I can't see his face, but I know it's Dylan strapped to the board, his body motionless. I don't know if he's alive.

I drop my head in my hands. It hurts and feels heavy with visual overload. The tears stop, I'm dried up. Then I feel a gentle hand on my back. It's Archie who holds me tightly and walks my feeble body back to his car. I wait in his ancient Lincoln Town Car as he goes back to confer with Carson who looks back at Archie's car before he quickly climbs into the ambulance after his brother. The ambulance speeds off ahead of Archie's parked car, lights and sirens blaring. I watch it disappear down the road, hoping they can save Dylan.

Archie speaks to the officers for a while before returning to the car. My car is still on the side of the road, but I know I'm too shaky to drive it so I stay in Archie's.

"We'll meet Carson at the hospital," Archie says to me as he gets in and buckles up. He is very calm and, in his three-piece suit and bowtie, he's a pillar of comfort for me.

"Is Dylan alive?"

"Yes, but he's unconscious. Carson said he was mumbling something when they pried him out of the truck. That's a good sign. We're heading to St. Francis."

I nod without any idea where we're going. I look out the window to watch the trees and houses pass by as if I'm stationery and everything else is moving. Archie pats my hand, yet is silent on our journey to the emergency room.

When we arrive, I jump out and run inside to find Imogene, Lauren, Bonnie, Lois and Eleanor along with the whole Blackard staff already there. We are relegated to a waiting room since none of us are blood relatives. Only Carson is allowed inside with Dylan.

"Is it true you were with Carson?" Lauren says in an angry low voice so others can't hear.

"Yes, I was at his house. I was driving home when I saw... when I heard Dylan's truck crash."

Imogene approaches and puts an arm around me. "Carson is with him. I think Dylan will be okay. I do," she says as if she's trying to convince herself.

"Jess, everyone is saying that Dylan walked in on you and Carson... you know... and then he intentionally drove the truck into a tree or something." Lauren is visibly upset and believes I have something to do with Dylan's accident.

"That's not what happened at all. Dylan saw me in my car, not in Carson's home. Then Dylan drove the truck—or he lost control of the truck on the bridge. It went off the bridge. He didn't drive it into a tree. I called for help." I can't believe everyone already has a manufactured story to go along with the incident where I'm the villain.

"But Dylan did see you driving, coming from the direction of Carson's house?" Lauren pushes.

"Yes," I admit.

"Lauren, enough with the questions. It doesn't matter what happened. We need Dylan to be okay." Imogene is protective of me and keeps her arm firmly across my shoulders.

"But it does matter," I say softly. "How it happens, matters greatly. Was it an accident or did Dylan intend to hurt himself, or worse."

Imogene hushes me as Lauren looks warily at me and then spends the next hour while we wait cautiously avoiding me. I feel ashamed. It's an easy emotion to trap yourself into, especially if you deserve it.

While everyone is quietly waiting, drinking bad coffee and murmuring hopeful thoughts to one another, I consider what I have done to these two brothers who have depended solely on each other for the last twenty years. I think of how cavalier I was with Dylan's affections and then how I moved on to Carson, accepting his love like it's a lollipop. I've used them up and neglected to accept the consequences.

After another hour, Carson comes down the hall; his tall figure stands out among the doctors and nurses in scrubs. Everyone jumps up to meet him and hear the news. I linger in back, not really sure of my place in this close-knit group.

"Dylan is going to be fine." Carson's voice is solid, no wavering. He looks over the group at me as he talks. "It's hard to believe, but his big fat head may have saved him. He wasn't wearing the belt and took a good beating when the truck rolled down the ravine, but all he has are some superficial lacerations on his head. They're stitching him up now."

Archie asks Carson about the scans on Dylan's head. Everyone is huddled around Carson, so I miss the rest of the story, but what I keep hearing in my head is "when the truck rolled down the ravine".

I hope that means Dylan didn't attempt to drive off the bridge, which would have been a straight drop down and could have been a more fatal prospect for him. I hope Carson is going to tell us that Dylan misjudged the turning circumference on the truck and ended up with one wheel off the bridge, causing it to roll. These scenarios play out in my head, different versions with different implications, however, I can't bother Carson with this when the only thing that matters at this point is whether Dylan is alive or not.

At least thirty of the people in the waiting room are there for Dylan and they all wait their turn to hug Carson and give him some cheery words. Then he looks through the crowd again until his eyes settle on mine. He moves through the tight space towards me. Imogene gives me a little smile and pushes me towards Carson. His face breaks into a strained smile of relief before he embraces me. I hold on to him and collapse against his body.

"My brother is okay," he whispers. I look up at him. A few feet away, I see Lois and Eleanor watching us.

"When can the rest of us see him?" I ask.

"Probably not until tomorrow. They shot him up with a lot of painkillers and they'll have to do some more tests, but I'm guessing tomorrow they'll move him to a regular room."

"Good and will they let you stay here tonight with him?"

"Yeah. He'll go to ICU for tonight, but they'll let me stay as long as I stay out of the way and don't fall asleep. Apparently, you're not allowed to sleep in a hospital." Carson attempts to lighten the stressful mood and tension. I try to smile along with him, yet it's difficult to pretend that this is a normal trip to the emergency room.

"Hey," he whispers to me. "You saved him. You called for help. It would have been much worse if you hadn't been there." Carson leans over to kiss me. Our lips linger together and I can sense others watching us.

"You go be with Dylan. I'll see you tomorrow." I want to get out of here now, but I also don't want Carson to think I'm hurrying to leave.

"I will. I'm going to have Archie drive you back home. Leo told me he picked up your car. You left the keys in it, so he drove it back to your place." He hugs me tighter and kisses my cheek. "Stop worrying, Jess. This could have been worse, but it wasn't. Dylan got lucky."

I just keep nodding along because I can't put two intelligent words together.

"I'll call you in the morning," Carson says.

After Carson goes back to be with Dylan, the others have a group hug as if we all survived some terrible tragedy together. Imogene and Lauren pull me into the cathartic hug along with Lois and Eleanor. Even Leo and the other odd friends of the Blackard boys embrace me as though we're all part of a whole. It's meant to make us feel safer and we do.

Archie drives me home and I have trouble keeping up with his perky conversation because I am as gloomy as ever. In front of my house, he turns off the car engine. "This is a time to count your blessings, Jessica."

"I don't think this would have happened if Dylan hadn't seen me coming across that bridge. We still don't know for sure if Dylan did this on purpose or if it was an accident, but I inadvertently had a hand in it, and for that, I am ashamed."

Archie leans across the seat with a pinched face. "You don't know that. Let me tell you, life is always full of pain and loss. Always, but this isn't one of those times. Dylan is young and strong and he will be healthy again. Besides, now more than ever, Dylan needs all of us to help him through this dark time. You can *feel* however you want about this situation, but it's a waste of precious resources. This is no time for self-pity, my dear." His words come through loud and clear. *Get off your pity wagon.* Yet that's easier said than done.

I will not sleep well tonight.

Twenty-Seven

I'm awake when Carson calls me early the next morning from the hospital.

"Are you still shaken up?" he asks. "I didn't want to send you off with Archie, you looked so upset, but I had to be with Dylan."

"Of course, you had to be with your brother. I'm fine, Carson." My words are clipped. I'm trying to hide my anger and sadness from him.

"Visiting hours start at eleven. I asked Lois to bring you then and everyone else will come later in the day so we don't overwhelm Dylan with too many visitors," he explains.

It appears that he's managing Dylan's life and mine, too. I could drive myself to the hospital, but apparently he thinks he needs to organize my day. I'm getting angrier and angrier thinking about this. I want to ask him why he watched my relationship with Dylan spiral out the way it did while he did nothing to intervene.

If Carson really did love me from the beginning as he says, why didn't he say something to me earlier so Dylan and I could have avoided this whole fiasco? Archie's words ring true. I like neat and tidy packages, like the numbers a computer spits out. Sometimes there's a bug, but I can find them and fix the problem. Unfortunately, people don't fit into nice and tidy packages and blaming

Carson for not being an accurate speculator regarding all things Dylan isn't becoming on me.

Imogene and Lauren are working at the diner, however, they plan to come to the house later with some of their things so they can start moving in. I'm looking forward to their company, even if it's a bit strained right now with Lauren questioning my antics with Carson. Are they antics? Or is this the real deal? He hugged and kissed me in front of everyone at the hospital; I can't imagine what kind of gossip about us is roaring through this speck of a town today.

I feed Bert and then shower, scrubbing myself with the coarse loofah sponge until my skin is pink and blotchy. I wear a black sweater tunic with black tights and knee-length boots. Lois picks me up at ten to eleven sharp, just as Carson said she would. I buckle myself inside her clean, little, red sports car. It is quite a hot car for a senior citizen, but then she looks pretty great with her silver hair in loose curls and her bright red lipstick that matches the color of her car and happens to make her eyes really pop.

"Very nice outfit, Jess, but for the love of Jesus Christ Superstar, couldn't you put on some make-up? And pull that ponytail out!"

Lois drives like Steven McQueen, so I grip the Hang-On-For-Dear-Life hand grip above my window as I yank the rubber band out of my hair with the other hand.

"That's better," she says. "Now, how about a spot of lipstick? It's right there in my bag on the floor."

"We're going to a hospital, not a disco."

"You should try to look your best."

"For whom?"

Lois races through the town of Woodstock disregarding the speed limit. "Don't be so pouty. You're not five anymore. You should know that playing that pouty girl doesn't help at this age."

"I have no idea what you are talking about. I'm not pouty," I say. "And you need to slow down before we end up in the room next door to Dylan."

"Dylan and Carson should see you at your best. You need to put up a good front despite what is going on inside of that mixed up heart of yours."

I pinch my mouth into a frown.

"Dylan needs to know you're there for him as a friend, as we all are. While Carson needs to know you're there for him. You have his heart. You know that, don't you? That young man has been pining for you for a long time."

I must have misunderstood her comment about Carson pining for me, or she's a confused old woman. "We don't need to talk about my love life right now, do we? Don't you need to focus on breaking more speed laws and endangering innocent pedestrians and drivers?"

"You can't avoid this. It's your love life that's sitting in that hospital."

"I knew it. Everyone thinks I'm responsible for Dylan crashing the truck. Well, that's just great because I've been thinking the same thing. I'm to blame," I practically shout at Lois, who parks the car in the hospital lot and kills the engine before putting her hand over mine.

"What are you talking about, Jess? No one blames you."

"If I hadn't gotten involved with Dylan, he wouldn't have been so depressed that he'd drive his truck off a bridge. Yes, I think he did it on purpose." I'm hysterical, yet also relieved to get that out.

"Oh, sweet mother of hash, you are very pretty. You're a real beauty, but don't think you're so special that men will drive off bridges because of you. No one thinks you're to blame. Dylan may have been surprised to see you coming from Carson's place, but it was an accident. Even if he was upset, it caused him to have poor judgment when he tried to turn that monster truck onto that little bridge. He rolled down the ravine by accident. He didn't want to kill himself."

I want to believe her. Her version sounds more reasonable and it doesn't incriminate me or make Dylan out to be suicidal. She sounds so grandmotherly. Of course, she's the kind of grandmother that smokes pot and swears like a drunken sailor.

"I'm still not sure what to believe," I say.

"I had my doubts about you being with Dylan. See, I knew how Carson felt about you even if he didn't admit it to the rest of us. I have always been worried about Dylan; however, he seemed to go after you with gusto and I was surprised that Carson sat back and let it happen. But who was I to get involved? Then I saw Dylan getting worse and Carson was suffering right along with him. He wanted to help Dylan, but he was also miserable watching you two, knowing he couldn't go near you. I could see those tortured looks on his face. It was awful when you and Dylan left my party together."

"Well, why the hell didn't Carson stop me? If he's in love with me, why did he let me go off with his brother?" I whine in the most awful, shrill tone. "Never mind. I know it was all about Carson protecting Dylan. I've heard it before."

"If it had been any other man, Carson would have stepped in. He would have been jealous, but it was Dylan. You have to understand how hard Carson has worked at protecting that boy. I don't think he felt right about yanking you away from Dylan."

"I had no idea Carson cared about me in that way until yesterday. At least Dylan was very upfront. Carson has been hiding this whole time."

"I know. It's been a confusing mess. Love can be like that, but Carson is the right man for you and it can be fixed now. That is, if you want to fix it."

"I don't know what I'm doing," I say, getting out of the car.

"Well, it's show time, so put on a good face, at least during visiting hours."

Lois goes in first and I wait in the hallway because only two people are allowed at a time. I hear Carson's deep voice and then Lois's loud barks of laughter. She makes no attempt to be quiet for the sake of all the sleeping patients.

After ten minutes she comes out into the hall with a big grin on her face. "They're all yours, doll."

Dylan's head is shaved, buzzed to the scalp, and he has two ghastly curves around the base of his head and over one ear where the black stitches are prominent. He has one black eye and half his face is swollen and covered in ugly bruises. The purple and black hues run down the sides of his arms and his torso. He's propped up in the hospital bed with the top of his gown turned down where he's hooked up to monitors and extra tubes that travel down his arm to an I.V. bandage. Carson is leaning on the ledge of the window talking to him when Dylan sees me and turns his head slowly towards the door to take me in with a big smile.

It's that big, baby-face Dylan, cute and adorable, but his eyes have a stoned look to them.

"The nurse was in here and gave him his meds so he's pretty doped up," Carson tells me.

"I'm not so bad that I can't see Jess," Dylan says. "But I'm loving the drugs. At least I can smile at you without it feeling like a knife in my face."

"Hi." I come around to the side of the bed near Carson.

"Hi, there, yourself," Dylan says. His voice is a little woozy from the painkillers, but it's my old Dylan. "I heard I scared the hell out of you. Come here."

I hesitate. Carson has his arms folded and is smiling at me. He nods in the direction of Dylan, giving me the go ahead. I appreciate that Carson doesn't attempt to kiss me or touch me in any way in front of Dylan. I move to the side of Dylan's bed where he has one free arm without needles and tubes.

He grabs my hand and rubs it on his head. "Feel this," he says groggily. "It's like when I was a kid. Remember my buzz?" I laugh because I think I do remember him having a buzz cut as a little boy; his dark blond hair was soft against his scalp like it is now.

"I'm amazed at your body's resiliency."

"You should have seen the truck. The trooper came by with the photos they took at the scene. The truck did a complete roll over and I bounced all over the inside of that thing like a bowling ball. My head pounded repeatedly against the steering wheel and actually dented it to half its original size. The trooper said anyone else would have died." Dylan slurs this last statement and closes his eyes.

I look over at Carson who shakes his head in disbelief, but I can see the gratitude in his expression as well. "It's true. I saw the photos. They think Dylan survived because he's young and packed with enough weight and muscle that it protected him."

"He was driving so fast..." I let my words trail off. This is a conversation I need to have with Carson at another time and place.

"Jess." Dylan's eyes are open again.

"Yes, I'm still here." I reach for his free hand again, which is now limp on his leg. His eyes flutter closed and then open again.

"I can't say what I'm trying to say, the words are coming out funny," he says.

"The morphine is kicking in," Carson explains. "He's going to fall asleep. We can leave him alone for a while. His nurse will be back to check on him."

I get up and follow Carson out into the hall. Lois is gone, so I figure she must have headed off for the waiting room.

"I need to go home and shower and shave," Carson says. I admit he is handsome with his one-day beard and his tussled hair, however, he looks completely beat.

"Did you get any sleep?"

"Maybe a total of twenty minutes. I would start to doze off, but there are too many beeping machines and the nurses were in his room doing checks and tests every half hour. I want to run home." He takes my hand. "I thought you could come with me and wait while I get cleaned up. Then we could grab a real meal some place and come back to the hospital together."

I take my hand away. "I don't think that's a good idea, Carson. You need to be with Dylan, not me."

"What's wrong, Jess?" His smile fades as he searches my face for an explanation.

"We can't start something now, not with Dylan in the hospital. You can't flaunt this in front of him or other people. I shouldn't have been at your house, Carson. I shouldn't have started anything with Dylan, either. This is messed up. I'm going to find Lois and have her take me home."

"We're not flaunting anything. You've got this wrong."

"We're not going to argue about it here. I'm going home with Lois," I say, moving away.

"This isn't messed up. You and I are good together."

I shake my head and start walking away. Carson looks back at Dylan's room and then at me.

"Don't walk away from me," he says too loudly for a hospital. "When I knock on your door later tonight, I expect you to answer it. Don't hide from this, Jess."

Twenty-Eight

Imogene and Lauren choose the two bedrooms that belonged to Carson and Dylan that one summer long ago. Lauren borrows her father's truck to bring all of their boxes to my house. They begin unpacking their clothes, toiletries and worldly possessions of junk. It takes all three of us to carry their jewelry supply boxes up to the playroom that belonged to the young Blackard boys and me. They are eager to get settled in so we eat Pop Tarts for dinner instead of taking a break to prepare an actual meal.

I keep checking the clock, noticing as the hour approaches the time of the end of visiting hours at the hospital; the moment when Carson will leave for home. I am on my knees, helping Lauren fill dozens of shallow trays with jewelry findings when she unexpectedly hugs me tightly.

"I'm so sorry," she says.

She has me in a crushing embrace and I am bewildered and touched at the same time.

"I was terrible to you yesterday. Dylan's accident was not your fault and I shouldn't have come down so hard on you about Dylan and Carson."

"Where is this coming from all of a sudden?" I ask as she lets go of me.

"It's a small town, Jess. Archie and Lois are very worried about you and I know you worry enough for one hundred people. You don't need me riding your ass, too."

"Oh." I sigh. "Thanks for being so understanding, but I've been thinking about everything a lot. Dylan and Carson. Dylan's accident was a wake-up call. I don't think it's as simple as everyone is making this out to be."

Imogene comes in the room with another box. "I heard that," she says. "Dating Dylan is one thing, but if you think you can win over a guy like Carson and then just walk away from it, you're crazy. It doesn't work that way."

"What do you mean?" I ask. Then there is a loud pounding on the front door, which could only mean that Carson is making good on his promise to bash my medieval doorknocker continuously until I respond.

"Hark! But what is that obscene pounding and which caveman could it be?" Imogene sings. "I know it's not Jeremy or Leo because they haven't grown big enough balls to ask us out."

Lauren starts laughing.

"I'll get it," I say.

"Damn straight you will. You have the makings of a perfect life and this is the guy you have been infatuated with all along. So you are going to talk to him and you are not going to blow it."

"I never said I was infatuated with Carson. How could I? I was dating Dylan."

"Sometimes we have stand-ins until the real deal comes along," Imogene says. "Some of us realized that Dylan was your stand-in."

"Oh." It's obvious I don't have a good comeback.

Carson doesn't stop knocking, so I take the stairs two at a time as fast as I can without breaking my neck on the way down.

I swing the door wide open. "It was unlocked," I say to Carson who's walking through the door before I finish the sentence.

"You told me to stop letting myself in. I'm not here to bully you into doing what I think is right. I'm here because we had the best day with each other yesterday," he says passionately, wild-eyed.

"Until it stopped being the best day," I say.

"Then, I guess I am here to bully you. Jess, I don't play games of any kind, especially guessing games. I've been completely honest with you, so you know where I stand. I want to know why you're angry at me and what you were thinking back the hospital earlier today. Something set you off and you left."

"You do play games, whether you realize it or not. You were interested in me from the beginning—that's what you said—but you let Dylan and I carry on, knowing full well that Dylan couldn't handle it and I wasn't serious enough for him. You knew this would blow up. If you had asked me out first, this wouldn't have happened."

Carson stares at me and then laughs. "Do you hear yourself?"

"Yes, I sound really stupid and it's not coming out the way I want," I snap at him.

"Do you think I'm the Dating Czar in this town? That I have the authority to control who everyone dates or doesn't date?"

"We could have prevented Dylan's accident, if it was really an accident," I retort.

"Maybe you haven't noticed, but I'm not like Dylan. I don't flirt, I don't remember to buy flowers and I don't keep track of birthdays, unless Archie reminds me. If I was the Dating Czar, then my two stupid, yet lovable employees would be dating the two unattached women you have upstairs," he shouts to the upstairs floors.

"Thank you, Carson!" Imogene interjects from the second floor.

"You're welcome," he shouts back.

"You're not listening to me," I say.

"No, you're the one who doesn't get it. I'm not known as Mr. Romance in this town. Dylan won you over the minute you saw him. I didn't have a chance. The one thing I don't do is date. I don't do the small talk and ask random women out."

"He doesn't date!" Imogene and Lauren both shout from upstairs.

"Hey! Greek Chorus, shut up!" I yell to the invisible pair upstairs.

"Thank you!" Carson responds to them again, but he glares at me. "Did you hear that? I don't date, not in ages, because I don't do it well. I don't take chances with women. I do it once. I waited because I wanted the time to be right to tell you how I felt."

"That is a stupid policy. You do it once, huh? You did have a chance with me. In fact, you had two chances; day one and then the two week period when I wasn't talking to Dylan before we actually got together," I say softly. "But you didn't take them. Dylan did. After the fight you had with

Dylan in my kitchen, you could have stepped in then."

"I almost did. I wanted to tell you when we were on the bridge and again when we were making those crappy pies." Carson is hovering over me, his face fallen, his hands out while he figures out how to touch me.

"But you didn't take a chance on me and by not taking a chance and telling me the truth, I ended up with the wrong guy and I hurt him. Badly. It's a mess. Dylan's alive; however, we haven't addressed the bigger problem."

"We will," Carson says, trying to be reassuring. "As soon as he's out of the hospital. I finally got space for him in that really good residential treatment program that will help him."

"That's great," I say. "Then that's what you should do."

"We'll do it together. You saw Dylan, he was happy to see you and his world didn't fall apart when you walked in the room."

"He was heavily sedated. I have no idea how I can be any help. Dylan's problems get progressively worse when I'm around him."

"Not true." Carson comes back at me with both arms open, but I push his hands away.

"Did you ask Dylan why he went over the bridge or are you and everyone else going to assume that Dylan couldn't handle the curve onto it? Dylan, who can drive any vehicle off-road, the same guy who's driven to your house a million times before without incident? Did you ask him?"

"He remembers parts—the tumbling truck—but as far as where his mind was at, we'll have to discuss that when he's healed." Carson looks down and then rubs his hand down his tired face. "I'm not trying to pretend that this wasn't a big deal. I know it's serious and I have to help Dylan, but the state police said the markings on the road showed the truck overshot the turn and hit the bridge from the side and that's why the truck rolled down instead of being projected in the air through the middle of the railing. They didn't see evidence that Dylan drove straight through the railing. They seemed satisfied with the responses they were able to get from him when he was semi-conscious. I can't interrogate Dylan while he's still recovering."

"I understand. You have to let him heal. You need to take care of him. You are a really great brother." I want to cry, although not in front of Carson.

"Jess," he says, his hands out again as though I'll take safety in them this time, but I put my hands up to stop him.

"Carson, we can't do this. I can't do this. One fuck up was enough."

"We're not a fuck up. Believe me when I say I love you."

"Right, you loved me so much that you didn't mind that I was sleeping with your brother? You were taking your sweet time because Carson Blackard only does it once," I say mocking him. "Believe me when I say I can't love you back."

I run back up the stairs to the third floor. I can hear Imogene on the second floor as she leans over the banister to talk to Carson. "She got you on that one, Carson. You don't let other guys sleep with the woman you're in love with. You didn't fight for her."

"Oh, for fuck's sake, I'm not Wyatt Earp. I wasn't going to shoot his balls off," he says before slamming the front door.

Twenty-Nine

"Are you ready to be a grownup?" Imogene asks, standing over my bed.

"This is a fuckervention," Lauren says from the other side of the bed. "Stop breaking his heart. And yours."

I try to open my eyes, but I'm still mostly asleep. Imogene's arms are crossed over her busty chest as she stares at me, waiting for me to wake up.

"God, what time is it?" I ask.

"Six in the morning. Lauren and I have the breakfast shift so we're leaving soon. Coffee is done and there's a gorgeous man sleeping out in his truck waiting for you."

"What?" Now I'm fully awake.

"Fuckervention," Lauren whispers loudly. "We're intervening so you don't fuck this up."

"Carson never left," Imogene explains. "He spent the night in his truck. You're going to go down there and offer him a cup of fresh coffee and you're going to talk to him nicely."

"Why is he here?"

Lauren groans.

Imogene puts up her palm up to Lauren. "Gee, maybe because he's in love with you and wants to work through your silly issues, so he can get over to the hospital to see his brother."

"Me, silly? How about a guy who sleeps in his truck?"

Imogene yanks my bed covers back. She is furious. "Stop it. I mean it. Get up and throw on some clothes and get down there this minute."

"What's with you? What happened to all the hugs and understanding I got last night from you two? Now I'm the bad guy again?"

"No, you're the stupid guy," Lauren says. "You have a wonderful man who is crazy about you and I don't mean crazy in the way Dylan obsessed over you and got jealous over every person who looked your way. Carson is a once in a lifetime deal. I would give whatever I could to have someone care about me the way he has for you. It takes a lot of fortitude for a man to pursue a challenging woman despite the fact that she slept with his brother, don't you think?"

I get out of bed and look out the window.

"He's still asleep," Imogene says. "I saw him when I let out Bert."

Lauren hands me a pair of jeans and a sweater.

"Carson is no saint," I say as I get dressed.

"No one is, but you're not going to find a man who's better than him," Imogene replies.

"I'm only twenty-one and you're trying to push me into marrying this guy?"

"I'm doing no such thing and he didn't propose. But it really pisses me off when people I love act like idiots and screw up great opportunities."

"I'm the idiot?"

Lauren nods. "Yes. Go talk to him."

"And say what?"

"I can't watch this train wreck again. God, I wish I could have a cigarette!" Imogene says, storming out of the room.

I turn to Lauren. "Well? What do I say?"

"The truth. He's not expecting miracles. He's not like Dylan at all, Jess. Carson doesn't expect you to shit rainbows and look like a goddess every day. Unlike Dylan, Carson is a realist and he's mature enough to know that relationships of a lifetime happen over a lifetime, not over a four week fuck-frenzy."

"Dylan did take dreamer to a whole new scary level," I mumble. "But I still don't know what you expect me to say to Carson?"

"You tell him what matters. What's important to him? You. His brother. Keeping everyone together. He's not asking for promises or guarantees from you. He's only hoping you'll consider him, even if it has to go on hold for a while."

I deliberate over her words and realize she's the first friend who has spoken so honestly about my own fears. She's right, Carson never placed demands on me to give or say anything that didn't come naturally to me, unlike Dylan who was practically begging for me to say 'I love you'. Lovable, adorable Dylan and his haywire mood swings.

When I step out onto the porch with a hot steaming mug of coffee, Carson is standing outside of his truck taking in a long, graceful, arching stretch. He doesn't notice me, so I use the opportunity to admire his incredible body, sculpted in all the right places with those strikingly serious eyes that make him absurdly handsome.

When he sees me, he smiles.

Ah, he is so forgiving.

I walk towards him slowly, making sure not to spill the coffee. He leans back against his truck and watches me with a tender expression.

I hand him the mug and he takes a sip, keeping his eyes on me.

"What possessed you to sleep out here all night?" I wrap my arms around myself to prevent my oversized sweater from letting in the cool drafts.

Carson is in a short-sleeved T-shirt and he looks perfectly fine with the chilling temperatures. I shiver and he rests the mug on the roof of his truck while he reaches inside the cab for his jacket. He drapes it across my shoulders and I smell him in the wool; scents of pine, musk and sawdust.

"You," he answers. "I stayed because the thought of going home and trying to sleep after our fight sounded impossible. I didn't want to stare at the ceiling all night, wondering what I should have said or done differently. It was easier to stay here and sleep in the truck, knowing that you were only ten feet away."

When he says things like that, it makes my heart sing and I want to hug him as I revel in the safety of his arms. Yet I know it would lead to sex and that seems to be the problem. These proffers of love are difficult for me to accept when they're attached to sex.

Perhaps it's my inexperience at both love and sex. They arrived in my life at the same time, so it's next to impossible for me to separate the two and ascertain if the love is genuine or if it's merely a side effect to making love. Besides, I never refer to what I did with Dylan as making love. To me it was sex, getting it on, or fucking. Then I reflect on that day in Carson's bed. I never once felt like we were fucking in the impersonal sense of the word. I could almost touch the joy that was surrounding me like a bubble when I was in Carson's orbit; whether it was at Barron's Creek, in my kitchen, or in his bed.

I look around, avoiding eye contact with him because I have to craft my words carefully. How do you tell a man that you want to be with him, but not yet? That you like him, although you're not sure you can return his love? How do say this delicately enough so that he waits for you?

I can't ask Imogene and Lauren since they have already left for the diner. Besides, they would give me a scathing speech about stringing Carson along. First Dylan then Carson, as though I'm one of the popular, bitchy girls in school. That's what this seems like. I've finally made it to the high school ranks of popularity.

Imogene's question is appropriate. Am I ready to be a grownup?

"Thank you," I say at a loss for a better response.

"Why are you thanking me?" He crosses his arms and stays in his relaxed position against the truck as if he's trying really hard not to touch me, not to set me off. It makes me feel like I'm a bomb.

"Because you have been very forgiving and kind through all of this and I made some very harsh statements. I'm not saying what I said last night is wrong, but the way I said it was distasteful. I am not proud of myself."

Carson looks down at the ground. I watch his jaw clench and flex. "So sleeping on it didn't help. We're still stuck where we were last night. You want to blame yourself for being with Dylan and me for not asking you out sooner?"

I don't say anything. I have nothing wise to add to my original argument.

"Tell me what you want, Jess. Do you want me to go away for good?"

"No." I definitely don't want him to go away. It might be a good test to see if my heart breaks, or to see if I actually have a heart, however, I don't think I could survive that test. "I want to... I'm going to use one of Lois's terms, so don't laugh, but I want to find my center. I want to figure out what I'm doing. I'm not a care-free spirit like my Aunt Virginia was. I'm very much a product of my upbringing and my parents taught me to figure out what I need to do. I'm good at that. But now I want to figure out what I *want* to do, too.

"My parents used to direct my life. It's my turn to take the reins. So I'm going to say those dreaded words and I don't want you to correct me. I need a break from romantic entanglements and relationships. I want to see Dylan get better, I want to know you the way everyone else in this town knows and trusts you, but I'm not going to be sharing anyone's bed for now. That's what I think I should do."

Carson studies me for a moment and then lets out a deep sigh. "Fuck. I didn't know I was an entanglement."

"You're not. It was a bad choice of words. I need to be on my own for a while."

"You've been on your own for years," he says. "Your parents sent you out into the world when you were fourteen. A kid making adult decisions is never easy."

"You did it, too, but you've also had a few years to be your own boss. I need to process everything in my own way and I can't keep accepting everyone else's opinions because it only confuses me at this point."

"How much time do you need?"

"This isn't something I can schedule onto the calendar like one of your renovation projects. I need time for myself and it will take as long as it takes. Is that okay with you?"

Carson gives me a hesitant smile and relaxes his arms. He looks positively gorgeous with his messy hair and unshaven face. "I'm fine with that. There's no statute of limitations on my feelings for you."

I wish he'd stop being so accommodating. It only makes me want to jump in his arms and have reckless sex with him.

"Ah..." I stammer, contemplating how to end this conversation without blowing it forever.

"Do you know why I could sleep out here all night?" he asks.

"Because you're made of steel?"

He smiles at my attempts to delicately diffuse the tension.

"Because you never fell in love with my brother."

"What?" I look at him with confusion.

"You didn't fall in love with my brother or any other guy for that matter. That gives me hope that I'll be the one and only."

I am floored and quite pleased that he would confess that to me.

"I don't care who you've slept with in the past. Okay, that's bullshit, but I can't change that. What I do want, however, is to be the first and last guy you fall in love with." He delivers this declaration with a confident inflection like an ambitious colonial statesman, except I doubt references to sex would ever be uttered in a John Adams speech. It's Carson's old-fashioned perspective on how people should behave that makes me fall harder for him.

Abandoning my earlier remarks about needing more time, I reach up and kiss him, putting my arms around his neck. He doesn't hesitate to seize the opportunity I've given him. He kisses me savagely. One of his hands holds my head while the other grabs my ass and pulls me in closer. I press into his hard body and it feels right. It would be so easy to think with my urges and the raging hormones that are begging me to give into Carson; to hold him, to make love to him, to love him. I don't trust anything that comes so easily.

The kiss ends slowly, neither of us wanting to stop since it means we'll have to get on with the business of real life.

"Everyone tells me that you are exceptional as a person. It's true. But I still need more time, Carson."

His façade is solemn.

"I owe you a huge apology for acting like a brute, at least that's how Imogene put it. I'm sorry." He hands the coffee mug back to me.

"I'm kind of getting used to you busting down my doors, but I really do need some more time."

"Okay," Carson says.

Thirty

Three weeks have passed since the accident and we're already being threatened with an early winter, a dusting of snow in October.

Dylan's bruising has faded completely and his follow-up medical exams have been clear. He started seeing a new psychiatrist two weeks ago when he went back to work. The new anti-depressant he's trying needs another week or so before its full effect kicks in, but Dylan thinks they're working and his spirits are up. He's hopeful.

I know this because, when I'm not bogged down in 5 Alpha work or attempting a yoga class, we meet for lunch at least twice a week at Bonnie's and talk like we're old friends. He sometimes brings Leo and Jeremy along so we can hang out with Lauren and Imogene while they work.

During those times our conversations are light, mostly about life in general, but when Dylan and I are alone, our conversations turn to our personal, yet separate, struggles. There's nothing sexual or romantic about it. Dylan is still beautiful in that angelic way, yet we have evolved into friends with a shared past and my affections for him have become more of a sisterly fondness. He seems more serene in general and is looking forward to moving into the residential treatment center in Massachusetts next week after the annual

Blackard Designs party that Carson hosts in his home every year.

I have been invited to the party, too, along with three hundred other people. Although I see Carson periodically, at this point, I don't trust myself and I'm still uneasy about spending any time alone with him. Dylan and I have been officially over for a couple of months and it makes it easier for me to talk to him since I'm not worried about how he perceives me sexually or romantically. That's what makes it tough, too. Dylan is my past, and Carson is my present and future; if I have a future with him.

We're sitting in a window booth, the last diners at the end of the lunch rush. The staff is in the kitchen eating their own meal and cleaning while I watch Dylan wolf down a burger and fries. He keeps his head shaved and it shows off the scars that have gone from a fleshy-neon pink to an opaque whitish-rose color. I want to reach over and rub his head, which I and the other women do often. His fuzzy scalp is irresistible.

"Keep your hair like that and the women are going to fawn over you, touching your head. And the scars make you look a little dangerous," I say as he grins at me.

"Just what I need, more women."

"They are going to be all over you at Carson's shindig. You wait and see. They'll come out of the woodwork."

"I have no doubt. I expect to get laid before I go off to the crazy house."

"Don't say that. I'm really proud of you. So is Carson."

"Did he tell you that?"

"No, we haven't spoken. Other than 'hello' when we bump into each other at the store."

"That's the problem. You have to talk to him, the same way you're talking to me. Well, except we're not together anymore, so maybe you want to talk to him in a guy-getting way. Whatever spells or Jedi mind tricks chicks do to get our attention. Does that make sense?"

"No, not at all, but I'm really relieved you and I are on speaking terms. We're better friends now, don't you think?"

"Yes." He finishes gulping his water and puts the glass down. "My new medication makes me really thirsty, or maybe I'm imagining it. Anyway, you should be with Carson." He blurts that last part out. I assume the medication makes him a little incoherent, except I understand him perfectly.

I sigh and avert my gaze to the empty diner.

"I'm serious. Carson is the best human being on the whole planet."

"That's quite an endorsement," I say dryly.

"It's true. You'll never regret being with Carson. He's been in love with you this whole time. I was so persistent with you because I wanted something that belonged to Carson."

"Gee, thanks. I don't belong to anyone."

Dylan leans across the table and takes my hands in his. "And you don't get to decide who Carson loves. He loves me and you. Maybe you're not ready to love him back, but Carson doesn't change his plans. He's like you. He thinks about something a long time and follows through on it. I wouldn't be here today if Carson hadn't picked up where my parents left off. He raised me and planned a future for me. I fucked up a lot of times, but here I am. Carson saved me again and again, and this time I'm going to follow through on the plan. I'm going to live and breathe that therapy program for however long it takes. Six weeks, three months. I'm going to succeed and then I'm coming back to make Blackard Designs even better."

"Good." I smile and squeeze his hand.

"Good? Did you not hear the part where I said you and Carson are alike? Stop putting me in this position where I have to talk about you and some other guy. Seriously." He's trying to be jokey, yet it's not an easy topic for either of us.

"I didn't ask you to talk about Carson."

"Yeah, but if you won't talk about him, then I'm sort of obligated to push this along. He's my brother and I screwed things up for him. Plus, you're my friend and I owe you some truths. I'm trying to point out how perfect you two are for each other."

"You don't have to." I don't think I can hear another lecture nor have someone sing Carson's praises to me.

"See, you sound just like Carson."

"Well, there you go. I don't want to date myself."

"Ha. Funny. Listen, you spent years following through on your academic goals and your painting. He did the same with his furniture company and me. I have been Carson's biggest project. You and Carson are both very strong, persistent people. You take your time and you do the right thing."

"You don't think I've made some hasty decisions since you've known me?"

Dylan laughs loudly. "You mean me?"

"Yes, you."

"In your defense, I got you when you were very vulnerable. I was like an eagle diving in on its defenseless prey."

I scoff and laugh with him.

"A lot has changed in the last five months, hasn't it?" He's serious again.

"Yes." I put my hands back in my lap. "I feel like a different person, too. Don't you?"

"Yeah," Dylan says quietly. "But not Carson. He's the same. You can always count on him."

"You could sell used cars. You can count on this one!" I mock.

Dylan chuckles. "You should call your parents more often."

"What made you think of them?" I ask.

"You've been here long enough. I don't know why you haven't asked them to come visit. It's nice that you have parents. I wish I did. I don't want to sound preachy. I know you haven't seen eye to eye with them over the last couple of years, or ever, but they did push you in the right direction, getting an education. They raised a great daughter. You should give them some credit and throw them a bone sometime. I bet they'd love to hear from you."

"Huh. Well, I'm still a little miffed about them keeping me away from my aunt all these years and they have never cared much about my art."

"Big deal. I used to complain about Carson being too bossy and controlling, but he was there for me. I'll give him credit for that. You need to stop acting like you're all alone, that you have to make every decision by yourself. You have parents and friends. Did you even notice I'm using the speech you gave me about not doing it alone?"

"Yeah. Clever."

We sit in silence for a moment. It's strange to be receiving advice about life from someone who is about to go into a therapy program for his emotional instability.

"I never got to apologize for being such a shitty girlfriend to you."

"You were perfect." He gives another devilish grin.

"Hardly." I laugh.

"I'm serious. You never promised anything more than what was offered. You were honest with me and I appreciate that. I'll never regret the time I spent with you."

I lean across the table and Dylan leans in to listen. "You were my first, so I'll never regret my time with you either."

"I know and I think everyone already knows your secret," he whispers loudly.

"Very funny."

"Jess, I have made some bad decisions in my life, but you were not one of them. I hope you listen or at least try to believe what I've been telling you. Stop thinking you could have prevented any of this from happening. I really didn't want to get married and moving in on you was a mistake. I dragged you into my screwed up brain; that's what happened."

"Okay. I believe you and now I want you to listen to me. I know you idolize Carson. That's understandable. But you're also a very good person. He's not better than you."

"Huh. Yeah, well thanks."

"Huh, yeah, you're welcome."

"Smarty pants, I want you to come visit the shop and see what we're doing. Carson's business deal came through a while ago and he's expanded the place. We're doing these weathered pieces of furniture—aged wood—and I helped get the operation going. Carson has a great appreciation for your art, so you need to see his."

"Maybe so.

"You see me moving forward, you don't have to tip-toe around me or feel responsible anymore. You are free to date Carson without feeling any guilt."

"Ah. It's not that simple, Dylan."

"It's also not as difficult as you make it out to be," he says.

Thirty-One

The Friday before Carson's party, the snow comes down like a thick, white, fluffy blanket. As I watch the peaceful flakes float down from my library window, Lauren is busy in the next room working on some new necklaces that she and Imogene want to post on their new website soon. She listens to classical music while she strings beads and crimps wire.

Imogene is cleaning the house. She's decided I am a slob and she will clean once a week in return for a hefty rent reduction. I don't argue with her, especially since I'm not sure I'm brave enough to hire Talia just yet. She's too close to Carson and it would put me in another very awkward position if I drag Carson down into the black hole where all my dates go to die.

Since Imogene and Lauren are both occupied with tasks, I convince myself to make a trek into town. I need the exercise and I want to take Dylan up on his offer.

Jogging through the snow along the main route to town requires more stamina than I expected. By the time I arrive at Blackard Designs, my wool cap and running shoes are soaked.

"Hi, Jess!" Daisy greets as I walk through the door of the shop. I tell her I'm just visiting, no need to buzz anyone.

I peel off my soggy watch cap and run my hands through my damp hair, trying to fluff it up. I hang my down vest on the front coat rack and wipe off any remaining snowflakes on my black running tights.

On the left side of the building, in the showroom, I can see Dylan talking to some men and women in business suits. He must be giving his pitch to some sales reps. I watch him for a moment, admiring how he's at ease talking with such authority on the subject of their craft.

I turn and walk back by Daisy's counter and through the right side to the actual workshop. I spot Leo and Daniel right away, both are wearing goggles and gloves, painting or staining furniture. They wave and give me silent hellos as I walk by. There are projects everywhere, most in the finishing stages, but the crew is unusually sparse in this part of the shop.

In the back I see where the extension has been added, the new addition Dylan mentioned. The back wall has been knocked out and a glass wall has been installed in its place that allows me to see the whole new addition without going in. It's very industrial looking with concrete flooring, a high ceiling, metal doors with rivets, metal skylights and tall windows, machinery that looks like ovens and lots of timber. It has an artisanal ambiance, a place for real craftsman who work with basic elements of earth, fire and wood. It reminds me of Carson's home. Every bit of this workshop has Carson in it. It even smells like him.

There are more people working here, even a few women, so Carson must have used the investment loan to increase production as well as number of staff. I'm watching the activity without really understanding their process when I see Carson. He is speaking to a man by the enormous oven with a tool that resembles a pizza paddle.

Carson looks up and sees me then says something to the man and walks towards the partition door. In that instant I realize how much I have missed seeing him. His dark hair hangs loose down to his chin and frames his handsome face. His stride is long and shows off the hard lines through his arms and legs. He runs his hand through his hair to push it back. I love that move. When he opens the heavy, metal door, the sounds of machinery and crackling wood carry into the workshop area.

"Jess," Carson says. He offers a conservative smile, a pleasant version for greeting business people.

"Dylan said I should come by and visit."

"He's in the showroom if you want to see him," Carson tells me. His jeans and boots are dusty with wood chips and he smells like a campfire. He holds his heavy work gloves in one hand and keeps the partition door open with the other.

"I saw him. He's with customers or reps. I wanted to see the new addition."

"Oh. Great," he says, genuinely surprised. "Come in, I'll give you the tour."

I walk by him through the door and feel like a panther in my body-hugging black attire.

"Did you run here?" he asks.

"No, I jogged and it turned into more of a brisk walk before the final half mile changed into a limp."

He smirks. "Well, you're here. I'm glad."

"Me, too. This looks impressive. You never told me about any of your plans to expand."

"I'll tell you whatever you want to know. Come here."

I follow him to the big oven where the man with the paddle is shoving wood inside the high flames.

"We're doing a new line of furniture. It's all aged wood. It looks similar to our recycled barn wood furniture, but waiting for wood to age naturally is slowing things down so we came up with our own process. This is a boiler where we cook the wood at high temperatures. Then we put it in the season chamber for drying." He points to a set of ominous, black metal, double doors. "After that, those guys over there use steel brushes on the cooked wood to give it a more weathered look."

"What about all the cracks and imperfections?"

"They add to the individuality of each piece of furniture," he says, walking me towards two women.

"Noelle and Gemma. This is Jessica." They smile and shake my hand. I'm struck by their attractiveness.

Gemma is a redhead like me, yet her hair is smooth and perfectly straight down to her shoulders. She is very pretty with a nice, slender figure. We study each other as if we're competitors. I doubt Carson picks up on this, but I sense Gemma is having the same thoughts as me about Carson.

314

"Very pretty hair," Gemma says with a lovely English accent. "I wish mine was thick and wavy like yours."

I smile, however, I'm no match for this woman who is closer to Carson's age and has much more experience and confidence. She is polished and beautiful.

"Noelle and Gemma are designers, too," Carson says. "They are creating the new line with me, but they also do some of the heavy lifting."

I notice the women wear the same heavy gloves; they look cool and trendy in their jeans and work boots. I envy them for getting to work here with Carson. Actually, maybe I even hate Gemma for being here where Carson can see her every day. Jealousy really does make us feel ugly inside.

Carson continues and there's excitement in his tone. "The business is changing since I started. It used to be guys who were good at carving and tinkering in their woodshops. Some of our new staff, like Gemma and Noelle, have college degrees in design and actual work experience in the craft."

His reserve is breaking down and the real Carson is coming through as he gets more animated describing his business to me. I admit I like having his hand on my lower back in a possessive way, which is noticeable to Gemma. I'm also relieved when he propels me away from the pretty women to introduce me to others. Everyone is looking at me with wonderment as though it's a novelty to see Carson with a woman who isn't a part of the business or trade.

I get caught up in his attention and relax a bit. It's being next to Carson that makes me heady.

There's something intense about the room with its crackling fire and the dry air that leaves my cheeks rosy and my hair curly and voluminous rather than limp. Aside from my paintings, I never have mystical experiences like this. I am Cinderella, transformed from a sooty cinder girl into a wild haired redhead. Maybe it's my active imagination, which is fine. What's wrong with finding happiness in my own world in my own way?

By the end of the tour, Carson and I have changed our demeanor. His hand is on my shoulder and I find myself standing closer to him, especially when I laugh.

"Can I take you out for lunch?" he asks.

"I can't go anywhere dressed like this." I sound like I'm fishing for compliments. I could see how Carson looked at me when Gemma remarked on my pretty hair; he had that glazed, lovelorn look of admiration that every woman enjoys. I have no shame and milk it for all I can to feed my sagging ego.

"You can absolutely go anywhere you want like this," Carson says.

"You came!" Dylan exclaims as he bursts through the partition door. Damn these Blackard boys and doors.

"Carson gave me the complete tour. I love it. It's amazing," I reply, thinking I may be overdoing it.

"Good." Dylan grins at us.

"Am I missing something?" Carson directs at Dylan.

"Your lunatic brother made you a very big sale."

"How big?" Carson asks skeptically. Dylan hands him a stack of papers I assume are wholesale orders.

"Wow. Cool, Dylan," Carson compliments as he flips through the pages.

"More importantly, are you going to the party tomorrow night?" Dylan asks me.

I look at Carson and then Dylan scoffs at his big brother. "Seriously, you didn't even ask her yourself?"

Carson's face blanches with embarrassment. We're both uncomfortable being directed by Dylan.

"I wouldn't miss your hillbilly hoedown for anything," I say in my best honky-tonk accent.

"Ha! We're not that backwards. Don't be surprised if you see some women in Prada," Dylan says. "But you can come in a burlap sack and you'll still be the prettiest girl there."

It's an awkward moment for all three of us, Dylan innocently flirting as comes naturally to him. I rub his head as a show of his impromptu jest.

"I'm more interested in your hoedown outfit than anything from Prada," Carson says, eyeing my hand that was touching Dylan. "Does it come with clogs?"

I laugh and slap my hand playfully against his arm. Dylan follows the move in slow motion, not as a jealous former lover, rather as a man who wants to bow out of this threesome.

"I have to give Daisy these orders." He takes the papers from Carson's hands and heads quickly to the front counter.

"It's too weird having me here," I say. "I'm going to go."

"No. I'm glad you're here." Carson takes hold of my arm to stop me from moving away. "Don't misread this. That was Dylan being generous to both of us."

"He is different," I say, searching for a better word to describe Dylan's small transformation.

"He has committed to going through with the program this time. He can do it." Carson releases my arm, but closes the space between us to make this more personal.

"I think he'll be very successful. There's an eagerness in him, he seems renewed," I say. As much as I care about Dylan and want to help him, I'm wondering if Dylan is the main thing Carson and I have in common.

"You've been a good friend to him over the last few weeks; I was wrong when I told you to stay away from him. He still talks about you a lot, but in a new way; he says his conversations with you help. Thank you for that."

Carson struggles to think of something else to talk about, but either we have nothing other than our shared concern for Dylan and our afternoon of sex, or we're both too afraid to go beyond small talk. That is my fault, of course. I wanted to slow my dating life down. Unfortunately, I've essentially put it in a coma and Carson is being too careful around me, or maybe he has lost interest. Regardless of his quest to push me and Carson together, Dylan's no prophet and I'm not very good at reading men.

"Sure," I say.

We're stalled for more dialogue. Moments ago, I thought I was in a magical realm and I thought the man I've been attracted to for months was experiencing the same desire for me; suddenly, I'm a nervous, doubtful ninny again. I hate that nag inside of me, however, she's very persuasive and I feel the need to leave immediately.

"I have to get going." I back away and then walk quickly through the work area to gather my clothing by the front door.

Thirty-Two

I'm out the door of Blackard Designs and running back up home, sliding and stumbling on the shoulder of the road, yet determined to keep moving away from the shop and Carson as fast as I can.

"Hey!" Carson yells through his window as he drives his truck alongside me. "Get in."

When I shake my head and keep running, he guns the engine and drives the truck farther ahead. He blocks my path by parking the truck at an angle across the shoulder so the only way I can pass is to climb down in the ravine off the shoulder or go left into oncoming traffic. There are very few vehicles, but intentionally running around his truck to the other side of the road would look juvenile, even for me.

I climb into the truck, out of breath and panting.

"You can't run along the side of the road in this weather. I'll take you home," Carson says.

"No, I don't want to go home." I look out the window, pull my wet cap off again and ruffle my hair. I am too anxious, sad and scared. "Take me anywhere else."

Carson starts driving. "What happened?" He looks upset. I turn away, keeping my gaze on the scenery.

"Nothing. Everything is great at the house. I just need a break from work and staring at the same walls and my sleeping dog."

"Okay," he says, however, he keeps glancing at me warily.

"Take me to the Ridge, the place where people hike and have picnics."

"Sure. I know the Ridge. I'll take you there."

Carson cranks up the heater and I take off my wet vest and my shoes, which are pretty much demolished. The heater gets my skin good and toasty, especially when I put my bare feet on the dashboard. "Do you mind?" I ask.

"Not at all," Carson replies, looking at my feet as I rub them.

He's not wearing a jacket so he must have left in a hurry to chase after me. I like the idea of that, but I'm not kidding myself with unrealistic fantasies anymore.

We drive in silence while I keep my focus on the passing houses and farms. After a few miles, Carson takes the truck off the main road onto a steep dirt road, which takes us to another smaller, inconspicuous, makeshift road. He shifts down into a lower gear and we begin crawling over the uneven ground. I could not have driven here on my own. Carson is obviously very experienced with the terrain and handling a vehicle that requires some clever uphill maneuvering.

"Goodness," I say when we reach the top and drive onto a flat area.

The Ridge overlooks a valley of smaller towns and hills buried in snow. There's no one up here since it's really only used by locals in the summer and fall months.

My initial anxiety dissipates as I ponder the fact that we are alone up here in our private snow tower. He parks the truck, although he keeps the engine and heat running.

"Do you want to tell me what's going on?" he asks.

My feet are hot, so I remove them from the console and pull my knees up to my chest. I rest my head back against the seat and sigh.

"Is it all about sex?" I ask. "Us?"

Carson looks confused for a moment before he then shakes his head. "No. If it were about sex, then I would have spent the last five months getting laid every day. With you, by the way."

I laugh nervously.

"We spent one afternoon together, Jess."

"And now?"

"Now I'm waiting. I've been waiting for you."

I unbuckle my seat belt and climb over to his seat. Straddling him, I kiss him before he can say anything. It takes him two seconds to register what is happening before his hands are buried in my hair and he's dragging a long, hungry kiss across my lips. My heart is racing along with my voracious desire to have him inside of me. The need is blinding and doesn't allow for any slow tenderness. We've been at a distance from one another for so long—too long—we're both fireballs of energy; grabbing one another, kissing and pulling clothing off.

My fleece top is off and thankfully, I wore a regular bra and not my running bra, which is more cumbersome to remove. This bra snaps off with a flick of the fingers. I remove my tights like an acrobat, my tongue probing Carson's mouth while my hands pull the clingy fabric from my limbs. I'm completely naked on top of him; Carson is unhinged, his hands roaming up and down my body. He undoes his jeans and yanks them down enough so I can pull his cock out.

"There." He points to the glove compartment. "I think there are condoms in there."

"Oh really?" I laugh. "You keep condoms in your truck?"

"From a while ago," he says, watching me handle his cock. "It's been a long time. Really. See if—" He groans.

I arch over and open the box to dig through papers until I find two condom packages.

"I wonder if they're still good," I say, examining the packages and torturing him with my stall. He grabs one from me and rips it open, sheathing himself before I can continue teasing him.

Then he gasps when I impale myself on him with one quick lunge.

"Oh, damn," he groans. "I would like to have this everyday with you. Every single damn day."

I smile down at him and keep lunging and thrusting against him with my knees planted on either side of his seat. I hold his headrest to steady myself as I move faster and let my head fall back. Carson is holding my ass and thrusting into me while his hands and mouth are on my breasts. I focus on one thing only, pumping and thrusting, building up to my release. I can sense Carson holding back so he doesn't come too soon, but he's in overdrive, too. He trembles beneath me, trying to maintain control, yet his quiet grunts give him away.

He begins rubbing two fingers against me where our flesh keeps slamming together. The sensation he creates with those two fingers and his lusty expression is enough to drive me over the edge.

"Come," he commands, but it is really a plea.

The delicious spasms come in robust waves and grow more intense as I look down at Carson and my naked body against him. I buck harder against him until the pleasure is pouring out of me like a sieve. Carson wraps one hand around my ass and the other behind my head so I don't slam into the steering wheel. Then he pounds into me, ramming quick thrusts until he shouts my name with his release.

We're both breathing hard as he wrenches me back into his lap with a full embrace. I wrap my arms around his shoulders and rest my head against his neck, still panting. It's only then that I feel my leg cramping from the tight space, but I don't want to disrupt our moment together.

"You've lived here five months and we've had sex twice," he says between breaths into my hair. "So, this should be enough evidence for your question. No, we're not about sex, but I sure like when we are."

I reluctantly climb off him and get dressed.

"You're so quiet," he observes as he fastens his jeans.

I lean against my seat and study his beautiful features. He plays with a few tendrils of my hair and caresses my face.

"I think I always wanted you. After a while, when I slept with..." I decide not to mention Dylan's name.

"What were you going to say?"

"I always imagined I was with you when I wasn't."

He smiles. "But that's a good thing, right? Lucky me."

"Is it a good thing? Or do I make poor decisions?"

"I don't understand," he says, his hand holding my chin.

"Never mind."

"Don't *never mind* me. Who do you think of when you're with me?"

"You. I always think of you."

He sighs with relief. "Good. Isn't that enough?"

"Enough what?"

"Enough evidence. Isn't that enough proof that we're good together?"

"No, it's lust and sex," I say and he groans with exasperation.

I know I'm making him more frustrated, yet we all must have our own process of determining what is right for us. Otherwise, my decision process would be like Carson's black and white version. My process on relationships has morphed into a very convoluted system of self-doubt and denial. It confounds me as well as him.

"My point is that I have made some poor decisions. Aren't you concerned that maybe this is one of those times? What if I'm with you because of the sex?"

"Do you know how many guys would love to hear a woman say that?" He laughs.

"Except I'm serious."

"Yeah. You're worried that, if you choose to be with me, it could all be based on sex. Ask yourself if you wanted me to fuck you or did you want to be with me."

"I want to be with you, but Dylan thought the same thing. Hasn't he always confused sex with love?"

"Seriously? You think Dylan's illness has spread to you? You're not related by blood. If anyone has a genetic predisposition to mental illness, it's me," Carson snaps. "Is all of this indecision you have going on because you have doubts about me or are they doubts about yourself?"

"It's all about me, Carson. You're..."

"What?" He searches my face for an answer.

"Perfect. You're perfect." I think back to Dylan saying the same thing to me in the diner.

He shakes his head again and gives me a worrisome smile. "I wish you'd stop doing this to yourself. I don't know what the hell your parents did to let you torment yourself like this."

"That's odd you'd say that. Dylan was telling me to reach out to my parents. He said they must be good because of the way I turned out," I scoff. "But then, you and Dylan are very different."

"I shouldn't have said that about your parents. I don't know them and all my beliefs stem from a pretty erratic childhood, along with my own ideas of what makes a person good."

"What makes me good?"

"You have sex with me and when you're not with me you think of having sex with me." He looks pretty proud of that answer.

I give him the thumbs up. "That was too easy."

Carson laughs, but he is guarded with me. "You're still not sure about me. About us, so we don't have to talk about it."

I can understand him being cautious. He gave himself fully to me weeks ago when he told me he loved me and I have hoarded his affections for me without giving him anything in return. He is politely letting me go.

"Yeah, I've talked in circles on this topic far too long. You have a business to run and I have to get ready for my art show," I say in my 5 Alpha business-like tone.

We don't speak at all on the ride home so Carson turns on the radio for background noise. It is dark when Carson drives up to my house.

"You're coming to the party tomorrow night, right?" he asks.

"Yes. If you still want me there."

He scowls. "Shit. You're the only person I care about seeing there. If you don't get that by now, then we really are screwed. My feelings for you haven't changed."

I inhale slowly. His words are a soothing balm.

Thirty-Three

We order our designer dresses online after searching for sales and have them shipped overnight. They arrive early and we gleefully pull them from their shipping boxes. Lauren is modeling her very skimpy dress for us in Aunt Virginia's room where there's a full-length mirror. We squeal, drunk on our excitement, as Lauren's lanky legs look ridiculously long in her platform stilettos. Her dress is made of a gold mesh fabric that resembles a snug, gauze bandage wrapped around her and it barely covers her lady parts. She's rail thin, but the dress gives her the appearance of a fuller bosom so she's pleased. The gold also complements her blond hair.

Imogene's dress is a rich burgundy velvet and, against her long, dark mane and her alabaster skin, she looks like a voluptuous, over-sexed, fairy princess.

My dress is simple, black, short and sleeveless with a plunging neckline that almost reaches to my belly button. The back scoops almost as much as the front. I will be very self-conscious walking into the party if other women are not wearing their sexiest dresses, too.

"Do I wear my hair up?" I ask, holding my hair in a twist on my head.

"No," Lauren says. "If you were accepting an Oscar tonight, I'd say wear your hair up. We're going for fun and sexy, so hair stays down."

"All-righty," I reply.

"I'm going to do your hair," Imogene says. "I need to keep my fingers busy because they really want to light a cigarette."

Imogene spends an hour making great spiral curls with the curling iron as well as extra curls with a twist of her fingers. She is meticulous and only sprays enough hair product on to hold the curl without making my hair sticky. Then she does my make-up, arching my eyebrows and filling out my lashes. When I look in the mirror I'm surprised and exhilarated to see my metamorphosis from computer geek to sexy maven.

"We all look fantastic," Lauren says. "We should walk around town like this every day."

Imogene and I laugh hysterically as we practice walking elegantly.

"I have an extra surprise," Imogene announces.

"You're pregnant?" Lauren asks and I gawk at her.

"No," Imogene snaps. "Jeremy is escorting us to the ball and he will be our designated driver." She grins and Lauren cheers.

"You asked him out?" I ask.

"No, I couldn't bring myself to actually say the words, but I masterfully manipulated him into asking me out," Imogene says.

"How?" Lauren asks. "Maybe I could try that on Leo."

"He came in for lunch at the diner and I mentioned that we really want to go to Carson's party, but can't risk driving my shit-mobile, so Jeremy nonchalantly said he'll swing by to pick all of us up."

"Was Dylan there when you said that?" I ask. "Because he knows my car runs fine."

"Yes, but Dylan is a good sport and played along. He never mentioned a word to Jeremy about your car." Imogene is smug with her conniving.

"Jeremy offered to drive because he wants to take you," Lauren says. "He wasn't fooled by your damsel in distress act. Please, he's probably relieved you gave him an excuse to take you."

"Well, but that's even better, right?" Imogene does her best Jessica Rabbit pose.

"Abso-fucking-lutley," Lauren adds. "The nice boy likes you."

I smile, happy for Imogene, yet it reminds me how I have squandered my rare opportunity with a nice boy. Two nice boys, in fact, but one boy in particular.

Imogene actually waits on the second floor and we yell to signal her when Jeremy's truck comes up the driveway. He stands in the front hall, looking like a timid businessman and watches Imogene descend the stairs in slow motion. He is bowled over when he sees her and stutters.

Lauren is less patient with Imogene's theatrics. "Get the lead out, Scarlet. Tara is burning and we've got a party to go to!"

We wear sneakers and carry our heels out to Jeremy's truck so we don't slip in the snow. Lauren brings along a beach towel to dry our sneakers and an emergency bag of who-knows-what for any wardrobe crisis we may have. These country girls have every angle covered.

My stomach is doing somersaults as we approach Carson's home. It's lit up and, within all the windows we can see the crowd of people already gathered in his home. All three of us hold on to Jeremy as we walk up the path to the front door. Jeremy has a sheepish grin as we enter and all these faces watch him walk in with three glammed up women teetering alongside him.

I look around and see Archie, Lois, Eleanor, and Imogene's parents taking over the living room couches. Bonnie's diner is closed for the night so everyone can attend the party, which is being catered by a popular restaurant from another town. There are servers everywhere in black outfits with white aprons, holding out trays of cocktails and appetizers. A deejay on the second floor is playing a mix of loud tunes and the dining area has been turned into the dance floor. My head is still roaming around, checking out all the people I don't know. They fill every room upstairs and downstairs.

Imogene stays with Jeremy while Lauren grabs my arm. "Let's find the bartender. That's where the single men hang out."

She steers me through the people with incredible determination and I'm impressed with her tenacity. I've never gone to a party with any agenda in place like Lauren's scheming. For me, showing up at a party at all is a success in itself.

Some young, attractive guy recognizes Lauren and reaches out to touch her and say hello. "Not now! Excuse me." She brushes past him.

"Who was that?" I ask.

"Who cares?" She continues dragging me into the casual dining area of the kitchen. "Bingo. The bar. The bartender. The men."

"You are good at this."

When the men at the bar see us, a path to the bar instantly opens up like the parting of the Dead Sea.

"You're like Moses," I whisper in her ear.

"Look again. Am I an ancient old man or do I know how to work this dress?"

"You have a wow factor that's off the charts, but I hope you remember you can't sit down in that dress without all your lady parts showing," I remind her.

"We'll be dancing, not sitting," she replies.

Lauren asks the bartender to make us dirty martinis with extra olives. I take a sip and make a face.

"Oh, grow up," she says.

"Stop saying that or I'm not going to be your sidekick." My roving eyes are searching for Carson.

"Geez, don't look so worried. Of course he's here. It's his party," Lauren says wryly.

"Lauren! Jess!" Dylan calls from across the room. He pushes his way through the men and gives us each a kiss on our cheeks. "You two look great." He looks positively dashing in his tailored black suit with a grey shirt and tie.

"Yes, we do," Lauren agrees. She holds up her empty martini glass for the bartender to refill.

"She's going to be plastered at this rate," I whisper into Dylan's ear. "You have to get Leo to ask her to dance and keep her dancing."

"I'm on it," he whispers back. "I need to talk to you, too." He rushes off, hopefully to wrangle the shy Leo into entertaining the most energetic girl at the party.

Lauren begins her second martini when Dylan hustles Leo over to her and takes her drink. "Lauren, Leo wants to dance," he says. "Have at it."

Lauren takes Leo's arm and dances her way over to the dining area and the hopping dance floor. Leo looks back at Dylan with an indiscernible expression.

"Is that fear?" I ask Dylan.

"No, that expression says *How did I get so fucking lucky?*"

"Really? You got all that from his bulging eyes and clenched mouth?"

Dylan laughs. "I live with the guy. He's gaga for her, but he's a little slow in doing something about it."

"Interesting."

We observe Lauren taking over the dance floor with her waving arms and leggy kicks. She could have been a Rockette. Leo is much more passive and looks like he's jogging in place. Dylan and I both burst out laughing.

"You're not drinking this," Dylan says, taking my martini and putting it on the bar.

"No, much too strong for me."

"Come over here," he says, leading me to the small passage between the dining area and the kitchen where a quiet reflection fountain blocks out some of the music and voices. We are alone in the space.

"What did you say to Carson at the shop yesterday?" Dylan demands and his abrupt change from party guy to inquisitor surprises me.

"Not much. He gave me a tour of the new addition. It's very impressive—"

"Yeah, yeah. I know that part. You left and he immediately left. Did you two meet up? Did something happen?"

I gulp air and let my eyes wander over to the wall of cascading water that plunges down the concrete wall into a rectangular pool of still water as I try to think of what to say. I'm certainly not going to tell Dylan that I had his brother drive me to the Ridge and then we had sex in the truck.

"I'm only asking because when he saw you at the shop he was happy. When I got here today to help him set up for the party, he looked like a guy who really didn't give a shit about anything and that's not like Carson. Did you say something to him?"

Wasn't I in this same conversation with Carson when he interrogated me about Dylan? "Carson has been very nice to me, but I'm still a disappointment to him. Nothing has changed in that area."

"Something has," Dylan says. Watching him cross his arms to contemplate the issue of his brother makes him look so much older, as if he has learned these skills from observing or mimicking his brother. "Have you spoken to him tonight?"

"I haven't even seen him yet."

"Great," Dylan mutters. "You look gorgeous by the way. Carson's going to have his heart ripped out when he sees you."

"Stop it, Dylan. May I remind you that you're known for blowing things out of proportion? Did it occur to you that maybe Carson is too busy having fun to even care if I'm here?"

"Yeah, right. Good one, Jess," he says and then looks past me and smirks. "Well, well, well. I'll let you two figure this out."

I turn around to see what he's looking at. Carson is striding through a group of women, including Gemma who looks stunning. He says hello to them, but doesn't stop to chat and doesn't take his eyes off me the whole time it takes him to make it across the large room to the little alcove where I thought Dylan and I were perfectly hidden.

"Hey, brother." Dylan smirks again as if they have some secret between them.

Carson glares at Dylan and then looks directly at me. "Jessica."

Is it ever a good sign when someone uses your full name with menacing eyes?

"If you'll excuse me, I see a few dozen women that want to dance with me. That's how popular I am," Dylan says, making me giggle and I have to cover my mouth to suppress them. Then Dylan winks at me and taps Carson on the shoulder. "Tell her how beautiful she looks. That's always a good way to start a conversation with a woman."

Dylan leaves us, laughing in a smug way now that he's the one to be the voice of reason.

There's something different about Carson. I'm so used to his tussled hair and beard stubble paired with his work jeans and boots. Tonight he shaved and looks very debonair with his hair slicked back more than usual. I can't see him using hair gel, although somehow, every part of his body and wardrobe is working his look. I know he doesn't have to spend any time on grooming the way we women slave over our appearance with sharp tools and dangerous appliances. It takes us hours to work those razors and hair devices, not to mention squeezing into the small, slinky fabrics. I imagine Carson showering, flipping his hair back and throwing on the first suit he sees in his closet. He has a casual elegance; dressy, cool and incredible sexy. The dusty jeans and tool belt have been replaced with a black suit, a black shirt without the tie and the top buttons undone. He's a masterpiece, made for that suit.

"Armani or Zegna. I'm guessing Armani."

He shrugs. "Who cares? It's a suit."

"You sure throw some hoedown." I'm trying mightily to make him laugh, but he's resisting my super powers.

"This only happens once a year. The other three hundred and sixty-four days, this place is like a monastery."

I was going to make a crack about us having sex in the monastery, but he doesn't seem to be in a joking mood.

"Well, thank you for inviting me. Your house is a fabulous place for a party and you've made a lot of people happy."

Carson takes in my dress with the deep neckline that slightly exposes the sides of my breasts. I've never worn anything so revealing and watching Carson's eyes roam slowly from my legs up to my face reminds me of the day I wore the red bathing suit and how naked I felt in front of him.

That may have been the beginning of when I started lying to myself. I agreed to a date with Dylan, but I was already thinking about Carson and, when I wore the sexy red swimsuit, it was Carson's attention I really wanted. He notices the necklace he gave me, the delicate gold key hanging between my breasts.

"Dylan called it. He said you'd be the prettiest woman here."

"There are hoards of pretty women here." I watch a group of giggling young women surround Dylan.

"I hadn't noticed," he says with a penetrating gaze that never leaves my face.

I suspect every woman in Hera jumps at the chance to attend a Blackard event, anything to be around Dylan and Carson. I stare at Carson's lips and so desperately want to kiss him. The thought of him sends waves of heated desire through me. I must surely be an awful person if I always want to jump into bed with him when I can't admit that I could possibly have strong feelings for him as well as possibly a future.

Guilt and shame, whether they are deserved or self-inflicted, are strong opponents to someone like me. I don't want to be the tart that jerks Carson around. I know many already believe I did the same thing to Dylan. I put my head down and pretend something is in my eye.

"I know you have another powder room hidden behind one of these passageways somewhere. Can you point me in the direction?" I ask, putting my hand up to my blinking eye.

Wordlessly, Carson takes my arm and drags me down the hall, further from the fountain and far away from the party guests. We round a corner by a window with more dramatic views and Carson pulls open one of those metal doors with rivets, similar to what I saw in his workshop. He walks right in with me, closes the door behind him and I hear the lock click. He flips a switch that lights the room in an amber glow.

It's more than a simple powder room, it's huge. It has a large, stone vanity with a rustic mirror covering the wall above it, a cozy chair and a toilet area that is separated by a bamboo wall and private door.

"Everyone uses the bathroom down the other hall. They forget that this one exists, so the room is all yours," he says, but doesn't turn to leave.

I forget that I'm supposed to have something in my eye and, instead of going to the mirror and acting out my fake eye problem, my hands are at my side. I'm staring hopelessly at Carson. In the amber lighting, his dark features are striking to the point that he takes my breath away.

There's a single moment where we must be experiencing the same thought, a glint of desire or need passes between us. Carson rushes forward with one hand cupping my face, the other under my ass and he backs me onto the vanity between the two sinks, kissing me. I wind my arms around his neck and arch into him as I return the kisses, touching him everywhere I can. His hands skitter across my bare back and one reaches into the neckline and palms my breast. Then he caresses my bare thigh and pushes up underneath the dress to cup my bottom flesh.

He pushes himself between my legs, so I feel his hardness between us. My tongue duels with his while he squeezes my nipples until they are aching with heat and sending spasms down between my legs. I reach down and rub Carson's bulge, which is straining against his pants. His hand leaves my breast and holds the back of my head while his other hand rubs against my bare leg and bottom. In that instant he pulls away from my mouth and holds my head firmly.

"Do you want me to screw you here because you're in the mood to get fucked by any guy?" He pauses. "Or do you want me?"

I'm yearning for him and the tug in my heart is louder than my libido. I'm afraid to answer. My silence suggests the worst; that I'm only seeking out a physical relationship. I am a coward.

He lets me go and steps back from the vanity to adjust himself. "I don't do casual sex with you," he says. "You can be platonic friends with Dylan, but I'm not your friend. I'm something more and we both know that." He walks out, slamming the door closed.

I sit for a moment and take deep breaths so I won't cry. Then I tidy myself up and put a handful of cold water up to my mouth to wash away the heat from his lips. I avoid looking in the mirror, sure that I'll see the person I dislike the most.

Thirty-Four

I can't go home yet since my friends are having too much fun dancing and I'm counting on Jeremy to be our designated driver. I'll have to wait out the evening, bury myself in the throngs of people I don't know and try to avoid Carson.

Not long after I've re-entered the party area, Archie and Eleanor flag me down and invite me to sit between them on one of the big sofas in the living room. Lois is propped on the armrest next to Archie. A waitress brings me a glass of champagne and tidbits of food that I can't identify, but it's all so scrumptious. I eat as much as I can while trying to remember the last time I really filled myself with food. My stomach has been clenched and nervous for the last few months, a painful reminder of my festering anxiety.

"Goodness, you're one hungry girl," Eleanor comments.

I shrug with my mouth full.

"You should be dancing." Lois sighs.

"We should all be dancing, but I'm very comfortable sitting here watching everyone else," Archie says. He is in a tuxedo and looks like he could be the unflappable butler in a BBC drama.

"That's fine for you, Arch, but Jess and Carson have had a spat and she really should be dancing with him," Lois says.

"What's the drama du jour?" Eleanor asks, lifting an eyebrow.

"Now, now. Leave her be. She's not used to this small town life. It's like one big family; sometimes happy, sometimes not." Archie pats my leg.

"No drama. We're not fighting," I deny. "We're simply not speaking."

Lois scoffs. "Fudge. I wish Ginnie were here to deal with this. She was so looking forward to knowing you as an adult and now you're stuck with us instead."

"Great, you can grow old with us," Eleanor adds.

I laugh. "I may do that."

"She's serious, Jess. At the rate you're going, you will sadly find yourself on the sidelines," Lois says. "Look at your friends and their new beaus. Isn't that a sight to see?"

Fortunately, two gentlemen I recognize from the diner ask Eleanor and Lois to dance and they sashay off to the dance floor in their flowing dresses.

Imogene and Jeremy are talking and smiling on the dance floor at the same time that Lauren is making Leo laugh with her moves. It is a sweet sight, but my attention is drawn to another part of the huge living room where Dylan and Carson are surrounded by a group of friends. They all look about the same age and some story with a famous punch line is being retold. I can't hear the words; however, the nods, shouts of laughter and high-fives tell me that these must be their childhood friends, the kids who saw what Carson and Dylan went through and how they survived.

The brothers are laughing together when Carson puts his arm around Dylan's shoulders and brings him in for a headlock and plants a kiss on the top of his head. I've never seen them so affectionate and loving with one another. I slip my cell phone out of my evening bag and watch them through the screen. In the second that Carson has his head against Dylan's forehead, smiling with his arms wrapped around his younger brother, I take the photo. The image is exquisite. I bring it towards me for a closer look.

"What is it?" Archie asks.

"It's beautiful," I whisper. "It's pure love."

Archie leans in to study the photo. "That it is."

I shove the phone back in my purse and take a deep, calming breath so I don't get emotional in front of Archie.

"We don't always get do-overs. Think very carefully before making a decision about love," he says to me. "Sometimes when it's offered, it may have an expiration date."

I snort. "If love has an expiration date, then love really does not last forever as the saying goes."

"No, it means that love isn't always available when you want it. When it comes, you grab on to it because you never know when that opportunity may disappear forever."

"I'm not really following you," I say, adjusting the hem of my dress while also trying not to allow my gaze to follow Carson's every move around the room.

"Do you want to end up in a big, old, empty farmhouse like me? All alone?" Now Archie has my full attention. "I fell in love with the only love of my life fifty years ago. I made her wait, though. I wanted to impress her. I wanted to make more money, buy more land and make more investments so I could offer her more."

"That's what we're supposed to do. Wait, build up our lives and our bank accounts before we get seriously involved with someone."

"I thought so, too. Why start poor? My love, Emily, agreed as well. She waited, but I kept putting off proposing because I wanted her to have more than the poverty of her childhood. After three years, though, she found someone else. She said she loved me, but she could not wait a lifetime for me and sacrifice her chance to have children and a family of her own. She lived in another county and, while we were broken up, I thought it was temporary; I did not know that another gentleman was also in love with her. He had no intention of making her wait.

"When I told her I had purchased this lovely home for her and had several profitable investments in place along with my growing law practice, she said *Archie, it's too late. You made my love for you the least important part of your life. I'm marrying George Weston because he carries my heart around like it's his most precious possession.'* I hated George Weston for that, and I thought he must be a real sap. Well, George had the last laugh. He and Emily are still happily married and they have six children as well as fifteen grandchildren. I never fell in love with anyone like that again. I never married and my house is empty."

There's something so suspiciously sappy about his story that I find it hard to believe. "Archie, are you pulling my leg?"

Archie smiles, yet there is a distant look of pain behind his wrinkled eyes. "No, my dear. People like me who live with this kind of regret rarely talk about it. It was a calamity of my own making. My point is that, in some cases, time is never on your side."

"I'm sorry that happened to you, but I'm not ready to get married."

"Oh, I know that. It's a different world, but people," he points to his chest, "in here, haven't changed. There's more to love than getting married. It's about treating someone's gift of love with the utmost care and respect."

I look down at my hands which are fidgeting in my lap. "I can create software for billion dollar companies... I can solve complex mathematical equations and I can paint everything I'm feeling even if I cannot express it verbally. Yet, being in love confounds me."

"I gather. Are you in love?"

"I think so."

"It's the most glorious reason to live, isn't it?"

"Yes. I believe you're right."

"And the problem is?"

"I'm afraid of mirroring my parents' relationship. It works for them, but it's not what I want; I fear it might be in my DNA."

Archie smiles. "No. You're too much like Ginnie. She had a great love. He died two years ago, but they had a great twelve-year run."

"Better late than never, right?" I force a smile.

"Yes, I wish that were true for me, though."

"Lois thinks I'm being unkind to Carson and I guess, in her own bully way, she believes I'm not being true to myself. Do you think that, too?"

"Jessica, the only opinions that matter are yours and Carson's. That being said, I think Carson is a very patient young man when it comes to people he cares about. Dylan, for instance. The door is open for you at this moment. It may still be open next month or even next year, but do not assume it will always be so."

"What about when one door closes another door opens?"

"Bullshit." Archie's final word on the matter is probably his most powerful.

Lois and Eleanor rejoin us, plopping down on the couches with an air similar to Imogene and Lauren, making both Archie and I chuckle.

"Are you all done with that stinkin' thinkin' of yours?" Lois says to me. "Are you ready to grab the bull by the horns?" She demonstrates with her fists in the air. Before I have to defend myself again, I beg off to find the powder room. I really just escape to stand in the hidden hallway by the wall with the waterfall.

There are a few older couples mingling by it, but I feel alone enough to gather my thoughts. I wander back to the end of the hall to peer out into the great room again. I see Carson talking to Gemma and my soul drops to the floor. Gemma is standing close enough for her arm to touch Carson and he's smiling down at her as she talks to him. They aren't in a group, it's just the two of them talking and it looks so intimate I want to retch.

"Hi," a nice voice says behind me. I turn around and face a handsome man, one of the guys I saw hanging around Dylan and Carson when I took the photo.

"Hi," I say, putting my hands behind me like a five-year-old.

"Would you dance with me?" he asks. A beautiful Van Morrison song starts playing. "Slow dance," he says, holding out his arm with a smile.

"Sure," I agree. It is a party after all. As we walk out to the dance floor we pass by Lois and her geriatric gang again. I give her a signal and toss my purse to her. Like a pro she stands and catches it then frowns and shakes her head in disapproval. She wants me to dance with Carson, but the dancing gods are not on my side.

"Jess, right? I'm Matthew," he introduces himself, taking my hands in his.

"Nice to meet you," I say. He pulls me in closer as Van Morrison croons about searching the world over for his love.

"No. No. No." I hear Carson's voice booming behind me. "That's enough of that. Move over, Matt, this is my dance and take this for me." Carson tosses his suit coat across Matt's empty arms still in their dance pose.

Matt looks from me to Carson, not sure if he should argue that he was here first. Most likely, Carson's sheer dominance in height and muscle causes Matt to apologetically bow out and allow Carson to take over.

My shocked expression must be apparent to everyone within sight of Carson's display.

"House rules. Host gets first dance." He yanks me close to him and we begin moving with the melody. My nerve endings are fired up as my hands rest on his hard shoulders. I can feel his heat through his shirt. *Stud in the house!*

"Did you have to humiliate him like that?"

"Matt? He'll get over it," Carson snaps. "I wasn't going to let this be your song with him."

"What are you ranting about?"

"Everyone has a song for their first dance; when they first meet or get married. I wasn't going to let this song belong to you and Matt."

I stifle a laugh. "You're jealous. I thought you never get jealous."

"I never have until you let that guy swing you out onto the dance floor like…"

"Like what?"

"Nothing," he says and holds me tighter. "Like he's your lover. This is a song for lovers."

I smile up at him and he begrudgingly smiles at me and then looks away. "I didn't think you were speaking to me anymore." It hurts to have to hold my head back to look up at him. I'd rather rest my head against his chest while we sway, but I think I lost that privilege.

"We're not really speaking. We're dancing."

"Carson," I admonish him with another smile.

"You think I give up that easily? You're more interested in me than you want to admit. You've already decided to live in Hera, you let the girls move in and you gave up your lease in the city."

"How do you know about my apartment?"

347

He tilts his head to the side as if I asked a stupid question. He smells so good; I really don't care about the answer to my question.

"I hope you're doing some soul-searching."

"What?"

"The song. Aren't you listening to it? This is our song," he growls.

I laugh so hard, I have to pull my hand from his and cover my mouth. He uses the opportunity to pull me into an embrace and keep dancing. His head is resting on mine.

"Stop ruining our song," Carson says.

"Carson, I think you'd be less sure of me if you knew my parents."

"What do they have to do with us?" His deep, rich voice rumbles into my ear.

"They are everything I know about marriage. They never ask if I'm dating anyone because they don't care. They taught me that the most important parts of my life are career, salary and ambition."

"They are just trying to protect you. All good parents do that."

"I know how to work hard and I know how to manage bank accounts. I don't know how to be a couple. You deserve someone who is as caring as you are with Dylan and your friends. You deserve someone who appreciates family the way you do."

He moves back to look at me. "Don't patronize me and most definitely do not preach some movie script to me. I can take care of myself. Do you judge me by my parents?"

"What? I didn't know your parents." I have a difficult time hearing him over the music and can't believe we're having this discussion on the dance floor.

He pulls me back in and speaks into my ear. "You know my mother died young and my father was a suicidal drunk. They left no will, no provisions for my brother and me. Do you think I would take the same path as them?"

"No," I answer. My skin tingles as his lips brush against my cheek. "I think you have faced extreme adversity and used it to make you stronger."

"So, you don't judge me by what my parents did or did not do, but you believe I should judge you by your parents. Who I don't even know. Christ. For someone who likes logic, you make the most illogical argument about us."

"I don't want anyone to get hurt," I say softly with my eyes focused on his chest peeking through his open collar.

"I don't, either. Shut up and dance." He's angry and disappointed that I would have to mention sparing anyone the hurt of loss. If anyone knows how to protect people, it's Carson.

The deejay announces the last song of the evening and starts spinning a sexy dance club song. Dylan comes jumping onto the dance floor with three young women following him. Their arms and legs are flailing everywhere. I decide this would be a good time to exit the dance area since Carson isn't a showy dancer like Dylan.

"Whoa. Where do you think you're going?" He grabs my arm. "We're still dancing, Babycakes."

That name infuriates me and he loves it. I put my hands back up for a traditional waltz hold, but

Carson rests his hands on my hips and slams my body right against his as he starts dancing to the fast pop tune. One of his legs is between mine as he does some kind of sexy rumba move, swaying and grinding.

"You have got to be kidding," I say loudly. I can't believe he's comfortable dancing so provocatively.

"Oh, I'm not kidding. Put your hands on my shoulders."

While everyone else is jumping, hopping and twirling, Carson makes us look like the hot salsa duo. I would never do this in public with any other man, but my surprise and anger dissipates as I begin enjoying our erotic dance. His muscles are thick and hard across his broad shoulders. His eyes bore into me as our bodies crush together and the heat between us soars. It's over too soon; the song ends and I push away to get some air. Carson is behind me and puts his hands back on my waist.

"I've changed my mind," he whispers into my ear. "You're staying here with me tonight."

I whip around so fast my elbow slams into his ribs. He winces.

"I'm leaving with the girls. Jeremy is our driver."

"Nope."

Carson heads to the door where people are milling around, putting on coats and saying goodbye. He says something to Imogene who looks across the room at me. I'm still standing there, not really sure if I should insist on leaving or follow my body's lead, which is begging to stay with Carson.

"Dear," Lois says. She raises an eyebrow with a hint of a smile, but she says nothing else before handing me my evening bag and leaving with the other guests.

Thirty-Five

I peer out the window into the blackness of the valley below and when I turn back to the large, quiet house, the catering staff has already wrapped leftover food and stored it in Carson's big, empty refrigerator along with swiftly collecting all the dishes and glassware. When the house is cleared of all people, the lights dimmed or shut off, Carson comes back in through the front door and locks it. We look at one another from across the room and I don't know whether to be excited or terrified.

He strides toward me and takes my hand to pull me towards the stairs.

"We're doing it your way," he says.

"What's my way?"

"No talking, no strings."

He walks me briskly upstairs to his bedroom and closes the door. Before I can say anything, his mouth is on mine, hot and frantic. My whole body responds immediately. I run my fingers through his hair and then his tongue and lips are on my neck. A rush of cool air envelopes my body as I realize Carson has pushed my dress straps off my shoulders and it falls to the floor.

"Keep the shoes on," he demands, still kissing me and pulling my panties down at the same time.

I am fully naked and standing in my heels while he is fully dressed and ravaging me with his mouth. I reach for the bulge in his pants and he groans, however, when I start to undo his zipper, he pushes my hand away.

"No," he says. "Here." He walks me to the window, a glass wall that overlooks the white valley, and plants my hands above my head, flat against the glass. He stands behind me and uses his leg to spread mine wider. I feel extremely vulnerable, yet excited. The sound of Carson unzipping his pants sends a flame of arousal through my body. I am getting wetter with anticipation.

His calloused hands do not caress me gently this time, they maul my breasts, kneading and pinching my nipples as his cock rubs against my butt cheeks. He keeps one hand on my breast and uses the other to rub my clit. He is rough as he pushes two fingers in me and rubs my folds with my own fluids.

"Carson, now." I am practically panting with desire.

"I don't want to use a condom this time. I want to feel you without it. Is that okay?" he asks gruffly.

"Yes. It's a safe time," I blurt it out, wanting him to know that I recently started the pill to be with him, but it sounds like a pretty lame statement, so I keep quiet.

From behind he pushes his cock into me, forcing me up against the window. I gasp, but then groan with pleasure as he grunts and pumps relentlessly into me. The more I moan, the faster he thrusts. His hand is still circling my wet center and I think I'm about to come when Carson pulls out. He swings me over to the bed, no easy move for me in heels. I'm on my back facing Carson as he strips his clothes off. It's a highly erotic sight and I scramble backwards to the middle of the bed to watch him.

Naked, Carson looks even taller, wider and more intimidating. Seeing his face darken with arousal, I gasp at the size of his cock. He puts one knee on the bed, grabs my ankles and yanks me back to where he's standing by the side of the bed. He shoves two pillows under my lower back and rests my left thigh over his hip so I'm exposed and titled up to him. The heels fall off when he puts his hand under my butt cheek and props my right thigh up with his other hand. I watch every muscle and ripple in his torso as he bends over and kisses my belly. He works his way down between my legs and pushes his tongue into me.

"Oh God," I whisper.

His tongue circles, licks and sucks until I can't stop moaning.

"That feels so good, don't stop... don't stop."

He stops and chuckles cruelly, obviously wanting to punish me. He stands up again and leans in with his cock circling me until he is dripping in my wetness. "Shit," he whispers and shudders. He can't wait any longer either, and plunges into me full hilt.

I gasp and a low groan escapes Carson's steely demeanor. He doesn't take his eyes off mine. I have the urge to close my eyes and let my head fall back, but I use all my resolve to keep my gaze locked on him. He slams into me with uncontrollable desperation. I arch up and run my hands down my sides and back up across my breasts and peaked nipples.

"Keep doing that," he says hoarsely, staring at my hands fondling my own breasts.

I slowly run my palms lightly over my nipples and watch Carson's intense gaze as though we're dueling for who can have the most pleasure without showing any affection. I want to stroke his face and remove the lock of his hair that has fallen forward, but he keeps enough distance between us so my hands can't reach him. His frantic thrusts slow down and he grinds in a full circle. It's an assault on my sensitive spot and I smile as a spiraling orgasm begins to build in me.

"Fuck, fuck, fuck," Carson groans as his own pleasure becomes too powerful. He pulls out of me and flips me over. "On your knees," he rasps.

Feeling bereft without him in me, I scramble to get in position, on my knees and elbows. He enters me from behind again and lunges forward covering my body. I've temporarily lost the climax that was building in me and I think that was intentional on Carson's part. Somehow, in his way, this angry sex is his way of getting back at me for being distant and noncommittal. He's putting on a good show, but I'm not fooled.

His emotions are running him ragged on the inside. If he only wanted to fuck me senseless and get pleasure out of it for himself, we'd already be done. This is going on and on because he can't touch me without an emotional investment. I consider this and how much I like having him care about me. He thinks this rougher version of sex will frighten me or turn me off, but truthfully, in

Carson's mind, he is making love to me, not screwing me. He's a terrible actor if he thinks I'm falling for his tough guy act.

His fingers rub my wet folds as he pummels into me with quick grunts. Having this animalistic effect on him arouses me more. I clench my inner muscles, making him groan louder.

"God, Jessica," he hisses. We both come.

Our undulation continues as his climax subsides. Another wave rolls through me and I yelp as a lingering flame triggers my nerves endings again. Carson holds onto me tightly before pulling me down with him still inside of me as he lies down on his side. My back is to his chest and he is breathing heavily against my neck. He keeps his arms wrapped around me. With a slight movement, he pulls out of me. I can feel when his tense body relaxes completely and his weight sinks further against me.

"Seventy million," I whisper to myself.

Carson laughs softly into my hair.

We stay like that until we fall asleep.

Thirty-Six

The sun is pouring through the bedroom when I wake. I am wrapped under Carson's thick arm, nestled against his naked body. Sometime in the night he must have put a pillow under my head and covered me with a blanket. I turn in his arms to look at him, hoping I don't disturb his sleep.

He is a gorgeous specimen of male virility. His thick, glossy, chestnut hair swept back from his face, his muscular torso that narrows down into a trim waist with abs that I trace with my finger. One of his giant, corded legs swings and pins me in place. His steel blue eyes open lazily, taking me in with a mischievous twinkle and a curve to his mouth. I feel his cock get hard between us. As it presses against my stomach, I know that, if I don't get out of here now, I'm going to be too turned on to leave.

"Huh, you didn't get away." His deep voice is sultry and relaxed.

"I shouldn't have slept here. I have to—"

"Get going," he cuts me off. "Yeah, that's the same line you always use. Not going to work this time."

"Carson, it's late, we overslept." I peer over his shoulder at the nightstand clock. "It's ten. I thought you like to work on Sunday mornings and I have plenty of work I need to get back to."

357

"Not today." He runs his finger along my cheekbones and jaw; the same thing I was aching to do to him before he woke up.

I wriggle my arms free and place my hands on his rock hard chest. "Can I take a quick shower and borrow some sweats from you so I don't have to do the walk of shame home in my dress?" I ask, remembering that Lauren left my sneakers from her emergency bag by the door.

Carson stares dreamily at me with a smirk. "We'll take a long shower and then think about food. I'm starving."

I'm pretty sure he's starving for sex the way he's devouring me with his smoldering eyes and my body is gleefully rejoicing as it responds with a growing heat and need to have him inside of me again. I barely recognize myself when I'm with him.

"Bad idea," I say as my nipples bud and a surge of wetness ripples between my legs.

His fingers begin playing with my hair, stroking my head. "You're not going anywhere, Jess. I'm hard and your hands are all over me. You can't touch me like that and think you're walking away."

I can't say anything when my hands are betraying me. Carson rolls me onto my back with him on top of me. My breath catches with unabated desire as his weight presses me into the bed. My hands immediately begin roaming his back as I reach down to caress his firm ass.

His mouth covers mine and his tongue is fervent at first before slowing down to a leisurely pace of swirling and probing my mouth and lips. I kiss him back with the same fervor and feel him reposition himself with his forearms, taking most of his weight so I can breathe. The kiss ends with a sweet sigh and the stormy Carson from last night is gone. He looks at me with a boyish grin that makes my heart swell.

"You're so beautiful," he says, looking down at me with a tenderness that he keeps hidden from everyone else. "I love this wild red hair and your big brown eyes floor me every time you look at me."

"Hmm," I mumble as I run my hands through his hair. "You're pretty gorgeous yourself but pinning me with your naked body is hardly a fair move. This will only lead to trouble. That's why I should leave now."

"I told you, you're not going anywhere. I'm hard and you can't keep your hands off me, so this is happening," he says before he kisses my neck. He runs his tongue along my collarbone and I let a moan coax him on.

"I don't know why you bother to put up with me," I whisper and then regret saying it aloud.

Carson runs his lips gently over mine. "Because I'm in love with you and I want you. Even when you're being obnoxiously neurotic, I can't stop thinking about you or wanting you."

Carson expertly rubs his fingers over my hungry parts and circles around the sweet spot until I'm soaking and writhing in his arms, greedily raking my fingers over any unexposed part of him. He has two fingers inside of me, probing in and out, rubbing my center, and I'm squirming with so much agonizing pleasure that the blanket falls down to the small curve in Caron's lower back.

I stroke his cock and I like to think it becomes longer and thicker in my grasp. He watches as I rub his tip against my wet cleft and his head swings up, throwing his dark hair back so he can look at me. He props himself higher up with his hands and as soon as I give him an inch of myself, he thrusts and grunts like an unleashed wild beast. I pull my knees up to his waist and take him in fully.

In a rapid-fire succession, I am assaulted with the joy, desire and ecstasy of having Carson inside of me. It is more than a primal need and lust for him. I want him to need me, to see through every part of my body and mind.

He sucks hard on my breasts until they ache and I let out a cry as he swivels his hips in a sexy motion that keeps striking the right spot. I moan and push my body against him, wanting more.

"I want you to come," Carson says between ragged breaths, "because I'm about to lose it. That's what you do to me."

I pull his head down to me so I can kiss him. "Oh man, Jess," he says gruffly between our lips.

I'm about to climax when I see a bright flash to my side. My head turns in that instant and I see a young blond woman with a laundry basket entering the room, singing to herself. She is lost in her song before seeing us. Then she screams, covers her mouth and backs out of the room, closing the door behind her.

"Shit!" Carson says as his cock pops out of me accidentally from the surprise intrusion.

"Who was that?" I slam my palms against his chest.

"Shh," he says, trying to calm me. "It's okay. That was Talia. I forgot she comes on Sunday mornings when I'm usually at the shop.

With our orgasms on hold, our bodies are thrumming with sensory overload. "I'm so embarrassed. Get off me. I have to get dressed."

"No, you don't." Carson holds my face still. "Stay here."

His cock is heavy as it bobs between us, Carson is flushed and barely holding it together.

"Carson, she saw us. I have to get out of here." I slap his chest again, but it's like slapping a boulder that won't budge.

"Big deal. We're in my bed, so it's not like getting caught naked in a car. We're going to finish what we started." His voice is low with need.

"Let me go take a shower." I 'm thinking about a quick rinse and then getting away.

"You want a shower?" he asks, gaining some composure despite his throbbing erection. "Good idea."

He picks me up off the bed quickly and carries me to the bathroom, to his large shower stall.

"I meant me," I say as he puts me against the cold tile wall and turns on the three showerheads that are positioned on two walls.

He closes the glass door and lifts me up, propping me against a corner of the shower. He lifts one of my legs, positioning himself between them and then begins rubbing my wet clit again.

"Carson," I begin to protest, however, his fingers are in me again. "Oh God."

He smiles and kisses me. I feel dwarfed by his height and powerful, naked body. "Let yourself go," he says, putting the tip of his cock in me. He hoists me up by bracing both of his arms under my knees and then he rams into me with a shudder. "Ah, fuck yeah."

I throw my arms around his neck as he grinds and thrust into me slowly while I salivate over his splendid form. My head falls back against the tile wall with the water spraying down on us. Carson has a heated expression of rapture as he studies my face and begins to thrust faster. Triumphant moans escape from him. The marvelous sensation of an impending explosion fills me and I groan as the orgasm shatters me into a million tiny pieces of extreme pleasure, sending my body into vibrating after-shocks.

"Carson." I smile as he continues to drive himself into me until his own release comes.

"Ah!" Carson groans with his slowing thrusts, pumping the last of his liquid into me.

He keeps swiveling and grinding his hips into me until he's empty. He frees my legs, but keeps me pinned against the wall, holding my face for a searing kiss that means more to me in the afterglow of our love-making.

I am completely sedated and less concerned about Talia seeing us. Carson pulls me under one of the showerheads and scrubs my head with shampoo before massaging my body with bath gel. I moan as his slippery hands slide up and down my arms.

"This feels too good," I say.

Carson gives a deep chuckle. The smile on his face is nothing short of bemused gloating.

"Spend the day with me." He wraps me in his arms with my back against his chest.

I groan, not wanting to battle with him again, especially when I'm naked. His soapy hands fondle my breasts, making them perk and fill with an ache. Then before I can build up any defense against him, his hand is slipping between my legs, rubbing me where I'm still vibrating from the first orgasm. My sex is wet and open and I feel my senses hum on a wave of arousal when I think of Carson driving his lust, need and want into me.

"One more time. We both want it. And then you stay here with me today," he says gruffly into my ear.

"You don't play fair," I say breathlessly as his fingers push inside me. I love that his large body can encompass me, trap me and titillate me so easily.

"I can't play fair. I have a lot of competition." His tone is guttural and I sense him turning into a feral creature of need, his cock getting hard against my back.

"There's no competition. How can you be ready for this so soon?"

"Look who's talking? You're so wet. I bet I could make you come with two more strokes." He talks low as though he can't control himself much longer.

I raise my arms, put my hands against the glass wall and arch my back, sticking my rear end out. "Now. I want you."

Carson rubs his full cock against me before inserting the head. "Are you ready for me again? I don't want to hurt you," he says, spreading my legs. His slippery fingers rub me from the front and caress me from the back as I pant with wanting him, arching my back more.

"Now," I moan.

"This will help," he says and it sounds like he's using more gooey liquid soap.

"Now, Carson," I beg as I face the shower glass.

He pushes upward into me with his hands on my waist like a vise, which is good because I can barely hold myself up.

"How's that?" he asks and I can picture his smug expression.

"Faster, harder," I plead.

On my command I can feel his excitement surge through him, an energy that also courses through me as long as we are touching. He holds me in place with one strong arm while his hand rubs my clit until I'm about to scream. The lubrication allows him to go deeper and faster, and I cry out with each thrust. My climax comes hard and spills into converging spasms that shake me into oblivion and leave me gasping.

"Yes," I moan.

"Fuck, that feels good," Carson mutters as his cock spurts into me. His arms wrap around my waist and he holds me firmly as he mounts me, slamming his length as deep as it can go until it is empty.

We are in a slow, hazy mind fuck after that. I have never spent this much time with any man in any of my sexual experiences. That's not saying much since I've only had actual intercourse with two men, two brothers. I cringe. One I liked, but one I am now falling hard for. I think about this as I regain my composure.

Carson cleans my body gently again with a washcloth, kissing each part as he does. Dylan could do this with anyone I think. He is affectionate, loving and able to throw himself into a moment with anyone. I suppose that's how he got a reputation as a ladies' man. Yet Carson is closed off to women when it comes to intimacy and I know how significant it is for him to have me in his personal space. Plus, all this time our bodies were touching, I only thought of Carson. Not once did I think of Dylan or any of the guys I've ever thought I liked.

Carson hangs up the washcloth and then pulls me in for a long, deep kiss. His hands cup my face and I gush inside, knowing that he loves me. At least for this moment, I have this beautiful man and his desire to please me. I still grapple with believing this could be permanent, however, it's this moment that I want to savor, so I return his kiss with the same loving attention.

"If you keep looking at me like that, I'm going to make love to you all day," he says, biting my ear lobe.

"Hmm, you have to be out of steam."

Carson looks down and smirks and I follow his gaze. His cock is semi-erect and bobbing between his legs.

"Good Lord. What are you made of?"

"Want to find out?" He laughs before kissing me again.

I have to push my way out of the shower.

"You're going to leave me like this?" he asks as I snatch two towels.

"You're insatiable," I accuse as I wrap a towel around my body and put my hair in a turban.

"Only when it comes to you." He laughs again and begins washing his hair.

As he showers, I find his hair dryer and work on my knotted mass with sneak peeks at his magnificent physique.

"I see you looking," he says as he shampoos his hair with his eyes closed.

I scoff and leave the bathroom.

"I'm going to have my way with you again in the bed," he shouts after me and I hope Talia can't hear us.

I rifle through his drawers to find some sweat pants and a T-shirt. I have to roll the pants and tie the drawstring waist band as tight as possible. Then I collect my rumpled black dress before heading downstairs.

The scent of good coffee hits me as I descend the staircase. I head into the kitchen where Talia is adjusting a mop head. She is not much older than me; petite, blond and very pretty. Carson never mentioned that.

With Carson naked on top of me and a skimpy blanket covering his ass, I wonder how much she actually saw. At least I feel less exposed now. My face and body scrubbed clean and I'm swimming in Carson's giant-sized sweats. Without make-up I look like I'm seventeen tops and that makes me self-conscious.

"Hello," Talia says with a heavy Polish accent and a big smile. "I'm so sorry. I didn't mean to disturb."

"It's okay."

"Carson is always out the door before seven so I didn't know he was here and the truck is not parked in front of the house. Really, I thought he was at work," she goes on to plead her apologies.

"Really, it's fine." I flit my hand in the air like getting caught in a sex act is something that happens all the time to me. "Did you make coffee?"

"Yes, for you and Carson," she answers. My discomfort is somewhat mitigated by her sincerity and sweet demeanor.

I help myself to a mug of coffee and relish the hit of caffeine.

"Are you hungry?' she asks. She takes a pan of burritos out of the oven.

"Did you make that?"

"Yes. I cook for Carson. I cook for you, too. It's shrimp and asparagus from the party and I scramble it with egg and cheese to make a breakfast burrito. You like?"

"I love."

Talia puts a burrito on a plate, gathers a napkin and utensils and then places it in front of me where I sit at the kitchen island. I pick the burrito up with my hands and start eating, realizing once again how hungry I am.

"I'm so glad you're with Carson," she says, putting another burrito on my plate and making a plate for Carson. "He likes you a lot. You were dancing last night."

I vaguely remember noticing a pretty blond on the dance floor with Dylan. It was Talia. She must have witnessed our silly scene while Carson and I were dancing.

"He talks about me?"

"No," she says, but she's nodding and smiling. "I mean, yes, in a way. When he's here, sometimes he mentions you, but it's how he says your name. He put up your paintings, did you see?"

I nod, my mouth full of her excellent food. I imagine Carson talking about me with Talia in a subtle way, although it's enough that she picks up the signals. She's a very attractive woman after all and looks like someone who has to fend off a lot of men.

"You blush. You like him, too. More than like, yes?" she asks.

We both turn and notice that Carson is standing at the far side of the kitchen, leaning against the passageway to the formal dining area. He's wearing relaxed jeans and a black T-shirt. His hair is wet and slicked back. He crosses his feet and arms in a very obvious way as he waits for my answer.

I turn back to Talia and feel my face redden even more.

"Oops," she says, smiling at me and then at Carson. "Too personal. I'm going to go clean." She slinks out of the room with her mop and bucket.

Carson approaches and sits down to eat his meal. He is quiet and I know, behind that steely façade, he is seething. He has professed his love for me more than once over the last few weeks, especially over the last ten hours.

I scrutinize my unfinished meal with an artificial interest and wish there was some way I could click my heels and beam myself home. I'm going to have to ask Carson for a ride since the snow is too deep and treacherous for walking.

"More than like?" Carson repeats Talia's question to me. "Jess?"

Our eyes meet and I immediately register the hurt behind his tone.

"You don't want to give the real answer," he says. "Whatever. I'm starved." He picks up his food with his bare hands and eats it like a bear discovering a fully stocked campground.

I want to tell him that I'm crazy about him and I want to reach out to tuck a lock of his glossy hair behind his ear, something to bring back the intimacy of the last few hours we spent together. I don't do or say anything.

"Fucking is exhausting," he says between bites.

I deserve that one.

Carson finishes his meal while I sip my coffee. His silence is punishing. If we can do this to each other, the sooner I leave, the better.

"Get your things. I'll drop you at your house." His tone is cold. It makes me feel sick to disappoint him.

Carson pulls his truck up to my house and keeps the engine running.

"Sorry," I say, looking at him for the first time since we left his house.

"Don't." He puts a hand up so I'll shut up. "I don't want to hear it."

"Fine. Tell me how a guy like you can surround yourself with so many beautiful women and yet you want me to believe that I'm so spectacular?"

Carson takes in a slow breath and clenches his jaw. "I really don't understand how your great mathematical mind works, Babycakes."

"Don't call me that. I told you I hate it. It's patronizing."

My rage over his silly pet name for me startles him. "I'll never say it again," he says curtly.

"You said you haven't slept with any women in a while, but there are plenty of condoms in your truck and your house. You're getting action somewhere. Talia is very pretty—"

"What?" he shouts. "I have never touched her."

"What about the women you just hired at work? Hell, what about Lauren or Imogene and the mystery woman at the Mohonk resort?"

"I'm confused," he says angrily. "Do you actually think I slept with all of these women or are you just jealous of every woman I know? What am I working with here? Irrational accusations or insane jealousy?"

"Oh!" I scream and kick the dashboard. "I don't know what I'm thinking, but I hate feeling unsure about you."

"How can you be so insecure about us? I'm a very direct guy; I thought I made my intentions clear."

"You paint a very enticing picture here, a nice package; the handsome guy with an incredible talent, who also happens to be super nurturing to others and he's surrounded by all these lovely available women, but he sets his sights on me," I mock. "Hmm, I don't know. Should I fall for this or should I use some common sense?"

Carson looks dejected and shakes his head. "You don't trust me. I don't know what I've done, but you don't trust me."

"I'm a realist and I'm not ready to live up to your expectations of me." I jump out of the truck.

"You're a cynic. Bottom line, you don't believe what I'm telling you, so end of story." Carson yanks my door closed and drives off.

Thirty-Seven

"Tell me again," Lauren says. "I'm trying to understand why you walked out on Carson."

I'm sitting at the kitchen table. Jeremy and Imogene are making grilled cheese sandwiches with bacon and tomato while Lauren and Leo are setting the table. It's a very homey, domestic setting with two lovey-dovey couples and me. I envy their comfortable simplicity when it comes to dating. It makes me more miserable watching them touch each other with loving gestures and little knowing smiles.

"I didn't walk out on him. You make it sound like we're married and this is a bad country song. Can we change the subject, please?"

They spend the next hour talking about their new projects at the workshop and the girls' jewelry business. Leo and Jeremy have nothing except good things to say about Carson's business acumen and the project ideas as well as the new furniture plans coming from the design team, Gemma and Noelle. Imogene explains her new marketing plan for her and Lauren's re-purposed vintage jewelry and everyone praises her for the research and business plan she has drafted.

I say little and mostly push my food around on my plate. I wouldn't say it out loud, but I'm longing for Talia's scrumptious breakfast burrito that was sitting so close to the guy who stars in my daydreams and fantasies. If I could go back and play that scene over, I don't know what I'd say differently, yet I would do it with more diplomacy and unselfishness. I would hope. Then again, I keep blowing it every time, so who knows.

After lunch, I check my emails from my 5 Alpha team and follow a thread of messages about a glitch that started about the time I left for the party. The team is worried that the first trial run and presentation to the client will have to be postponed, so I begin reading through the code. I'm sitting sideways against the massive desk with my feet propped up while I scroll through one of the monitors. I'm mindlessly lost in a particular section of the software when Lauren walks into the library and plops herself on the couch with an exaggerated huff.

"Where's Leo?" I ask.

"He and Jeremy just left. Is this a good time to talk or am I interrupting your work?"

"I can't concentrate, so we can talk. Let me guess. Carson?"

Lauren is wearing a Syracuse sweatshirt and fleece shorts, looking like a cheerleader with her blond hair pulled back in a high ponytail. She's the popular, pretty girl on campus that I wanted to be in high school and college, but I could never muster up the confidence to be as outgoing as Lauren.

"You spent the night at his place and you came home in his clothes. How long have you really been seeing each other?"

"We're not. We've..." I take my feet off the desk and bring them to my chair, hugging my legs.

"You've hooked up a few times, right?"

"Yes." I don't like using that term. "Hooking-up" isn't the right word to use with Carson. Maybe he did that with other women in the past, but it's not how he sees me. At least that's what I tell myself because it's not how I see him.

"But it's more than that, right?"

"Lauren, get to the point. What are you asking me?"

"Leo says that Carson doesn't even realize when he's talking about you, but he brings you up a lot; at work, at lunch. Leo says Carson has been like this for weeks, and I'm no idiot. Carson didn't leave a date and drive through a tropical storm to see me. He does these things for you. Not to mention the party last night. My God, the guy only has eyes and hands for you. How do you not see this?"

"I do see it, but I find it hard to believe that it's real. It wasn't long ago I was going through a similar situation with Dylan and look how that turned out. It seems kind of creepy of me to date his brother even if he thinks he's in love with me. I don't—"

"What?" Lauren practically shouts. "Carson told you he's in love with you?"

"Yes."

She beams. "That is so fucking amazing. Carson is a great guy. He's not screwed up like Dylan. I mean, I love Dylan, he's adorable, but Carson has his shit together and he lives like a monk. Seriously, if he did date a woman, it was a secret and it never happened here. I always wondered if he'd find someone and settle down and now he has his eyes on you. I love this."

"Well…" I hesitate.

"Oh God, no. I know that face you make. What did you do?"

"Apparently, I'm not doing enough. I've discovered Carson is a very direct, no holds barred type of guy when it comes to a relationship. He has an idea or opinion and that's it, he puts it out there. It's all or nothing with him. There's no in between."

"Oh, let me see if I get this straight. He's in love with you and you probably haven't said it back to him because you're chicken shit after what happened with Dylan. Because if you get involved with Carson and it goes south," Lauren winces, "yikes, you'd have the small town gossip girls shredding you. Oh, wait a minute. I'm the biggest gossip in town, so you don't have to worry about that, and um, you're already involved with Carson. You can't sleep with him and pretend like nothing happened. Besides, I don't think it's creepy. The Dylan thing was months ago and they're not related by blood so there's that."

"What? Dylan and Carson aren't brothers? I mean, of course they're brothers, but they are not biologically related?"

"You didn't know? Carson was adopted. His parents adopted him when they didn't think they could have kids and then Dylan was a surprise baby that same year."

"Carson was adopted when he was three?"

"Yeah. He was removed from a very violent home and the state put him in foster care. The Blackards took him in and adopted him. He never,

I mean never, talks about it. I got all this information from my parents and Ginnie when I was younger. He probably didn't tell you because he thinks of Dylan as his only family and nothing can come between them. Carson has hammered it into Dylan's head that they are brothers, regardless of blood ties. He had to in order to get Dylan to listen to him over the years. Carson has worked his ass off trying to protect Dylan."

"Yeah, I know, that's one of the things I admire about him."

"So why are you pushing him away?"

"Because I'm not sure of this. I'm not sure about me and if this is what I want."

"Stop trying to process this like it's one of your computer programs. What do you feel in your gut?"

"My gut jumps up and down every time I'm around Carson. It's been like that from day one. Even when I was with Dylan," I admit to her.

"Wow." Lauren smiles and it's the hopeless romantic in her that makes me cry.

I put my head in my hands and start sobbing. Lauren jumps off the couch and hands me a wad of tissues.

"It's not that bad, is it?" She rubs my back.

"I want to be normal. I like Carson. I wish I wasn't afraid to act on this. Any normal woman would jump at the chance to be with him and I keep screwing up by running away. He wants a straight answer, no games, and I'm behaving like a child. Am I intentionally trying to sabotage this?"

"I don't think so. You're too smart for that. What has he said to you?"

"He's told me more than once that he loves me, that he's in love with me, and today he wanted me to spend the day with him. God, I'm awful. I have sex with him and then I say I gotta run."

"That's a guy thing," Lauren adds. "Just saying. Kind of funny you'd do that. Is that what started your fight today? You had an argument, right?"

"You could say that. Talia walked in on us in the middle of getting it on." Lauren's eyes grow big and she covers her mouth to stifle a laugh. "Oh, it gets worse. When we came down for breakfast, Talia was very happy for us and she asked if my feelings for Carson are stronger than 'like'. Believe me, nothing was lost in her broken English translation. She wanted to know if I am in love with Carson. I didn't say anything and Carson was standing in the doorway and heard the whole thing. Breakfast was miserable. The ride home, even worse."

"Poor Carson. He's whipped and you crushed him," she says.

"I thought you were trying to make me feel better."

"What did he say after that?"

"Well after my diatribe about him and other women that I don't want to repeat, he accused me of not trusting him. He's right. I'm cynical and cold when it comes to talking about..."

"Love and commitment. Yeah, I dated enough guys who had the same problem."

"You're not making me feel better."

"Why should I? Carson is the one getting his heart battered around."

"It's my heart, too. That's why I'm crying."

"Oh, boo-hoo. Say it then."

"Say what?"

"That you're in love with him. What is with you? Do you think a bomb is going to go off if you say the three little words to him?"

"They're not little words and I can't be cavalier about it. That's how people end up getting hurt."

Lauren rises on her long legs and moves to sit on the armrest of the couch.

"Then decide how important it is to you. Is it worth having Carson in your life or would you be content without him? Stew on it. Get pickled and really miserable over him, or not."

"You think I'm an idiot, don't you?"

"I think you know what you want, but you're afraid to go after it. You like to plan things out and your methodical approach has been very successful for you in school and work, but this is love. There's no blueprint to follow. Carson is waiting for you to tell him you feel the same way as him. It's not unreasonable."

"It's not easy."

"Then don't do it. Baby," she accuses. "You tell me that you've been in love with Carson for months, but you can't tell him?"

I've lost Lauren's sympathy. She's completely on Carson's side at this point.

"Okay, I'm going to take your advice and stew," I concede.

"Great. You'll be known as the woman who single-handedly brought down the Blackard boys. Hope you're happy." She stalks out of the room.

Thirty-Eight

Dylan meets me at our usual booth at Bonnie's. Imogene is our waitress and in between serving other customers, she sits down with us and chats about Dylan's upcoming stay at the mental health facility in Massachusetts. Carson will be picking him up after lunch and driving him up there. My heart clenches when I think of Carson.

"This is what the place looks like," Dylan says, sliding a brochure across the table. "Nice dorm rooms, right?"

I flip through the photos of the well-appointed grounds, amenities for patients and the images showing smiling concerned doctors as well as therapists in one-on-one and group sessions.

"It looks very nice, Dylan. Kind of like a retreat with spa services."

"No shit. It comes with a hefty price tag, too."

"It's really that expensive? Does insurance cover it?"

"No. Affluent brothers cover it. At these prices, I better leave there feeling great."

Dylan is his usual cute self. His hair is growing out and his athletic good looks haven't suffered since the accident; in fact, he is probably more attractive since taking his anti-depressant and following a dedicated program he prescribed for himself of alcohol abstention and daily runs. He said Carson works out with him in the makeshift weight room in the back of the shop and then they go for a six-mile run before they start their day.

He explains that he was diagnosed with bipolar disorder as a teenager and how his classification has changed since then to bipolar II. When he describes the symptoms he's tried to manage over the last ten years—extreme depressive episodes, decreased need for sleep, talkativeness and excessive participation in risky behaviors—I think of his past experience with his dangerous motorcycle racing and all the wild partying he did in college. Yet it's the last symptom he tells me about, hyper-sexuality, that triggers remorse in me.

Dylan is kind and never discusses our past sexual relationship. We have built a stronger friendship over the last few months and I'm pleasantly surprised since I've never maintained a friendship with any of the men I dated; I use that term loosely. Dylan is like the sibling I never had and, despite our crazed few weeks of dating and sex, that period seems like events that happened in a different lifetime with a different person.

Dylan talks openly about his disorder as if the accident has freed him from a lifetime of secret shame, his illness, and his father's suicide. I am happy for him and reach my hand across the table to hold his hand that is fidgeting with a fork.

"Dylan, this is so wonderful. I'm happy you're going to one of the best places for treatment and that you're so enthusiastic about it."

"Don't get too excited. My enthusiasm could be one of the symptoms of the disorder. *Grandiosity*," he says, rolling his eyes.

We laugh over that and eat our burgers and fries, which he refers to as his last meal before imprisonment. Of course, the treatment center has a gourmet chef in residence since they cater to wealthy people and celebrities because, if you're going to suffer from depression, there's no reason your refined palette should suffer, too.

"Can I ask you something?"

Dylan swallows his last bite of food and gives me a questioning look. "What haven't you asked me, or better yet, what I haven't I told you?"

"It's not about you. It's about Carson. It's personal and you've never mentioned it and neither has he, so this is kind of awkward."

"Ah," Dylan says, putting his napkin on the table. "Shoot."

"Carson is adopted. Is that true?"

"Yes. My parents didn't think they could have kids. My mom and dad took in Carson as a foster child and then they adopted him. I was a surprise baby."

"That's what I heard."

"Is there a problem?" Dylan is concerned and, considering his big heart, perhaps it's for both Carson and me.

"A while back, Carson referred to his family as having the genetic component, a predisposition to depression. But if he isn't your biological brother, I'm wondering why he felt the need to say that to me. Why didn't he tell me that he was adopted?" A sudden chill makes me shudder, so I pull the long sleeves of my heavy black sweater down over my hands and clasp them on the table.

"Carson never refers to himself as the adopted son. It doesn't matter that we're not related by blood, there are no brothers closer to each other than us. I think he decided a long time ago that whatever happened to him before the age of three is irrelevant and his real family was my parents and me. Loyalty is one of Carson's strong suits. He never forgets and he takes care of his own."

"Does he remember his biological family?"

"Nothing good. He was only three when the state removed him from his home. He remembers the trauma, the violence, the yelling and his fear. He told me about it when we were kids and I was old enough to understand. I brought it up and asked a lot of questions, but this isn't something he talks about. I doubt he's talked about it in over a decade unless he's seeing a shrink that I don't know about. Why are you asking?"

"Don't you think it's odd that he's never mentioned this to me in all these months I've known him?"

"You mean because you two have hooked up a few times?" Dylan says this as if hooking up for me is as trivial as sharing a cab.

I clamp my mouth shut in surprise and the heat in my face rises.

Dylan smiles. "Sorry. Did I embarrass you?"

"A little. How did you know?"

"About you and Carson?" He scoffs. "No one knows my brother like I do. He has had a thing for you forever. The day of the accident, I assumed you were stopping by his house. But by the look of your face now, I'm guessing you got more than a tour."

I look down at my hands. "We don't have to talk about this."

"I can handle it," Dylan says softly. "It's not my favorite topic, but I'm not going to slit my wrists over this."

"Don't make jokes like that. Please," I say quietly, hoping other customers can't hear us.

"Fine. Well, I also know of another time when Carson came into work, really worked up, muttering about you. This was after you visited the workshop and he gave you a ride home. You're pretty irresistible, so I kind of put two and two together," he says with a little smirk. "And then I heard about the party and you spending the night. So, there's that."

"I guess everyone knows."

"Pretty much. It's good I'll be gone for a couple of months or so. You two can figure out what you're doing without me being in the way, if that's what's making you uncomfortable."

"Why are you so supportive of this after what you and I went through?"

"Because I love my brother and he deserves to be happy for a change. He's always taking care of other people; me, his employees, his friends. If he wants to be with you, I hope it happens."

"I don't understand the secrets. Why wouldn't he tell me about his past?"

"Maybe he doesn't think what happened to him before coming to our family matters anymore. If he had a criminal record, then I'd say yeah, he should be upfront about it. But Carson does whatever he thinks is best to protect other people. It's rarely about him."

But that isn't true, I think. Protecting other people is what makes Carson feel stronger and in control. It is about him, but I really can't hold his intentions against him. It's one more damn thing I have to admire about Carson. Someone should smack me for being so tough on him.

My silence annoys Dylan enough that he feels he must intervene on Carson's behalf. "Carson is in love with you," he spits out with a tinge of anger. "Okay, maybe I'm full of shit and act like I'm okay with all of this, but the truth is, I'm jealous of my brother. Always have been. But he deserves to be with someone who is good to him and honestly cares about him. He is a better man than me. If you could start something with me, then what is holding you back from Carson? He's better than me in every way. I've been a handful for Carson since we were kids; I did bad things out of spite because I was jealous of him. He never cut me off, though. He kept pushing his way into my life to help me. He's never let me drown in my own mistakes. Never. Is that what this is about? How you feel about Carson?"

I sigh nervously.

"That wasn't fair of me," Dylan says and then rubs his chin, the gesture I assumed was a genetic trait, but now I realize it must have been a characteristic of Carson's that Dylan emulated after observing his big brother do it so many times.

"There are parts of Carson that make me question how I feel about him. This little secret doesn't help."

"Shit, women love him; think he's some unattainable gift. He is unattainable because he's

384

been in love with you for years." Dylan shakes his head in disbelief.

"Years? You mean months or weeks maybe."

"Years," Dylan says emphatically. "How do you think Gin kept up on you? Who got her the photos of you?"

"Carson told me about the private detective she hired to track me down and he took photos of me at different times in my life." My seriousness is drowned out by Dylan's boisterous laugh.

"Holy crap! Is that what my brother told you? A detective?" He keeps laughing.

"What is so funny?"

Dylan wipes the tears from his eyes with a napkin. He has a big grin on his face. "There was no private detective. The year you graduated high school from the posh private school you went to, Carson was in the city working on his first contacts for distributing and selling the furniture. He swung by the school on the day of your graduation and took the photos of you outside of the school talking to your parents and friends. When you were at Columbia, he walked right into the big lecture halls and got photos of you sitting and taking notes. It was easy. Carson had his own school ID. He was accepted and took classes part-time. He wanted to study engineering, but he never finished because he had to deal with yours truly."

By this time, my mouth is hanging open in a stupor. I can't believe this is the same Carson. "Go on," I say, dying to hear the rest of the whole cockamamie scheme.

"Carson got a lot of photos of you for Aunt Gin. He kind of prided himself on being so inconspicuous, but then you wouldn't have recognized him as an adult. Gin was thrilled to keep up with you."

"It is so weird."

"Weird?" Dylan asks annoyed. "How about impressive? Carson didn't start out falling for you. He was doing this as a favor to Gin, but then something happened and I could tell he was very interested in you."

"Well, he wasn't charged with stalking because I didn't know what was going on. So what happened?"

"You became a woman," Dylan says in all seriousness.

I lean back in the booth, my skepticism faltering as I listen to Dylan.

"You left for M.I.T.; two years and two Master's while Carson kind of watched over you."

"Carson went to Cambridge to follow me?"

"No, by that time he had clients there selling his furniture. Instead of sending me, he went on store visits. He would spend a few days there seeing clients and attending some interesting consortiums in math and computer science."

"That's absurd."

"Yeah? How many guys would sit through a two-hour lecture on algorithms or math and computer jargon so he could hear you speak? Carson, that's who."

"That's amazingly insane," I say but inwardly, I am glowing with joy that Carson saw that confident intelligent side of me when I was a graduate student.

"He loved bringing back information to Ginnie. I could see it in how he acted, he was excited to do this for Gin and even more excited to show us the photos. That's when I knew my brother was falling for you in an epic sort of way and a part of me always wants what my brother wants.

"We knew when your bus was arriving last June. What Carson didn't know is that his brother had a plan to usurp him. Carson thought he'd catch up with you at Gin's house when Archie took you there. He didn't know that I planned on being there front and center, your escort to the house, your date, your boyfriend. He didn't have a chance, unless of course you were repulsed by me."

I scoff. "You were diabolical."

"I was an asshole."

"Why did Carson let it happen?"

"Carson doubts himself when it comes to you. He was second-guessing how he would approach you. I didn't give him a chance to find out."

"That's not true. I met Carson first, in Archie's office. He stormed by me. He didn't seem to give a shit who I was."

"That's not true. You don't think guys get stage fright when it comes to women? How did I end up at the diner, falling all over you, Jess?"

I shrug, more disturbed as his story progresses.

"Carson came back to the shop like he'd seen a ghost. He was on a total high that you were here, but he was torpedoed. A total mess. Had no idea how to talk to you. So while he wasted time pacing the office, I went to the diner to zoom in on you."

"You fiend." I'm not being playful or smiling along with Dylan.

"I know."

"No, really. You were a fiend. You undermined Carson, but you also played me," I snap.

Dylan's smile fades to concern. "No, that wasn't my intention. I didn't think I would actually end up in a relationship with you. I planned on flirting and making Carson jealous, but I really fell for you."

"It doesn't matter now," I mutter. "What's done is done."

"I regret fucking everything up for all of us," he says. "But on the bright side, you know more about Carson, maybe things he was afraid to tell you. I hope it works in his favor and you don't shut him out."

"Well, I did get that very inspiring story from Archie on missed opportunities."

"Oh right. The story about making his fortune and losing the girl he loved to someone else?"

"Very sad."

"Yeah, he's used that story on everyone under the age of thirty."

"You mean it's not true?"

"No, it's true and very sad, but Archie has been milking that one for years, trying to get all of us to settle down and get married. He's lonely, especially without your aunt around. He wants us to all settle and grow roots in Hera so he has some company."

"I'm not sure this was the best decision for me to give up the anonymity I had in New York and all the action there to be the center of small town gossip and scandal here."

Dylan comes around to my side of the booth and hugs me. "You are definitely in the right place. You need this place as much as it needs you. No one should go through life being anonymous."

I lean my head against his and he kisses me on the temple.

"Walk me out. It's time for me to go." He pulls my hand as he stands up.

Before we can get out the door of the diner, Imogene, Bonnie, Lauren and Imogene's parents, Pam and Mark, all give Dylan long embraces. A few of the women are crying and I feel my eyes well up, too. The customers give him a cheery loud sendoff of *Go Dylan! Go Dylan! Go Dylan!*

I walk him out to Carson's truck, which is idling in the street. Dylan is still smiling. "It's nice to know that people will miss me."

"I'll miss you," I say and look over to the driver's side window where Carson is waiting patiently for Dylan. He's wearing aviator sunglasses and he's looking straight ahead at the road and not at us.

When I stand on my toes to give Dylan a peck on his cheek, I notice Carson glance our way. Dylan quickly kisses the top of my head and I push him forward. "Leave before I start crying for real," I whisper.

Dylan jogs around the truck to the passenger side and gets in. Carson turns towards me at the last moment and raises his hand in a solemn wave.

"Seventy million," I whisper to myself, teary-eyed.

Thirty-Nine

The first two weeks that Dylan is gone are the worst for everyone. The town seems too quiet and somber without him.

Leo is painfully lonely in his home without Dylan there talking and cooking, so he spends as much time as he can with Lauren at my house. He speaks in a soft, reserved manner, although it's apparent he's got it bad for Lauren. He follows her around, pulling out chairs, getting her coffee and generally touching her arm or back in a possessive way that I miss having in my own life.

Imogene is very industrious and focuses on growing their jewelry business and her relationship with Jeremy. Both women party less and put more structure into their day, so when they aren't waitressing, they are working in the room dedicated to their business. When I'm lonely, I wander in and sit at their craft table and watch them make their intricate pieces.

Bert follows my moods and mopes along with me. We drag ourselves around the house from the studio so I can paint, to the library where I unravel mangled code and rebuild weak platforms and then back to eat my umpteenth bowl of cereal before I make my way to bed. Bert lounges against me to give me some comfort in that special way dogs can read their owners.

I miss Dylan's friendship, but I ache for Carson in every way, emotionally and physically.

"Why don't you send him a nice friendly text? It's not as scary as a phone call or seeing him in person. That way you can connect to him in a less terrifying way," Lauren suggests one morning at the kitchen table as I scroll through emails on my phone.

At first I think she's referring to Dylan, but then I realize she's not.

"That's an excellent idea," Imogene says, looking up from her laptop. "Let him know you're thinking about him."

"How is that a good idea? Then we're right back where we started from. He wants a sure thing and I'm wishy-washy. We'll have the same argument." I put my phone on the table.

"You've been sad long enough. You drag your sorry ass around the house like some maiden who lost her sailor-pirate-husband-lover at sea!" Lauren shouts.

Her outburst surprises Imogene and me.

"You need make-up sex and then you'll come to your senses. You're just as crazy about Carson as he is about you," Lauren continues. "You're not fooling anyone with your *I'm-not-ready-for-a-serious-relationship. I'm-not-sure; poor-me!* Enough, Jess, you're the surest person I know. Your whole life has been about planning and following a very specific path and you nail each objective perfectly. I think you are madly in love with Carson and yeah, maybe it scares you a little, but you can't throw it all away because of a little fear of the unknown."

"Take it easy," Imogene says to Lauren. "Jess has to figure this out on her own."

"No. She won't figure it out because this isn't one of her number problems that add up to a nice perfect sum. She's so used to being the girl genius and having all the answers. Nothing is a mystery to her." Lauren leans over the table to me. "Quit being an asshat and go after this guy before you lose him. Who says he has to wait around for you? Another pretty genius could come along and snatch him up. You're not the only one on the planet."

"God," I say. "Why are you flipping out over this?"

"Because you're making a problem where there doesn't need to be one. Are you in love with Carson?" Lauren asks.

Imogene looks at me. "Well?"

I take a deep breath; the question is a punch to the gut that stirs a whirlwind of emotions in me. "Yes," I say softly.

"Give me this," Lauren says, grabbing my cell phone.

"What are you doing?" I panic.

"Thinking of you," Lauren says as she types furiously. "There. Done."

"What did you do?" I shout and lunge for the phone.

"I sent Carson a sweet text from you." Lauren tosses the phone back to me.

Imogene huddles next to me as I read the text. *Thinking of you.*

"Oh God. This is so not like me. What do I do if he responds?"

Lauren huffs and puts her hands on her bony hips. "You have a big, fat I.Q., so I'm sure you'll have no problem sending a reply. Imogene, we have to finish those necklaces and get our shipments out today."

Before they leave, my phone pings with an incoming message.

Lauren runs around the table to see my phone. She and Imogene lean in to read the screen while I'm holding it in my hand like it's a live grenade. They giggle at Carson's response. *Good. I'm always thinking about you.*

"There. Now who's a genius?" Lauren says, waving her arms above her head. "Me, that's who. I got the ball rolling for you. You'll thank me when this nonsense is all over."

Several hours later, the paintings for the show are finished and packaged, ready for Tom's assistant, Griffin, to pick up. I leave my studio, still wearing my black leggings and oversized painting smock, which is really one of my father's old, white dress shirts. It is covered in faded, dried paint and it's almost tissue soft from years of washings. My hair is pulled into a ponytail on top of my head, making my curls fan out like a mop head. I keep my big, black, retro-style glasses on since I'm going to sit in front of the computer for a few hours. Lately, I've been wearing my glasses more when I paint or have to look at screens for a long period of time to prevent eyestrain. They make me look like a total geek, though.

I go back to the library and sit in front of the monitors, pulling up the work I'm doing for Lauren and Imogene. One screen shows the website I set up for them. Another screen shows the simple program I set up for their financial records and inventory. The screen I'm currently working on shows photos of individual pieces of their jewelry collection. I'm creating a product gallery so people can purchase items directly from the website.

As I play around with a photo, I hear my phone ping. I look down to see Carson's text. *So? What were you thinking about? Bed? Truck? Shower?*

I laugh and quickly type a response. *Not sex. You.*

I try to concentrate on the photo position I keep changing, but it's hopeless. I'm waiting to hear if my phone will ping again. I'm more excited about the prospect of engaging Carson in a remedial texting conversation than working.

He texts back. *I like that. Can I see you?*

I respond. *Yes. When?*

After a few minutes, there's still no response, so I figure he must have had something to do at work. I put my heavy, noise cancelling headphones on and decide to listen to some music while I work on the website design. Lauren comes in from the room next door that has been dubbed *L & I Creations,* as their temporary business title. She hands me the SLR camera she has been using to take photos of her jewelry. I can't hear her over Adele's deep voice wailing in my ears as I dance and play with the website, but I nod and take the camera, knowing there are more photos I need to download for the gallery portion of the site.

After Adele, I have my music library shuffle through dance songs. Rick James's "Superfreak" comes on and I have to sing and dance along.

I feel a tap on my shoulder and scream. I jerk around so fast, the headphone cord yanks my head back and I hit the floor on my ass.

It's Carson and, as I scramble to my feet, he watches me with an expression of amusement. His hands are clenched at his sides as he searches for something to say.

"You scared the hell out of me." I put the headphones on the desk. "I'm doing some stuff for the girls; their website."

He looks at my bare feet, my freshly painted pink toenails and works his gaze up to my leggings and tattered shirt before his gaze then settles on my face. "That's a good look on you."

I look down at my grungy clothing and adjust my glasses with a nervous laugh. "Yeah, no one is supposed to see me looking like this. Except Imogene and Lauren, that is. They always see me like this, unfortunately."

"I envy them," he says, his voice wavers and I know that look he gets when he's turned on.

"Ah!" I scoff.

The blood is rushing through me, starting those exhilarating waves of searing heat. I try not to stare at his blue eyes or his biceps bulging underneath the long-sleeve, black T-shirt he's wearing, but he has that sexy five o'clock shadow I love to touch and his hair is falling in careless waves around his face. The sight of him puts my sexual drive into warp speed, and this, after I texted him that it wasn't about sex.

"What are you doing here?" I ask, gripping the edge of the desk so I won't fall down.

"You said, ' *Yes.'* I got here as fast as I could."

"I thought you wanted to set up a date and time. I didn't know you meant now."

He's eyeing me like I'm his prey and he's toying with me. Who doesn't love being pursued by someone they're crazy about?

"I meant now," he says, moving closer so we're only a few inches apart.

"But it's the middle of the work day. You must have furniture... stuff... things, and I'm in the middle of work... here." I struggle to sound coherent.

"You're not working. You're dancing and singing "Superfreak". And I like it. I also really like those glasses on you. You've got some kind of sexy-librarian-slash-bohemian artist thing going on here."

"Oh," I say. My vocabulary bank is completely empty.

Carson has inched his way forward so his body lightly touches mine. I can feel his breath on me and the electricity he puts out makes me shiver and tighten my inner muscles. I am trapped between the desk and him with my ass practically on my keyboard. He reaches down to touch my face and put a hand on my lower back so I don't crash backwards into the computer equipment. He bends his head down to kiss me tenderly, tugging at my lip with his teeth and circling my lips with his tongue. He keeps his eyes locked on mine. My breathing becomes heavier, however, I don't want to lunge at him, instigate sex and then be accused all over again of being heartless.

"What are you doing?" I ask breathless.

"Seducing you," he says calmly as he continues to kiss my lips and trail down to my neck.

"I thought you didn't want casual sex with me. I thought you were angry at me and you don't want me near you unless I'm willing to sign myself over with some kind of rights of exclusivity or declaration of dependence." He licks around my ear and my nipples get hard, so does the bulge he has pressed against my belly.

He sighs and then pulls back to look at me with a curved mouth. "It's been a long three weeks since you slept at my house."

"I wouldn't call what we did sleeping," I say and he smiles.

"I miss you. Every day. The first thought I have when I wake up is *you* and the last thought I have before I fall asleep at night is *you*. I don't want you to forget about me."

"Don't worry; Hera is hurting for available good looking, young studs, so you're always in the running."

He laughs and runs his hands around my waist. "I also miss your sense of humor."

"I miss you, too." Saying it out loud is liberating and for the first time, I feel like I'm making myself available for real intimacy. I've been hurting over missing him, so rather than doing it in silence, I might as well summon up some bravery and say how I feel.

"Thank you," he says. "Thank you for saying that."

"I'm not just saying it. It's true."

Carson kisses me harder, with more purpose, and I melt into the strokes of his tongue, letting my hands rest in his hair.

He presses into me and the zing of arousal is instantly amplified.

"I can either take you on this desk or the couch. Either works for me," he says into my ear with a husky voice.

"We can't. The girls are right next door, working in the other room."

"That's what doors are for."

He grabs my hand and pulls me across the room to slam the door to the hallway closed. I turn the bolt to prevent any surprise visitors. Then he swings me around to the couch so I land on my back against the aged leather cushions. He pushes my legs apart and nestles his body on top of me. He kisses me with a grateful brutality. His erection feels like a brick against my pelvis and I get wet thinking about it being inside of me.

"I have been hard since this morning when you sent the first text. So, I decided I would either have to jerk myself off while thinking about you, or I could drive up here and convince you that Tuesday afternoons are the optimum time for sex."

"Take off your clothes," I command, pulling the bottom of his T-shirt up.

Carson stands up and hurriedly takes off his shirt, yanks his boots off and then throws his jeans and boxer briefs off. I'm lying on the couch as he pulls my leggings and panties off with such force that I slide across the leather cushions. I slip my oversized shirt over my head without unbuttoning it. Carson's eyes widen when he sees that I'm braless.

He kneels on the couch between my legs as I take in his beautifully sculpted features; his olive skin that looks so dark against my fair complexion when he runs his fingers up my leg and his handsome face that shadows with lust and love when his eyes meet mine.

As he leans down, propping his arms on either side of my head, I take his erection in my hand and rub it against my wet folds. "I'm so ready."

"Good," he chokes out. "I've been waiting all day to do this. I need you now. This second."

I put him partially in me and grab his back to drive him into me. He obliges without delay and goes deep with the first thrust. "I'm sorry, baby, but this is going to be fast and hard."

"Yes," I whisper as he pummels me with his thickness.

Our moans and grunts escalate with each thrust. Suddenly dance music with a heavy, thumping bass starts blasting from the other side of the wall where Lauren and Imogene are working. Carson and I laugh as he pumps into me with more force in sync with the quick beat of the music. I lock my legs around him and he moves in closer, changing his long thrusts to faster, shorter pumps so his hips are doing most of the work. As soon as I start arching upwards, the friction on my special spot makes me tighter and hotter.

"Carson," I moan as an orgasm takes command of my nervous system and I fall into a delirious series of aftershocks.

"Ah, shit," Carson says as his own release takes over him. "God, fuck; I love you." He covers my mouth with his as he rams his last shred of hardness into me.

He collapses on me, all two hundred plus pounds of him, and I hope the couch doesn't collapse after all that creaking and crunching coming from the wood frame. His mouth travels down to my breasts and sucks on each nipple. "And I love these," he says then kisses my ears, shoulders and hands, proclaiming his love for them as well.

I roll to the edge of the couch so Carson can lie behind me against the back of the couch and hold me. He grabs the throw blanket from the armrest and covers us. I snuggle against him so he can spoon me.

"Thanks for the booty call," he says and kisses the nape of my neck.

"My pleasure."

"Trust me, it was mine. I wasn't kidding; I've been carrying a hard-on all day over you. A guy can only adjust his dick so many times before he loses his vision and implodes. I was ready to hunt you down; I couldn't think straight at work."

I laugh. The music volume suddenly goes down and we both laugh again.

"Guess we were rocking the house," he says.

"Carson," I say softly.

"What?" He plants another kiss on my neck.

"Thank you for not hating me. I can't bear the thought of you hating me."

He holds my chin and directs it slowly towards his face. I have to turn my whole body towards him to see his blue eyes that exude warmth for me, creating a tight spasm in my heart. "I could never hate you," he says.

My head rests on his bicep as I trace the outline of his jaw. He closes his eyes and then inhales and exhales slowly.

"Carson, I know Aunt Ginnie had some photos of me from school. I think she had some from the conferences I spoke at. There was one I did on computer analysis, if I recall." I pretend not to remember the name.

"It was a symposium on software testing and analysis. You were the third presenter that day," he rattles this off with his eyes closed, enjoying my light touch.

He remembers every detail; the titles of the conferences don't fluster him in the least. He must have been paying very close attention when he was stalking me. The thought of Carson navigating the conferences then sitting and listening to the dry material is more than thrilling, knowing he was near me.

"Yeah, that was it. And then I had a bigger one on numerical computations."

Carson jumps right in, not aware that I'm testing him. "That was the conference on computational methods and function theory. You gave a talk on theory and algorithms," he says matter-of-factly. "You were very good, professional and entertaining at the same time."

"Carson?"

"Yes?" He opens his eyes and looks at me.

"What was my Master's in?"

"Science. You specialized in computation for design and optimization."

I smile. "And how do you know so much?"

"Oh." It finally hits him. "You know."

"That there was no detective? I can't believe I fell for that malarkey."

"Dylan told you?"

"Right before he left town, he told me. I had no idea you knew so much about me and shadowed me through school."

"It started as a favor to your aunt. I was going into the city on business and she mentioned you were graduating. I didn't ask how she got her information. I suppose through old friends of hers in the city. I didn't think anything of it. You were a kid. Fourteen? Almost fifteen? I got some shots of you outside the high school and it made Gin really happy."

"How did you recognize me?"

"Your long, red hair, big brown eyes and you looked like you could boss any guy around."

I laugh. "I grew out of the bossy phase when I became the youngest person in every school I attended. I became timid."

"No matter. I found you."

"And the other photos in college?"

"It was easy at Columbia because I was enrolled part-time, so I found some of your information. I knew where you lived and I sat in some of your classes—the big lectures—and nabbed some photos on my phone. It was harder to keep tabs on you at M.I.T., though. But when I saw you..."

"What? When did you see me?"

"You were eighteen. I sat in the different conferences they had your last year of graduate school. I checked agendas to see where you were speaking. By then I could get partial videos for Gin and some very good shots. You were—"

"I was what?"

"Fearsome, beautiful, and so fucking smart. You took my sanity away. And then, after graduation, you turned nineteen and went to work for 5 Alpha. I have a huge client in the Village so I actually passed you a few times on the street near your apartment."

"I can't believe you recognized me. There are beautiful women all over New York. Those fucking Amazonian models on every goddamn street corner who make people like me look like shlubs."

"No, you are beautiful. I couldn't miss you. That's about the time when I started falling for you."

"You didn't know me."

"I knew your voice. I also knew it was at least two octaves higher when you talked to your girlfriends about tacos or shoes."

I start laughing and slap him on the shoulder.

"No, really. Your voice was deeper when you were giving lectures and you'd wear glasses and put your hair up to look older. You really *were* a fearsome creature. You spoke with so much confidence and you were graceful and poised; I was blown away by your maturity and intelligence. That's how I started thinking about you. It was about the time Gin was diagnosed and she wanted to plan what to do with the house. She didn't think you'd want it, but I probably pushed her more than anyone else to give you the house instead of the proceeds from a sale. I wanted you here and Gin agreed that a home with a solid community would be good for you since you didn't have the happiest family situation growing up."

"Like you, right?"

"Yeah," he says and kisses my forehead. "I thought we could both use something better and it seemed like the ideal opportunity for you to come here and experience something other than dance clubs and fine dining in the greatest city in the world. Hera has sushi you know."

We both laugh. "Thanks." I kiss his neck and inhale his manly, musky scent of sweat.

"You can text me anytime for this," he jokes, but this isn't just sex for him. He's already revealed so much about himself and how he feels about me. My insides are like jelly, I am turning into a big pile of mush around him.

"No, I was thanking you for this home, helping my aunt and finding out who I am. Thank you. I'm not sure I deserve this."

"We both deserve this."

I snuggle against him and he holds me tightly. I feel safe asking him anything.

"Okay, maybe you never mentioned this to me because it's not something you like to talk about, but why didn't you mention you were adopted?"

Carson is quiet and then focuses intently on me. "Does it matter?"

"That you're adopted doesn't matter. It's that you chose to omit it from any of our conversations that's strange. You even alluded to a genetic predisposition to mental illness, but you're not biologically related to Dylan."

"He's my only family regardless of what circumstances brought us together. Just like your parents are your family and someday you'll see that you want them in your life. I want to have a family even if Dylan is the only member I ever have. Family is everything. But I hope my family grows. I want Dylan and myself to have more than this. It's one of the reasons why I supported the idea of you taking over Gin's home. I wanted you near me. I did everything for my own selfish reasons."

Finally, the knot in my chest loosens and I exhale. Carson keeps giving me more reasons to love him and it's beginning to seem incredibly easy.

"Will you tell me about your family?" I ask.

"The only parents I remember are Abby and Robert Blackard. I remember the day they drove me to their home. I remember how the car smelled. My dad was driving and my mom was sitting next to me explaining that they were my parents now. She made me feel safe. It was a good feeling."

"She was very caring, like you. She gave you the beautiful name, didn't she?"

"Yes, she told me it was so I could start over."

I kiss his cheek and run my fingers along his jaw. Carson closes his eyes as I touch him.

"I thought my new parents were pretty great," he says, looking at me again. "I had my own room with a lot of toys, but it didn't last long. Soon there was a crib and then a crying baby. Dylan. I thought he was pretty great, too. I liked having a little brother. We had about five years of being a perfect family. We loved each other and my parents never fought. It was good and it was safe. Then my mom got sick and my dad fell into a bad depression. You know the rest of that story. It's those five great years that I try to remember more than the bad stuff that came later. We lost the house because of the medical bills. Then, when my mom died, we moved to a rental in a run-down trailer park. That's when everything went to shit."

"I sound petty when I complain about my parents," I whisper "It makes me sad to think of you and Dylan as young boys, struggling to survive all that pain. I don't know how people overcome that."

"I figured out what was important and put everything into that. It came down to Dylan and making a living. If you have someone you care about, you figure out a way to make it happen."

"Your dad couldn't do that. I don't know if I'd be strong enough to do it, either."

"Like I said, you figure out what's important and you do it."

"Carson, *you're* fearsome."

"Why do you think I'm here?" he asks and kisses me thoroughly before I can say anything.

Forty

When we open the door to the library, Lauren is leaning her hip against the second floor railing with her arms crossed, looking expectantly at us. I'm a little uncomfortable with her scrutinizing expression, but Carson is unfazed.

"Hello, Carson," she says.

"Lauren," he replies.

"Imogene is cooking a scrumptious stew for dinner and wants to know if you'd like to join us?"

Carson looks at me.

"Please?" I ask.

"Absolutely," he says to me and then turns to Lauren. "Tell Imogene I wouldn't miss it."

"Very good." Lauren smirks at me before turning on her heel to run downstairs.

"Let's go freshen up." I take him by the hand and lead him up to the third floor. When we enter my bedroom I see him look at the bed with a grin. "No. No bed. Shower, and don't get any ideas."

"You first. I want to get something for you," Carson says.

I shrug and take a scalding hot shower, but leave my hair in a ponytail so when I step out of the water it curls up around my head. I wrap a towel around me and go back into my bedroom. Carson is sitting on the bed with only his jeans on, rifling through boxes of photos and discs. He's not wearing a shirt and his bare feet are crossed at the ankle. It's a rare vision where he looks vulnerable, as though he's let a wall down and I'm seeing the real man who is willing to do anything for me.

"What ya got there?" I ask.

"The photos I took of you for Gin. These were in a box in her closet. You must have missed them when Lois was going through the closets with you. The discs are videos of your conferences or whatever I could capture on my phone. Not the best quality, but some are pretty good."

"Lois must have decided not tell me about them." I walk over to the bed and lift up one of the photos. It's a close-up of my roommate Marissa and me. My head is thrown back and I'm laughing exuberantly. I recognize a store window behind my head.

"This is on Bleeker Street," I say as if that matters.

Carson nods. "That's one of my favorites. I have a copy of that one, too."

"You do?" I look more closely at the photo and notice part of someone else in the foreground, someone with red hair. A woman. "How did you take this photo so close to me without me noticing? It looks like you were taking a photo of someone else, but moved the camera slightly to the left of that person to capture me."

Carson looks at the photo, yet doesn't elaborate.

"Carson, you were with a woman here. She thought you were taking her photo, right? But you were really taking a photo of me?"

"Yes."

"Who was the woman? I see she has red hair. It's Gemma, isn't it?"

"Yeah, it is." Carson's good mood disappears as soon as I say her name.

"Was she your girlfriend?" I have a million questions and I feel myself about to hyperventilate if I don't slow down.

"No. I dated her a few years ago."

"She's the one everyone jokes about you seeing in the city, the mystery girlfriend. Oh God. And now she works with you."

"That's not how it is, Jess."

"Did you sleep with her? I know I probably don't have a right to ask these kinds of questions since I dated your brother, but fuck if this doesn't piss me off." I start crying.

"Jess, I went out with her a few times, but we weren't serious. Ever."

"Did you sleep with her?"

"Yes. Once. When I was in the city. Not at my house and it's been two years."

"Who was the woman who you met at Mohonk for a date, the night of the storm?"

Carson stands up to hold me.

"No, Carson. Was it Gemma? Is that who you met?"

"Yes. Okay? Yes, I met her for dinner and then I left her so I could be with you."

"Were you two trying to make it work again? Were you planning on sleeping with her?"

"No." Carson's steely eyes look at me. "She may have wanted more, but I told her I wasn't interested so we talked about business. That's all that happened."

Everything about him seems sincere and I want to believe him, but I've never felt I could be a match for someone like Gemma or most women.

"I didn't sleep with her because I'm in love with you. The only reason I met her for dinner was because, maybe I was lonely, but I wasn't going to sleep with her. I thought I could pass the time talking about business. At that point I was willing to try anything to get my mind off you."

"But then you hired her. Why her?"

"She's a good designer and has a good reputation in the business. She's an asset to the company. Jess, she lives in the city and only works from our shop two days a week. The rest of the time she works from the city and, when she is here, I don't spend that much time with her. She works with everyone in the shop. I'm not interested in Gemma, other than her business knowledge."

"But the way she looked at me at your shop. I get it now. She was checking me out like I'm the competition."

"No, that's when she realized you're the one I'm interested in. You're the mystery woman, at least to my business colleagues and associates. When I walked you around the shop, everyone got that."

"But she was all over you at the party. You didn't see the way she was looking at you."

Carson scoffs and smiles. "Jess, you're jealous. I like that. But you're also wrong. We were talking about business at the party."

"I am jealous."

"You don't need to be. I'm only interested in you. Besides, if it makes you feel any better, I think Gemma has been dating someone for the last two months. I think she's serious about him so she doesn't have any interest in me."

"You men are so stupid when it comes to women," I mutter.

Carson's mouth curves and I think he wants to laugh. "Do you want me to fire her? Should I tell her I'm in love with a woman who doesn't want to be my girlfriend, but she's also jealous of any woman who comes near me? I'll certainly do that for you if it will put your mind at ease."

"No, that's ridiculous and it makes me sound like a moron." I push him back on the bed and he laughs. "So, you have all these photos, too?"

Carson picks up the photos again and rests his hands, clenching a stack of them on his leg while he looks at me with amusement. "Yes. I gave Gin the copies. I kept all the originals."

"What did you do with them?"

"They're on a memory card and I have a shoe box like this with hard copies, but mine are probably more worn out than Gin's. I looked at them a lot, and then, you moved here so I got to see the real thing."

I rifle through more photos of myself as I stand in front of him and blush. "Do you remember much about me when I was a kid?"

Carson sighs and smiles. "I remember everything. I was eleven. You used to bust my balls over everything. '*Carson, this sandwich has too much peanut butter. Carson, fill the baby pool with more water. Carson, get out of the pool, your weight displaces too much water! Carson, you're a meanie! Carson, I'll marry you if you buy me a red convertible!*'"

I am laughing so hard at his impression of a little girl, I think I'll pee my pants. "I didn't really say those things." Although, I know without a doubt I did.

"Yes, you did. You said it so often I couldn't possibly forget. Gin and your mom gave you a party for your sixth birthday. I got to light the candles on your cake and you actually said, *'Carson, you have to give me a kiss for each candle. That's six, in case you didn't know."*

"I did not say that, Carson. You made that one up."

"Scouts honor."

"You were never a Boy Scout."

"Okay, but it's the truth."

"So did you give me my six kisses?"

"Yes, I did. On the cheek. Your lips were full of blue frosting."

"That's funny. You must have hated me then."

"You drove me insane, but I thought you were pretty cute."

"Like a little sister?"

"No, I never thought of you as my sister, I told you that before. It was more like you were the girl who would grow up to be my impossible boss someday. You'd be the CEO," he says and slaps my rear end.

"That's cute." I smile because his grin fills me up with so much promise.

"Can I buy you a red convertible?"

I let out a little gasp at the meaning behind his question and quickly dismiss it. "It's your turn. Get in the shower."

While Carson takes a quick shower, I put on a fresh pair of skinny jeans and a flattering black sweater that hugs my slender frame while it also makes me look more curvy and busty than I am. I take out the ponytail holder, fix my hair and brush on a little mascara and lip gloss. I study myself in the dresser mirror and think I look infinitely better than when Carson arrived to see me in my working duds.

When he comes out of the shower with a towel wrapped around his waist, he takes one look at my transformation, strides towards me and plants a leisurely kiss on my mouth.

"No, no." I push his hands away. I can already see myself as one of those women who have no self-control and drops everything for her irresistible man. I want to get naked again and have him all over my body, which is why we have to get out of my bedroom.

"One more round," he says, holding my waist and leaving a trail of wet kisses down my neck.

"No, get dressed, please." I don't have to beg long before we hear the front doorknocker banging.

"Jesus, that thing is loud," Carson says. "Are you expecting someone?"

"Yes, the gallery is sending someone over to pick up the rest of my paintings."

We hear Lauren answer the door and her high-pitched voice carries upstairs as Carson gets dressed.

He follows me downstairs and, when I see Griffin, I feel Carson fill in every breathable space behind me like an ominous presence. I sense his growing heat like he's protecting his turf.

Griffin is a twenty-three-year-old graduate student who interns for Tom and is one of the few people that likes talking to me about my science background. Griffin dotes on me and happens to be very cute in an academic way with his wire-rimmed glasses and khaki pants. He's getting his Ph.D. in art history and is wiry and slender. He also doesn't emit any dangerous pheromones like sexy, hunky Carson. Yet our recent sexcapade is still fresh in Carson's mind, his head is running low on blood and he can be a big, dumb male. I suppose it's fitting since I've proven that I can be a stupid female on occasion. Carson does the territorial dance as if Griffin is a threat, so he immediately walks in front of me and circles Griffin like he's Carson's next meal.

"Carson, this is Griffin," I introduce, trying to diffuse Carson's detonation trigger.

"Hello," Griffin says to a towering Carson and sticks his scrawny hand out. Carson captures his hand with a little too much pressure.

I give Carson my best stare down. "Griffin, the portfolios are over here." I point to the living room and Griffin follows with Carson inches behind him.

I have ten portfolios stacked on the table with all my recent paintings. Earlier in the week I photographed them and emailed them to Tom so he would know what to expect. He and Griffin have been very supportive of my grunge style paintings with their whimsical and chaotic compositions, so I am immensely grateful that I have this opportunity. I offer to help Griffin carry the cases to the SUV he parked outside, but Carson interjects and insists on helping Griffin. When they return to the house, Griffin is carrying a large tote bag and Carson is carrying a large, flat cardboard box.

"I brought you something. It's a gift from Tom and me. This has brushes, watercolors, ink; all your favorite brands." Griffin says hands the bag to me with a big smile. "And that's more paper. Arches and Fabiano. The one hundred forty pound weight ones are in there, too," he says, pointing to the cumbersome cardboard Carson is setting against the wall.

"Griffin, that is so nice of you. I've been meaning to make a trip in to visit Lee's and New York Art. You saved me a drive." I give him a kiss on the cheek. Carson watches me without blinking.

Lauren is about to invite Griffin for dinner, however, I intercept and tell him to be careful on his drive back to the city. Griffin looks a little disappointed to be rushed out of the house, but his smile returns when I tell him I owe him a dinner in the city sometime.

"Well, that was very rude," Lauren says when we see Griffin get in his SUV. "Why didn't you invite him in for dinner?"

"Because The Hulk over there looked like he was going to have Griffin for dinner." I wave my hand in Carson's direction.

"I didn't do anything." Carson scowls.

"You didn't have to. You were practically breathing fire down the guy's neck, hovering over him."

Lauren starts laughing.

"The guy is totally into you. He's bringing gifts and he drove out here at night so he could get invited in for a drink. That was at least three hundred dollars' worth of supplies he gave you." Carson stops and tries to think of more ways to inflame the situation.

"Carson, he's doing his job. There's nothing more to it," I say in a huff.

"Did you see his face when you said you owed him dinner? He's one of those guys who hear, *I owe you a blow job.*" Carson mimics and crosses his arms.

Lauren can't contain her laughter. "Dinner is ready," she says and heads back to the kitchen.

"He did not think that, Carson. You're being ridiculous and jealous."

"Sound familiar? I'm only jealous because every guy thinks you're available. If you were with me, I wouldn't worry about other men because I'd know that you're *mine.*"

That shuts me up. I stand back and think for a moment. There's nothing I can say that hasn't been repeated to Carson too many times already. I don't want to drive him away, but I'm not ready to give him the three words he wants. I feel powerful and cruel at the same time.

"I don't want to argue," he says, noticing my discomfort. "Let's go eat Imogene's dinner and try not to say our trigger words."

"I agree, but every word seems to be a trigger word for us."

"I'm going to go eat," he mutters, raising his arms above his head in defeat, "before I consider doing something else with you."

"No, wait. You don't get to have the last word and walk away. I have thought about this a lot and I have something to say."

"I'm not going to like this, am I?" Carson's hands clench and open at his sides as he watches me.

"I believe in you, Carson. I do. I screwed up. Anyone in town will tell you that. I shouldn't have been with Dylan, but I'm not entirely to blame. I do think you're Mr. Romance. I also think you're Mr. Take Care of Everyone. But you screwed up big time, too. You like 'should haves'. Well, you should have been strong enough to stop Dylan and me from going out in the first place."

"Here we go again," Carson mutters.

"It's true!"

"I know," he growls. "You don't think I play that over and over and regret not doing something then. I was afraid of hurting my brother. Seeing you two together made me sick. Sick! But I failed to act on it immediately from day one."

"Why?"

"Because for a long time I thought Dylan was my weakness. I couldn't be happy because I worried about Dylan. I couldn't go to college because I had to take care of Dylan. I couldn't have more in my life, other than work, because Dylan consumed all of my energy. I allowed myself to believe that I was doing the right thing by letting Dylan be with you even though it felt so wrong."

"So you're not made of steel. You do have weaknesses?" I give a small smile to restore the peace.

"I do. But I can't blame Dylan. He's not really my weakness. I actually think he makes me stronger. I have to be... for him... for me... because failure isn't an option."

"Geez. Now we're back to Mr. Perfect again."

"I'm not perfect at all. As you know, I can be too uptight, too controlling, too opinionated and too stupid when it comes to you. You're my weakness."

"Really?" The thought that I can bring this impressive man to his knees inflates my ego with a jolt.

"You're a weakness in a good way. When I'm with you, I let part of my tough exterior down and you bring out a side of me that I like. Do I make any sense to you?"

"You make perfect sense to me."

Forty-One

I put on the final touches of black ink, splattered in some places. The photo of Carson hugging Dylan at the party is captured in my own style. I blew the photo up and hung it on my wall so I could paint my own rendition of it. The goal is to capture their love for each other and their stand-out charisma in a sea of bodies. I am pleased with the finished product and it gives me pause to memorize Carson's loving gaze on his younger brother. It makes me miss Carson more and it's the reason I could never really leave Hera to move back to New York. Knowing he's a short distance up the road from me is a geographical significance that I don't want to lose.

I pull off my smock and take a quick shower to scrub the paint from my nails and arms. The house has a distinct, ever present chill, like any old Victorian home, so I put on a black tunic sweater with a mock turtleneck and my black leggings, topped off with my chunky glasses to remind me of my afternoon with Carson in the library. I put Carson's key necklace on over the sweater. I wear the necklace every day and flip it between my fingers when I think of Carson.

I try out the new flat iron I bought online. Imogene showed me how to create a new look. It makes me look a little more sophisticated, I think, when I straighten my hair out to its full length, letting it drape in thick, silky strands.

The third floor is the warmest part of the house, so I stay in my bedroom and work on the bed with my laptop on a lap desk. It's these times of day when the girls are working at the diner that I daydream too much, thinking about Carson.

Sometimes I get funny texts from Dylan, sent to a wide circle of his friends; photos of a sandwich he's eating, or his feet propped on a table. His messages are optimistic and are meant to reassure us, especially Carson. However, when my phone pings, I am always hoping it's Carson. He will no longer initiate anything between us. Lauren called it; he's waiting for me.

I run some tests on a program and take a few work phone calls while Bert snuggles on the bed at my feet. I like to run my toe over his jowls and under his chin. He flips over on his back with his legs in the air, hoping I'll rub his belly. "You males are all the same," I say to Bert.

"What about us males?" Carson fills the doorway, his hands raised above his head, gripping the doorframe, and one bare foot bent slightly forward in a casual stance.

"I didn't hear you come in. What are you doing here?" I try to fight back a smile so I don't look too eager.

He shrugs. "I still have a key. I decided that I need to show you what you're missing."

"You mean sex?"

"Nope. By the way, your hair looks great like that."

"Are you trying to get in my pants?"

"Nope. There will be none of that."

"Did you bring your handy dandy tool belt to hammer something senseless? Something to drive me insane?"

"Nope. I'm making dinner. I'll let you know when it's ready."

"But you can't cook."

"Imogene gave me some tips. It won't be as good as Dylan's cooking, but I've got some moves." He is serious and it occurs to me that he is intentionally staying outside of my bedroom.

"Dylan used to cook for me. Is that what this is? I thought you weren't jealous of Dylan and our short affair." I had to put that out there since it seems to be one of the main reasons why I can't give myself completely to Carson.

"I've never been jealous of Dylan. I know how much he has struggled. I would never want to live with the demons that battle in his brain." He's about to say more and then clears his throat to end our conversation. "Be downstairs in an hour or I will come and carry you down. Don't cross me on this one." His lovely mouth curves and I am tempted to ask him for a kiss, but I will follow his rules.

An hour later, when I walk downstairs, I smell tomato sauce and burnt garlic and enter the kitchen to a scene of Carson flinging spaghetti noodles against my new refrigerator. There's a pile of cooked noodles on the floor and a trail of them sticking to the fridge.

"What are you doing to my new appliances?"

"Imogene told me how to test the pasta to make sure it's al dente. I think I got it." He picks up potholders and takes the boiling water off the stove and dumps the noodles in a strainer in the sink. He moves fast, sliding on his bare feet, tossing olive oil in the pot and then tossing the drained pasta back into it. He adds more olive oil and a touch of marinara sauce from another pan. I see empty jars of Rao's Marinara Sauce on the counter.

"You got me Rao's?" I am excited.

Carson smiles. "Sit down. Imogene told me it's your favorite and you miss it. I bought two cases for you when I was on the Upper Westside yesterday." He nods to the boxes on the floor.

I put my hands together gleefully as if he just unveiled a pony to a five-year-old. He dresses our pasta bowls with more sauce and freshly grated Parmesan cheese. "So what's the nasty smell?"

"I annihilated the garlic bread. Apparently the two-step directions were too complicated for me."

I laugh, seeing the charred bread log on the counter. "It's the stove. It's made for a professional chef and it's easy to ruin your food if you don't know what you're doing."

"Now you know why Talia is the only one who uses my range." His remark is meant to be funny, but I feel a pang of envy that Talia spends several days a week cooking for Carson and handling his laundry, folding his boxer briefs!

He fills two glasses of wine. "Eat," he commands.

I dig in and eat with a craving for my favorite starchy carbs, twirling mounds of spaghetti on my fork against the pasta spoon before shoving it in my mouth. "Forgive me, but no one looks attractive eating spaghetti and I'm really hungry."

"Go ahead. Slurp all you want." He is pleased with himself. "Oh, and I fucked up the salad, too. It was supposed to be arugula with shaved fennel. I accidentally pulverized the fennel in the food processor, so the salad is arugula with a side of arugula. But this is very good wine and there's ice cream for dessert."

I bark a laugh. "I thought you would offer yourself up as dessert. Isn't that a guy move?"

"Nope. No sex, babe. And if that's what your previous boyfriends offered, I don't want to hear about it. Got it?"

"Sure." I twirl a smaller amount on my fork and try to look a bit more elegant, if that's possible with spaghetti. I like that he calls me babe, a new endearment. "There weren't any other boyfriends, Carson. And Dylan was... you know, a moment in time."

He nods and keeps eating and re-filling my wine glass.

When I work on my dish of caramel ice cream, he gets up to do the dishes. With his back to me at the sink, I watch his butt like it's the swim relay at the Olympics when the hunky anchor is coming down the lane for the photo finish. My eyes never leave Carson's ass.

"Getting enough there?" he asks without turning around.

"I have plenty of ice cream, thanks."

"No, I meant the view." He turns around and points to the window over the sink where my reflection looks back at me.

"Oh. Yeah, it's a nice view." Caught red-handed. I smirk and lick my spoon.

"Don't do that." Carson is looking at my tongue. "That new hair, with those glasses? It's like having a horny, sexy librarian staring at my ass."

"How do you know I'm horny?"

"Because I'm horny," he growls. He takes my bowl, finishes loading the dishwasher and washing the pots by hand.

"Thanks for dinner and doing the dishes. It was a very nice surprise."

Carson turns around and leans against the sink. "It doesn't have to be a surprise. I'm happy to do this anytime. I'm happy to do a lot of things for you that have nothing to do with sex. Believe me, when I get horny, I don't cook for any old girl."

Our conversation is interrupted by Imogene and Lauren making a commotion as they come in the front door. "Who made dinner?" Imogene yells as she comes down the hall.

"Ah! Mr. Blackard, did you follow my instructions?" Imogene smiles to me, sniffing, looking for some sign of how the dinner went.

"I got about fifty percent of it right. There are leftovers in the fridge for you and Lauren."

Lauren pops into the kitchen with snow still in her hair. She stands next to Carson at the sink and looks at me, waiting for the game replay.

"Lauren, your eyes are about to pop out of your head," I say, getting up to put my wine glass on the counter.

"Babe, don't forget I'm coming tomorrow to fix the downstairs toilet that keeps running and I'm going to measure the windows. I'm not going to replace them when it's this cold, but I can order them." Carson kisses me on top of the head and starts for the front door. I am a little tipsy and giddy that he called me babe again, another obvious move on his part.

"Babe?" Lauren whispers.

I ignore her and head to the door as Carson puts his boots and coat on.

"Is this your new strategy? Show up and fix things, cook for me, call me babe?"

"Yep," he says and looks past me to see if the girls are listening. We both know they are staying perfectly quiet in the kitchen so they can hear us. "You told me you didn't want me barging in anymore, but I'm thinking *fuck that*. I'm going to be around and you're going to know it."

"To what end? Why?"

"So you'll know how good it feels to be wanted and needed; to know that it's what you really want."

"You think so?" I linger, hanging back at the far end of the front hall.

"Yeah, I do."

He strides toward me and covers my mouth with his lips that taste like marinara sauce and wine. I let a small moan escape and he probes further, running his tongue inside every part of my mouth before tugging on my bottom lip with his teeth. We slowly pull apart, not wanting the kiss to end.

"I'm going to get in my truck and think about you on the drive home. Then I'm going to go to bed and think about you until I fall asleep. When I wake up, I'll think about you again and then I'll have to take a cold shower. I'm going to pick up lunch because I know you like when Sushi Dan is town. So I'm going to bring you lunch. I'm going to work in your house the rest of the afternoon, not because I want to fuck you, but because your house needs work. I wouldn't mind if you think about me, too. Even if it's my ass that turns you on."

I am touched by his thoughtful assertiveness and insistence and he's so goddamn sexy. "I love Sushi Dan."

His mouth does that slight curve again. "I have to leave before I kiss you again."

"Wait a minute. Who is Talia cooking for? Are you going to sneak home and eat the good stuff?"

"Nope. I gave her three weeks off. So it's you, me and my bad cooking."

"That was generous of you. It's paid time off, right?"

Carson shrugs. "She needs to see her family in Poland."

"And I bet you paid for the trip. You're such a nice person."

Carson picks up my hand and kisses it. "I'm coming back for you."

He sure knows how to shut me up. I bask numbly in his flirtation before he leaves and I lock the door behind him.

"What was that?" Lauren asks, running down the hall towards me. "Babe?"

I shake my head. "He wants to come over and fix things." I shrug.

Imogene joins us and crosses her arms. "He wants to fix you.

My cell phone pings with a text from Carson. *You're always on my mind.*

Lauren reads it and does one of those spastic cheerleader jumps. "He's courting you. He's wooing you until you admit that you're in love with him."

Imogene is more reserved and, for some reason, I trust her advice more than Lauren's. Something about Imogene's dark red lipstick and dark wavy hair with her Jessica Rabbit body makes her seem like a woman who reads men well. "He's very serious, Jess. It may look cute and innocent, but make no mistake. Carson is deadly serious about what he's doing. Do not fuck with his heart on this. If you have a problem, you tell him now."

Her warning carries a great weight, this time I understand. I can't dismiss her the way I brushed off Carson's warning about Dylan.

Forty-Two

For the next two weeks leading up to my show, Carson arrives every day to work on my house and to cook dinner. I work in the library or paint in the studio and sometimes I wonder if he's downstairs breaking things so he has projects to work on. I really don't care. I listen like a hawk for any sign of the door opening and grin to myself when I know he's arrived.

Sometimes he comes in the morning and stays all day. Sometimes he brings my lunch and then works, but he always informs me when dinner is ready. Afterward, I always come downstairs to eat his stinky tuna casserole, his crunchy dry meatloaf, his tacos made with store bought rotisserie chicken, his sub sandwiches that could feed four men, or his pasta that he tops off with my favorite Rao's sauce.

If the girls are here, we all eat together and he openly refers to me as babe and kisses me whenever he pleases, but he never takes it further. His hand doesn't reach under my shirt to cop a feel and he never lets his lower extremities brush against me. He's making me insane with wanting him.

When we do finally meet at the end of the workday for dinner, I'm dying to hear his voice and have him talk to me about anything. I find his observations on amendments to an IRS code for businesses in particular to be a real turn on. I don't care if he is talking about wood varnish, rotating his tires or the weather report, I just need to be near him and hear his voice.

Carson is playing for keeps and my heart is tugging me towards him. Everything I was taught and all that I've perpetuated about keeping a distance from men is being tested daily and hourly; my feelings for Carson are breaking down the defenses in my brain.

The day before my show, Carson doesn't show up. By lunchtime, I'm worried. Maybe Archie is right and I waited too long. My phone pings with a text from Carson. *Something came up. See you at dinner.*

I sigh with relief. He's coming, but not until dinner. Carson has rendered my brain useless. I think about him moving around my house, cooking in the kitchen, eating dinner with me and talking about his shop or his clients, the furniture designs he's working on and about the sex I'm not getting. The kind of sex that addles my brain and fills my heart with a gush of love for Carson. *I love him!* My brain screams this over and over.

I shower and change into clean jeans and a flouncy cream blouse with a scoop neck which hits me at the hips. I play with my hair, making long waves with the curling iron and I put on some mascara and a dusting of a light eye shadow. I wear my favorite black, knee-high boots over my jeans that also give me a two-inch boost. Nothing Carson would notice since he's six four, yet it makes me feel sexier to walk on longer legs. I put on my wool coat and grab my purse, car keys and a portfolio case.

"Wish me luck," I say to Bert. He licks his chops and plops back down on the bottom step so he can greet me when I return.

As I drive through the snow, rumbling up the snow-packed road to Carson's house, it occurs to me that he's probably not there. The "something" was most likely work-related and I'm wasting my time. My worries are eased somewhat when I see Carson's truck in front of his house. Then a new set of fears set in. What is he doing home when he should be at work or at my home?

My heels sink and crunch in the snow as I make my way to the door. I hesitate, my finger hovering over the doorbell. I push it and exhale. I hear voices and wonder how many people are behind the door. Before I can consider crunching my way back to the car, the door swings wide open and Carson is inches from me, towering like the giant I found intimidating on my first day in Hera except he's shirtless. His jeans hang lower than usual, a sign that he's going commando. Combine that with the angles and planes of his brawny arms and torso, and I'm rendered speechless.

I'm in love with one of those beautiful god-like men I used to assume were brainless. He's anything other than brainless, though. He's the only guy I have lusted over who enjoys listening to me rattle on about function theory and computational testing. How have I gotten so lucky

430

as to have the biggest and hottest star in my little galaxy?

He is surprised to see me and it takes a moment for him to quickly scan all my body parts with concern as if I might be injured before he understands that I'm there to see him.

"Jess." A smile breaks across his face. He steps back. "Come in."

I walk in, clutching the portfolio, my nerves threatening to revolt on me.

"Did I interrupt something? I heard voices."

"I was talking to Dylan on the computer. That's why I stayed home this afternoon and couldn't come to your place. The facility monitors all outside communication, so he has to sign up for computer time for live chats. We're finished, though. Come in, give me your coat." He finishes unbuttoning my coat for me and hangs it up in the hall closet. Dying embers are glowing in the living room fireplace and I see his open laptop on the coffee table.

"How is Dylan?" I ask as Carson picks up the key on my necklace. His mouth curves before he lets the key drop from his hand.

Carson pauses and looks down, a moment of reverie for his sibling. "He sounds really good. Dylan's good at fooling people, but this time he sounds genuinely good."

"Great. Everyone is rooting for Dylan. I bet he has made friends there."

Carson smiles, yet seems apprehensive. I'm giving off mixed signals again. My knuckles turn white as my grip on the portfolio increases and I begin to crush the cardboard.

"Hey," he says and takes the portfolio from my hands. I bend down to remove my boots. My recent pedicure shows off bright red toenails and baby soft feet. In the excitement to see him, I forgot to put on socks and I'm glad. Carson takes in a slow breath as he watches my toes when I arch my foot from the boot.

"I brought you something. I hope you like it." He turns his focus to the portfolio.

"A gift? You made this for me?" His mouth curves into a lopsided grin.

I nod.

Carson opens the case and takes the painting out. He lets the portfolio fall to the floor as he holds the painting with both hands and studies it. I can't read his solemn face. Maybe including Dylan in the piece was a mistake and Carson is uncertain whether I am secretly holding a torch for his brother.

"This is—" He stops mid-sentence when his voice catches and a sadness crinkles around his eyes.

"I'm sorry. Does it upset you?"

"No. I'm astonished," he says, studying the painting. "You captured the part of me and Dylan that means the most to me." He looks at me and then again at the painting. "You got it."

"So you really like it?" I can't hold my smile back.

"Are you kidding? I'm framing this." He walks over to the coffee table and sets the painting down to admire it from a distance.

I stay by the door and put my fists up to my chin, anxious to finish what I came to do.

"Are you going to come in?" he asks, turning back to me. "You can sit down and relax. I don't bite." That's not entirely true when I think back to him taking a few nips against my butt cheeks.

"I have something I want to tell you." I clip the words out and can't hide my uneasiness.

"Ah. This sounds serious." Carson comes back to me by stepping on the couch and flying over the back of it, landing at my feet. He's my personal super hero, shirtless of course, so I can marvel at his beauty. "This is about you and me."

"Yes." I hold my elbows across my chest and let my gaze wander down to his chest which is eye level for me.

He puts two fingers under my chin and lifts my head up to meet his gaze. "Say it. Whatever it is. Say it," he demands and releases my chin.

"Okay. Here it is. I push back because I am scared about many things, mostly because I'm young and stupid when it comes to men. Because I was with your brother and I thought that made me unworthy of you." Carson grimaces at that. "Furthermore, I really didn't believe that anything good would come out of being with you because I was so afraid of being hurt. It felt like I was giving you a power over me, but the truth is, I feel stronger when I'm with you. When you tell me those beautiful things about myself like telling me I'm fearsome, I feel the same way about you. I do feel the same way about you in every way possible."

Carson moves closer to me and settles his hands firmly on my waist. "Say. It."

"I love... I love you. I love you, Carson."

433

"Yes, you do." He smiles and leans in to give me a tender kiss.

I take a breath and struggle to say more.

"You have something else to say. It's okay, tell me."

"I'm also terrified that I fell in love with you too fast."

"Fast? It's taken you months!" Carson smiles.

"It goes against everything my parents taught me about being a practical, responsible person," I ramble.

"You make it sound like loving someone is the same as paying your phone bill. Should I be concerned?" Carson squeezes my waist and moves his palms up my back before giving me another soft kiss.

"No, you don't have to be concerned. I don't want to be without you," I whisper between kisses. "It's too empty when you're not near me, it hurts when you stay away from me."

"Same here."

"Carson?"

"What?" he asks, brushing his lips against mine.

"I'm not as strong or as smart as you think I am. Don't break me."

"Never." He holds me tightly. "We're going to make each other very happy. You and me, babe."

"You're the first man I have ever been in love with." I curl into his embrace, my heart racing.

"I'm also the last. And you are the only woman I can imagine loving forever. So we're even." He picks me up with an arm under my legs and behind my back. I wrap my arms around his neck.

"What are you doing?"

"Kiss me," he commands before he carries me up to his bedroom without ever removing his lips from mine.

When he sets me down on the floor in the master suite, he kicks the door closed.

"Lock it," I say, thinking of Talia showing up.

Carson laughs. "Talia is still in Poland. Take all of your clothes off. Every last stitch."

I remove my blouse and, when Carson sees my black lace bra, he begins undressing me himself. His hands pull down my jeans and panties and then he unclasps my bra, palming the mounded skin beneath before the bra falls to the floor. His jeans fly off and his mouth is instantly on my breast; I gasp from the heat of his mouth and the sensation that ripples through my body. I go boneless and he carries me to the bed. He reluctantly reaches for the condoms in his nightstand.

I put my hand on his arm. "Carson, I went on the pill. I decided to go on the pill so I can be with you."

"Excellent," he chokes out.

His cock, long and hard, rubs against my belly as he kisses me gently and slowly. He lavishes his talented tongue down to the sensitive zones on my neck and I moan as I close my eyes.

"Babe, keep your eyes open." He pulls me up to the headboard so my head is on the high pillows. I look down to see Carson spreading my legs and kissing at the top of my thigh before licking into my wet center. I moan his name and encourage him to keep going. When he sucks on my special spot, my hands fist in his hair and I buck into his mouth. He doesn't slow down. Tongue, circle, tongue, suck, repeat. I come in a dizzying frenzy of moans that end with me shouting his name.

"Damn," I whisper.

I am still with pleasure which paralyzes every cell and limb. Carson props himself above me. "You should see your face after you come. You're gorgeous."

I smile lazily as my eyes close, enjoying the rapture.

"No, look at me," he says, straining over me with his own need.

I stare into his eyes as they glitter with love and bliss. He rubs himself against my clit. "You're so wet."

I replace his hand with mine and stroke his cock, rubbing it against me.

"Jesus. Shit. It's been so long that it's going to make me come." He pulls my hand away and lies down next to me. His cock rests on my thigh as he begins kissing me hard. I taste myself on his tongue.

I begin to stroke him as we kiss and a guttural moan escapes from him. I get up and push him on his back. "My turn," I say, pinning his biceps down, a purely symbolic gesture since the muscles in his arms are too wide for my hands to grasp.

I get between his legs and hold his length, running my tongue up and down the shaft, taking extra time to circle the tip so it releases its creamy fluids.

"Babe, stop, I'm going to come if you keep doing that. I can't hold on and then it will be over too quickly," Carson says this between his panting moans.

"Carson, I'm not going anywhere. We have all day and night." I put him in my mouth and watch his expression glaze over with surrender.

I'm certainly no expert, but I put everything I know into worshipping his cock. I suck and take as much of him as I can into my mouth, hoping that he doesn't feel cheated that there isn't enough room for all of him. My jaw aches between the ferocious sucking, licking and stroking. Carson's hands move from balling the comforter in his fists to holding my head and pushing me as far onto him as possible.

Carson comes, shouting my name, and I feel a little self-satisfaction in that. I swallow the spurts of semen and take breaths while I can, so I can continue my assault on his favorite appendage. When he's empty, I bend over his thigh and wipe my mouth on the comforter before I kiss my way up his torso to relax against his side. His arm pulls me in snug against him and he kisses me again so our tongues share everything—every fluid—a marking of territory, taking possession of each other in the most primal way.

"I'm the only woman you've had in this bed?" My fingers flit lightly across his chest in dancing circles.

"Yes. Are you going to stay?" He sounds cautious. I don't blame him. Given his unstable, sad family history and my ability to put myself and my career choices above all else, he must still have reservations about me. "Your show may launch a whole new sphere of clients who want your art. To be successful in that business you need to be tenacious and you may want to live in the city again to maintain contacts and work full time on your painting. Have you thought of that?"

"I thought you were opposed to me moving back to the city? Are you trying to get rid of me?" I try to sound flighty and sweet the way a girlfriend would behave.

"No. You know I want you to live here, but I want to make sure you've worked out all the issues in your head. If you change your mind and end up leaving, it will destroy me."

I lift my head up and lean on my arm to look at him. His blue eyes against the backdrop of his chiseled, handsome face; his prominent cheekbones and strong chin make him look too beautiful to be a sad person. He is blessed with beauty and intelligence while he's also very serious about me. I wish he had made that clear from day one. I wish he had been the Blackard to ask me out first.

"You don't really trust me," I say.

He puts his hand on the back of my head to pull me in for a sweet kiss. "I do," he says. "I believe your intentions are good, but sometimes that isn't enough. If you're not one hundred percent sure of being here, you may change your mind."

"So you think I'm fickle. In other words, you don't trust my emotions."

Carson grimaces and shakes his head. "I love you and I want you to share the same degree of love I have for you."

"I came here, nervous as hell, and told you that I love you." I don't like sounding pouty, but I don't know where he's going with this.

"Fucking 'bout time. Thank you for that." He smiles and kisses me again.

"Everyone gives me a hard time about my plans and these rules of order I have set up for my personal goals, but you're worse. You keep changing the rules. You want me to stay. I stay. You want me to love you. I love you. Now you question if my *degree* of love is great enough to keep me grounded or keep us together?"

"I'm not doubting you. Shit. I'm sorry." He kisses me again, deeper. "Tell me where you see yourself in the future."

"Ah. The future. I don't have a crystal ball."

"Tell me what you want, Jess."

"I want harmony. I want my art and I want to be with you. I want both and I want it to be harmonious. Is that a cop out?"

"No. I'll take it." Carson smiles.

Carson moves on top of me, holding my hands and pinning them down on either side of my head. His leg pushes mine apart and he positions himself at my sex. He's already hard and eager to resume his quest to keep me in his bed.

My eyes begin to drift closed with arousal. "Look at me, Jess. Look at me."

I stare right into those steely blue eyes as he teases my body with the tip of his cock, light thrusts dip into my wet folds before filling me up completely. Since my hands are trapped and I can't touch him, I arch up so he'll use that perfect tongue on me. He sucks and bites my nipples and then finds that good spot inside of me that he caresses with his length in a sideways motion which brings me to an early climax. The orgasm is short, though explosive. I bring my legs up and wrap them around Carson and it sends me off on another round of spasms; smaller in intensity, but deliciously long.

"Don't stop looking at me," he says with a raspy voice.

"You are so demanding, Blackard." However, I keep focused on his eyes that bore into me with love. Carson keeps rocking me through my pleasurable moans until he gets even harder and rubs against me in a way that makes him come with violent thrusts and grunts.

He releases my hands, but stays inside of me and lets the bottom half of his body weigh me down. He holds himself up on his forearms and positions his hands in my hair. "I just want you to be mine," he says.

"You have me; body and soul, and all the parts in between."

Forty-Three

The gallery is spectacularly crowded. Most people are here for Martin and Yvette, who have representation in several major cities in Europe as well. They are the artists with the star power, but I'm thrilled to ride behind on their coattails. Tom is working the crowd, introducing the artists to potential buyers.

I do my best to talk about my paintings and answer questions like a seasoned pro, however, people take one look at me and start peppering me with questions about my age and education. Tom is rather proud of that and uses it to our advantage. I feel a little like a sideshow circus freak, but then it is selling paintings. The little red dots start going up next to my paintings on the wall and a little bell inside my head tinkles like when an angel gets its wings.

Imogene has put my red mane up in a high, loose twist, so the curls still fan out casually, but my neck is exposed, showing off a glittery, vintage rhinestone necklace with pearls, rosary beads and a hundred year-old locket, courtesy of L & I Creations. I wear Carson's necklace triple wrapped around my wrist along with Aunt Ginnie's diamond stud earrings, a black wrap dress, black tights and my black boots. I have an understated glamour thanks to Imogene who didn't want me to look like the amateur, over-eager artist.

Everyone I know from Hera is in Tom's Chelsea gallery. Everyone except Carson who said he'd meet me here. That is a little disappointing. I wanted to walk into the gallery with him on my arm, but he said he had something important to do before the show.

Lauren and Imogene are walking arm in arm with Leo and Jeremy. I've already introduced them to Kate and Marissa who immediately found common ground and hilarity in what young women their age share. Archie, Lois and Eleanor are wandering by the various pieces together, chatting and sipping champagne. They look right at home in a New York gallery. Bonnie and her crew from the diner are here as is Carson's staff from Blackard Designs. Even Harvey made time to come see my show. Not that I'm expecting him, but if Sushi Dan happens to show up before Carson, I'll really be livid.

Finally, my head is drawn to the door of the gallery and I see him. Everyone sees him. Heads turn when the tall, sexy man—my guy—steps into the gallery. My heart stops, squeezes and then bangs loudly in my chest. I am trembling, awash simultaneously with relief and joy. He is wearing a black leather jacket, a black T-shirt, jeans and boots. He shaved, although his hair is pushed back in its usual mop of sexy. Just the way I love him.

He looks around the room, not noticing the pretty, leggy models and all the other people in the room before his eyes lock on me. His mouth curves and he stalks towards me. I swoon watching my tall, hunky boyfriend come for me with a swagger and a smirk that puts me on the moon.

"Hey." He smiles and slips an arm behind my back before he kisses me on the lips. "Nervous?"

"Very. I wish we drove in together. My stomach was so nervous when I got here; I thought I'd throw up."

"You never had a problem speaking at conferences and you don't have to give a lecture here. Relax and enjoy the ride." His deep voice is very soothing.

"This is different. Talking about numbers is one thing. Talking about my art; it's personal and subjective."

"Ah, Ms. Channing is out of her element," he teases me and picks up my twitchy right hand. Both of his large, warm hands envelope my hand and he looks at it with purpose then at me. "You don't have to prove any theorems or yourself. I was here earlier today and spoke to Tom while they were setting up. You're going to be fine."

"You were here?"

"I told you I had to come in early before the show to do some business and I stopped by to see the paintings. I saw most of them at your house, but I wanted to see the set up before the crowd came in. Tom gave me a personal tour."

"Hmm. I guess you already know him since you bought my other paintings last year, right?"

"Yeah." He kisses my hand and puts it down at his side, keeping it clasped in his.

"Oh farfegnugen," I mutter, looking past Carson to the gallery entrance.

"What?" Carson asks, laughing.

"My parents."

Carson turns and we both witness the attractive, well-dressed, middle-aged couple stop to look at one of my paintings.

"Well, aren't we going to go talk to them?" Carson uses his free hand to touch my earlobe and inspect the diamond stud.

"Yes. Can we wait a moment, though? They're looking at my paintings and I can't judge their expressions. Can you?"

Carson looks back at my parents who float through the crowd, studying my paintings with complacent facades. "Do they always look so serious?"

"Yes," I say, but then, I thought the same thing about Carson before he let me see his light-hearted side.

"Do you think they'll like me?" he asks, watching them.

"Do you really care?"

"It would be nice if your parents like me, sure. It will make holidays easier, but I'm not going to worry about it. Too much."

"No. They probably won't like you. They don't like most people. I don't even know if they like me."

"They love you. That's why they are here," Carson reminds me.

"Yes, they love me as their child, but I'm not sure they like me. They obsess too much on my faults and it makes it hard for us to talk in a friendly way."

"You don't have any faults. They're insane." Carson squeezes my hand and smirks.

"Right. I've got all the right moves. How can my parents not see that?" I scoff.

"Let's get to it," he says, leading me by my hand to my parents. I like that he treats it as a team effort.

"Jessica," my mother exclaims when she sees us approach. She gives me a peck on the cheek before standing back, putting a comfortable distance between us. She is dressed impeccably in a grey, fitted dress that complements her short blond hair and lovely face. For someone who eschews pop culture and trends, she looks very pretty and trendy as well as looking a decade younger than her fifty years. My father looks fit and handsome, a math professor who resembles an investment banker.

"Jess," my father says in his authoritative, professor voice. He kisses my forehead and I smell his aftershave.

There are no hugs or tight, smiling embraces about how long it's been even though we live only a two-hour drive apart. My parents are not touchy feely in anyway, although in this second, maybe for the first time, I see that they love me. Maybe it's because I recognize love now. Their faces flush and their thin, stern lips curve slightly upon seeing me and maybe knowing that is enough as far as parents go.

Yet I know it's not enough as far as I feel about Carson. I want the thrills of being in love; the giddiness, the laughter, the sparkly, lust-filled eyes and the outward passion. I want to shout and jump with joy when I see Carson, the same way my

445

insides turn into a bounce house when I think about him.

Carson's left hand squeezes my hand as if he knows what I'm thinking.

"Carson, this is my mother, Michelle Channing."

"Mrs. Channing." Carson shakes her hand while his other hand holds mine in a vise grip.

"And this is my father, Robert."

"Mr. Channing." Carson shakes his hand, too.

"Congratulations, Jessica. A fine show and your work is so unusual," my father says.

"But do you like it?" I ask, trying to decipher his comment.

"I suppose I thought you'd have more traditional compositions similar to the portraits you used to do in high school," he says, not answering my question.

"No, this is what I expected." My mother surprises the hell out of me. "A girl who spends her life studying numbers and science isn't going to do anything traditional. She's going to do the unexpected and I suspect there are a lot of interesting ideas in that head of yours. I like the messages you put into your paintings, Jessica. You have a lot of passion and it shows."

A happiness I haven't felt with my parents in a long time reappears like an old memory, but this unexpected delight leaves me mute. Without waiting for me to respond, my mother turns her head to examine Carson. I can't imagine what she thinks of the towering, attractive eye candy next to me; her once geeky prodigy of a daughter.

"Carson Blackard," my mother says with recognition in her tone. "You were such a responsible young boy. More like a little man back then, so grave."

Carson gives a very reserved smile.

"Well, those were difficult times for all of us. How are you and your brother doing?" she asks and if my mother was the huggy type, I'd give her good one for remembering the Blackard boys.

"We're both doing well, thank you." Carson isn't nervous like me. He looks very confident meeting my parents.

Then my mother glances at our hands tightly clasped around each other's fingers.

"Are you two dating?" she asks, looking from Carson to me.

"Mom." I laugh lightly. "When have I ever really dated? Seriously. We're not dating," I say and Carson shoots me a deadly look. I ignore him and turn back to my mother. "Carson and I live so close to each other that we don't need to date. I'm ninety-nine point nine percent sure I'll be marrying him someday, though." I blurt it out, confident that it's the right thing to say because it's the truth. My mother's composure droops a little when her mouth falls open at the same time that my father gives an uncomfortable cough and Carson barks a little laugh.

My mother looks confused. "You're not dating, but you're going to get married?"

"We're together," I clarify. "Boyfriend sounds like such a juvenile term. Carson is more than that."

"Oh." My mother regards Carson again, trying to sum him up based on what she remembers about the sad little boy who tried to take care of his family.

"Blackard," my father says gruffly. I'm pissed that he addresses Carson by his last name.

"Yes?" Carson is polite.

"No, I meant, Blackard as in the furniture. That's your company, correct?" my father asks and I sigh with relief.

"Yes, I have a furniture company and another business that does renovations. I also have some home construction projects going. Sustainable, green homes." Carson states it as simply as possible even though he has earned a solid reputation in his business and could elaborate, perhaps even brag if he weren't so modest. I'll have to start bragging for him.

"I read an article about you," my father states. "Let me think, what magazine was that?"

"Should we take a walk around and see Jess's work?" Carson puts an end to the discussion about himself.

Carson never lets go of my hand. We follow my parents around the gallery like they are two bored tourists who feel obliged to look at every painting on display. They compliment a few pieces, some of which are mine, but for the most part they regard everything with a silent scrutiny. My father did have a good laugh when he saw *Grenade Girl.*

"Jess, this one reminds me of you," he says with the first smile of the evening. My mother reads the caption and winces before moving on to another painting. Carson sneaks a kiss on my temple when he sees my troubled face observing my mother.

"I suppose it could be worse," I whisper to Carson.

"It could always be worse." Carson laughs. "How do your parents look when they are pleased? Do they smile much?"

"Not that I'm aware of. Maybe this *is* them being pleased. I don't know anymore."

"They're here. That's what matters."

Tom walks by us and flashes ten fingers at me with a big smile on his face.

"What's with the jazz hands?" Carson asks when Tom is gone.

I laugh. "He's sold ten of my paintings so far tonight. Not bad."

"You're hot shit."

"It feels pretty good," I say. "It would be better if we weren't hanging with my parents. They're like the walking dead. Look at our friends across the room. They're laughing it up and having fun."

"Take it easy." Carson keeps his voice low. "Your parents don't know what to make of your new career path and having me next to you isn't helping. You should tell them you want them to visit you at the house sometime soon."

"You're *shoulding* all over me again. Sometimes you're very practical. My father will like that about you."

"I think he already likes me," Carson says, swinging our hands playfully back and forth between us.

I sigh, enjoying the moment.

Before my parents leave I do offer an open invitation to have them visit for a weekend or even a dinner. My father seems amiable to the idea while my mother smiles in one of those noncommittal ways.

The exhibit hours have officially ended, so I don't have to keep performing, explaining my paintings to inquisitive lurkers. We all leave the gallery together and I'm riding on a thunderous high, complete exhilaration over being part of the show and having Carson on my arm. Our group has grown to include friends of Marissa and Kate, the Blackard employees, the employees from Bonnie's and some of my colleagues from 5 Alpha.

Archie, Lois and Eleanor beg off, choosing to go dine at a quiet restaurant on the Upper Eastside before they drive back to Hera. The rest of us gather on the sidewalk with the chilly snowfall nipping at us. It's a beautiful, wintery evening in the town that never sleeps and my friends want to live it up.

"Let's go to Cielo!" Marissa says to everyone. Lauren and Imogene squeal with approval at her choice of dance clubs in the meat-packing district.

"You're finally legal, Jess. You need to dance and celebrate this great night," Kate adds.

I turn to Carson. He shrugs. "It's your call. I'll go dancing if that's what you want."

"You guys go without us," I tell them. "Carson and I have dinner plans." He arches an eyebrow at me, but doesn't complain.

When the group disperses into five separate cabs to head off to the club, Carson and I are left alone, walking on West 25ᵗʰ Street. "Do you really have dinner plans for us?" Carson asks.

"None. Sorry. It did not occur to me to make reservations anywhere. I know it's shocking that I did not plan ahead, but I got caught up in the excitement of today. Although, I'm finally coming off my nervous high now."

Carson chuckles. "Good, because I made plans for us."

"You did? Where?"

"I have a room booked for us at The Standard. You mentioned once that you like the restaurant and the High Line."

"I love the High Line Park and I've always wanted to stay at The Standard. It's perfect, but Carson, it's so romantic and, as I recall, you were the one who gave the speech about not being Mr. Romance." I elbow him and he puts his free hand on my waist.

"I figured I'd be a pretty shitty boyfriend if I didn't at least treat you to something special on your big night. Besides, you're ninety-nine point nine percent sure that you'll marry me someday. I'll take those odds."

"Aww, shucks. Don't let it go to your head." I pull his head down and kiss him hard, starved for his warm mouth.

"Damn. I should have offered this plan back when I saw you in Archie's office last June. It would have saved me a lot of grief."

"You and your goddamn *shoulds*. And yes, you really should have asked me out then."

We hail a cab and head to the meat-packing district. As much as I love dancing, I want Carson to myself, so we skip Cielo and head straight to The Standard. At the restaurant, I go overboard on clams, crab legs and Lobster Thermidor, however, Carson keeps ordering food and I keep eating.

"Does this make up for all those chewy tuna casseroles and crunchy pasta dishes I made you?" He wipes a piece of caviar from my lip with his thumb.

"Oh yes. This is heaven."

"Save room. There's more."

"Not possible. I'm stuffed."

"We're going to walk in the park before it closes and then we'll go back to the room."

"I didn't bring an overnight bag."

"I did. I had Imogene pack some things for you. It's already in the room." He gives me a sly smile and it warms me all over.

"Is that why you came late to the show? You were arranging this?"

"That's part of it. You'll see."

Our walk through the park is more of a chase to beat the curfew before they lock it. I am slipping and laughing in my boots. Carson picks me up, cradles me in his arms and jogs to the end of the park, amusing the other people strolling through.

Our room is on one of the highest floors with palatial views of the Hudson River.

"Who knew Jersey was so cool?" I stand at the floor-to-ceiling window as Carson puts his arms around me and rests his chin on my head.

"I have something for you and I don't want you to freak out," he says.

I turn in his arms and look up at him. "Jesus, when you put it like that, how can I not freak out a little? What's wrong?"

"Nothing's wrong." He laughs and goes to the closet to retrieve a small, light blue, square box with a white ribbon.

"Oh sweet pancakes! I know that box. You went to Tiffany's." I jump back, pointing my finger accusingly.

"You spend too much time with Lois. Settle down." He places the box in my palm.

"Carson, what are you doing?"

"You know what I'm doing," he says, tugging on the white ribbon. "Listen, my brother had the right idea, but he was the wrong guy for you. Open it. Now."

I stare at the box and then at him.

"Jess. Now." He's very good with demands because his sexy voice and gorgeous face make it difficult to resist.

I pull off the ribbon and drop the velvet box into my palm. When I flip open the lid and gape at the wide platinum band with diamonds all around it, Carson drops to one knee on the floor.

"This is why Imogene had me pick out a ring when she was looking at jewelry sites. I thought it was for shits and giggles, but she was doing research for you. That's how you knew to buy a band and not a solitaire."

"I prepared." He smiles.

"You're really going to do this?" I ask, feeling thrilled and scared at the same time.

"Yes, I am." He takes the ring out of the box and holds it out to me. "You're not the only one with plans. I came up with my own and I want you to hear me out before you say anything, okay?"

I nod.

"I can't be shown up by my little brother and I know what you said about being too young for marriage, but I decided I'm going to propose to you anyway. A wise old man once told me that he waited too long to propose to the woman he loved and—"

"Oh God, not the Archie story. Carson, I've heard that one."

"Yeah, who hasn't? Bag that one. Okay, how about this? I want you to live with me. I want to turn my home office into your studio so you can paint out on that terrace you like so much. We'll set up your computer equipment in the downstairs bedroom and turn that into your office. You keep Gin's home, rent it to the girls or have them live there for free, whatever you want. Naturally, Bert will live with us. I want you to accept this ring now and wear it. Then, for the next one thousand and ninety-five days, we can say we're engaged until you feel ready to get married. I know you generally like bigger numbers, especially seventy million for some reason, but how does one thousand and ninety-five work for you?"

"Yes, I like that number. It's a good one."

"Are you saying yes?"

"I love you. How about thirty?"

"I love you, too. But thirty? The number thirty? Are we talking about the same thing?"

"Yes, the number of days until we get married. Dylan will be back home, so he can be your best man and we can have all the important people there. Our family." The confidence surges through me, dispelling any and all doubts that have ever crossed my mind about Carson.

Now it's his turn to gape.

"Damn, that's a really small number and you're good with that?" His mouth curves into a wide smile.

"Yes. I love you, Carson. I want to marry you now, not later. I've put in so many years of school, studying and preparing while also putting off happiness for work and academic accomplishments. My parents and professors said my rewards would come later. I've had a lifetime of *laters*."

"Me, too." Carson stands and puts the ring on my finger. "It's Mrs. Blackard in thirty days, baby."

"That's Babycakes to you."

Carson embraces me and we kiss hungrily as I begin to cry joyfully, tears of contentment pouring out of me. "You're happy, right?" Carson asks, wiping a tear with his thumb.

"Unbelievably happy." I laugh. "Never stop kissing me.

"Never."

Acknowledgements

Much love and gratitude goes to my family. While writing, I ignored them a lot, often forgetting meals and civil conversation. They are truly a forgiving bunch, and despite my ability to be lost in my own world most of the time, my family keeps encouraging me to write.

To my friends, thank you for being so patient while I ramble on about fictional characters as if they are a part of our circle of friends · and for the great input you all provided. I couldn't ask for a better support system.

To my wonderful editing team at C&D Editing, Kristin Campbell and Alizon Duckwall, thank you for making Fearsome a better book. Your professional skills and virtual hand-holding were an absolute necessity, and Serenity Valle's keen eye added the perfect polish.

To Aaron Campbell, thank you for my cool website and being patient with all of my inane questions and ideas.

And to all my author buddies online and in the real world, thank you for being so generous with advice and support!

About the Author

S. A. Wolfe lives with her wonderfully loud, opinionated children and husband. She is a voracious reader and passionate about writing, and when those two activities don't keep her locked away in her room, she loves hiking mountains as much as she adores all the thrills New York City has to offer.

Dear Reader-

   If you enjoyed *Fearsome*, please consider leaving positive feedback on Amazon, Goodreads, or any book blogs you participate in.
   Oh, and I love interacting with readers, so if you want to visit, please contact me at:

www.sa-wolfe.com
https://www.facebook.com/sawolfe24
https://twitter.com/sawolfe_
sawolfe24@gmail.com

Thank you!
S. A. Wolfe

Leave a review at Goodreads:
http://www.goodreads.com/book/show/184612
47-fearsome

www.ingramcontent.com/pod-product-compliance
Lightning Source LLC
Chambersburg PA
CBHW030536260626
47157CB00006B/2052